THE BLUE JOURNAL

THE BLUE JOURNAL

A DETECTIVE ANTHONY WALKER NOVEL

L. T. GRAHAM

SEVENTH STREET BOOKS®
AN IMPRINT OF PROMETHEUS BOOKS
59 JOHN GLENN DRIVE • AMHERST, NY 14228
www.seventhstreetbooks.com

Published 2015 by Seventh Street Books®, an imprint of Prometheus Books

Cover image © Bigstock
Cover design by Grace M. Conti-Zilsberger

This is a work of fiction. Characters, organizations, products, locales, and events portrayed in this novel either are products of the author's imagination or are used fictitiously.

Inquiries should be addressed to
Seventh Street Books
59 John Glenn Drive
Amherst, New York 14228
VOICE: 716–691–0133
FAX: 716–691–0137
WWW.SEVENTHSTREETBOOKS.COM

19 18 17 16 15   5 4 3 2 1

Library of Congress Cataloging-in-Publication Data

Graham, L. T., 1950-
    The blue journal : a Detective Anthony Walker novel / L.T. Graham.
    pages cm
    ISBN 978-1-63388-060-3 (paperback) — ISBN 978-1-63388-061-0 (ebook)
    1. Psychotherapy patients—Crimes against—Fiction. 2. Diaries—Fiction.
3. Women—Sexual behavior—Fiction. 4. Murder—Investigation—Fiction.
I. Title.

PS3619.T47676B58 2015
813'.6—dc23

                                                              2014027005

Printed in the United States of America

To Bob Diforio, with thanks

CHAPTER 1

There was no reason for Elizabeth Knoebel to suspect that this was going to be the last day of her life.

It was a radiant autumn afternoon. The trees and plantings that surrounded her spacious home were awash in sunlight. Inside all was quiet. She was alone in her comfortable den, holding a glass of wine, working on the memoir that had come to consume her over the past several months.

She stopped typing and stared at the screen. Odd, it occurred to her, that she was more at ease contemplating her personal history this way, rather than sharing secrets with a confidant, a friend, or even one of her lovers. Odder still was the perverse satisfaction she felt from knowing that someday she would reveal all of this to her husband— and that she would revel in the pain it would cause him.

That last idea filled her with a strange mix of amusement and loathing, driving her back to the keyboard. She leaned forward, placed her wine glass on the desk and prepared to add something to the scene she had begun yesterday. She typed:

```
The next time we met he arranged for a
luxurious suite in a downtown hotel.
When we arrived, he poured us each a
drink from the bar, led me into the
bedroom, then took me in his arms and
kissed me, our mouths wet and sweet.
    As he began to undress me I offered
no resistance. He said very little, nor
did I. He lifted my dress above my head
and draped it over the back of an arm-
```

chair. Then he turned and took my hands in his. I stood there in my high heels, bra, and panties.

"You are so beautiful," he said and kissed me on the neck. Then he led me to the bed where we sat on the edge and embraced, engaging in another moist, hot kiss.

He felt the soft shape of my breasts, then took his time removing my bra. When he tossed it to the floor I kicked off my shoes and laid back, stretching across the soft duvet cover. He unbuttoned his shirt and pulled it off, then kneeled beside me, reaching down, now taking hold of my breasts with both hands. He massaged me with great tenderness, then leaned forward and began gently sucking my nipples. I moaned appreciatively in response.

I reached out to unbuckle his belt and pull down his fly, urging him to finish undressing, then felt inside for him. He was already hard.

He finished undressing and we lay on our sides, facing each other. I still had on my panties. He was naked. We kissed again, then he took my ass in both hands and pulled me to him. His tongue meandered its way up and down my neck and tickled my ear, then entered my eager mouth as our bodies pressed together. He slid my panties off, then turned so that his head was between my legs. He covered me with his mouth, his tongue flicking at my moist pussy, his hand pressing down on my pubis. I took hold of him, gently stroking his shaft with one hand, exploring beneath it with the other.

I was already wet, and I groaned with pleasure as he licked me, sometimes quickly, sometimes slowly. His fingers began searching inside me, and from behind as well. He stopped for an instant to tell me that I was delicious and, when his tongue resumed its path up and down my damp opening, my entire body tensed and I cried out. Then I grabbed for him, urging him to climb atop me, and he did.

Even as he had prepared me for the moment, he penetrated me slowly. Even with the lubrication of my own juices, he was careful and attentive. Then, in a final push, he was inside and I forced a gasp of delight. I moved with him, rocked with him as his thrusts grew faster and faster, then uttered a throaty shriek, my back arched, and he exploded inside me and we found ourselves side by side again, still in each other's arms.

⚜   ⚜   ⚜

In the end, the greatest aphrodisiac for a man is the pleasure he thinks he has given his partner. This is the way to own him, to invade his thoughts and control his desire—simply convince him that he is your greatest lover. To be sure, there are other factors in every relationship. But in the rites of sex, you must make him believe that you have never, and will never, achieve ecstasy the way you can with him. You must persuade him that you live for the pleasure only he is able to give you.

His ego will be nurtured, his sense of self-importance fulfilled, and his craving for sexual dominance will be tied to you and the way he makes you feel.

And then, ironically, he will be yours.

Elizabeth pushed away from the laptop, rose from her chair, and picked up her glass. A full-length mirror, framed in polished brass, stood in the corner of the room. She turned away from the computer and slowly scanned her reflection. She studied her fine features, intense eyes, dark complexion, rich full lips and thick auburn hair. She looked herself over as if searching for something familiar that had once been there but could no longer be found. Her face was still young, although informed by a bitterness she refused to see. She was approaching forty, and it seemed all that she valued in herself was what remained of her physical beauty.

She placed her wine glass on a side table. Dressed only in a blue satin robe, she held it open, then shrugged slightly, encouraging the sleek fabric to slide from her shoulders and float slowly to the floor. A gust of cool air wafted in through an open window, caressing her skin as she studied her naked figure, admired the fullness of her bosom, the curves of her womanly hips, the dark texture of the narrow line of manicured hair that gave musky focus to the smooth flesh between her legs.

She held her breasts in her hands, then ran her palms roughly across her nipples until they hardened. She was pleased as she watched herself in the looking glass, but this wasn't enough.

She suddenly uttered a hollow, mirthless laugh that resonated beyond the confines of the small room, carrying through the open window and piercing the quiet outside.

Her murderer, standing beside a large oak at the near edge of her property, flinched at the familiar sound.

Elizabeth's home was set amidst proud old maples and stately oaks, a large stone Tudor with leaded glass windows and an imposing slate roof. It was not actually *her* home, as Stanley would be quick to remind her—he had bought and paid for it, just as he had paid for all of the other extravagances she enjoyed as his wife. Elizabeth would never voice a response when he launched into these tirades about possessions and entitlements and rights. After all, Stanley did not give her everything she wanted, but he certainly provided her comfort. And comfort was important to Elizabeth.

Stanley was working at the hospital in New York today, as he was on most weekdays, performing surgery. He told her that he would be staying overnight in their New York City apartment, leaving Elizabeth to amuse herself.

Amusing herself was Elizabeth's favorite pastime.

This afternoon she would indulge in the ultimate humiliation of her cold and disapproving husband. In an act even more degrading to him than merely giving herself to someone else, Elizabeth would have one of her lovers in her home. *Stanley's* home.

She thought of how she might taunt her husband with the details of this latest infidelity. The thought amused her, excited her, but did not make her happy.

She picked up her robe and headed upstairs.

In the bedroom, Elizabeth sat at the dressing table facing another mirror. She was fond of mirrors. This time she regarded herself with the vacant stare of a stranger. Noticing the scratch marks on her neck, she absently touched them, then picked up a brush and began running it slowly through her thick hair.

When she heard the front door open and then close downstairs, it only vaguely occurred to her that he had arrived early. She listened as the footsteps faintly echoed through the quiet, as if real life were suddenly intruding upon her fantasies. She had told him he should let himself in, that she would be alone, but she wondered for a moment why he had not called out her name. She did not trouble herself about it. Instead, she placed the brush on the table, rose from the cushioned bench, and walked to her bed.

Champagne was chilling in an ice-filled bucket on her nightstand. She twirled the bottle once, then fluffed up the pillows against the mahogany headboard and climbed between the sheets, pulling the comforter over her naked legs. She waited, listening to the sound of muted footsteps as they made their way up the carpeted stairs.

When the door to her bedroom slowly swung open she did not conceal her surprise. "What are you doing here?" Elizabeth demanded.

At first no answer was given, then, "Under the circumstances, don't you think I should be the one asking the questions."

"Don't be a fool," she replied. "I want you to leave right now."

The murderer strode slowly into the room without speaking.

"What are you doing here?" Elizabeth asked a second time.

Again, there was no response.

"Don't be tiresome," Elizabeth said with growing anger. "I want you out of here. Right now!"

"You've done so much damage, Elizabeth. Far too much. It's time to put an end to all this."

She forced a laugh. "What damage have I done?"

"You asked me not to be tiresome. Please don't play the fool, it doesn't become you."

"What do you want?"

"I told you, I'm going to end all this."

Elizabeth responded with a disgusted look. "Get out," she said.

Only then did the murderer raise the gun for her to see.

Shock turned to fear, then almost at once to defiance. "Put that away," Elizabeth said.

There was a momentary hesitation followed by a grim smile. "I can't," the murderer replied.

"Is that the best you can do? 'You can't'?"

The murderer moved closer, staring down at Elizabeth, not speaking.

"You want to frighten me, is that it?"

"No. I already know that frightening you won't be enough. By tomorrow you'll be back to the same games, the same destructive behavior. No, I've come here to kill you."

"Don't be absurd," Elizabeth said, doing her best not to sound scared. "Put that gun away."

"I told you, I can't. I can't allow this to go on."

"Allow what to go on?"

"You."

It seemed there should be something else to say, but for a moment neither of them spoke. Then Elizabeth raised her hand as if to wave all of this away as some nonsensical raving. "You take everything too seriously. I've told you that before. Put that away so we can talk."

"Talking is done." With that said, the murderer moved to the edge of the bed and yanked back the sheets to expose Elizabeth's naked form. "This is all it's about for you, isn't it?" the murderer said, then raised the gun and pointed it at the side of Elizabeth's head.

"You're so pathetic," Elizabeth replied.

Then it was over.

CHAPTER 2

That evening, Lieutenant Detective Anthony Walker arrived at the bank building in the center of town. Paper coffee cup in hand, he stepped from his unmarked SUV into the dusky night.

Officer Kovacevic was waiting for him.

"He still up there?"

Kovacevic pointed skyward. Walker spotted the young man, leaning over the edge of the roof of the four-story building. It was tough to see much at this hour from that distance, but Walker guessed the kid was in his late teens.

"How long has he been there?"

"At least fifteen minutes."

Walker had a quick look around. Two police cruisers, an ambulance and a fire truck were already on the scene, along with a growing number of spectators. Walker pulled out his badge and hung it on the zipper of his jacket, an old New York City habit that was unnecessary in this small burgh where it seemed everyone was pretty much acquainted with everyone else. "The chief on his way?"

Kovacevic shook his head. "He told us you'd be in charge."

Walker nodded. It was no secret within the town's small police force that Chief Gill was not a fan of Walker's big city style, but it was Walker he turned to whenever things became messy.

"Any idea who the boy is?"

"That lady over there recognized him." Kovacevic pointed to a middle-aged woman in the crowd who, along with everyone else on the scene, was staring up at the roof. "Told us his name is Kyle Avery, local high school kid."

"She say anything else about him?"

"Sir?"

"You know, is he a bad kid? Trouble maker? Nut job?"

"All she said was he comes from a good family."

"Don't they all?" Walker had a quick look at the team of firemen who were assembling a net just below where the boy was standing. "Get that goddamned thing ready," he called out, then turned back to Kovacevic. "He talk with anyone yet? Say what he wants?"

"Kevin Chambers went up there and tried to talk with him, but the kid got all kinds of nervous. Kevin came back inside and called the chief. That's when he told us to wait for you."

"The kid could have jumped in the meantime," Walker said, more to himself than his junior officer.

Kovacevic waited.

"Any indication of drugs or alcohol?"

"Don't know, sir."

"All right." Walker took a sip of his black coffee, which had become lukewarm in the cool night air. He tossed it into a nearby trash can. "We reach his parents?"

"The mother was out to dinner, they just tracked her down. The father was at a meeting in New York. Both on their way now. Mother gave us the name of their family psychiatrist, said she would call her."

A woman's voice came from behind them. "I'm a psychologist, officer, not a psychiatrist."

Walker and Kovacevic turned to face a tall, attractive blond. She was wearing a black skirt, gray jacket, and a serious look.

Walker gave her the once over, then said, "Well I'm a detective, not an officer."

"Oh," she replied, her anxious gaze moving from Walker to the boy on the ledge.

"He's your patient?" Walker asked.

"I work with the family, yes." She extended her hand. "Randi Conway," she said. "I'm here to help."

He liked her grip, it was firm and sure. He also liked her looks. She appeared to be in her midthirties, with warm, brown eyes and soft features. Her sandy-colored hair was straight and shoulder length, a style he figured she didn't waste a lot of time on but looked great all the same. She was a couple of inches taller than Walker, but he wasn't the type to hold that against a woman. "What sort of help you figure you can be? You gonna talk him down, like in the movies?"

"I would like to speak with him, yes."

"Look, uh, miss . . ."

"Conway, Doctor Conway."

"Look, Doctor Conway, this kid doesn't want to jump and I don't want you giving him any reason why he should."

"He doesn't want to jump?"

"That's right."

"And what qualifies you to make that judgment?"

"I'm told he's been up there for more than fifteen minutes. If he wanted to off himself, he could have done a swan dive already, right?"

"I appreciate your professional analysis, Detective, but I'm Kyle's therapist and I demand to see him right now."

"Oh, I see, you *demand* to see him. Sorry, I didn't get the demand part the first time. Well, Doctor, I would love to accommodate your *demand*, but I think it's a little late for an hour of therapy, don't you? I'm in charge here, and I'll be the first one to speak with the boy. Whatever he's up to, it's my job to bring him down safely. After that he's all yours." He turned to Kovacevic. "Run over to that liquor store and get me a couple of cans of cold beer, pronto."

"Seriously, sir?"

"Seriously. Now move it." Kovacevic took off at a trot across the street and Walker returned his attention to the activity at the front of the building. "Get that damned trampoline set up," he yelled out. "You're a rescue unit, not Barnum and Bailey's Circus."

Kovacevic quickly returned with a six-pack of Budweiser. Walker took it from him and strode through the crowd. Short and muscular, he moved with purpose, arms akimbo, his unforgiving gray-brown eyes announcing his attitude without the need to utter a single word. He did not bother to acknowledge any of the familiar faces he passed. The only thing Walker cared about right now was the young man on the roof, and how the hell he was going to get him down.

He entered the lobby of this four-story building, the tallest structure in town, with Dr. Conway and Kovacevic in tow. They rode the elevator to the top floor in silence, then the three of them hurried up the staircase leading to the roof. At the door, two police officers greeted Walker.

"You spoke with him?" Walker asked.

Sergeant Chambers nodded. "He's a touchy kid," he warned.

"Right," Walker replied.

"When I opened the door and tried to say something I thought he was going to fly right off the edge."

"Got it."

Randi Conway began to speak, but Walker showed her the palm of his hand and said, "Stay here," then he slowly opened the door and went outside alone.

As Walker stepped onto the roof, Dr. Conway turned to Kovacevic. "Your boss had better know what he's doing."

"Don't worry," he told her, "he does."

When Walker strode through the door, the boy was so startled he nearly fell backward.

"Take it easy, son, I'm only here to ask a couple of questions."

Walker could have scripted the kid's next line.

"Don't come any closer or I'll jump." The boy was standing just a few feet from the edge of the roof. He had turned away from the crowd below as he watched Walker and waited for the policeman's next move. "I mean it," he said.

"Fair enough," Walker replied. He let the door close behind him and moved slowly toward the ledge. Looking down, he said, "Quite a show, huh?"

The young man offered no response, keeping his eyes on Walker as he took another step away from the policeman.

Walker knew from years of experience that there's a world of difference between gazing up at a jumper and meeting him face-to-face. He felt his stomach tighten as he eyed the boy, knowing that whether the kid was going to live or die was now in his hands. Over the course of the next minute or two, the things he said and the moves he made were going to determine this young man's fate.

"I hate heights," he told the boy, doing his best to sound matter-of-fact about it. "Scares the hell outta me." Walker turned his back to the crowd below and sat on the concrete parapet. He placed the six-pack of beer beside him, then pulled a can from the plastic holder and popped the top. "Want one?"

The boy shook his head.

Walker drank down a long swallow without taking his eyes off the kid. "They tell me you're Kyle Avery, that right?"

The boy nodded.

"I'm Anthony Walker."

Kyle just waited.

"You drink beer Kyle?"

Kyle appeared confused.

"It's not a trick question," Walker assured him with a grin.

"I'm under age," Kyle told him.

Walker nodded thoughtfully. "How old are you?"

"Sixteen. Almost seventeen."

"Well, under the circumstances I think it'll be all right." He smiled again. "I am a cop, you know." He pointed to the badge that hung against his chest. "I can give you permission."

Kyle stared at him without speaking.

Walker pulled another can from the plastic sleeve and tossed it underhand to the boy. Kyle took a step away from the edge of the tar-covered roof and grabbed the can as it spun toward him.

"Nice catch," Walker said.

Kyle popped the can open and beer foamed over the top. He took a gulp and began to cough.

Walker reacted with a warm laugh. "Easy," he said.

The boy surprised himself as he began to laugh too.

"So," Walker said, "here we are, just a couple of guys having a beer. Isn't life something?"

"Yeah," Kyle said, "I guess it is."

"So what're you gonna do now? You gonna drink that brewski and come with me and enjoy the rest of your life, or you gonna jump off this building and break your legs?"

The smile vanished from Kyle's face.

"Hey, I'm just asking." Walker took another swig of beer, then nonchalantly held up the can. "A lot of those foreign brews are tasty, but there are times when you can't beat a cold Bud."

Kyle took another drink of the beer, more carefully this time, but said nothing.

"You have anything to drink before you came up here? Do any drugs or anything?"

Kyle frowned, then shook his head.

"Hey," Walker said with another of his friendliest smiles, "don't be so offended, I had to ask."

The boy nodded.

"Look, I don't know what brought you up here, Kyle, but it's still your choice how you get down."

Kyle hesitated, then said, "I'm in a lot of trouble, huh?"

Walker pursed his lips as if he was thinking it over, then shrugged. "Not as far as I'm concerned. You came into the building, it's a free country, right? You decided to have a look at the roof. Okay, not a great idea, but not the end of the world either. Then everyone down there got excited when they saw you, so you started watching them, they got to watching you, and next thing you know everyone is watching everyone else and trying to figure out what all the excitement is about. That about right?"

Kyle responded with a shy smile.

Then he took a step closer to the ledge.

When the boy saw Walker tense, he said, "I'm just going to sit down."

Walker let out a breath. Then he watched as the boy sat, his back to the street, just as Walker had positioned himself. They were about eight feet apart now.

"Things get so complicated," Kyle said.

Walker nodded. "You're telling me."

"I mean it," he said. "I really screwed up."

"Not yet you haven't."

"Yeah, I have."

Walker sighed. "We all screw up."

The boy said nothing.

"You've got a lot of people worried about you."

Kyle nodded.

"I think they'll all be glad if you come down with me."

"Sure they will," Kyle said, "at first. Then they'll just be pissed off." He paused, then added, "*As usual*," in that way young people have of making things clear with just a couple of words.

"Maybe so, but not for long, right? They'll be a lot more upset if you jump off this roof, I can promise you that."

Kyle thought it over. "I guess so."

Walker laughed. "You guess so?"

"All my parents do is argue anyway. This'll just be something else for them to fight about."

Walker watched as the boy took another gulp from the can, then said, "I figure their problems are their problems, even if they are your parents. No reason to make their problems yours."

Kyle shook his head. "Some of their problems *are* mine," he said.

"That could be so, but whatever they are you're not going to solve them up here."

"I guess not."

Walker eyed him seriously for a moment. "Big problems?"

"I think so."

For the first time, Kyle looked him directly in the eyes, and it struck Walker how young the boy really was—and how pivotal these next few moments would be. "Anything you want to tell me about?"

Kyle was quiet for a few seconds, just staring at Walker. Then he said, "Maybe. But not now."

"These problems with your family, they what brought you up here?"

Kyle nodded.

"That's lousy."

"Yeah." A sad look crossed his young face.

"Whatever these troubles are, trust me, things have a way of working out."

Kyle managed a sad smile. "That's something adults always say."

Walker could not help suppress a genuine laugh. "Damn, and I thought I was doing so well up till then."

The boy laughed too.

"Look Kyle, just cause we say it a lot doesn't mean it's not true. Big troubles today become ancient history in no time."

"You think so?"

Walker responded with a serious look and said, "I know so."

Kyle took a long gulp of the beer. "Adults can really be fucked up."

"Tell me about it. I'm a cop."

The boy looked at him again. "I mean it. They can do some rotten things."

"You mean, like parents?"

"Sure. But not just them. Other people too. Really bad, you know?"

Walker gave him a serious look. "I do."

Kyle nodded to himself, as if confirming a thought. "I guess I've got some stuff to figure out."

"Everybody does. You ever want to talk about it, I'll be around."

"Thanks."

Walker stood. "So, you ready to go?"

Kyle looked up, then held out the can. "Okay if I finish this first?"

CHAPTER 3

An hour later the crowd in front of the building had dispersed, Kyle Avery was in the care of the psychiatric staff at Norwalk Hospital, and Anthony Walker was preparing to spend another night alone in what he referred to as his comfortable townhouse apartment.

He described the place as "comfortable" only because the alternative was to admit that it was small.

Walker was thirty-nine, New York City born and bred, son of a tough Irish American father and a doting Italian American mother. His destiny, as a second-generation police officer, was written the day he first saw his dad in uniform. He attended public schools in the Bronx, graduated with honors from John Jay College, then joined the NYPD. He served with distinction for ten years, fighting the good fight and getting a practical education in the realities of the American criminal justice system.

He dealt with junkies who would slit an old lady's throat for the price of a dime bag; inner-city scum who acted as if raping a child was an acceptable way of life; violent thugs who preyed on their own people; and a court system that kept spitting these vermin back out onto the street. He became sick of risking his life without ever making a real difference. More than anything, he grew tired of worrying about the life he was providing for his wife and daughters.

After ten years of wrestling with all that, he decided it was time to get out.

That was just over five years ago. He left New York and accepted a position as a detective with the Darien Police Department. Moving his family to the suburbs of Connecticut meant a substantial pay cut and an increase in his cost of living. But Walker felt it was the right thing to do for his wife and daughters.

Then he discovered that financial concerns were the least of his problems.

There was the cultural change, of course, like going from a rock concert to a library reading room. Darien was not a hotbed of crime, and there was not much of consequence to detect, not for a cop of his experience and ability. Taken together, all of the incidents of vandalism and burglary he had handled over the past five years were considerably less dangerous than a single midnight-to-eight tour in his old Manhattan precinct.

But those changes were nothing compared to the personal issues that turned his life upside down—and the worst of it was that he never saw any of it coming.

He beat himself up over that last part during many a lonely night. *What a lousy detective I turned out to be*, he kept telling himself.

It began in subtle ways. His contact with old friends in New York became less frequent. He was in the prosperous suburbs now and, although Walker was the same person he had always been, there was a change in the calculus of those relationships.

New friends were tough to find in this affluent area, where he was regarded as little more than the hired help. He never really clocked his wife's growing disenchantment with their limited means, never saw her increasing fascination with the wealth around them. When she walked out on him she told him there was nothing to discuss. It was over. She took their two girls and moved in with the guy she had been sleeping with while Walker was working at keeping their lives together. The divorce was cut and dry—as Walker knew, fighting anything in court is a rich man's game—and so now she was married to someone else and living in a fancy house up the coast in Westport.

Walker was alone.

He was not big on regrets, never saw the point in that. His decision to move from New York had been a personal disaster, but it was what it was. He wasn't about to head back to the city, not with his two daughters up here. All he could do was keep his head down and continue moving forward.

Tonight, for instance, he did what he was accustomed to doing on most evenings in his comfortable townhouse apartment—he changed into sweats, switched on the TV in the kitchen, and got ready to pour himself a bourbon. Then the telephone rang, the sound telling him that his plans were about to be undone.

"Walker? It's Gill."

"Hello Chief."

"This Avery matter. The hospital tells me they'll be releasing the boy after twenty-four hours of observation."

Walker stared at the television. The Yankees were playing the Blue Jays. "That's good news, Chief."

"Yeah. The kid's a minor and they won't hold him under these circumstances, not with the family insisting there was no overt action toward a suicide. But we've got to get a statement from the parents. Just routine, you know. Best if you get over there tonight and get it done before the boy comes home."

Walker felt his jaw tighten. "All we need is a statement. Can't you send Kovacevic? He was there with me, and I was just about to eat." He stared at the bottle of Woodford Reserve that seemed to be beckoning to him.

"Kovie's too green," Gill said, making no apology for disturbing Walker's evening. "You were in charge, and I don't want any more flak about how this was handled."

"Flak about how it was handled? The kid was on the roof and I brought him down."

"I know, but it seems everyone in town has already heard about the beer. He's under age and was a possible suicide attempt. You can imagine how that might be viewed."

"How about with gratitude?" Walker shook his head. "Jesus, I would've given the kid the six-pack if I thought it would help."

"I know, I know."

"Who complained? Not the parents, I'll bet."

"Not so far."

"The shrink?"

"No. Heard you were a little rough on her, but she gave you high marks." Gill hesitated. "You know this town, bunch of magpies, but we've got to keep the natives happy." He paused. "You still don't get that."

"I suppose not."

Gill exhaled into the phone, as if to say that Walker would never get it. "Look, we've got a job to do, and around here we do it by the book."

Walker figured that was about the eleven-thousandth time he'd heard that line from the chief. "Right."

"So, when you're there, if you've got to say you're sorry about the beer, just say it."

"That I'm *sorry*?"

"This whole episode is upsetting enough for the parents," Gill reminded him, then recited the Averys' address. "Get on over there and finish this, you copy?"

"I copy," Walker agreed, then listened as the chief hung up. He placed the phone down, said, "Shithead," plugged the cork back into the bottle of bourbon, and trudged to the bedroom to change back into his street clothes.

✣   ✣   ✣

Randi Conway pulled into the driveway of her small home, which was set on a tree-lined street just south of the Merritt Parkway. She turned off the car and dropped the key in the ashtray. Stepping into the cool night air, she reached into the mailbox and pulled out a handful of bills, notices, and catalogs, then strolled toward her front door.

She did not notice the sedan, parked across the street, or the driver sitting in the dark, watching her.

Randi's house was a traditional Cape Cod, but the interior featured her own style, an incongruous mix of modern and traditional pieces. This was no designer showcase, and it mattered not at all to her that chrome and glass tables should not be mixed with Queen Anne armchairs or bead board walls and crown moldings. It was hers and it worked for her.

She shut the door and made her way past the living room, straight ahead to the kitchen.

The house was silent.

She opened the refrigerator. It was empty but for fat-free milk, ketchup, an assortment of mustards, a variety of other condiments, and several bottles of spring water. She settled on water, picked up the mail again, and went to the dining room.

Randi had never been married. She had been engaged once, but that fell apart three years ago when her former fiancé—whom she had come to affectionately refer to as "that miserable sonuvabitch"—walked out on her and moved to California. That was when she began using the dining room as an office, since she figured dinner parties were not in her immediate future. The table held a telephone and a pile of papers to which she now added this latest stack of envelopes. She fell wearily into a chair, reached for the phone, and retrieved her voice mail.

"Hi Randi, it's Sharon," the first voice announced. "Talked to a great guy at our sales meeting today. Single, or I think he's almost single. Anyway, I told him about you and he asked for your number. Should I give it? He's a good-looking guy . . ."

Randi groaned, then deleted the message before it was finished. A beeping sound gave way to the next voice.

"Hello sweetheart, it's your mother. You haven't called me this week. Are you all right? I'm fine, if you care to know. I was just worried about you, that's all. Are you busy this weekend? Give me a call if you have a minute."

Randi deleted that one too.

"Hello Randi, it's Bob," the next message began. "Look, I'm having dinner at the club Friday night with some of the usual suspects. Linda may or may not make it, she's got one of her charity things, off to save the whales or something. Either way, I'd love to have you join us. Give me a shout."

After saving that one, an electronic voice told her the messages were finished. She sighed, then returned to sorting through her mail when the chime at her front door rang. She was not expecting anyone, but surprises were part of her profession. She made her way back through the foyer and, when she opened the door, she found Kyle Avery's mother standing on the small wooden portico.

"Joan."

"I'm so sorry to bother you. After we spoke on the phone I went to the police station, but he'd already been taken away. To a hospital," she added with pained look. "Then they told me they need to get a statement from us about what happened tonight."

"I understand. They have to speak with you because he's a minor," Randi explained. "Come in, please," she said, then shut the door behind them.

Joan said, "Yes, that's what the police chief told us."

"Did they ask for the statement there?"

"No, Mitchell's on his way back from New York and I didn't want to do anything without him. They said they would come to our home." Her distress was mixed with confusion. "What can we possibly tell them?"

"They're only going to ask for some very basic information. It'll be fine. When are they coming?"

"Right now," she said. "I'm so sorry to impose, but I would feel so much better if . . ."

"It's all right, Joan. I'll follow you. Let me just get my bag."

In the dark, as they climbed into their cars and headed off to the Averys', neither of them noticed the car that remained parked across the street from Randi Conway's house. Or who was seated at the wheel.

CHAPTER 4

Walker parked his Explorer in the circular driveway at the address Gill had given him, walked to the double doors and rang the bell.

A few moments later, he was greeted by a man who looked to be in his early fifties, about a dozen years older and a couple of inches taller than Walker. He had a spreading middle, broad shoulders, and a balding head. He was wearing neatly creased slacks, a crisply pressed shirt, and an embarrassed look.

Walker was dressed in the wrinkled trousers and shirt he had been wearing all day, having tossed off his sweats and pulled his clothes back on after the chief's call. He suddenly felt he should have done a better job of dressing for this visit.

"Mr. Avery? I'm Detective Anthony Walker from the Darien Police. I hope my timing is all right, coming over here like this."

Avery stuck out his hand and forced a smile. "It's Mitchell," he said. "Chief Gill told us you were on the way. Just got back from New York myself."

Walker looked directly into the man's eyes as they shook hands. He generally gave himself high marks for the ability to judge people quickly, but he figured Kyle's father was going to be a tough read. Just a couple of hours ago Mitchell Avery was told that his son had spent the early part of the evening peering over the edge of a four-story roof. Then he was informed the boy would have to be held for psychiatric evaluation in a high-security hospital ward. Now a police detective arrived at his home for questioning, all of which might throw the average guy off his game. But, other than that first uncomfortable grin, Mitchell Avery acted as if an old crony had dropped by for cocktails.

"Come on in," Kyle's father said, leading them into a two-story-high foyer, which Walker judged to be about the size of his entire apartment. It was adorned with textured wallpaper, had a granite tiled floor, and featured an impressive crystal chandelier.

"Nice place," Walker said. He was not a jealous sort, at least not when it came to possessions. All the same, since coming to Connecticut he had wondered more than once what it would be like to exist in this sort of world, feeling that you really belonged, that you really deserved to be here.

He reckoned he would never know.

"This way," Avery urged him, "the ladies are inside."

They passed through an arched entrance into a spacious living room where Avery said, "This is my wife, Joan. Joan, Detective Walker. And this is Randi Conway. My wife asked Randi to be here. She's our, uh . . ."

"Doctor Conway and I have had the pleasure," Walker told him.

The two women were seated on the other side of the room, and Walker took the dozen or so paces he needed to navigate the expanse of a very large Oriental carpet to get there. As he approached them, he noticed that Randi had removed her dark jacket to reveal a cream-colored blouse. He also noticed, in the soft light, that she looked even better than she had before.

"Didn't expect to see you again so soon, Doctor," he said.

"No," she replied, "likewise I'm sure."

Joan Avery was seated beside the therapist on a long, ivory-colored sofa. She was a smart-looking woman, smartly dressed, with smart eyes that were green and warm and sad. She looked somewhere between distraught and exhausted.

Walker liked her.

"I really hate to bother you folks like this," he told them. Joan Avery stood up and they shook hands. "This is one of those routine things we have to do."

"We understand," Joan said politely, although her turned-down mouth told him she really did not understand at all.

Randi Conway, who remained seated on the couch, said, "Perhaps you could explain to the Averys exactly what this routine thing is you have to do?"

"Well, in the case of, uh, a case like this, we have to get a statement from the parents." He turned back to Joan. "Your son is under age, and he's, uh, well, the subject of, uh . . ."

"All right," Mitchell intervened. "Let's get on with it then. Sit down, Detective." When he pointed to a plush armchair, Walker sank into it, grateful to be rescued.

"Can I get you something?" Joan Avery asked. "Coffee?"

Walker smiled. "No thanks, I'm fine. Funny though, how people think policemen want coffee all the time."

"That is funny," Randi Conway said with a knowing smile, "especially in your case."

Walker turned back to Mrs. Avery, who had resumed her seat beside her therapist. "Look, about the beer . . ."

"Detective Walker," Joan interrupted wearily, "Doctor Conway told us what you did. I'd prefer to think that Kyle was confused and never really intended to . . . to . . . do himself any harm. Whatever part you had in putting an end to the incident, I just want you to know that we're very grateful."

"Glad we got that out of the way," Mitchell jumped in. "So how about it, Walker? Beer? Gin and tonic?"

"No sir, but thanks. On duty, you see." Walker turned back to Joan Avery. At the moment she seemed to be the only one there concerned about Kyle. "For what it's worth, ma'am, I don't believe your son was the kind of kid who really wanted to hurt himself."

"Tell you the truth," Kyle Avery's father said, "I'd like to know exactly what kind of kid he is."

"Please, Mitchell," his wife intoned in a way that provided Walker some additional insight into the Avery family dynamic.

"You know, Mr. Avery," Walker jumped in, "I've dealt with a lot of kids over the years. Good kids, confused kids, some real punks too. Everything from serious crimes, when I was with the NYPD, to suburban pranks here in town. In fact, I just realized, wasn't your son one of the boys who tore up part of the golf course with a Ski-Doo last winter?"

"That was him, all right," Mitchell sighed.

"I didn't put that together till just now," Walker admitted.

Randi tilted her head slightly, as if about to say something, but remained silent.

Walker stayed focused on Kyle's father. "Hell, kids do that kinda stuff all the time. It's not right, of course, but it happens. Point I'm trying to make is that a kid who actually wants to, uh, who really wants to hurt himself, believe me—and this may sound harsh—but they know how to do it. Kyle has some concerns, that's why he was on the bank roof."

Walker saw Mitchell wince at that statement. "What concerns?" the man asked.

Walker decided not to push the issue. He said, "I think your son just needed a little attention, is all."

"Thank you for your psychological evaluation," Randi Conway interjected. "Are you giving a statement here or taking one?"

"Right." Walker turned to Joan Avery. "I had a chance to speak with your son for a while. Up there on the roof and afterward."

Joan responded with a curious look.

"Obviously Kyle has issues, I understand that, but there was one thing in particular seemed to be gnawing at him. You have any idea what that might be?"

Joan shook her head and began to say something, but her husband broke in.

"Do you?" Mitchell asked Walker, the question sounding more like an accusation than an inquiry. When Walker met his gaze the man did not blink. "Did he say something?"

"Not much in the way of detail, but whatever's eating at him, he certainly believes it's a big problem."

The look on Avery's face was more relief than concern. He said, "Too bad he didn't tell you more," then leaned back in his chair. "So, what else do you need to do here?"

"Just a few questions and I'll be out of your way."

❖   ❖   ❖

Walker completed the remainder of his *pro forma* interview as quickly as he could, pulling out a notebook and making a show of jotting down a few things. Then he stood, assured the Averys everything would be just fine, and said good night. Mitchell escorted him to the door, where he shook his hand energetically and thanked Walker as if he'd just delivered some extraordinarily good news. It was obvious, of the two of them, Avery was even more relieved the interview was over than Walker.

Walker strode down the driveway, then decided to wait.

A couple of minutes later he watched as Randi Conway bid the Averys good-bye at the front door. After Mitchell and Joan went inside, Randi turned and saw Walker leaning on her car.

He said, "You're pretty tough, you know that?" Randi began walking toward him, so Walker straightened up. She was taller than he was, so he figured there was no reason to make it worse. Before she could speak, he added, "I was just doing my job in there. I was also trying to help."

"Help? These people are in distress. When you mentioned the golf course vandalism, was that your idea of being helpful?"

"A little perspective can be a good thing. Kids do crazy things for all different reasons. Haven't you ever done anything crazy?" Before she could respond, he said, "No, of course you haven't."

They stared at each other for a moment. "Was there something else?" she asked. "I've had a very long day."

"I don't know. I just wanted to say it's been interesting meeting you."

Randi tilted her head slightly to the side. "Interesting? I wonder what that's supposed to mean."

"You're the psychologist," he said with a grin, "you figure it out." Walker turned toward his SUV, then stopped and looked back at her. "You know," he said, still smiling, "you're kind of edgy, even for a shrink."

Randi Conway stood there without responding as he climbed into his Explorer and drove away.

CHAPTER 5

The following morning the Knoebels' maid, Nettie Sisson, arrived at their home, made her way up the winding staircase, then quietly approached the door to the master bedroom. It was closed. She listened, heard nothing, then knocked and, getting no answer, turned the knob and pushed it open.

She stood there, stock-still, and viewed the scene.

Elizabeth was lying in the comfort of the soft sheets, the goose down duvet thrown back exposing her naked form, her long, well-formed legs parted slightly. Even from the doorway, in the dim light that peered through the curtains, it was apparent that Elizabeth's skin, always silky and smooth, had turned gray.

Elizabeth's arms lay peacefully at her sides, as if she were resting. The only evidence of her violent end was the blood that stained the pillows and headboard and her once beautiful face.

Nettie did not scream. There was no one to hear it. She drew a deep breath to steady herself, then went down to the kitchen, picked up the phone, and dialed 911.

When police dispatch received the call, Chief Gill immediately summoned Anthony Walker to his office, briefed him on what little they knew, and sent him out to lead the investigation into Elizabeth Knoebel's death.

Walker arrived at the house just after the forensic team and the first wave of uniformed officers. He was pointed upstairs, found his way to the bedroom, and had a quick look around. Kovacevic was already taking some preliminary information from a stocky woman. One of the other officers told him she was the housekeeper. Walker did not interrupt. He walked over to the bed and stood over Elizabeth's body for a moment, staring down at her lifeless face.

"Doesn't matter how many times I see it," he said to no one in particular, then kept the rest of the thought to himself. He turned away and joined Kovacevic, who made the introductions.

Nettie Sisson was a squat, plain-looking woman he figured to be somewhere near sixty. She had a timeworn face that age had chosen not to favor, and she would have been utterly forgettable but for the hazel eyes that seemed haunted, perhaps by Elizabeth Knoebel's death, perhaps by something else.

"You live here?" Walker asked.

She shook her head.

"Where were you yesterday?"

"I was home mostly, it was a day off." Her voice was timid and she seemed incapable of looking directly into Walker's eyes. "I only work here three days a week."

"You married?"

There was an almost imperceptible flinch before she shook her head and said, "I live alone," which did not exactly answer the question.

"Where?"

She gave her address, a garden apartment complex just outside town. Probably not unlike his own place, Walker noted.

"Got all that?" he asked Kovacevic.

"Already wrote it down," the officer told him.

Returning his attention to the housekeeper, Walker said, "You were the one who found Mrs. Knoebel?"

The woman nodded. She was still avoiding his gaze while also refusing to look in the direction of the corpse on the bed. Walker made it a habit of interrogating witnesses at the crime scene whenever possible. He believed it helped to bring out the truth from people.

"You always have Tuesdays off?" he asked.

She shook her head. "Usually, but not always. Mrs. Knoebel would sometimes change the days."

Walker turned back to Kovacevic. "Where's the husband?"

"On his way, sir. He's coming back from New York, he was in surgery. They couldn't interrupt him."

"I understand from the chief he wasn't here last night."

"They have an apartment in New York."

"Uh huh." Walker glanced around the bedroom again. It was decorated with dark wooden antiques and brocade fabrics. Not a very feminine decor, he observed, full of ornate furniture and heavy drapery. "Mrs. Sisson . . . it *is* missus?"

She nodded tentatively. "I'm divorced," she told him.

"You say you got here about eight o'clock this morning, right?"

"Before eight. I got here before eight."

"And no one else was here."

"No."

"And you didn't touch anything in this room, correct?"

"Yes. I mean, no, I didn't touch anything. I knocked on the door, then I opened it."

"Uh huh. Why did you open the door? Wasn't it possible Mrs. Knoebel was just sleeping late."

"Mrs. Knoebel never sleeps late. I always come up here first thing to see if she wants coffee or tea or something."

"You notice anything strange in Mrs. Knoebel's behavior lately?"

She replied with a vacant look. "Strange?"

"Unhappy, nervous, upset?"

"No sir," she replied, her voice barely audible now.

"Appear to you that anything is missing from the house?"

She treated him to another blank stare. "I don't know," she said. "I didn't touch anything."

"So you said. Well, spend some more time with Officer Kovacevic here. Tell him anything you know about where the Knoebels keep their valuables, jewelry, silver. See if you notice anything that might have been taken. We'll be in touch."

Nettie Sisson again nodded solemnly. Before she followed Kovacevic from the bedroom she bowed her head, crossed herself, and kissed her bent thumb.

Walker watched her leave, then turned to the coroner. "What have we got?"

Jake, a balding, bespectacled man wearing latex gloves and a grim expression, looked up from the notes he was making. "Time of death, sometime yesterday, probably afternoon or early evening. We can get more specific after the autopsy. One slug to the right temple seems to have done the trick."

As he listened, Walker moved back to the side of the bed, looking down again at the inert figure of Elizabeth Knoebel. He shoved his hands in his pockets and wordlessly surveyed the bloody death scene. "Go on."

"You want some general observations?"

"Sure."

Jake used his middle finger to push his eyeglasses up the bridge of his nose. "Okay. Her body is in a strange position. She looks incredibly relaxed for someone about to have her brains blown out. The force of the gunshot snapped her head to the side, but otherwise she looks like she just laid down for a nap."

"You think someone rearranged the body after she was shot?"

"If they did, it was only a minor adjustment. The blood pattern is consistent with her having been shot right here."

Walker nodded. "What else?"

"Why does she get undressed and go to bed in the middle of the afternoon?"

"You want me to take a guess?"

"Okay, I'll give you that. It just struck me as peculiar, is all."

"Any evidence of drugs or alcohol?"

"The autopsy will tell us. I don't see anything to indicate drug use, but I assume you noticed the champagne."

"Uh huh," Walker said. He had another look at the bucket on the night table.

"Expensive bottle of bubbly," Jake said. "Unopened."

"Right," Walker said with a sigh. Jake, master of the obvious. "Get me what you can on sexual activity before death. Or after, for that matter. I don't see any signs of a struggle, although I noticed there are scratch marks on her neck."

"Old news," the coroner replied. "Those marks are partially healed, had to be made at least twenty-four hours before death, probably more."

"All right, do your thing. I'll speak with you this afternoon."

"We won't have all the autopsy results done by then."

"That's fine, Jake, just call me with whatever you've got. I love the sound of your voice."

Kovacevic returned and reported that Mrs. Sisson was downstairs in the kitchen with Kevin Chambers.

"Anything on the burglary angle?"

Kovacevic shook his head. "She says there doesn't seem to be anything missing. Silver in the dining room is intact, jewelry boxes upstairs don't look like they were touched."

Walker nodded, then scanned the room again. The headboard was mahogany, but the dresser and armoire were made of some wood he did not recognize. He noticed that the deep burgundy bedding coordinated with the rich patterns of the drapery. Obviously pricey stuff, but awfully dark.

"Kind of a masculine room, don't you think?"

Kovacevic had a look around, as if seeing the room for the first time. "I guess so."

"Looks like a man's room."

"Maybe," Kovacevic said with a shrug.

"In my experience the bedroom is usually decorated by the woman."

Kovacevic nodded. "I wouldn't know, sir."

Walker smiled. "The housekeeper tell you anything else about the Knoebels' relationship I might be interested to know?"

"Not anything specific, although I get the impression from Mrs. Sisson that they didn't have the greatest marriage in town. I've got notes," he added and began to thumb through his pad.

"All right Kovie, we'll go over that later. Meanwhile, speak with the neighbors. I don't suppose anyone phoned in a report of a gunshot?"

"No such luck, sir. But this is a big piece of property. Wooded.

Houses are shut up tight with their central climate control systems. I had a look at the windows. Solid double-insulation jobs. Even if someone heard something, it wouldn't have been real loud. They could've figured it for a car backfiring."

Walker held up his hand. "Easy," he said with a grin, "I was only kidding."

"Right."

"But it *is* possible someone might have seen or heard something."

"Jake says it was a late-afternoon shooting. Wouldn't most of the neighbors be at work?" He hesitated. "Assuming the people around here go to work."

"Don't assume anything, just spend some time with the local gentry."

"Yes sir."

A uniformed officer came into the room looking for Walker. "Lieutenant, there's something I think you should see."

"What have you got?" Walker asked.

"It'll be better if I show you."

Walker and Kovacevic followed the officer along the corridor, down the stairs, and into the small den on the ground floor. The officer led them toward the laptop on the desk.

"I was poking around, you know, looking for anything that might help, and I saw the computer was on. I just touched the mouse here." The young officer used his latex-gloved hand to move the mouse again. The monitor revealed the passage Elizabeth Knoebel had been working on less than an hour before she died.

Walker and Kovacevic leaned forward to read. When they were done Walker looked up. "Go to the next page."

The officer scrolled down, but they were at the end.

"Anything before it?"

The office hit the *Pg Up* button, and the screen displayed the start of the file. They began reading again:

SEXUAL RITES
By Elizabeth Knoebel
NOTES FOR CHAPTER 5
The Power Seduction

Confident men are often attractive men, a combination that makes them the easiest to seduce. A man with a superior ego has the feeling he deserves to be flattered and desired.

Insecure men tend to be suspicious. They have reasons to doubt your interest, to look behind your subtlest advances for other motives. The egotist has no cause to question your attraction to him. He will not worry that you might be after his money or his position or any of his other assets. He is therefore easy game.

One of the more interesting aspects of seducing a powerful man is the control you can exert over him once the seduction is complete. His opinion of himself is so high he could never doubt your desire for him. You can therefore control him by playing to that vanity. He will be trapped by a fatal combination of two forces.

The first is his own desire. Fueled by your sensuality, he will believe not only that he deserves your favor, but that you are fortunate to be his lover. A married man in this category—and most of them are married—will also be certain he can manage the risks. Like most men, he will have that incredible capacity to ignore the obvious consequences of his actions in order to justify a present need. (How else could we explain every husband who cheated on his wife and was then surprised at getting caught? Every one of them thought they could "handle the situation").

The second factor, somewhat paradoxically, will quite literally bring him to his knees. It will come from your ability to convince him that he is correct, that his attention, his passion, his very being are the things that you lust after, the things you cannot live without.

Remember, you must proceed with caution, for it might cause him to turn away. If overstated, your infatuation will be seen as a sign of instability or desperation. Even a man filled with sexual desire cannot ignore those dangers.

Be prepared for his lies—to you, to himself, to the other people in his life. Still, in the end, the balance of power will have shifted in your favor, as long as you stay focused on the fulfillment of desire.

✣　✣　✣

Our first encounter involved cocktails, suggestive conversation, a chaste kiss, and a subsequent date for lunch in New York. He chose a fashionable bistro on upper Madison Avenue. It was a lovely meal, fueled with wine, and we talked about everything but the truth.

Afterward, we left the café and took a short walk up the avenue. The sky was clear and the autumn air felt crisp and cool as the breeze whipped around us. He had a friend who loaned him the use of his apartment, a small one-bedroom just off Fifth Avenue near the Metropolitan Museum of Art.

We spoke less and less as we made our way to his friend's building. He unlocked the front door to the small brownstone, then led me upstairs.

The apartment was dark, the sunlight shut out by heavy curtains drawn tight across the windows. He switched on the music system in the living room and it began to play a Mozart piano concerto. He poured drinks and placed them on a small round marble table in the corner of the bedroom. It was obvious he knew his way around the place.

He led me to the bed where we sat side by side. He took my hands in his and told me how happy he was to finally be alone with me.

I turned to him but said nothing. I just stared into his eyes. Then he gently kissed me on the lips, letting go of my hands and tenderly holding my face. I responded, his tongue sweet with the taste of whisky as he explored my mouth. I pulled him close, kissing him with a growing passion as I pressed my breasts against his chest.

His hands slowly traced the curves of my sides, my hips, and my ass. I pushed away, giving myself enough room to stand and pull off my silk burgundy dress. Then I sat again, my face warm with modesty and desire.

He laid me back across the width of the bed and slipped off my lace panties. My pussy was already becoming moist from my natural flow. He lifted my legs high in the air and then, bending over me and supporting the underside of my thighs with his hands, he began to lick me. As he probed the lips and depth of me with his wet, hot tongue, I moaned. After enjoying several minutes of this intense pleasure I moved away and turned on my side, encouraging him to lie alongside me so I could take him in my mouth as he continued to explore my tender regions.

He became even more passionate now, with a faster motion, then moved slowly again, and I writhed with the increased rhythm and intensity of his effort.

He reached up to massage my breasts and play with my nipples, all the while licking and sucking me, joining the wetness of his mouth with that of my own engorged flesh. He pushed the heel of his hand against my mons veneris, released, then pressed down again, creating a sublime pressure that made me shudder.

He was large and stiff and I begged him to get inside me. He obliged, turning around and entering me as I lay on my side. After I came—loudly and with obvious delight—he changed positions, moving me onto my knees and taking me from behind. I came again and then he turned me onto my back, got astride me, and we rocked together in a furious motion until we climaxed together.

✥ ✥ ✥

He was clearly pleased with his performance, and I made sure he felt even more than that. I told him that I had never had multiple orgasms before and, with tears in my eyes, said I was completely overcome by the experience.

He was both gracious and confident in his response, but I could see the truth in his eyes.

I could see, from that moment on, that I owned him.

Walker looked up at the other two men. "Nice lady. See what else she's got in here."

When the officer closed the file and attempted to enter the directory, the screen became blank, displaying only a box in the center of the monitor requiring the reentry of the password.

"Damn, must have been on some sort of default screensaver."

Walker nodded. "All right. Kovie, have the computer dusted for prints, then take it with you and get started on a warrant to have it impounded. Grab the maid again and find out if she knows which of the Knoebels used this computer. Find Teddy Blasko, tell him we need to get access to whatever's in there. Anything recent, especially e-mails. And you guys, you keep this to yourselves, you hear me?"

The two younger officers nodded.

"Meantime, make sure the forensic boys do a good job sweeping this room. And for God's sake," Walker said, "tell them to finish with the photographs upstairs so they can cover that woman with a sheet."

CHAPTER 6

That evening, Randi Conway stood in her dining room, the telephone clutched tightly in her hand. Phyllis Wentworth, a diffident woman who was one of the members in Elizabeth Knoebel's therapy group, called to deliver the news.

Randi sank slowly into her chair.

"It's been on the radio. I didn't know if you'd heard."

"No, I hadn't," Randi said.

"It was on the radio," Phyllis repeated.

"What else did they say?"

Phyllis paused, then provided the few details that had been broadcast. A local woman, wife of a prominent New York surgeon, was found dead in her home, victim of a gunshot wound. They gave her name and said an investigation into the death was underway.

Randi did not respond.

"Doctor Conway? Are you there?"

"Yes, Phyllis." Randi drew a deep breath, then asked, "Are *you* all right?"

"I'll be fine," Phyllis said.

"I do appreciate you letting me know."

"It's awful, Doctor Conway. Isn't it awful?"

"Yes. It is awful." When there was no response, Randi said, "Please call me if you want to talk."

"Thank you," Phyllis said, but she did not say good-bye.

"Did you want to say something else?"

"I don't know. Maybe I just want to say that I can't believe it."

"I understand," Randi said. "Neither can I."

Phyllis paused again, then said, "Good night, Doctor Conway," and hung up.

Randi put the phone down and turned to her computer, bringing up the link to the local news station. The evening's top headline was the death of local resident Elizabeth Knoebel. The few details given were those Phyllis had shared. Elizabeth died some time the previous day. Her body was discovered this morning by the housekeeper. More to follow.

Randi sat back, remembering a group session she had conducted just two days before.

They met at Randi Conway's office each Monday afternoon, the gathering of her so-called Wives Group. This past Monday all five women were present.

One of them, a dark-eyed brunette named Fran Colello, was holding court on her favorite subject. "We have their children and make their homes. We cook for them, clean for them and lay on our backs for them. All for what? We're treated like indentured servants, and in the end we get dumped on the garbage heap of life. We can't even be recycled."

A couple of the women managed sympathetic laughs, but Fran responded with a dismissive wave of her hand. She was on her usual roll and didn't see any humor in it.

"I'm forty-five years old and my husband treats me like a piece of furniture. I might as well be in one of those cabinets that hold the junk we've collected over the years, souvenirs that no one even looks at anymore. It might not be so bad if someone took the trouble to dust me off and play with me once in a while, but no one does. My kids are old enough where they don't need a thing from me. I haven't had a job for more than twenty years, unless you count live-in slave as a profession. I'm about as useless as a fondue set." She was staring at Dr. Conway now, as if, somehow, some part of this was her fault.

Randi leaned forward in her seat. "You said 'useless,' Fran. Is that what you meant?"

"What?"

"You described yourself as useless. Is that accurate?"

Fran pushed back her straight brunette hair, revealing a plain face that would be far more appealing if she could lose the fifteen or so pounds she had picked up during those years she now regretted. Her eyes were dark and troubled, her mouth framed in lines etched by anger. "I suppose 'useless' is the right word," she answered defiantly. "I said it, right?"

They were seated in the windowless room Randi used for her groups, chrome and cane armchairs forming a circle, cool fluorescent lighting, and bare, eggshell colored walls creating an antiseptic space designed to generate the fewest possible distractions.

"Do any of you have a response for Fran?" Randi asked.

None of the women answered the challenge until Elizabeth Knoebel spoke up.

As was her custom, Elizabeth came to the session intending to show off her sultry beauty to its maximum and most irritating effect. Her dark green dress featured a low, revealing neckline and the slinky fabric clung to her trim waist. Her makeup was applied with care, her auburn hair brushed perfectly in place. When she turned to Fran a thin smile crossed her lips, but her voice was as cold as the overhead lighting. "If you feel useless then you are useless."

Fran sat up a little straighter in her seat and said, "That's just great, coming from you."

"What is that supposed to mean?"

"It means you haven't spent a single day of your life as a real wife or mother. You don't raise your own daughter, you send her off to school so you won't have to be bothered with her. And you probably couldn't find the kitchen in your own house with a map. Who the hell are you to be making judgments about my life?"

"I didn't. You made the judgment, Fran. I simply agreed." Elizabeth's tone was positively frigid now. "And I must say, I'm sick and tired of you taking out your pitiful frustrations on me. The fact that you got fat and out of shape is a choice you made. The fact that you don't have a job is a choice you made. The way you've lived your life for the past twenty years is a choice you made. If you don't want to hear my thoughts, don't ask."

"I didn't," Fran said angrily. "She did."

All five women looked to Randi Conway as if she were a referee in a wrestling match.

When Randi offered no response, Fran turned back to her antagonist. "You're a bitch, Elizabeth, a conceited, self-centered, bitch. You come here dressed like a hooker with your red lipstick and your big tits hanging out and you think you can tell the rest of us how to live. You're not even a real part of this group. You've never shared a single genuine emotion with us. What the hell are you doing here if you're so damned smart and so damned perfect?"

"I never said I was perfect." Elizabeth spoke slowly now, her lovely face set in a hard stare, her jaw clenched, her dark eyes aflame. "If you see me that way, it's your problem Fran, not mine. I'm not going to sit here and make apologies for the way I live my life. You claim I should reveal more of myself? What a laugh. Why would I want to share anything with a bitter, jealous, used-up old housefrau like you?"

Everything else in the room stopped as Fran launched herself out of her chair, moving so quickly that Dr. Conway could not prevent the attack. Fran lunged toward Elizabeth's throat, her outstretched nails clawing their way across her neck. Elizabeth responded quickly, lashing out with the back of her hand, slapping Fran hard across the side of her face just as Randi Conway sprang forward and managed a deft tackle around Fran's knees, dragging her to the carpeted floor. The other women, including Elizabeth, jumped to their feet. They all stood, watching as Dr. Conway got control of Fran, the two women ending up in a heap in the middle of the circle.

"That's enough," Randi hollered into Fran's face, and the woman suddenly became still. Randi looked up at Elizabeth. "Are you all right?"

Three bloody scratch marks ran across Elizabeth's throat. They stung, but she would not say so. "I'm fine," she sneered. "As long as I don't get rabies."

"That'll be enough from you too." Randi looked back to Fran, who lay beside her on the carpet, appearing now like a meek child just roused from a nap. "Are you okay?"

Fran looked up uncertainly, then nodded.

Randi got to her feet and offered her a hand. "Let's resume our seats, ladies."

Fran ignored Randi's outstretched arm, lifted herself to her knees, then stood, taking care to straighten out her blouse and skirt. When she sat, the other women also took their seats. All except Elizabeth.

"You see, Doctor?" Elizabeth demanded. "You encourage us to share our feelings and then what? I speak my mind and what do I have to show for it. This . . . this . . . lunatic tries to strangle me." She reached up and gingerly touched the red marks on her neck.

"Please sit down, Elizabeth." Randi spoke as calmly as she could, fighting the awful sense of professional failure, knowing that she had lost control of the group. "We have time left in this session and we obviously have some things to work out."

Elizabeth shot a venomous look at Fran, then turned back to Dr. Conway. "What's the point?" she asked in a derisive tone. "To discuss our feelings?"

"That's one thing we can certainly do," Randi Conway responded.

"You want to know my feelings?" Elizabeth replied coldly. Then she turned slowly toward Fran. "I think you're pathetic," she said.

Now, just two days later, Elizabeth was dead and, as Randi sat in the darkness of her dining room recalling that afternoon, her shock slowly turned to anxiety—and then to dread.

CHAPTER 7

As Randi Conway dealt with the news of Elizabeth's death, Thomas and Fran Colello were spending another unpleasant night at home. As Fran saw it, she was trying to make sense of their failed marriage. As far as her husband was concerned, he was merely fending off his wife's latest angry tirade.

She claimed to want answers about why things had gone so wrong between them, but there were no answers he was willing to give. More than that, he didn't believe she wanted to hear anything he had to say.

He swore that he still loved her, but she dismissed that idea as if it were utter nonsense. He did love her, he insisted again, but he was not prepared to explain how his love had changed over the years—that was something he could not bring himself to say. There was no way to describe how passion had given way to familiarity, how lust had been replaced by companionship.

Instead he reminded her that they had children. They had history. They had shared moments that neither of them would ever live again. In some ways, he insisted, his love for her had grown richer over the years.

"Bullshit," Fran responded.

The Colellos were in the bedroom of their modest ranch-style house. Thomas was sitting on the loveseat in front of the bay window. Fran was pacing furiously back and forth in front of him, her pink cotton dressing gown flowing behind her. She puffed furiously on a cigarette, stopping her determined march only long enough to stub out the remains in a crystal ashtray and light another.

Smoking, like her use of profanity, was a habit of recent vintage.

"I wish I could believe you're lying to both of us instead of just trying to fool me," she said. "But I know you're a deceitful, scheming bastard."

"Take it easy, will you please? We're trying to have a conversation here."

"A conversation?" She took a long, theatrical look around the bedroom. "What a joke. Conversation is all we ever have in this room anymore."

"You're not fair, Fran. We're trying to work things out. I'm seeing the therapist like you asked me to, right? You can't expect miracles."

She forced a laugh so bitter it actually made him cringe. "A miracle? I guess it *would* be a miracle to think you'd want to fuck your own wife once in a while." She uttered another empty chuckle. "That *would* be a miracle, wouldn't it, fucking your own wife instead of one of your sluts?"

"Keep your voice down, will you please? The kids'll hear you."

"Oh great, Thomas. Now you're worried about the children. Let's have a round of applause, shall we? First you go to a marriage counselor and now you're worried about the kids. You're the perfect husband."

"I never said I was perfect, goddamnit. I know I'm not perfect. But you've been getting yourself so worked up lately, I'm worried about you." As soon as he said it, he wished he could take back every word, swallowing one letter at a time.

"You're worried about *me*," Fran repeated in a mocking tone. She had stopped her aimless marching and now perched on the ottoman a few feet from her husband. She drew on the cigarette and exhaled a gray cloud of smoke in his direction. "I don't want your goddamned pity," she said through clenched teeth.

"This isn't about pity," Thomas Colello said quietly as he began to get to his feet.

"Sit down," she snapped. "I don't want you touching me."

Thomas sank back onto the loveseat. "Jesus Christ, Fran."

"Don't *Jesus Christ* me," she snarled, struggling without success to hold back the tears that were beginning to flow. "I want you to tell me why it's better with someone else, some . . . some whore." She struggled to speak more slowly now. "I want you to explain why you're willing to humiliate me this way. I want to know why you act as if your dick is some sort of a divining rod you're entitled to follow wherever it leads.

Make me see all of that, Thomas. Can you do that? Do I at least have a right to understand?"

He took a deep breath, then said, "You're wrong about all this, Fran," but it didn't even sound persuasive to him.

She stared at him with as much hate as she could muster. "Cross you heart and hope to die?"

Thomas couldn't look at her now. He reached up with the thumb and middle finger of his left hand and began slowly massaging the corners of his eyes, temporarily blinding himself to her grief. *Now if only I were deaf,* he thought. *Or better yet, if I had the ability to disappear.* "This isn't a discussion," he finally said.

"Look at me," she answered quietly, but when he did not remove his hand from his face she growled, "Look at me, damnit." He slowly raised his head, watching as she used the back of her hand to wipe away the tears that filled her eyes and stained her cheeks. "I'm calm, all right? I'm calm now, and I want to hear what you have to say. I really do. All I want to know is the truth. Whatever it is, at least allow me the dignity of knowing the truth."

Thomas drew in another deep breath and exhaled slowly through pursed lips, as if reluctantly blowing out the candles on a cake for a birthday he preferred to ignore. He was a handsome man, with dark wavy hair, dark eyes, and a dark Mediterranean complexion. At the moment, however, under yet another of his wife's verbal assaults, he felt as if all of the color had been drained from his face. "I love you very much, Fran."

"Thomas, I told you . . ." she cut him off, but this time he was the one who raised his voice.

"Come on, Fran, you asked me to explain my feelings. Just listen for a minute."

She nodded slowly.

He said, "I know you think this has something to do with love. That I don't have the same feelings toward you that I used to have. Or maybe that I love someone else. But none of that is true." He hesitated before adding, "Then you imagine I'm having all these affairs."

"Well aren't you?" she demanded.

He shook his head as if deflecting an assault. "I hate these discussions. They never get us anywhere except a bigger argument." He shook his head again, hoping she would interrupt him so he wouldn't have to go on, but she remained silent. "Look, men get older, they start to worry about death. In your twenties and thirties you feel immortal. You feel like nothing can happen to you, you're invincible. Sure, business goes up and down, careers take the wild swings they take, but you always figure you're going to get through it. Then you hit forty and you realize you've lost a step. You realize it's been ages since the last time the guys got together and played a game of softball or touch football. Your kids are growing up, but you're just growing old. The hair is going, the muscle tone is gone, you exercise a couple of times a week, not to stay trim, just to keep from getting flabby. And then one day it hits you. You're on the down side of the mountain. You'd be a fool not to realize you're deep into middle age." He paused, but she did not respond. "You start worrying about what you missed, what you still might miss if you don't start to take every opportunity there is to live. I mean really live, and experience things."

"Like screwing young women?" she asked as politely as if she were asking him about the weather.

"Jesus, Fran. Is that all you're getting out of this?"

"You must be joking," she replied. She was actually smiling now. "This is the best you can do? A speech about how life is short and you're struggling with your mortality? You must think I'm some kind of moron."

Thomas was truly offended. "I'm expressing my deepest fears and you're saying it's all bullshit?"

Fran shook her head vigorously. "Of course not. I actually believe every word of it. But so what? Where's the big revelation? I'm growing older, too. What about me? We were supposed to do that together, wasn't that the deal?"

He wrung his hands but did not answer.

"You're a child, Thomas. A selfish, middle-aged, alcoholic child.

You're shoving your peas underneath your mashed potatoes and you actually believe you're fooling someone." She stood again. "Last night you told me you worked late, but I called your office just after four and they told me you'd already left for the day." She glared at him and waited, as if that statement was some sort of question.

"I had a meeting outside the office. Is that so unusual?"

She responded with a disgusted look. "It's not just that you lie to me, it's that you don't even make an effort to sound convincing." She looked around for a moment, as if she might find an answer written on one of the walls in their bedroom. When she turned back to him she said, "Get the hell out of here. I'm truly sorry Thomas, but I can't stand the sight of you tonight."

He sat there for a moment, wishing there was something to say that might matter, knowing there was not. Then he stood up and left without another word.

Thomas Colello trudged into the den and readied himself for another night sleeping alone, which was fine with him, especially tonight. He switched on the television and turned to the news, waiting. It was the lead story, being covered by a young woman standing in front of Darien Town Hall. She reported what Colello already knew—a local woman had been found dead of a gunshot wound in her own home. The woman had been identified as Elizabeth Knoebel.

He stood transfixed as the reporter described the preliminary details obtained from the local police.

Wife of a prominent surgeon. Too early to name any suspects. No murder weapon found.

Colello shuddered as if an arctic breeze had just blown through the room. He couldn't move, couldn't think, he was only capable of feeling the chill that engulfed him as he thought about Elizabeth.

What was I doing? he asked himself.

Was he really that vain? *Yes*, he admitted. And that stupid. He fell for her like a punch-drunk heavyweight walking into a left hook. He never saw it coming until he was stretched out on the canvas.

But how could he have known what she was up to? *I couldn't*, he told himself, and yet he felt he should have. He should have at least suspected something.

After all, why would this gorgeous, voluptuous woman come on to him the way she did?

He had been with different women over the years, beautiful women, exciting women—but none of them were like Elizabeth. He could say she seduced him, but *seduced* wasn't a strong enough word. It was more like she hunted him down and captured him.

He had been with passionate women before, but they didn't know what Elizabeth knew. They didn't understand what Elizabeth understood.

He had made love to women who delighted in sex, who reveled in the intimacy and the pleasure, but they didn't have the intuition about men that Elizabeth had. She was willing to be everything. Yes, that was it. She was willing to be everything a woman could be to a man.

He had no way of knowing she was Stanley Knoebel's wife. They had been together several times before she told him, and he was stunned at the absolute delight she took in revealing the truth. He could still envision her face and the sense of joy she had in explaining who she was and what she was about. It was only at that moment he began to understand her game, but it was too late. What was he supposed to do? Confess to his wife? Confront Stanley? Make an announcement in Dr. Conway's group?

No, it was already too late for any of that, and Elizabeth knew it. Instead she teased him, used him, and threw him away.

And the maddening part, the part he could not bring himself to deal with, was that even after he understood her sick game, he still wanted her, needed her, ached for her.

He shook his head as he stared at the television screen, wondering if Fran had heard what he already knew.

Elizabeth was dead.

He was not going back into their bedroom to ask.

CHAPTER 8

Early the next morning, when Randi Conway arrived at her office, she found Detective Anthony Walker waiting at her door. He was dressed in jeans, cowboy boots, a white shirt, and a suede zipper jacket. He didn't bother to display his badge as he said, "Sorry to bother you first thing, but something's come up. Got a few minutes?"

"I have a patient arriving soon."

"This shouldn't take long."

"Is it about Kyle?"

"No."

Randi hesitated, about to ask the obvious question. Then she said, "You're here about Elizabeth Knoebel." Without waiting for a reply, she unlocked the door.

There was an envelope lying on the floor. Before she could react, Walker bent down and picked it up. He noticed there was no name or address on the outside.

"Rent bill?" he asked with a smile.

Randi took it from him without responding, showed him in, and gestured to the couch. She went to her desk and placed the envelope in the drawer.

Walker figured that she either knew what it contained, was one of the least curious people he had ever met, or was simply not willing to open it in front of him. He let it go.

"Nice place," he said.

"Thank you," she replied.

Unlike the adjoining room, where Randi held her group sessions in minimalist surroundings washed in cold, fluorescent lighting, this was a warm, well-furnished office. In the corner was a captain's table with two arm chairs facing the front and a swivel chair behind. The walls were covered in a gray grass cloth. On the wall in back of her desk hung a group of diplomas and plaques announcing her various professional qualifications. The other wall space featured modern art, including a series of Folon prints framed in lacquered wood.

Walker's lower lip covered his upper as he stood there, taking a moment to have a look around. The couch she pointed to was plush and comfortable, upholstered in a striped cotton fabric. Across from the sofa, separated by an oblong coffee table of polished brass with a smoked glass top, was a black leather chair.

He sat on the couch, watching as she took her place in the leather seat across from him.

"Looks like you do all right," he said.

"Thank you."

He waited for more, but Dr. Conway was obviously not in a chatty mood. "So then, you've heard about Mrs. Knoebel."

"I still can't believe it," she said.

"Mind if I ask how you found out?"

"One of my patients called. Then I had a look at the report on the Internet."

"You want to tell me which patient called?"

"I'm sorry. That would be privileged."

Walker nodded. "I need to ask you a few questions."

"What sort of questions." She noticed that he had not bothered to take out a pad or pen.

"You were Elizabeth Knoebel's therapist."

"How did you know that?"

"The police chief called her husband last night, took some preliminary information."

"I see."

"You're aware of how she died?"

"Yes," she said.

"Gunshot to the right temple. Awful thing." He waited for a reply that didn't come. In her line of work, Walker figured she got to be pretty good at waiting people out. "When was the last time you saw Mrs. Knoebel?" he asked.

"Monday afternoon. In a group session."

He took another look around the small, homey room. "You hold group sessions here?"

Randi shook her head. "In there," she said, pointing at the door behind him.

"Uh huh. Was she particularly distraught or upset over anything? Mrs. Knoebel, I mean."

"I'm a psychologist, Officer Walker."

"That's *Detective* Walker, but we've already been through that tap dance. You can just call me Anthony, if you prefer that."

"I'm a psychologist, Detective Walker. People come to see me with problems of one kind or another."

"Fair enough. Putting aside her usual problems, then, did you notice anything out of the ordinary in Mrs. Knoebel's behavior the last time you saw her?"

Randi Conway stood up and walked to the window overlooking the town's main street. She watched the morning traffic crawl by as she recalled the scuffle between Elizabeth and Fran. She also thought about some of the many other things she could tell him about Elizabeth. "I would like to help you, Detective, I really would." She turned from the window and faced him again. "As you know, whatever my patients discuss with me is strictly confidential. Elizabeth's death doesn't change that."

"Look, Doctor, would you mind sitting? I have trouble with people talking down to me." Walker smiled in apology. "Must be some sort of hang-up I should look into. What do you think?"

Randi returned to her chair without answering.

"Thanks," Walker said. "You do a lot of marriage counseling, that right?"

"That's the basis of my practice, yes."

"Your specialty is working with couples—talk with them about their relationships, their personal lives, deal with their children, all that?"

"You've come here prepared, Detective."

"It's my job. Sorry."

"You should never apologize for doing your job well."

Walker grinned. "Is that free professional advice?"

"Call it an observation."

"That's all I'm asking for. Some observations about Mrs. Knoebel."

"No, in her case you're asking me for specific information about a patient."

"Former patient."

Randi shook her head slowly.

"You say the last time you saw her was in the group?"

"Right."

"Was that a regular meeting?"

"That group usually meets on Monday. I occasionally saw Elizabeth for private counseling."

"No regular date for that?"

"It varied. Some of my patients need flexibility in their appointments."

"Mrs. Knoebel worked, did she?"

"She was a freelance software consultant. But I assume you knew that already."

"Did you ever see Mrs. Knoebel anywhere else?"

"Besides my office, you mean?"

"Yes, anywhere else."

"No."

"Never saw her socially?"

"Never. She was my patient."

"Never ran into her on the street, in a grocery store, nothing like that?"

"Not that I can recall."

"It's a small town, Doc."

"If I see a patient on the street, I generally head in the other direction. Protects their privacy, avoids embarrassment."

"She ever phone you?"

"Certainly, from time to time."

"Would she talk about her problems or would she just call to make appointments?"

"From time to time patients call to talk things over."

"She call at your office? Your home?"

"My office. I also have a line for patients to call me at home in the event of an emergency."

"What about Mrs. Knoebel? She ever have an emergency?"

"I can't recall Elizabeth ever telephoning me at home."

"Did you speak to her at any time after Monday's group meeting?"

"No."

"Did she ever mention that she was having an extramarital affair?"

Randi frowned. "Come on, Detective. You can do better than that."

Walker offered another smile. "Just doing my job. You said you can't blame me for that."

"No, I said you shouldn't apologize for doing your job well."

Walker sat back and rubbed his eyes with the palms of his hands. "No offense, Doc, but this isn't a whole lot of help. I have a dead woman in the morgue and I need to know where to go to start chasing down her murderer. I realize you've got to preserve her reputation—and your own ethics—but I need help." He looked directly into her soft, brown eyes. "I'm not asking you to tell me any of her deep, dark secrets."

"That's precisely what you're asking."

Walker shrugged.

Randi leaned forward, her voice quiet. "Elizabeth was an exceedingly smart woman. Complicated, troubled, no question about it." She shook her head again, dismissing an unwelcome thought. "Look, Detective, as a human being, not to mention as her therapist, I'd like to give you whatever help I can if it would identify the person who did this. At the same time—how did you put it? I've got to preserve her reputation. And my own."

Now Walker leaned forward. "What about her husband?"

"What about him?"

"She ever say anything about him?"

Randi laughed, breaking the tension Walker was obviously working hard to create. "We've already established that I specialize in marriage counseling. I think it's fair to say she discussed her husband."

"Think he could've killed her?"

"No."

"That's a fast answer, Doctor."

"That's because I've seen the question coming since I found you waiting in my hallway."

Now Walker laughed.

"That's what you came to ask me, isn't it? If I thought Stanley Knoebel was capable of murdering his wife?"

"That's one of the reasons," Walker admitted. "How about this one . . ."

"Is there anyone else she ever mentioned who might have had a reason to kill her?" Randi said.

Walker offered an appreciative nod.

They heard a knock. Randi excused herself, went to the door, and opened it slightly. Speaking to someone out of Walker's view, she said "I'm just finishing up. I'll be with you in a couple of minutes, just have a seat in the group room." Then she closed the door and turned back to the detective. "That's my next patient."

"*Next* patient? Am I being analyzed?"

She showed him a slight smile but said nothing.

It was apparent she would not be sitting down again, so Walker stood up. "You still haven't answered my question."

"Whether she ever mentioned that someone might want to murder her? No, I would remember that."

"All right. Anything else she might have said about anyone that might be useful, anything at all you can share with me?"

"I'll have to think about this. I'm sorry. I probably need to get some legal advice."

"What a world," Walker sighed. "Everybody's got to call their lawyer for everything." He shook his head. "All right. You look into it and we'll talk again."

Randi paused. "I'm not sure how far I can go with this, but I feel I can tell you that she never said anything about being in danger."

"Nothing that might suggest a problem with someone?"

Randi stared at him without responding. That was a different question with more answers than she was willing to contemplate right now. "That's not what I said. I mean that she never expressed any particular fear that someone might want to harm her that way."

"*That way*? Meaning what? Did she ever say someone might have wanted to hurt her? Other than murder, I mean."

"No, she didn't."

"Elizabeth Knoebel had scratch marks on her neck. The coroner says they were made a day or so before the murder. Know anything about that?"

This time, Randi Conway's silence spoke volumes.

Walker nodded. "You know we found Mrs. Knoebel in bed. Naked. Probably late afternoon when someone put that bullet in her brain."

Randi shook her head. "Is that a question? Because if it is, I really don't know how to respond."

Walker sighed. "They're working on the autopsy. You never know if someone might have drugged her first or whatever. Anyway, it was sure a strange setup." He shrugged. "Look, you and I know that in a homicide investigation a judge can sign an order that overrides your confidential privilege. Then you'd be forced to give sworn testimony about anything you know that might help in the investigation. I'm just trying to keep things simple. I'm not interested in hurting your practice or broadcasting any of the woman's secrets, but there may be things you know that have a bearing on this case. Things you may not even realize could be important."

"I understand. For now it doesn't change my obligation."

"Right." Walker decided to give it one more try. "Suppose she had mentioned another guy—just suppose, you don't have to say if she did or not. Would she have given a name?"

There was a long pause. Then Randi said, "No, she wouldn't. She wasn't the type."

"Wasn't the type. Perfect." He took a moment to think that one over. "The shooter was probably someone she knew well, maybe even trusted. Someone got extremely close to pull that trigger right beside her head. No sign of a struggle or forced entry into her home. Think about it—someone she knew and trusted." He watched her. "You might want to consider helping me here." They were standing face-to-face as Walker reached into his jacket and pulled out several photographs. He held them out to her.

They were graphic, providing several views of Elizabeth Knoebel's corpse, her blood-stained bed, and close-ups of her fatal wound. As Randi looked at them, she was no longer involved in a clinical discussion with a police officer. She felt as if she was in Elizabeth's bedroom, a witness to her violent death. She drew a deep breath, then handed the pictures back to Walker. He gave her his card in exchange.

"You know, Doc, your answers, or should I say your nonanswers, make me think you might just know something you should be telling me. So what gives? What could possibly be so confidential you wouldn't want to tell me if it could help find her murderer?" Walker shoved the photos back in his jacket pocket.

Randi was still thinking about the pictures.

"There's one more thing," he said, "something you may have considered yourself. Mrs. Knoebel was your patient. She talked to you, confided in you. Whoever murdered her might feel the way I do, that you know enough to help us solve this case. Which means you're a potential liability to the killer. Like I say, something you probably thought of yourself."

Randi stared at him. "Yes," she admitted, "I have." She did not reveal any of the other fears that were already forming.

"Well then, give me a call when you're ready to talk. And if you think any of your other patients might know something useful," he gestured toward the business card she was holding, "you know how to reach me."

✢   ✢   ✢

As soon as he was gone, Randi closed the door and hurried to her desk. She opened the drawer and pulled out the plain white wrapper. It was not sealed. Inside was a single sheet of white paper. On it was typed:

DR CONWAY
I AM SORRY

She read the short message twice, turning the note over to its blank side and back again, as if there might be something else to see, something she was missing. She returned the note to the drawer, placing it beside the other plain envelope she had received just a day earlier. Once again, there was no name or address on the message or the envelope.

Randi slowly closed the drawer and then, before attending to her waiting patient, she sat back and stared straight ahead without seeing.

CHAPTER 9

Stanley Knoebel was a renowned vascular surgeon with a successful practice in New York City. A talented professional, he enjoyed the stature society accords those who trade, quite literally, in the business of life and death.

Charm, however, was not one of his skills.

Knoebel had a reputation for condescension and coldness that was unusual, even for a surgeon. He was arrogant toward subordinates and colleagues alike, and his social interactions were not much different.

Born in Romania, he spent his early years in strict parochial schools that left him with a stiff bearing, and his heavy accent only added to that haughty persona. He valued intelligence and serious debate, despising banal chatter and cocktail party conviviality. As a consequence, he had many valued colleagues but very few friends.

Knoebel had no difficulty accepting that he was not a popular man. He was actually proud of his values, having long ago realized it was not easy to play God without offending someone.

On Thursday morning, the day following the discovery of his wife's body, Dr. Knoebel telephoned Darien Police Chief Henry Gill. Foregoing any sort of social preamble, he demanded to know when his wife's body would be released.

Gill informed him that the coroner had not finished his examination.

"As we discussed last evening, Chief Gill, it is evident that Elizabeth died of a gunshot wound, is it not? Any general practitioner could see that." His English was excellent, but those unmistakable inflections of Eastern Europe fortified his peremptory style.

Chief Gill mustered all the compassion he could, compassion not being his long suit. "I understand, Doctor Knoebel. Unfortunately, in a case like this we're required to follow our procedures and conduct a thorough autopsy."

"All right," the doctor responded with undisguised exasperation. "When do you expect these procedures to be completed?"

"Hopefully in the next day or two. We need to verify the time of death and finalize some other forensic tests." Gill glanced at Anthony Walker, who was standing in the doorway of his office, listening to the chief's half of the telephone conversation. "Detective Walker will be in touch with you so you can make the appropriate arrangements."

"I have *already* made the appropriate arrangements," Dr. Knoebel insisted. "My wife's will makes it clear she wished to be cremated. This is upsetting enough to my daughter without prolonging her suffering with bureaucratic delays."

"I apologize, but we do have certain rules."

"Rules," Dr. Knoebel said derisively.

"Detective Walker will also need to conduct an interview of you, Doctor. Perhaps we can set some time that would be convenient for you."

"Frankly, there is no convenient time."

"All right," the chief said, looking up at Walker as if he might offer some help. "How about the least inconvenient time, then?"

There was silence. "My house," Knoebel said. "Eight o'clock tonight."

"Your house at eight," Gill agreed without asking Walker how he felt about it. "That'll be fine."

"My daughter has returned from boarding school. She will be at home. I trust your Detective Walker will exercise some discretion. Obviously we will have this discussion privately."

"Of course. I'll pass that on."

"If you learn anything else before we meet, please call and leave word with my receptionist."

"All right," Gill answered, but the line had already gone dead.

Walker waited for Gill to put the phone down, then said, "Seems he's all teary-eyed over this thing."

"Spare me the sarcasm," Gill snapped. "Knoebel is a respected member of this community, and we have his wife on the coroner's slab with a bullet in her head. We owe him some answers."

"He owes us some answers too, don't you think?"

"Easy Walker." Gill, who spent more effort in maintaining his relationships with the local gentry than actually preventing or solving crimes, was not the sort of superior officer Walker was ever going to warm to. He had simply reconciled himself to the fact that Gill came with the job.

"I'm happy to take it easy, Chief. It's Doctor Knoebel who seems in a hurry to claim the body."

"Wouldn't you be?"

"Maybe, but they tell me cremation is forever. I wonder what the rush is."

The chief let that go. "Make sure Jake does a thorough job on this," he said.

"Of course. Meanwhile, if Knoebel can get one of his doctor friends to sign a death certificate saying she died of natural causes, we can release the body today."

Gill frowned. "Look, Walker, this is a town where people don't lock their doors, where they leave their cars in the driveway with the keys on the seat, where this sort of thing just doesn't happen. Now my friends' wives are calling, asking if they should be worried, if this was a random act or if we might have a serial killer on our hands."

"People watch too much television."

"Maybe so, but I work for those people." He treated Walker to his sternest look. "And by the way, so do you. Go do what you have to, but be sure you don't step on any toes along the way."

"I'll dance around like Fred Astaire."

The chief shook his head. "Local reporters are all over, but I can deal with them. Problem is, we're already getting calls from the New York stations. I want this wrapped up, and I want it done pronto."

"Yes sir."

"What'd the psychologist have to say?"

Walker recounted his conversation with Dr. Conway earlier that morning. "Not much help so far."

"What do you suggest?"

"I told her we could get a court order, force her to cooperate."

"Not yet," the chief said quickly.

Walker had guessed what Gill would say about that—he was just a bit surprised the reaction came so quickly. "All the same, we need to apply some pressure, right?"

"Maybe so, but we don't want to turn this into any more of a media circus than it has to be." He shook his head. "All I need is a local therapist giving up her patients' secrets. God, we'll all be on *Entertainment Tonight* before you know it."

"I also reminded Doctor Conway that the murderer might figure she was the one person Mrs. Knoebel would have confided in, the one person who could help us solve this case."

"You believe that?"

"I do. And I'll tell you something else, I think Doctor Conway believes it. I think she realizes the danger."

Gill groaned like someone had just hit him in the solar plexus. "Wonderful."

Walker waited.

"That's it," the chief finally said, dismissing Walker with a wave of his hand.

Walker returned to the room he shared with the two other detectives on the force. Officer Kovacevic was waiting for him.

"You don't look happy, sir, if you don't mind me saying so."

"Gill's in one of his moods, that's all. What've you got?"

"We received preliminaries from Jake, the work from forensics, and the narratives on the area sweep." He was holding the various reports.

"Anything helpful?"

"Afraid not. How'd it go with the psychologist?"

"Doctor Conway? It was interesting." Walker dropped himself into the old padded swivel chair behind his metal desk and took the papers Kovacevic held out for him. "As expected, she hid behind confidential privilege. I showed her the photos. Bet it was the first time she ever looked at a gunshot victim. For a second I thought she was going to toss her breakfast on my shoes." Walker realized the younger officer was still standing. "Take a load off, Kovie."

Walker leaned back and stretched his legs across the corner of the desk. He went through the report from the coroner's office. No surprises.

Elizabeth Knoebel died of a single gunshot wound to her right temple. The shot was fired from a .38 caliber revolver at close range, causing extensive internal damage. Death was virtually instantaneous.

Based on the extent of rigor mortis when the body was first examined, and the undigested food substances in her stomach, they put the time of death at about four o'clock Tuesday afternoon. There was no evidence of any narcotics in her system. There was minimal alcohol ingestion, less than two glasses of wine. There was no sign of recent sexual penetration, before or after death.

Walker tossed the report on his desk and picked up the lab results. No unidentified fingerprints. The only matches were for the Knoebels and Nettie Sisson. No helpful DNA findings, not so much as a shred of skin under the victim's nails. Walker nodded to himself. Elizabeth Knoebel knew her murderer. Someone who just strolled in, got close, pulled the trigger, then walked out. He put those papers down and went to the statements from the officers who had canvassed the area.

As expected, most neighbors were not at home in the afternoon. Of the few that were, none heard anything like a gunshot. Kovacevic's observations had been correct. These were large houses, well built, well insulated, and separated by generous stretches of land. Added to that was Walker's suspicion that anyone who might have heard anything resembling a shot would be inclined to deny it anyway. Why get yourself in the middle of something so messy if all you could report was that you heard a sound an acre away that might have been nothing more than a car backfiring?

There was one neighbor who did have something to say. Mrs.

Fitzmorris, who lived just down the road from the Knoebels, spoke with Kovacevic. She said that she returned home from grocery shopping on Tuesday afternoon around five. When she went back outside to pick up her mail she noticed a gray sedan go by—she thought it was a Mercedes or a BMW or something else foreign. Whatever it was, it was speeding away from the Knoebels' driveway. It struck her as odd at the time, a car moving so fast on their quiet back road. Must have been a BMW, she said, because you know how fast they drive, those people with BMWs. She did not get a look at the driver, but she was sure of the time. And no, she didn't recall hearing anything that sounded like a gunshot.

Walker dropped the report on his desk and leaned back, staring up at the ceiling.

The chief's comments about the fears in town had actually struck a chord with him. Walker knew from experience that any time a murder is committed there's a chance the killer will strike again. Serial murderers are rare, despite their frequent appearance in popular fiction, but murderers are capable of killing again for reasons other than sheer psychosis. Sometimes they haven't finished the job they started. Or they use a second victim to misdirect the first investigation. Or they need to take someone out to cover their tracks—a co-conspirator, perhaps—or someone who stumbles on incriminating evidence—or someone who just knows too much.

Which brought Walker back to Dr. Randi Conway.

"Sir," Kovacevic interrupted his musings, pointing to the reports. "What do you think?"

Walker slid his boots off the desk and sat up. "Let's check with Jake again about the time of death. His estimate is more than an hour before Mrs. Fitzmorris told you she spotted the car zooming out of the Knoebel driveway. I'd like to see if we can tighten that gap. Then you and I will pay another visit to see how sure Mrs. Fitzmorris is on *her* timing—maybe get a better read on identifying that car."

Walker had another look at the photographs. Elizabeth Knoebel was certainly attractive, even in death, that much was apparent.

"Not a very friendly woman," Kovacevic volunteered as he watched Walker study the pictures. "At least that was the word I got from the neighbors I spoke with."

Walker nodded for him to go on.

"Not the country club type, no junior league stuff. Not well liked, let's put it that way."

"There was certainly someone who didn't like her."

"Doctor Knoebel isn't going to win any popularity contests either, although it seems he's home a lot less than his wife. They say he's a big deal surgeon in New York. Keeps to himself. Apparently left the missus alone on a regular basis."

Walker pulled out a cigarette and stuck it between his lips. Bad habits from his days in New York died hard, even though he couldn't light up in the office. "You know, Kovie, gossip has a bad reputation, but in this business it can be more helpful than an eyewitness account."

"Yes sir," Kovacevic said, having heard that one before from Walker. "So what's next?"

"When we visit Mrs. Fitzmorris again let's bring some pictures of several different late-model foreign cars. Get some brochures of BMWs, Jaguars, Mercedes, Audis, whatever. Maybe we'll get lucky."

"I'll pull it together."

"Jake is a competent guy. If he says the time of death was around four, that's at least an hour earlier than her sighting of that sedan." Walker shook his head. "If it wasn't the murderer Mrs. Fitzmorris saw, maybe it was someone else entirely. Maybe someone got there after Elizabeth Knoebel was dead, saw the body, and took off. Or maybe the murderer came back, maybe he forgot something."

"Like what?"

"That's what we have to figure out once we nail down the timing. How are we doing with that computer?"

"Teddy is working on it."

"Where are we on the warrant?"

"We'll have it today."

"Good. Who knows, maybe we'll find something there to help us."

CHAPTER 10

A short time later, Walker was still in his office when he received word from the front desk that Teddy Blasko had arrived to see him. Blasko was the outside consultant the department used for all things computer.

"Have Kovie bring him up," Walker told the receptionist.

Kovacevic accompanied Blasko to the detectives' office, where he greeted Walker and then promptly set Elizabeth Knoebel's laptop on the desk and powered it up.

"Just busted the main codes this afternoon," the techie told them proudly.

Walker and Kovacevic watched the screen flash a series of changing images as Blasko tapped on the keyboard.

"I'll run the list of programs for you. I've already printed the directory," he said, reaching into his pocket and handing Walker a sloppily folded group of pages. "I've only had a quick look at the software she's got loaded in this baby. Some programs are custom. She has different passwords for each of those."

"Of course," Walker said. "Goes without saying."

Blasko ignored the sarcasm.

"She used to work as some sort of software consultant," Walker said.

"Kovie told me," Blasko replied without looking up. "Looky here."

"What is it?"

Blasko pointed to a list of symbols on the screen that Walker found indecipherable. "All the subdirectories seem to be intact," Blasko said. "That doesn't mean some of the information wasn't erased from within the files themselves. We can cross-check that afterward."

"Naturally," Walker said with a grin.

"Right. Anyway, she has a lot of technical data stored here, some of it is for the programs she wrote herself."

"Is that good?"

"Might make it tougher to get into them."

"How tough?"

"We'll find out. Haven't cracked that group yet. They might have to do with her work, not necessarily personal. I assume you're after the personal data."

"The name of her murderer would be nice."

Blasko frowned.

"You know the drill, Teddy. Anything that might help us identify a suspect. Threatening e-mails. Intimate e-mails. Whatever you computer people write to each other on these things."

Blasko laughed his goofy laugh, which sounded like he might choke unless he spit out whatever was gagging him. "*Computer people?*" He chuckled again. "What are computer people?"

Walker liked the guy too much to share any of the half dozen clever responses that leapt to mind. "Just show me what you found."

Blasko went back to the keyboard. "No reason to look at her finances."

"You know where she lived."

"Right. Let's have a peek at her e-mails." Teddy played with various access codes until he entered the program directory.

"Impressive," Walker said.

"Nothing to it," Blasko admitted. "It's Microsoft Office, standard stuff once I got the first password." He hit some more keys and then said, "Here you go. You can read through all of her e-mails, even the ones she sent and the ones she deleted."

"Good." Walker turned to Kovacevic. "Hope you didn't have any plans tonight. Looks like you've got some reading to do."

The young officer nodded. "I'll be on it."

After Blasko hit a few more keys he said, "This is a list of all the document files she created. You'll have to go through each of these too, see what they're about. I've already been through some, but this is the one you asked about." Blasko opened and closed a few windows, then brought up a folder titled SEXUAL RITES.

"That's the one."

In just a few seconds, Teddy had the screen glowing with a directory of files that read:

BVLCO.DOC
CLDTM.DOC
DVFQO.DOC
FINAL.DOC
FVDPD.DOC
FVHFX.DOC
INTRO.DOC
JSDPB.DOC
JWJCR.DOC
LMVCH.DOC
MMWEI.DOC
NIWKF.DOC
PEXNH.DOC
PLBNT.DOC
RIJPB.DOC
RSETU.DOC
SHAKE.DOC
SXQNZ.DOC
TLROT.DOC

"These file names look coded, probably to discourage anyone from having a quick look at them. I got into them. Based on the content, I'm guessing she wanted to hide them from her husband."

Walker nodded.

"Which one you want me to open first?"

"How about the one that says INTRO? That name doesn't look coded."

Teddy brought up the file marked INTRO.DOC. At the top of the screen, in the center, flashed the words:

SEXUAL RITES
INTRODUCTION

Walker pulled up a chair and sat down beside Blasko. Kovacevic stood behind them.

Notes for Introduction

Life is a series of experiences to which we assign many different names, a process that begins at birth, reaches a zenith, then follows its inexorable decline, and, ultimately, ends in death.

Infancy. Adolescence. Puberty. Teenage. Adulthood. Middle-age. Maturity. Old-age.

We grow. We mature. We decay. We die.

Men and women are as susceptible to this inescapable process as every other living thing on earth. Yet we are uniquely empowered with an intellect that causes us to try and comprehend its meaning, to come to terms with the significance of the rites of passage that mark our lives. We learn from them, draw from them in the hope of improving ourselves and, ideally, we seek out every source of gratification they can provide.

Sexuality is woven through the fabric of every stage of this evolution. Scientists tell us that a newborn infant is capable of sexual stimulation. Psychologists tell us that sexual urges can rule the psyche and affect our earliest emotions and deeds. Experience tells us that our yearning for sex can be the source of our most powerful desires, needs, and fears.

So what are these rites of sexual passage that exert such control over our lives? What are the forces that affect us as we mature beyond our pubescent longings and youthful adventures? We are intrigued by our early experiences and the wonderful, mystical unknown that offers a fulfillment of body and spirit. We often use the expression *innocence* to describe that phase, a most interesting choice of words.

So what changes occur along the way to cause the loss of such innocence?

What are the influences of love?

The constraints of marriage?

The demands of trust?

The consequences of infidelity?

The suffering that comes from cruelty?

The unrealistic expectations that lead to disappointment?

The inhibitions that come from insecurity?

The forces that drive us to hatred, violence, degradation, or even depravity?

And, most important of all, what are the rules and regulations we call civilized behavior that ultimately cause most of us to resist the impulses of our basic lust? What compels us to hide, ignore, divert, or struggle against this most primitive, visceral hunger?

Where do these inhibitions begin?

Just imagine if those limitations were removed. Who among us would not crave unrestrained sexual excitement? What passionate discoveries would we welcome if there were no boundaries or social taboos? Why then do most of us deny ourselves, every day, that which is so sublime and so readily available?

What have we done to civilize our most basic urges? And why have we done it? What takes place in our society to create the pretexts that mangle or destroy our sexuality?

Do you want to understand these sexual rites, to find the way to free yourself from their restrictions?

Come with me on my journey of exploration.

"Go back to the list," Walker said.

Blasko soon had the screen glowing with the column of file names. "Any way to tell which of these was most recently opened?"

"Sure. They all have an electronic date stamp, every time you edit one." After checking through them he said, "This one here, this is the last one she worked on." Blasko opened the file named RSETU.DOC. Walker recognized it.

"We've seen that," Walker said. "Open another."

Blasko worked the keys and, once again, the screen was transformed when TLROT.DOC was opened. The heading said:

SEXUAL RITES
NOTES FOR CHAPTER NINE

After scanning the first few lines, Walker asked, "Can you print this for me?"

"Sure thing. This laptop has a wireless connection, I just have to load your printer info."

"Print all of them then," Walker told him.

"Right."

With a proficiency that would be the envy of a concert pianist, Blasko went to work on the keyboard. Walker watched as the screen kept changing images until the printer atop his file cabinet began noisily feeding pages.

"Doesn't appear that anyone has been on this computer since Tuesday afternoon," Blasko said. "Last entry of any kind seems to be the one you saw."

"All right. Can you keep printing the other files while we have a look at the one you just opened?"

"Of course," Blasko said, then hit a series of buttons to return to the file titled TLROT.DOC. On the screen, Elizabeth Knoebel's "Notes for Chapter Nine" reappeared.

The three men leaned forward and read.

SEXUAL RITES
NOTES FOR CHAPTER NINE

T believes he is a great lover. He is certainly a good-looking man. He is also well endowed, which leads most such men to feel they are worthy bedmates. Like most men, T understands far more about the physical dynamics of sex than about its nuances; or about women; or about emotions; or even about himself.

T proved to be an easy seduction. He's the sort of man who needs to feel he's in charge, the easiest sort to manipulate.

T and I had never met, but I knew who he was, a fact which he only discovered after we became lovers. I sought him out at a lounge he frequented, a quiet place not far from a small suburban motel. I stood near him at the bar, looking at my watch, about to order a second drink when he offered to buy it for me.

"Waiting for someone?"

"A friend," I said. "I guess she's not going to make it."

"My good fortune," he said.

We drank together. I allowed him to control the conversation. He obviously thought himself amusing. I smiled at his awkward attempts at cleverness. I reacted with appropriate embarrassment at his increasingly suggestive remarks, but uttered no reprimand. I offered an occasional blush or, even more effective, a gentle tap on his arm. The third time I reached for him, I let my touch linger, giving his bicep a squeeze until he took hold of my hand and brought it to his lips. A short time later he suggested we move to a quiet table in the corner. Not long after, he was kissing me on the neck, then the lips, and I responded.

Too many women simply do not know how to kiss. They withhold their tongues, as if their mouths are something the man should enter and explore. They do not understand how excited a man becomes by a woman who freely offers her warm, wet tongue, fully meeting his as the passion grows.

So it was with T. He was warm with vodka and desire and feeling very sure of himself. He suggested we make our way to the nearby motel.

I feigned sufficient protest to satisfy his need for conquest, then gave in. We stopped at the bar on our way out. He reached into his pocket, took out some bills, and made a show of leaving a tip that was far too generous. Then he took me by the arm and led me into the night.

Once outside, his movements became cautious. He quite literally looked over his shoulder more than once. We drove a few blocks to a small inn where he arranged for the room. I waited in his car. As he stepped inside the office he had another look around—the actions of a married man. When he returned to the car I was amused to see him make a quick and subtle inventory of everything, as if to be sure I hadn't removed something or, worse yet, dropped my lipstick on the floor for his wife to find the next day. I was certain he would make another inspection when he arrived home later that night.

"You seem worried," I said.

"Do I?"

"Are you married?" I asked, already knowing the answer.

He hesitated, then asked "Does it matter?"

"That depends," I told him.

"On what?"

"On how the evening goes," I said.

Once we were inside the motel room he was sure of himself again. We were safe, alone in the darkness, and when he took me in his arms it was a gentle embrace. It was clear he was taking time not to hurry or offend. Our lips met, softly at first, then in a long, moist kiss.

He was patient in ways I knew he would never be with his wife. This was not just sex, it was also a seduction.

We sat on the edge of the bed, and he began to remove my blouse. He acted as if he were unwrapping a gift, yet still not rushing, not wanting this part of the ritual to be done too soon. Next he removed my bra and began caressing my breasts with his hands. Then he lowered his head and sucked at my nipples.

After a few moments I laid back, allowing him to gently pull off my skirt. I had my panties on and remained on my back with my legs crossed in a chaste pose that offered him one last little challenge before claiming his prize.

He stood, and I let him undress himself. Not only did I want to retain an air of indecision, but I also wanted to see if he would persist in his controlled pace or if he might simply tear his clothes away. He did well, moving quickly but without clumsy haste. Then he lay beside me on the bed and we kissed again. I reached for him and began stroking him softly. He made his way back to my breasts, kissing and sucking at my now swollen nipples.

When he reached down to slide off my panties, I lifted my ass slightly as he pulled them off. I parted my legs and he bent over and covered me with his mouth. I began writhing in appreciation, sighing as he alternated deep thrusts of his tongue with a gentle sucking motion on my clitoris. I arched my back and let out a soft cry, then pushed his head away and rolled him over onto his back.

I moved astride his legs and bent forward, taking him in both hands and then into in my mouth, sucking and licking him until I stopped and pulled back, allowing him to grab hold of my ass with one hand and then guide himself inside me with the other. I was wet and hot and he entered me in one smooth motion.

I remained on top, leaning forward so that my breasts brushed against his lips as we rocked back and forth, slowly at first, then faster and harder. And then I stopped. For a moment I did not move. I looked into his dark eyes, then sat up straighter and began riding him with reckless abandon. I cried out, louder this time, as my body shuddered, sounds coming from deeper inside me. His hands kneaded the flesh of my thighs and my ass as we rose and fell together, my hands reaching behind me now, scratching at the soft skin on the underside of his scrotum. I began to shudder, and then tense, and then I felt him give in to his own trembling release.

As he stopped moving, so did I, except that my chest continued to heave and my groans of delight were replaced with sobs. I uttered these sounds of joy as I fell forward and let him hold me to him, my body continuing to quiver in his arms for what must have seemed to him a long time after he was spent.

My performance complete, I told him that he was incredible, having already done my best to demonstrate that. I said I was embarrassed by my tears at the end, but the pleasure was like nothing I had ever known. Could this be only the first time we made love together? Could it ever be any better than this? Could he imagine how wonderful it might become the next time and the time after that?

Walker finished and leaned back in the chair. "You've had a look at the other files?"

"Just a few, then I figured I better get this over here for you to see."

"The others are all like this?"

"Pretty much," Blasko said. "Some with women, some with other men, some just about sex in general."

Walker had him open a couple of other files and they quickly scanned them. Just as Blasko said, the partners were different, but Elizabeth Knoebel's subject matter remained the same.

"You know I trust you Teddy, but you've really got to keep this to yourself."

"Understood."

"I'm sorry to even have to say it."

"No offense taken, Anthony."

Walker looked back at the screen. He took a deep breath, then said, "Wow."

"No kidding."

"Mrs. Knoebel was certainly making the rounds. Now we have to find out who her playmates were."

"Might help if I can decipher the file names. The code appears to be relatively simple."

"Can you figure it out?"

"Cake," Blasko said. "Give me till tomorrow."

"Any chance someone other than Elizabeth Knoebel got in here and deleted things? Like her husband, for instance."

"There are hard disk imprints, we can recover them."

"How do you check that?"

Teddy responded with a look that said, "Please don't waste my time having me explain something like this to someone like you."

Walker got it. "All right," he said. Then he turned from Blasko to Kovacevic. "Time for me to visit the good Doctor Knoebel." He stared back at the computer screen. "I wonder how much he knows about this."

CHAPTER 11

That evening, Walker arrived at the Knoebel home ten minutes early. He drove the long stretch of gravel driveway slowly, his car window down, the crunching sound of the rocks beneath his tires. He wondered how they plowed across all of this loose rock after a heavy snowstorm—wouldn't it kick up all the stones? Then he realized it was a question only a city kid would ask.

The morning newspaper, still in its filmy blue plastic cover, was lying on the ground. He considered bringing it to the door, then thought better of it and drove on.

The approach to the house ended in a circular sweep around a tiled fountain, a dramatic effect enhanced by outdoor lights that bathed the trees and stonework in a soft glow. This was Walker's second visit here, and he thought the place was even more impressive at night. He decided to have another look around before visiting with Dr. Knoebel.

The main house was faced in stone, two stories high, with arched windows and wood trim capped off by a gently sloping roof of slate tiles. The front entrance featured a large oak door, lighted on either side by brass sconces. He took a quick inventory of the other means of ingress—the kitchen door on the side of the house, French doors leading from the living room to a stone patio, another set of French doors leading from the spacious dining room to the stone terrace, and a single door from the family room to the backyard area. There were also a number of ground-level windows. *A burglar's paradise*, Walker noted. Like many of these homes, there were alarm systems that went unused; doors left unlocked for children, servants, or visitors; and windows an intruder could easily step through. Walker wondered if Elizabeth Knoebel's murderer might have simply used one of these, or if she had left the front door open for someone.

He wandered down the sloping lawn to the right, toward a stone swimming pool and bathhouse. The evening was growing colder and he stood with his hands in his jacket pockets, his right hand absently playing with his car keys. A mist rose from the surface of the heated water to meet the cool air of the autumn evening.

"You might have come to the front door," a voice behind him suggested with a touch of impatience.

Walker turned to face a man he assumed to be Dr. Knoebel. "I knew how concerned you were about your daughter. I was a few minutes early and didn't want to disturb you."

The doctor responded with a short nod, his neck and back remaining so rigid that it seemed a formal bow. "That was considerate of you."

Knoebel was almost a head taller than Walker. He was trim, stood perfectly erect, and appeared fit enough to run a marathon, if it became immediately necessary. He had a large forehead, owed partly to a hairline that had retreated long ago, and partly to an intellectual look Walker figured he must have had since he was a kid. His lips were even thinner than his long, angular nose, and his pale blue eyes seemed like they could bore a hole through a steel plate, not to mention a police detective. All in all, Walker thought Stanley Knoebel looked just about as friendly as advertised.

"We haven't been introduced. I'm Detective Anthony Walker." He held out his hand. "I'm very sorry about the circumstances."

Knoebel's grip was firm and warm, even in the cold night air. "Shall we go to my study?" His Eastern European accent was sharper than Gill had described.

"If your daughter is home, I'm comfortable right here. Might make it easier."

"Fine," the doctor replied. Then he looked away, as if searching for something in the distance. "I was told the remains will be released tomorrow morning."

"So I understand."

"We are anxious to be done with that part of this tragedy. Once Elizabeth has been laid to rest, I believe Kara can begin to heal."

"Laid to rest, doctor? I thought Mrs. Knoebel was going to be cremated."

"She is, yes." He returned his gaze to Walker. "It's a figure of speech, Detective. I was referring to her soul."

"I see." Walker waited for Knoebel to go on. His basic interview technique was to encourage as much voluntary information as a witness might offer, not unlike his attempts to elicit information from Randi Conway early that morning. As unsuccessful as he had been with the psychologist, it appeared using that approach with Knoebel might end up a duet in pantomime. "Nice swimming pool," Walker said.

"Did you have something you wanted to ask me, Detective?"

"Just a few routine questions."

"I understand routine," he allowed in his imperious manner. "Please proceed."

Walker began to take out his note pad, then thought better of it. He shoved his hands into his jacket pockets. "You didn't come home the night of your wife's death."

"Correct."

"You were in surgery that day."

"Correct."

"You keep an apartment in New York."

"Correct."

"And you stayed at your apartment that night."

"Forgive me, Detective Walker, but thus far you haven't asked me a question. You seem to be repeating statements I've already made to your chief."

"I apologize, Doctor, but I'm in charge of this investigation. I need to corroborate all of the facts myself."

"Very well." Knoebel turned away again, giving his attention to the stillness of the swimming pool and the haze that floated just above the surface.

Walker joined him in silently admiring the view, noting that the pool was kept heated, even at this time of year. He could not help wondering about the cost, not to mention that it must be one hell of a chilly walk from the pool to the bathhouse after a nighttime swim.

Knoebel finally said, "I had a full slate of surgery and rounds on Tuesday. I was due in the OR early yesterday. My custom is to stay in the city on those nights." He looked at Walker. "That is one of the reasons we bought the apartment in New York, in case you need an explanation for that."

"Do you recall what time you left the hospital Tuesday?"

"I was in and out all afternoon." He made an attempt to smile, but the effort seemed painful for him. "Are you asking for my alibi, detective?"

"Yes," Walker said simply. "An alibi would be helpful."

"My last procedure was done by two. I had rounds in the late afternoon. I was all over the hospital that day. I also went out to the park for some air."

"Central Park?"

"Yes."

"Alone?"

"Yes. Alone."

"And that evening?"

"What about it?"

"Were you alone?"

Knoebel thought that one over. "I had drinks with two of my colleagues. That was around seven o'clock. They can verify the time, although I'd prefer not to have them troubled with this. I'm sure you can understand."

Walker ignored Knoebel's irritation as he asked for and received the names of the two doctors. He finally took out his small pad and made some notes. "And then you went to your apartment?"

"I did."

"Alone?"

"I see that tact is no concern of yours, Detective." This time he made no attempt to smile.

"Tact has no place in my line of work, Doctor."

"Very well, then. I was alone."

"Do you recall what time you returned to your apartment?"

"Not exactly. Incidentally, when am I read my legal rights and asked if I want to consult with an attorney?"

"Would you like to consult an attorney?"

"Should I?"

"It's not really for me to say. At the moment you're not the target of this investigation. If you'd feel more comfortable with a lawyer present..."

"No, that's quite all right. Although I would be more comfortable if we sat down." He led Walker around the far end of the pool to the lawn chairs that sat on the flagstone deck.

"Are you sure it's not too cool for you?" Walker asked.

Knoebel was wearing a plaid shirt, open at the neck, and a tweed sport coat. Walker had on his suede jacket, zipped up tight.

Knoebel said, "I quite enjoy the fresh air after a day in the hospital. Have a seat."

Walker perched on the end of a chaise and crossed his arms, the notepad back in his pocket, his hands secure and warm against his chest.

Knoebel sat on the lounge chair beside him, sliding all the way back and putting his feet up, reclining with his hands behind his head, as relaxed as a man lying out in the sun. "It's getting dark much earlier now."

"Yes, it is," Walker agreed.

"Where were we?"

"I was asking what time you got home that night. To your apartment in New York."

"I don't recall exactly. Nine, nine-thirty."

"Did you call your wife that evening?"

"I don't recall. I don't think so."

"Was that unusual?"

Knoebel was staring up at the dark sky. "Not really. I told Elizabeth I would be staying in town that night. She always had my schedule in advance. At least as much in advance as I have it."

"What if you had called her that night? What if you called and got no answer? Would that have been unusual? Is it something you'd be likely to remember?"

"Not particularly. We often communicated through voice mail and e-mail and text." He let out a long sigh. "Elizabeth and I did not have a good marriage, Detective Walker. That is no secret. We spent many nights apart. Many of those nights we did not speak. Sometimes I would call. Sometimes she would call. Sometimes one or the other of us was out for the evening. Do you understand?"

Walker was not sure he understood, but nodded anyway. "Did your wife have enemies, Dr. Knoebel? When I say that, I mean . . ."

"You mean, can I think of anyone who might want to shoot my wife to death." He turned to face the detective. "Other than me, of course."

"Yes, that's the question."

Knoebel pursed his lips as he considered his response. "My wife was a nasty woman, Detective Walker. Making enemies was a hobby of hers. If you want to know whether I think any of those people would come into my home and murder Elizabeth, I must admit that it is beyond the realm of my imagination."

"I can understand that. But is there anyone who especially comes to mind, someone who might have hated your wife that much?"

Knoebel pondered the idea again, returning his attention to the star-filled sky. "I'll think about it." It was obviously not the first time the question had occurred to him, either before or since Elizabeth's death.

"I'd appreciate any help you could give us."

Knoebel offered no reply.

"Did you get home in time to, uh, see your wife here?"

"Before her body was moved? In the room? No. She had already been taken to the coroner's office. I asked our housekeeper to clean up, once your people were gone. I certainly had no interest in seeing her that way."

Walker nodded, as if confirming a thought.

"As you know, I was required to identify her body at the morgue," the doctor added.

Walker waited a moment for that image to fade. "Your wife hadn't received any threats, had she Doctor Knoebel? E-mails we might find in her computer." He waited for some reaction to the mention of the computer, which Nettie Sisson had confirmed was used exclusively by Mrs. Knoebel.

Knoebel responded with a blank stare.

"Just a possibility, that's all."

Knoebel gave his head a brisk shake. "No. If she had, I believe she would have told me."

Walker turned on the edge of his chair so he was facing Knoebel directly. "Excuse me for mentioning this, but your wife was found, uh, in the nude."

"So I was told," Knoebel replied curtly.

"We place the time of death at about four in the afternoon. Do you find it . . ."

"Unusual that my wife might be in our home, undressed, at four in the afternoon?"

Walker nodded.

"No. I do not."

Walker thought better of pursuing that line of questioning for now. "It seems there was no burglary, nothing missing from the house."

"That appears to be correct."

"Which means that the motive was personal, not monetary."

Dr. Knoebel nodded slowly, for the first time allowing a facial expression to betray something. It was as if he found the idea unspeakably sad.

"Did Mrs. Knoebel have life insurance?"

Sorrow was replaced by another of Knoebel's feeble impressions of a smile as he sat up and gave a theatrical look around his property. "No, Detective, she did not."

Walker nodded. "Had to ask."

Knoebel did not reply.

"Mrs. Knoebel was some sort of a computer consultant, correct?"

"Yes, and a very good one," he said. Then he added, "When she chose to work."

"You're aware we impounded your wife's laptop."

"Yes, although I am not clear about the reason."

"To check her e-mails and so forth."

"I see."

"Might help us with the case."

The two men were facing each other now, and Knoebel took a moment to close his eyes and rub them slowly. He had long fingers, Walker noticed, like a musician. "I will need to consider that. I never have time to bother with computers for social purposes." He paused, then added, "I really don't know what manner of unrelated private information she may have entered."

Walker took a moment to study the man. *Helluva poker player*, he reckoned, given what Blasko, Kovacevic and he had just spent the afternoon reading. "You have any idea what password your wife used to enter her programs?"

With no hesitation, Knoebel replied, "I do not."

Walker looked directly into the doctor's cold eyes. "I figure if you believe there's anything embarrassing in her files, you'd be likely to try to stop us from gaining access. Like denying you know her passwords."

"You certainly are a blunt man, Detective Walker. It is not a pleasant quality, but I must say, it saves time." He shook his head stiffly, just once, back and forth. "I presume, despite your warrant, that I may still have some rights to its return." Walker did not reply. "I will consider the issue of Elizabeth's computer and let you know tomorrow."

The way Walker had it figured, Stanley and Elizabeth may have had their problems, but there was no husband who would refuse anything that might lead to the discovery of his wife's murderer—except if the husband pulled the trigger. "It would be helpful if you'd give us your cooperation on this."

"Tomorrow," Knoebel repeated.

Walker stood up. "I've taken enough of your time. We'll call you about the arrangements for your wife's release."

"Very well." Knoebel stood also. "You can contact the funeral director. Your chief has the information."

"When we have anything else on the investigation I'll get back in touch with you."

Walker hesitated and Knoebel said, "You have another question?"

"Yes, Doctor, I do. You first learned of your wife's death when we called the hospital yesterday afternoon."

"Correct."

"Then you finished your surgery before coming up here."

"That is correct."

Walker hesitated, then asked, "How is your daughter holding up through all of this?"

It was clearly not the question Knoebel expected. "Kara is a bright young woman. It is a sad time for her, of course, but she is doing fine. Does that satisfy your curiosity?"

Walker did not feel the question required a reply. He said, "Good night, Doctor."

Knoebel said, "Good night, Detective Walker." Then he turned and walked back to his house, leaving Walker to find his own way to his car.

CHAPTER 12

The next morning, Walker was back in the detectives' squad room with a database printout concerning Nettie Sisson. Kovacevic had done a preliminary investigation into the backgrounds of some of the people involved with Elizabeth Knoebel. He discovered the housekeeper had an interesting personal history.

Walker poured himself a cup of coffee, then had a look at the information. "Looks like we'll be having another chat with Mrs. Sisson," he said. "First we need to find someone in that police department in Ohio who was familiar with her case."

"Already on it," Kovacevic told him.

"What about Mrs. Knoebel's e-mails? You find anything useful in there?"

"Zero. Nothing threatening or anything close."

"What about her calendar?"

"Whatever dates she had with any of the people in her diary, she wasn't recording them in her computer."

They were interrupted by the sound of the intercom, followed by a summons from Gill. Coffee in hand, Walker followed Kovacevic into the chief's office.

Gill was standing behind his desk, waiting. "Shut the door," he told them.

Walker obliged. "What's up?"

"You had your visit with Doctor Knoebel last night."

"That's right," Walker said.

"Sit down, sit down," the chief said as he took his place behind a large wooden desk strewn with files and forms and various items of unfinished business.

Walker sat in the armchair facing Gill. He was careful as he took a sip of the steaming coffee, but it burned his tongue anyway. "Damn," he said, "I should learn to use milk."

"How'd the talk go?" the chief asked.

"It went all right. Is there a problem?"

"No problem. What'd you think of him?"

"Let's say I've met warmer icicles in my day. I hope when I die my family's a little more broken up than he seems to be."

"You think he killed her?"

Walker rocked back on the hind legs of the chair and perched there while he thought it over. "It's a little early to say. I'll be looking over the coroner's report again this morning."

"You're not testifying at an inquest here. I just want your gut reaction."

"Okay," Walker nodded. "I can't say I liked the guy, but my gut tells me no. I don't think he killed her." He looked at the coffee, decided to wait before having another go at it.

"They can release the body this morning," Gill told them. "Jake says he's gotten everything he can from his examination, fully documented."

"I heard. Still bothers me though. Cremation."

Gill nodded, a reluctant admission that even he was troubled.

"What about putting the brakes on that? I'll take the hit," Walker said. "Tell them I asked Jake to run a different test or something."

"Not a bad idea," the chief agreed, "let me speak with the coroner's office." Then he got to the point. "Your new friend Dr. Knoebel already called here this morning, just before you came in. He was looking for you."

"About the release of his wife?"

"No. He said you're looking through her computer?"

"Right."

"He didn't sound happy."

Walker brought his chair down with a thud. "I don't think happy is in his repertoire. He say anything else?"

"He said when you're done he wants a chance to review everything you find."

Walker nodded. "That's it?"

"So far."

"Wonders never cease," Walker said. Then he leaned forward and said, "I have something to tell you, Chief." Then he treated Gill to a brief description of what they found in her computer.

At first Gill was silent. Then he said, "A diary of sexual adventures, is that what you're telling me?"

"Something like that," Walker replied. "A diary, a novel, we're not sure yet."

"Elizabeth Knoebel kept a diary?" the chief asked again, as if the notion was completely foreign to him.

"That's what I'm calling it. We printed it out, if you want to have a look. I have a sample here," he said, holding up the sections he brought with him.

Gill gave his head a determined shake. "I'm not leading this investigation, you are. The fewer people who see it, the better."

"Agreed, but there are names in here. They're in code, but Teddy said it should be easy to figure out. If her diary isn't pure fiction, if she really was having these affairs, she named the men. And some women too."

The chief looked as if he had just been told his tax returns for the past ten years were going to be audited. "What if there are names? What if they're real people? Local people? You'll turn this town into Scandal City." He pointed at the pages Walker was holding as if they might catch fire. "We'll have every tabloid reporter in the country camped out on Main Street."

"Maybe so, but I've got a murder to solve."

Chief Gill tilted his head back and peered at Walker down his long, uneven nose. "You just said this thing might be fiction. Even if it's not, you don't actually know it has anything to do with her death. You use it the wrong way and a lot of innocent lives could be ruined."

Walker frowned. "From what I read, these lives aren't so innocent. And as far as I can tell, the only life that's been ruined so far belonged to Elizabeth Knoebel. Who knows, she might have given us a clue to her murderer in here, whether she knew it or not. We've got to do something with the information."

"Not we, Walker, *you.*" Gill shook his head again. "You go figure out if there's anything in there that helps the investigation. And do it discreetly. We don't make another move on this until you determine whether or not it's relevant to solving this case."

"Got it."

"Good. Find out what you can from this . . . this . . . diary, then let me know where we stand. No court orders, no public announcements, no leaks. You clear?"

"As crystal," Walker said, then stood up. "How about Doctor Knoebel? He told you he wanted to see what we found. That could be interesting, right?"

Chief Gill grimaced. "Let me think about that one," he said, then waved them out.

In the hallway, Walker told Kovacevic they needed to make some phone calls. Then they would visit Mrs. Fitzmorris, the neighbor who spotted a car leaving the Knoebel driveway on the evening of Elizabeth's death. "See if you can set that up with her."

"Right," Kovacevic said, then he hesitated. "What do you think the chief is going to do about Doctor Knoebel and this diary?"

Walker smiled. "Are you kidding? He isn't going to do anything. He's going to hand that little hot potato to me."

CHAPTER 13

Since Walker's visit to her office on Thursday morning, Randi Conway had been haunted by the images of those photographs of Elizabeth.

Then there was the second anonymous note.

Whatever the persistent Detective Walker thought about lawyers, it was time to call hers.

Robert Stratford had been Randi's attorney since she opened her office in town, and along the way they became friends. Collecting friends was actually Stratford's principal gift. He had parlayed that talent into a successful law practice that had grown into a political career on the rise. After a stint on the Town Council, he became a Selectman, and he was now First Selectman. He currently had his eye on a legislative post in Hartford, and wherever that might lead him.

He was married to Linda Hope, daughter of a wealthy businessman who owned four car dealerships and considerable real estate holdings in the area. The marriage proved helpful to the growth of Stratford's law firm as well as his political aspirations. To everyone's disappointment, he and Linda had no children after more than fifteen years together. All they had, as his wife was fond of saying, was each other.

Since becoming a Selectman, Stratford had cut back on his law practice, but he always had time to help out his friends. When Randi telephoned him at his office that morning, the first thing he did was remind her of the invitation to dinner he had left on her machine a couple of days ago.

He said, "I was wondering if I'd ever hear back from you," doing his best to sound hurt rather than annoyed.

"I'm sorry," she said. "It's been a rough couple of days. I'd love to come if the invitation is still open."

"Done. Now that we have that settled that, what's been so rough?"

"Elizabeth Knoebel," she said.

"Awful thing, yes. I was just on the phone with Chief Gill about the case."

Randi hesitated, then said, "She was my patient, Robert."

"Oh. I hadn't heard that," he said.

"She was." Randi then described the visit from Detective Walker.

"You have to be careful here, Randi."

"That's why I'm calling," she replied. "I told him Elizabeth's death did not change my professional obligations to keep her confidences."

"You're certainly right about that."

"He threatened to get a court order to compel my testimony."

"I see." Stratford took a moment to consider her position. "You obviously need to avoid that at all costs."

"Yes I do."

"So does the town, I assure you. This could become a nightmare for everyone."

"It already is, Robert."

"Of course, of course. Let me look into this and get back to you."

"Okay."

He could hear the hesitation in her voice. "Something else?"

She thought about the notes but decided not to say anything about them, at least not yet. "Nothing," she said. "We can talk more about this when I see you."

"You know that I'm here for you."

"Thanks."

"Not a problem. And the good news is that you're coming to the club tonight."

"Yes," she agreed. She felt better already.

✣   ✣   ✣

Walker telephoned Stanley Knoebel, who was in his customary state of distraction and arrogance.

"I told you to contact the funeral director about arrangements for . . ."

"I'm calling about Doctor Conway," Walker told him.

"All right then," Knoebel demanded impatiently. "What about her?"

"You told Chief Gill that you and your wife were seeing Doctor Conway. I was wondering if you've been seeing her in a group format, as well as privately."

"Yes."

"I wanted the names of the other men in your group."

Dr. Knoebel paused, then without asking the reason for the question, he slowly intoned the names, "Mitchell Avery, Fred Wentworth, Thomas Colello, and Gorman, uh, Paul Gorman."

"You wouldn't happen to know the names of the women in Elizabeth's group, would you?"

"I do not. I believe they were the wives of the men I have just named. Does that satisfy your curiosity?"

"Isn't that sort of odd?" Walker asked. "Husbands in one group, their wives in the other."

"I'm not in a position to make that judgment. The format was devised by Doctor Conway. We all agreed to honor the confidentiality of our sessions and not discuss them with our spouses."

"May I ask if you honored that commitment?"

Knoebel's sigh came through the phone like a blast of cold air. "Yes, I did, and so did my wife."

Walker told him that was all for now and hung up. He decided it was not time to tell him anything about his wife's diary—assuming he didn't know about it already. He looked forward to another face-to-face with the good doctor, especially after Blasko determined which, if any, of those files referred to Elizabeth's husband.

For now, Walker had the names of Paul Gorman, Fred Wentworth, and Thomas Colello, not to mention the interesting coincidence that his recent acquaintance Mitchell Avery was also part of the group. On the department computer, he quickly matched them up with their wives: Lisa, Phyllis, Fran, and, of course, Joan. For a moment he wondered how her son Kyle was doing.

He noted that Thomas Colello was the only one in the group with *T* as an initial, the initial used in the file name they had read in "Notes for the Chapter Nine." He realized that might not mean anything, that he would have to wait for Blasko to finish his work on Elizabeth's code. Meanwhile, he decided to make a phone call, just to confirm what he had learned so far.

He tried the Wentworth house first, punched in the numbers, but got no answer. Then he tried the Gormans. A woman picked up.

"My name is Detective Anthony Walker, Darien Police Department. I'm calling with regard to the recent death of Elizabeth Knoebel. With whom am I speaking?"

"Poor Elizabeth," the young woman volunteered before he finished his introduction. Then she said, "I'm Lisa Gorman."

Walker nodded to himself. "Was Mrs. Knoebel a friend of yours?"

"Well, no, not exactly. We were in group together. I guess you know that. Isn't that why you're calling?"

"Actually no," he said, "we didn't have that information." Walker realized that if any of these people thought he learned about the group from Randi Conway, it might cause a problem for her, and therefore for him—no point in unnecessarily antagonizing a potential ally. He still had hopes of enlisting her assistance with the case. Walker, in his best 'golly gosh' tone, said to Lisa Gorman, "I didn't know you were in a group together, but that information may be very helpful to us. Actually, we found your name in Mrs. Knoebel's address book," he lied.

"You did?"

"Yes. This is just a routine call. We're following up on all leads, contacting anyone who knew her."

"I would like to be helpful, if I can."

"You know, Mrs. Gorman, because you're being so candid, I can admit this to you. We did know that Mrs. Knoebel was seeing a psychologist. Let me check my notes here." He riffled through some papers on his desk like a Foley artist, creating the proper sound effect. "Here's the name. Doctor Conway. Is she the therapist you were seeing in your group with Mrs. Knoebel?"

"Yes, yes, she is," Lisa replied earnestly. She had begun the day feeding her four-year-old son and cleaning the house. Now she was working with the police, helping to solve Elizabeth's murder. "Doctor Conway runs our group."

"Uh huh. That really is very helpful. And who are the other people in the group?"

"Joan Avery. And Fran Colello."

"Anyone else?"

"Oh, yes, sorry. Phyllis Wentworth."

"Anyone else?"

"No. Just the five of us." She paused. "Five, including poor Elizabeth."

Walker nodded to himself, confirming all the names.

"I hope I'm not doing anything wrong," Lisa Gorman said, "by giving out the names, I mean."

"No, no, of course not. And I'll keep our discussion confidential."

"Thank you."

"Well, you've been of great assistance, Mrs. Gorman."

"I have?"

"Yes. Very much so."

"Is that it?"

"That's all for now. But I'm sure we'll be in touch."

"Oh yes, please do. I mean, if I can be any more help."

They said their good-byes and, as soon as she hung up, Lisa pushed the speed-dial button for her best friend, Karen Martin. "Karen? Listen to this," she began.

CHAPTER 14

That afternoon, Mitchell Avery was seated comfortably on the striped couch in Randi Conway's private office. His right arm was outstretched along the back cushion, his legs were crossed, and his foot was wagging up and down like a metronome. He said, "Joan and I had a rough time after you and that cop left the other night."

"What do you mean 'a rough time'?" Randi asked.

"Just kind of tense." Avery shook his head. "Arguing is easy. Yelling and shouting are no problem. I can deal with conflict." He shrugged. "Silence is much worse. It's like she's giving up or something."

"Giving up?"

"You know, disgusted, depressed, whatever. Really morbid, actually."

"Did you talk about Kyle?"

As obvious as that question should have been, it caught Avery short. He stopped shaking his foot and sat up a bit straighter. "Not much," he said. "What the hell is there to talk about?"

Randi leaned back in her chair. "How about the fact that Kyle made his way to the rooftop of a four-story building earlier that night?"

Avery could not look her in the eyes. "Let's not discuss Kyle right now."

"All right. What would you like to discuss?"

"I don't know."

"How about you and Joan?"

"Like there's anything about us you don't already know?"

"Indulge me."

He was silent for a moment. Then he said, "Joan wants to know what went wrong between us, and I don't know what to tell her."

"Why not start with the truth?"

He responded with a disapproving look, as if the notion of telling his wife the truth was nothing less than absurd. "How can I? How can I can tell Joan that too many years have gone by, that things have changed, that she got older. How can I say that to her?"

"I'm not even sure what that means."

"What?"

"You said that *she* got older."

"Did I?"

"Yes, you did. What does that mean?"

"That's a stupid question, Doc. What the hell do you think it means? She got older. She looks older. She acts older."

"And what about you?"

Avery allowed himself an embarrassed laugh. "It's different for me."

"Do you feel you haven't gotten older?"

Avery looked genuinely puzzled.

"Mitchell, you said that Joan acts and looks older. Don't you also look older?"

"You mean, what do I see when I look in the mirror?"

"Let's start with that."

He pressed his lips together in a thoughtful frown, then said, "I'm heavier. A lot heavier, although I try and kid myself about it. I have less hair. Lines around my eyes. I'm closer to death than birth, if we're going to be blunt about it. That's what a midlife crisis is all about, right? Fear of mortality? But I don't really feel any of that. Somehow I don't feel older in the things that matter. Attitude. View of life. I feel as if I can still hack it. I feel . . ." He stopped.

"Go on."

"It'll sound ludicrous to you."

"Don't worry what it sounds like."

"Okay." Avery uncrossed his legs and leaned back, his arms folded across his chest. "I feel I'm still attractive to women. Including younger women. Maybe even more now than I was twenty years ago. Does that sound ridiculous?"

"Why would it?"

"Why? I've already admitted I'm a paunchy, balding, middle-aged guy."

"But one who believes he's attractive to younger women."

"Yeah," Avery chuckled. "Yeah, that's exactly how I feel. Who knows why, who knows what these women are after? My life experience? My money?" He laughed again. "Maybe it's the story about older men being better lovers."

"You rattle those off as if it doesn't matter what the reason is."

"I didn't say that."

"No, you didn't, but I want to know. Do the reasons matters to you or not?"

Avery paused, thinking it over before he replied. "If you want me to be totally honest about it, I don't think I care."

"So you don't care why you're attractive to younger women, as long as they find you sexy, is that right?"

"This may sound foolish all over again, but it's not just about the sex. It's about the romance."

Randi responded with a simple nod.

"It's about the excitement of a new relationship," he went on. "The idea that a beautiful young woman would want me, want to be with me."

"And maybe even love you?"

"Sure, why not?" He laughed. "Love is good, right?"

"But it's not that important to you?"

Avery tilted his head to the side and gave her a knowing grin. "Who are we kidding here, Doc? It's enough if a younger woman is willing to be with me. I'm not foolish enough to think she's really in love."

"So romance doesn't have to involve love?"

"Of course not."

Randi nodded, as if finally getting the concept straight. "Okay, then tell me how much younger we're talking about."

"How's that?"

"You keep referring to younger women. How much younger?"

Mitchell Avery smiled. "I'm fifty-three, so twenty-eight or twenty-nine sounds about right."

"Thirty is too old?"

"Come on, Doc, you're teasing me now."

"I really don't mean to tease you. What about a forty-year-old woman?"

"What about her?"

"Would you be interested in an affair with a forty-year-old woman?"

"I might. Depends on the woman."

For a moment, Randi wondered if they were both thinking of the same woman. "What would it depend on, Mitchell?"

He was obviously uncomfortable with the question. "Who knows?" he asked.

"But it's not as exciting as a woman in her twenties or thirties."

"I guess that's true."

"Do you mean it's not as flattering to have a forty-year-old woman want you as a twenty-eight-year-old?"

"Maybe. Maybe that's it."

"What if Joan wanted to be with a younger man?"

He shook his head as if he was incapable of imagining such a thing.

"You think a woman in her late forties couldn't attract a younger man?"

"Sure, I guess so," he replied. "But not Joan."

"I see." Randi hesitated, then said, "Elizabeth Knoebel was almost forty."

Avery's brow furrowed into tight little lines and he leaned forward. "That supposed to mean something to me?"

"It just came to mind, is all."

"Anything else come to mind? About Stanley's wife, I mean."

"Did you know her?"

"Elizabeth?" He sat back again, taking his time now. "Yeah, we met."

"You never mentioned that before."

"You never asked."

"Fair enough."

"What do you want to know?"

"Only what you want to share with me."

Avery forced a laugh. "A perfect therapist's answer."

"Elizabeth was an attractive woman."

"I'm not disagreeing."

"Would you agree that she could have attracted a younger man?"

Avery became increasingly uneasy, but repeated a casual, "Why not?"

"Much younger?"

"What is that supposed to mean?"

"You seem to be interested in much younger women, correct?"

"I'm not talking about children," he replied with a sudden flash of anger.

"No, I know you're not. I am."

"Are you?"

They stared at each other without speaking. Then Randi said, "I won't if you don't want me to."

"She was a demented bitch," Avery responded angrily.

Randi waited for more.

"How about we skip the whole Knoebel saga for the time being?" Avery said.

Randi stared at him for a moment, then said, "It seems the Knoebel saga, as you call it, has become part of your life."

"I don't want to talk about my son right now."

Randi nodded. "All right, we can discuss Kyle another time. Let's get back to you. I mean, all of this talk about other women. You said it's not just the sex. It's the romance, the thrill of new love, right?"

Mitchell Avery nodded.

"What about your wife. Doesn't she love you?"

"Of course she does. And I love her. I love her very much. But it's different."

"Or, it's not different. Isn't that the point?"

"How do you mean?"

"I mean it's the same old thing. There's no sense of discovery anymore. No risk."

"I suppose."

"No excitement," she added. "No romance."

"Exactly."

"So is that the problem for you? The need for something new?"

Avery forced a smile. "There's an old joke about the necessities of life for a man stranded on a desert island. He needs food, water, shelter, clothing, a woman." He paused. "And another woman."

Randi shook her head.

"Hey, I cleaned it up for you."

"Your wife is still very attractive."

"Hell yes." Mitchell looked into her eyes. "Joan's a great-looking woman. Sheer class, you know? Dresses like something out of a magazine. Takes care of herself, too. Exercises. Stays in shape. And for what? We go to bed at night, and all I want to do is sleep."

"And how does she react?"

"She's hurt, and she says so. She says I'm ignoring her, rejecting her. Then we argue. Or worse, we go through the goddamned motions, and then sex with her is about as thrilling as watching reruns of *I Love Lucy*." He stopped at the harshness of his own words.

"How do you think Joan feels about all this?"

"Women are different," he said reflexively. Then he smiled. "It's like that comedy routine about cavemen. Women nest. Men hunt."

"Thank you, Tarzan."

Avery forced a laugh. "We should go on safari some night. I'll show you what I mean."

She knew that he intended it as a joke, but there was something about the comment that troubled her, something disturbingly familiar. She was tempted to ask him about Elizabeth Knoebel again but let it pass for now. "So sometimes it's not about romance, or feeling younger, sometimes is has nothing to do with anything but the sex. Is that right?"

"Maybe."

"There are serious things we need to discuss to help you get clear on where you're going with all of these feelings."

"Oh sure. So you can convince me I'm a selfish egotist. Well, guess what—it's too late, I already know that." Avery averted his gaze again. "This is going nowhere, you see that, don't you? I can't go on fooling myself like this."

Randi watched him for a moment. Then she said, "Don't sell yourself short, Mitchell. People do it all the time."

CHAPTER 15

K ovacevic spent time processing each of the names Walker had gathered thus far, using the Department of Motor Vehicles, matching license plates and registrations, identifying the automobiles owned by each of the families. He had already gathered brochures of various cars that bore any resemblance to the description of the sedan given by Mrs. Fitzmorris, the neighbor who remembered a car speeding away from the Knoebel house on Tuesday afternoon. He now printed a few more examples from online ads, pictures of other cars that matched those registered to the people on their newly formed list.

"Good work, Kovie," Walker said as he looked through the photos. "Detective work isn't usually glamorous," he reminded the young officer, "but sometimes it can be easier than people think." He smiled. "You might want to keep that last part to yourself."

They arrived at the Fitzmorris home at the appointed time. Mrs. Fitzmorris was waiting for them at the front door. She was a stylish woman Walker figured to be around sixty, but looked better than that. She was dressed in a pink cashmere top and matching cardigan, her style well manicured and well kept.

After an exchange of polite greetings, the two policemen followed her into the house.

Shutting the door behind them, she said, "You know, Detective, it's terrible to have a thing like this happen right here in our neighborhood."

Walker nodded sympathetically at the idea of the privileged class having their idyllic lives disrupted by something as tawdry as murder.

"Believe me," she assured him, "I want to help if I can. It's just that I don't really know very much."

"That's all right," Walker assured her in his most studied manner. "You never know what little detail you might provide, and believe me, everything helps. If you'll just answer a few questions, we'll be out of your way."

Mrs. Fitzmorris led them into her kitchen and seated them at the polished gray granite island in the center of the room. Walker had a look around, at the Wolf stove and double oven, the Sub-Zero side-by-side refrigerator, the pantries and glass-fronted expanse of shelves. As she moved to the other side of the counter, facing them, she appeared ready to host a cable channel cooking show. "I feel as if I should offer you coffee but I never drink it myself," she said with a nervous giggle. "Can I make you some tea?"

Walker politely declined. "We'll only take a few minutes of your time. We just need to review a few things." He pulled out a typewritten report and began reading. "On Tuesday afternoon you returned home with some groceries at about five, came into the house, and placed the bags here, in the kitchen."

"That's right."

"Then you went back outside to collect the mail. That was when you saw the car coming from the Knoebels' house."

"Yes."

"And you noticed it because it was going so fast."

"That's right," she nodded, looking from Walker to Kovacevic. "That's right."

"And what time was that?"

"As I told this young man, it was just about five. I put the bags down and went right back out for the mail."

"Uh huh. Just as you had said." He turned to Kovacevic, who handed him a group of brochures and photographs. "We want you to spend a moment looking at these. They're pictures of several different cars. We think it's possible that one of them might be the type of car you saw leaving the Knoebel property that day."

She nodded dutifully.

"Just take your time and have a look at them."

Mrs. Fitzmorris spread the prints and color fold-outs across the countertop.

"I believe you said the color of the car was . . ." Walker paused, offering her the opportunity to fill in the blank.

"Gray. I'm pretty sure it was a medium gray."

Walker smiled in appreciation. "Excellent, that also confirms your earlier recollection."

Mrs. Fitzmorris appeared pleased with herself, and Kovacevic made a show of writing something in his notepad. Then Walker and Kovacevic watched as she carefully scrutinized each of the pictures.

"This could be the one." Mrs. Fitzmorris was pointing to a late-model Mercedes-Benz sedan. "I'm not very good at cars," she admitted. "They all kind of look the same to me nowadays."

Walker smiled. "I know what you mean. Let me ask you, would it be helpful if we began to eliminate some? Take out the ones it couldn't possibly be?"

"Yes," she nodded enthusiastically, "that might help."

They spent a few minutes setting aside the pictures of cars that were not close to her original description. That included the models of Jeeps and Explorers driven by the Colellos, the Gormans, the Wentworths, and the Averys; the type of small sedan owned by Nettie Sisson; the make of Fred Wentworth's station wagon; and Mitchell Avery's sports car. That left them a few sedans. Of those, Mrs. Fitzmorris still thought it might be the Mercedes.

"But I'm not sure," she warned them. "I'm really not sure."

"That's all right," Walker said soothingly. "You've been very patient. I just have one more question. I apologize, because I know you've been asked this before."

"Go right ahead," Mrs. Fitzmorris said.

"I want you to think back to Tuesday afternoon. I want you to concentrate on the period of time from when you first drove up to your house, right up to the moment you went out to get your mail. All right?"

She nodded.

"I want you to think back and tell me, did you hear anything at all that might have been a gunshot? Anything?" She was already shaking her head when he added, "The sound of a car backfiring? Something loud falling? A cracking sound, like a tree branch breaking?"

She was still shaking her head. "Nothing. Nothing at all like that," she told him.

"All right. I just needed to be sure." He offered up another approving smile. "If we get any additional information, we may ask to bother you one more time."

"That'll be fine," she said pleasantly. "I'm glad to help."

"Just one more thing. You're sure the time was around five in the evening?"

"I am," she said.

Outside the house, Kovacevic organized the pictures as they walked to the car. Walker said, "I don't think we're there yet."

"You don't think it was the Benz?"

Walker shook his head. "There was no real flicker of recognition, no *Aha* moment. It seemed like she picked it because it wasn't any of the others." He thought it over. "Some of these people probably lease cars through their businesses. Cars that wouldn't have matched up on the basic DMV name check. You need to run that down, then we'll have another crack at Mrs. Fitzmorris."

"Okay, but just so you know, a couple of the cars we identified here were leased, but they were registered in personal names. I'll drive by their houses and check the license plates, then match them up with company leases."

"Good," Walker said. "Do it."

They climbed into Walker's Explorer, then sat there for a moment before he started the engine.

"What is it, sir?"

"I'm not sure. It's Doctor Knoebel, I think. I can't shake the feeling that this is all too easy, you know?"

"Easy?"

"When I met with him I mentioned his wife's computer, but he didn't say much about it. Then, when I called him today, he didn't ask anything about what we found." He shook his head. "We've got to know if Teddy is absolutely sure the files weren't tampered with recently. Get him on the horn."

As Kovacevic tracked down Blasko, Walker fired up the engine and drove off, turning left out of the Fitzmorris house and past the tree-lined entrance to the Knoebels' property. As he passed the now familiar gravel driveway, he wondered if this was the same route Elizabeth Knoebel's killer had taken, just three days before.

CHAPTER 16

Back in his office, Walker found a message from Kettering, Ohio. He returned the call to Sgt. Fitzgerald.

"I appreciate you getting back to us," Walker said. "You know what I'm calling about?"

"Nettie Sisson."

"You're familiar with the case?"

"Very."

"I don't have much in the way of detail," Walker admitted. "We have a file, some of which was sealed, so we had a local judge open it. Was hoping you could fill in the background."

"Mind if I ask what this is about? Nettie in any kind of trouble?"

"I hope not. She lives in this area now. Employed as a part-time housekeeper. The woman she worked for was found murdered a couple of days ago. Nettie discovered the body when she got to work that morning."

Sgt. Fitzgerald whistled softly into the phone. "Cause of death?"

"Single gunshot to the woman's head. No struggle, no evidence of a break-in or a robbery. Appears the vic knew her killer."

"I see."

"Given Mrs. Sisson's history, you could see why I'd be curious about her."

Walker could almost hear the man nodding at the phone. "You want me to start at the beginning?"

"If you have the time, that'd be great."

"All right," Fitzgerald said. "Nettie grew up here. Most people thought her mother was nuts. Everyone knew her father was a drunk." He hesitated. "All right if I give this to you straight, or you want an official presentation?"

"I prefer straight talk," Walker said.

"Okay. The father was an abusive prick. Beat the wife, beat Nettie, died of cirrhosis before he made fifty. Nettie's mother died soon after."

"Natural causes?"

"Yeah, if there is such a thing for a woman who suffered the way she did. Anyway, Nettie became the usual story. Battered kid finds her way into an abusive marriage of her own. Married a local guy, Ralph Sisson, a real beauty. Another violent alcoholic. Had a couple of visits from our department when he got out of hand, but given the years she spent with her father, Nettie had plenty of experience in dealing with his type. Most of her married life she ran interference for their two daughters, struggling to keep her husband from getting at them, bearing the brunt of his drunken bullshit. When the girls were old enough they took off, leaving Nettie to face him alone. Things got worse, but for reasons no one could understand, Nettie hung in there. I guess she figured she could handle it."

"Nice life."

"Nettie was actually a popular woman. Baked pies for her neighbors, brought homemade soup to the elderly, all that sort of thing. Seems she looked for friendship anywhere she could find it, and everyone clocked her as a good person with a shithead for a husband. Problem was, Ralph wouldn't even allow her the pleasure of her good deeds. Mocked her in public, humiliated her every chance he got. He'd call her ugly and stupid and useless, right in front of people. Like I said, a real beauty." Fitzgerald paused, thinking about something. "I suppose the physical abuse got worse too, after the daughters skipped town, but Nettie never complained. People told her to get the hell out of there, get a protective order, get a divorce. She wasn't having any of it. One night Ralph comes home, a little drunker than usual. Nettie was going to be on the committee for the Fourth of July festival that year, and he must've found out about it that day. According to the story, he tells her he won't let her do it. Says she's a doormat for everyone in town, that they all think she's a joke, stuff like that. Starts screaming at her, calling her 'Nettie the Chump' over and over again. Neighbors heard that part."

"A real sweetheart."

"Oh yeah. Anyway, best we could re-create what happened next, she was in the kitchen cooking dinner when he started in on her. She told him she was going to work for the festival no matter what he had to say about it, so he knocked all of the dishes off the table, sent them crashing to the floor. Then he came at her and started pounding her pretty hard. By then he was shrieking at her, or so the neighbors said. Nettie was holding a chef's knife, or maybe she grabbed for it at that point. Tell you the truth, no one really cared. All we know is that she planted the thing into his chest, right up to the handle."

"Takes a lot of strength to do that."

"Exactly. Which is why we figured he must have been stumbling forward when it happened. Anyway, by that time all his yelling had people banging on the front door. Cool as a cucumber Nettie calls 911, then lets the neighbors in."

"I'm usually not a fan of homicide, but sometimes it can work out just fine."

"No such luck here, Walker. Ralph recovered, and let me tell you, there were a lot of folks disappointed about that. All those people Ralph told Nettie about, claiming they thought she was a chump, well they had a much different view of her, and they all rallied to her defense. They came forward, admitting they'd seen the cuts and bruises she'd suffered over the years. Some even apologized for not doing something or speaking up sooner. They promised they would march into court, one after the other, prepared to testify on her behalf if the case ever went to trial."

"So what happened?"

"A deal was made. Nettie was voluntarily confined to a state mental hospital for at least two years. Her husband was required to attend meetings of Alcoholics Anonymous and out-patient counseling for his history of violence. The court issued mutual protective orders, they got a divorce, Ralph left town. Finished business."

"According to the report I saw, Mrs. Sisson spent five years in the state institution."

"That's right. After those first two years it was pretty much voluntary, or so I was told. Nettie became a trustee, helped other patients. Eventually they told her it was time to go. When she was released, the head psychiatrist at the facility sent her to some woman in your area."

"Doctor Randi Conway."

"That's the name. The honcho in charge knew this Conway from graduate school, thought he'd be a good choice for Nettie's out-patient treatment."

"The he is a she. Randi Conway is a woman."

Fitzgerald laughed. "No kidding, never knew that. Anyway, it was also an opportunity for Nettie to move away, which was another recommendation on her release. That's the last I heard of her until you called."

"She's been here over two years." Walker looked at the file notes. "Began working part-time as a clerk in a gourmet food store, also does volunteer work at the local library. Doctor Conway introduced her to the Knoebels and she's been working for them as a housekeeper."

"Until Mrs. Knoebel turned up dead."

"Far as I know Nettie is still working for Doctor Knoebel. The husband."

"Doctor Knoebel, eh? Another psychiatrist?"

"Surgeon."

"Well, all I can say is that I hope she had nothing to do with your case. I came to know Nettie, and I would find it hard to believe she's capable of that sort of violence."

"Despite the history."

"*Because* of it. Last time I spoke with her, at the time of her release, she told me the years of state confinement were the best of her life. She was finally living without fear. She received professional help. I thought she'd be okay, I really did."

"I hope she is," Walker said.

"Anything else I can do for you on this?"

"No, you've been very helpful."

"If you need to see our official file, you let me know."

"I'll keep that in mind, thanks," Walker said.

Then they said good night.

✤   ✤   ✤

As her background was being revealed to Anthony Walker, Nettie Sisson was sitting alone in her apartment, considering the prospect of returning to work at the Knoebel home. Dr. Knoebel had called to say that he wanted to assure her that he still expected her there.

As reluctant as she was to return, she needed the job.

She sat in her small living room, staring down at her hands, wondering how she would go on, dreading the thought of entering that house. It was not Elizabeth's death that haunted her as much as conflicted memories of Elizabeth in life, the memories of her own past and the inevitable moment when all of it would be exposed.

Elizabeth was gone, and now she was on her own, the demons from her past once again her closest companions. She realized she had to learn how to trust again, just as she had been taught how to hate.

When she first arrived, Randi Conway was the only person there who knew the truth of her secrets, about the stabbing, about her internment, about all the things she had done back then, in her pathetic attempt to fund her escape from Ralph.

And then she made the mistake of trusting Elizabeth Knoebel.

Only Dr. Conway knew the depth of her relationship with Elizabeth. Not even Dr. Conway really understood what that relationship had become.

CHAPTER 17

Randi arrived late for dinner at Bob Stratford's country club. The maître d' led her through a maze of round, linen-covered tables to the far corner of the dining room, where her host and friends were already seated.

"Hello everyone," Randi said. "Sorry I'm late."

Bob Stratford stood and greeted her with a warm hug. "No worries. You're only one cocktail behind us."

Stratford was a reasonably handsome man. He had a firm jaw line, even nose, and clear complexion. He managed to keep trim with regular workouts, a lot of tennis, and a competitive streak most men outgrow at a younger age. His hair was straight and brown and always carefully combed and sprayed. But his opaque brown eyes were his most striking feature. They could change from pensive to puckish, then suddenly transform into a piercing gaze that explained his success as a ruthless negotiator and attorney. They could also convey a look of pure empathy, which was helpful as he burnished his political persona.

He was dressed, as always, in the conservative uniform of his dual profession—lawyer and elected official. He favored dark suits, white or blue shirts, and colorful silk ties that cost more than most people pay for a pair of shoes.

He stepped back, still holding Randi by the shoulders. "You look terrific."

"Thanks," she replied as she looked past him to the others seated at the table. She smiled at Jeannine and Bill Reilly, then saw that Bob's wife had decided to come along after all. "Linda," she said. "Robert told me you were going to be at a charity event or something. I thought I was filling in."

Linda Stratford made a move to push back her short blond bangs. "Filling in?"

Before Randi could answer, the Reillys stood and said how wonderful it was to see her, and she responded in kind.

Then they all sat down and Stratford ordered a round of drinks.

"So, we heard you were there with the Avery boy on Tuesday night," Bill Reilly said. "What's the inside story?"

Randi explained that she could not discuss the matter.

"What's to discuss?" Bob Stratford asked. "Obviously another rich little malcontent, am I right?"

"I don't even know the kid," Bill Reilly told him, "but that seems like an awfully tough appraisal."

"Yes," Linda Stratford agreed. Turning to her husband, she asked, "And what would you know about raising a child?"

If Stratford's look was intended to turn her into a pillar of salt, the only thing that became petrified was the conversation.

Bill Reilly rescued them again. Turning to Randi, he said, "At least tell us about the policeman and the six-pack of beer. True or not?"

Randi smiled. "True. And that is something I *can* talk about." She regaled them with her account of Detective Anthony Walker's primitive tactics, surprised at how much she enjoyed recounting the story.

From there, the discussion moved on to local gossip, and even Linda joined in as they dissected one couple after another, until Jeannine Reilly finally cut them off.

"Forget all this small-time stuff," she insisted. "What about the murder?"

Randi turned to Bob Stratford. The last thing she wanted was a discussion about the death of her former patient, and she looked to him for help.

Stratford said, "I think I've met the husband. A surgeon in New York."

"That's what I read," Jeannine said. "I never met either of them, but I've heard a thing or two about her around town." She raised an eyebrow and added, "If you catch my drift."

Randi remained silent as Stratford suggested they order dinner.

The subject of the Knoebels was dropped as they concentrated on the menu. They placed their orders, finished their cocktails, and moved on to wine. As best they could, Randi and Bob worked to navigate the conversation away from Elizabeth Knoebel.

Dinner was served, with colorful mixed salads followed by grilled salmon and pasta covered by julienne vegetables. When the wine was done, they turned to after-dinner drinks and dessert. The discussion meandered from town politics to local real estate values, but their interest in those events was soon exhausted. When Jeannine Reilly returned to Elizabeth's death, Bob Stratford again ran interference. Eventually they found their way to their favorite topic, Men and Women.

Jeannine began by turning to Randi. "We need a professional opinion here. You're a psychologist."

Randi smiled politely, knowing how discussions tend to go when they start with that observation.

Bob Stratford said, "Yes Jeannine, Randi is a psychologist. Thank you so much for pointing out the obvious." Then he picked up his glass and drained off what was left, mostly melted ice flavored by the memory of Irish whisky already consumed.

"You didn't let me finish."

"Oh, I'm sorry," Stratford replied with a raised hand, as if prepared to fend off a blow. "Finish, Jeannine, please finish. I really want you to finish. We all want you to finish." Jeannine's husband uttered an inebriated laugh, and Stratford nodded his appreciation.

Jeannine turned to her husband, narrowed her eyes until they were no more than two slits, and warned him, "Later for you, dear." Then she returned her attention to Stratford. "I want to talk about rituals, Bob. My friends were discussing it at lunch the other day, and I say that men are much more ritualistic than women. You disagree?"

"I can," Stratford said with a dismissive tilt of his head, "and I shall." He was still holding his empty glass, which he now gave a forlorn look. "First, let's have our waiter bring one more round to lubricate this complex conversation."

Almost on cue, all three women issued refusals to the offer of another cocktail.

"You see!" Stratford exclaimed triumphantly. "Exhibit A has been submitted."

Jeannine Reilly frowned. "All right, counselor, what is the significance of Exhibit A?"

"You speak of rituals and I've given my first example. Women will almost always refuse a drink. It's reflexive. Women will insist on being talked into the next round, as if it couldn't possibly be their idea, or their fault, or whatever. Men just say, 'Sure.' Or they say, 'No more for me,' and really mean it." He looked to Bill Reilly. "All right, maybe we don't always mean it," he conceded with a grin, then turned back to Jeannine. "But women go through the ritual of refusal, seduction, and submission. By the way, I believe you practice this for other purposes as well."

When the waiter arrived, Bill Reilly said, "Okay, who really wants another drink?" Amidst some grudging laughter all five of them raised their hands.

But Jeannine persisted. "That's a lousy example," she said. "Men have real rituals they follow."

"For instance?"

"Peeing on the golf course," she offered defiantly as her first point of proof. "I never met a man who played golf who didn't have to go into the woods and urinate at least once a round. And it doesn't matter if there are toilet facilities all over the course. You all just love to go into the woods and pee."

The men reluctantly nodded their agreement and Bill Reilly said, "If it's nice out, leave it out."

Jeannine shot him another of her disapproving looks, then soldiered on. "And all that teasing you men do. That locker-room banter. Stupid nicknames and insult humor. It's strictly a male thing, right?"

Her husband shook his head. "Not necessarily, Miss Butthead."

"That's right," Stratford agreed. "Although we can include you if you like, dorkface."

"Grow up," Linda Stratford said.

Her tone turned the table quiet for a moment, but then Bill Reilly said, "You know what they say in my business, Linda? Husbands are like long-term bonds, they never seem to mature."

That won him a couple of laughs, but not from his own wife, who said, "It's too true to be funny."

Linda Stratford turned to her husband. "What about the ritual of introducing your single friends to the unattached women you know? Surely, Robert, you must know some eligible bachelor for Randi. This way she wouldn't have to come to these dinners alone." She turned her sharp gaze to Randi and offered a smile that was as warm as the ice in her husband's glass. "That is, unless it's one of those nights you're filling in for me, dear."

Randi managed a smile of her own but did not reply, expecting Stratford to answer his wife.

He said nothing.

"Okay then," Bill Reilly barged in again, "what about some of that female stuff you all do?"

"What stuff?" his wife asked.

"You know, the way women are so catty about other women. Men may joke and make funny insults face-to-face, but women are really evil."

"Evil? We're evil?" Jeannine demanded of her husband.

"You know what I mean."

"I'm not sure that I do, *Bill*," somehow managing to wring three syllables from her husband's name.

"Come on, Jeannine, you're always talking about your friends behind their backs."

"I see," she replied, her face making it clear how she felt about the accusation, particularly in front of Linda Stratford. "As if men don't do the same thing."

Bob Stratford and Bill Reilly exchanged a guilty look.

"What about it, Randi?" Jeannine continued. "You *are* the professional here. Aren't men more ritualistic than women?"

Randi slowly shook her head. "Generalizations can be dangerous."

"Fine," Jeannine said. "Give us a specific then."

"Sex, for instance," Stratford suggested as he turned to Randi. "That's the main event, and your area of expertise, so to speak."

Bill Reilly lifted his glass and did his drunken best to focus his uneven gaze on Randi. "I would like to take a moment to congratulate you for choosing sex as your area of expertise."

After all of the cocktails and wine, three of them thought that was funny. Linda and Randi did not.

"If you want a serious answer, I can tell you that in my experience, men and women aren't so different," Randi said. "Basically they all behave the same way when it comes to sex."

"What does that mean?" Jeannine asked.

Randi slowly looked around the table, then said, "Men and women all have habits and patterns, no matter how dull or outlandish. And in our society, the truth being told, men and women spend much more time talking about sex than having sex."

"That's for sure," Jeannine Reilly said in her throaty voice, earning some approving laughter from both sides of the debate.

"I will admit," Randi went on, "when it comes to sex, it seems to me that men and women do share one basic ritual."

When she paused, Jeannine demanded impatiently, "What? What ritual?"

Randi took a long swallow of her fresh drink, then looked directly at Linda Stratford. "They lie," she said.

CHAPTER 18

Anthony Walker arrived at the station house early on Saturday morning. The Knoebel file was sitting atop a stack of papers on the steel cabinet in his office. He grabbed it, dropped into his chair, and began looking through the folder, trying to determine what, if anything, he might be missing.

After a brief but frustrating review he finally leaned forward, tossed the file on his desk, and grabbed the phone. He dialed up voice mail and retrieved his messages. The first call he returned was to Teddy Blasko.

"Hey, I've been trying to reach you," Blasko told him.

"What've you got?"

"For starters, there's no evidence anyone tampered with her computer. It also doesn't appear any of the files have been edited lately, except what we read together. Someone worked on that one the day she died."

"When you say 'someone' . . ."

"I mean anyone who had access to her computer. Could've been her, could've been someone else. No way of knowing that."

"The fingerprints lifted off the keyboard were all hers. She had to be the last one to use it."

"Right," Blasko said. "Forgot about that. Kovie went through her e-mails?"

"He did. Nothing helpful there, coming or going. If her stories are real, she wasn't communicating with these people by e-mail."

"Agreed. I checked for deleted messages, the trash bin on her hard drive, nothing useful there either."

"Okay. What about the file names?"

"Turns out to be a variation on a Caesarian code with a real first initial and a progression starting with the second letter."

"Simple English would be helpful."

"Right, right. She used real first initials, added four letters to the second letter, three to the next, then two, then one. Kept all the names to five letters."

"Names, Teddy. What are the names?"

"Right, right. Using those names you gave me as possible matches, that made some of them easy as pie. Others don't fit at all. I mean they don't match the pattern. Got your list handy?"

"Hold on," Walker said as he grabbed the sheet from the file. "Okay, go."

"In order, I'll spell out what we've got. Remember, the first initials remain the same. I get BRIAN. CHARL. DRCON. FINAL—that one appears to be uncoded. FRANC. FREDW. INTRO—another one that's uncoded. JOANA. JAMES. LISAG. MITCH. NETIE. PAULG. PHYLS. REGNA. ROBRT. SHAKE is another one that does not seem to follow the code. STNLY. THOMS. That's it."

Walker sat there and stared at the list he had just made. BRIAN, JAMES, REGNA, and ROBRT were new. He would have to look at the file called SHAKE, see what that was about. The other names were becoming increasingly familiar. He riffled through the pages for what he now knew were the DRCON and the STNLY files. They were blank. "What about the backup you mentioned?"

"Nothing different there."

"Tell me about the two empty files."

"Whatever they might have had in them, they were wiped clean a week before her murder."

"Okay."

"What do you want me to do with the laptop?"

"Drop it off here today."

"Done," Blasko said, then hung up.

Walker's next call was to Kovacevic.

"Still sleeping?"

"It's Saturday, sir."

"Right. Here's what you're going to do on Saturday."

Walker told him about the results of Blasko's work and explained what he wanted him to do with the names they had matched between Elizabeth's computer and Randi Conway's patients. He hung up, pulled another number from the file, and punched it in. When he got an answering machine he ended the call and dialed a second number, the one for her office.

She picked up the phone and said, "Doctor Conway."

"This is Anthony Walker."

"Good morning, Detective Walker."

"Working early on a Saturday?"

"Catching up on some paperwork."

"Yeah, me too. Look, I think I might have been a little heavy-handed the other day."

"A little?"

"Let's just say that you and I have gotten off to a bad start, how's that?"

"I'm not sure what you think we're starting," she said in an unfriendly monotone, "but, yes, I agree that we've given bad starts a new meaning."

"So what do you say to a truce?"

"A truce?"

"Is that what you therapists do, you answer every question with another question?"

"Someone else just accused me of that. Is that what everyone thinks?"

"See, that's another question. I'm catching on."

"Is there a point to this call, Detective Walker?"

"I think we should talk."

"Is that right?"

"I'm actually calling to ask if you'll have dinner with me."

"Dinner?"

"There you go again."

Randi allowed herself a brief laugh. "Maybe I can't help myself, but I do have another question. Why would we want to have dinner together?"

"Let's just say I have some new information you might find interesting, and I could use your help. You pick the spot, I'll buy."

"When would we be having this dinner?"

"How about tonight, at seven?"

"I can't do it tonight, I'm busy," she lied reflexively. It was a Saturday night, after all, and she was not about to admit she had no plans.

"Something you can change?"

She paused. "Is this like you're calling me in for questioning?"

Walker laughed. "Not exactly, no. But it is important."

He waited through a long silence. Then Randi said. "Can I call you back?"

"You can, but it'd be a whole lot easier if you just said yes and named the place."

"All right," she said, her tone making it sound very much like 'Why not'? "Seven o'clock."

"Good," he said. "How about Roberto's, in Stamford?"

"I thought I got to pick the place."

"You can, sure, I was just trying to move things along. I know them, a table won't be a problem."

"Your regular hangout?"

"No, but I once did the owner a favor."

"And it'll be better for us to meet in another town, rather than here in Darien, am I right?"

"That was my thought. Figured it might be more comfortable for you."

"Roberto's is fine," she said.

"Can I pick you up?"

"That's all right. I know the place. I'll meet you there."

He felt a bit uncomfortable about that—he was old-school about such things—but he decided not to push it. It wasn't a date, after all, it was a dinner meeting. "Okay," he said. "See you there."

After Randi hung up, the first thing she thought about was the typewritten notes she had found in her office. She took them out of the drawer and looked at them again.

She had not mentioned them to Bob Stratford and she already knew she was not going to tell Walker about it, at least not yet.

But why? she asked herself. What was she afraid they would discover? What was she afraid *she* might discover? The notes were anonymous, after all.

She leaned back, her gaze unfocused, recalling a private session with Elizabeth Knoebel, nearly a year ago.

It was near the end of the hour, and Elizabeth's face wore the sardonic smile that had become so familiar to Randi.

"Doctor," Elizabeth said, "I don't think you realize that you may actually be the one in need of help."

Randi did not respond.

"It's obvious to all of us."

"All of you?"

Elizabeth nodded. "Of course," she said. "You may be the analyst, but you're as needy as any of the rest of them in that pitiful group."

Randi stared at her without speaking.

Then, in a whisper, Elizabeth said, "I know what you need."

Randi looked away, which caused Elizabeth to laugh. "You see how tense you are, Doctor? You need a release for that tension."

"You believe I'm tense?"

"I believe you're tight, yes. Are you tight, Doctor? I believe you're tight."

Randi resisted the urge to say what she really thought. Instead she said, "What I believe, Elizabeth, is that we should be talking about you."

"But we are talking about me, don't you see? We're talking about us."

Randi remained silent.

"Fear is a disabling emotion, Doctor. What are so you afraid of?"

When Randi gave no answer, Elizabeth leaned forward, the low cut of her blouse offering a view of her fleshy breasts. She was not wearing a bra. "What are you so afraid of?" she asked again.

Randi lowered her gaze. She could not bring herself to answer. Elizabeth was so close they seemed to be sharing the fragrance of her musky perfume. Randi could almost feel the warmth of Elizabeth's breath as she spoke.

"Ah, Doctor, what a pity that you live your life this way, allowing opportunities to pass. It's true, isn't it? You lead a life of lost opportunities."

"I don't know what you're talking about," Randi answered, feeling foolish for having said it.

"Don't you? Isn't this an opportunity for you? For both of us?"

Randi began to stand up, but Elizabeth reached out and touched her arm. *"Don't run away,"* she said teasingly. *"Stay with me."*

Randi sat down, slowly pulling her arm back, now looking directly at Elizabeth. She said, *"Whatever you think you're playing at, Elizabeth, this is not a game. This is not a game,"* she repeated.

Elizabeth nodded slowly. *"No,"* she said, displaying as warm a smile as Randi had ever seen her manage. *"It's not a game, Doctor."* Then Elizabeth stood up and, without another word, left the office.

Randi rubbed her eyes, picked up the phone, and called Stratford.

CHAPTER 19

Elizabeth's murderer was faced with a problem, and her name was Randi Conway.

It had always been an issue, the existence of a psychologist with intimate knowledge of Elizabeth Knoebel, as well as some of the critical players involved in the drama Elizabeth had created. The detective in charge of the investigation would conclude the same thing, and it was inevitable that he would begin pressuring Randi Conway for information.

The built-in firewall was Dr. Conway's obligation to protect the confidences of her patients, especially those who were most troubled, those most in need of her care. Leaving the anonymous notes was intended to reinforce the therapist's commitment to her patients and to send her in the wrong direction.

Now it was time to intensify the effort, to add a measure of fear to the equation.

It would be a shame to have to kill her, but whatever needed to be done, it was a decision that would have to be made soon.

✤　✤　✤

That Saturday afternoon, as Elizabeth's murderer pondered the next move, Walker and Kovacevic were alone in the squad room, mulling over the various notes, papers and photographs on the case. Walker tossed a folder on the desk, looked up, and asked, "So, what have we got here?"

"Sir?"

"We've got this coded list of names from her computer, some of which seem to match the names of the women in her therapy group and their husbands. The contents are a lot of sexy stories about men. And women."

Kovacevic nodded.

"One of the unidentified files is probably about the Sisson woman. A couple of the others are wild cards, at least so far. And the files that appear to be named for the good Doctor Knoebel and our friend Randi Conway are blank."

"What about those?"

"Teddy says if anything had been erased since her death, he would have found it," Walker said. "Something about checking the backup and the hard drive and all that other cyber-talk."

"That's right," Kovacevic said. "Even if they were erased, he could go back and see when they were last edited."

"Okay, so we've got a murdered woman who was some sort of sexual predator, at least according to what's in here." He pointed to the pages of the journal. "And the way she manipulated these people, any one of them who read this might have wanted to blow her brains out."

"Even if they hadn't read it. Maybe even if they just knew she was writing it."

"Good point. Or if they knew what she was up to."

"Especially her husband?"

Walker grinned. "The thought has crossed my mind. But it raises another question."

Kovacevic waited.

"What if the murderer had no idea about her journal? I mean, whoever shot her was right there, inside her house. They could have taken the laptop. Or Teddy would have found evidence that someone tampered with it."

The young officer nodded again.

"Or there would have been some indication the house was searched for a hard copy, a printed version."

"Good point."

"If I'm going to kill her because her memoirs are going to embarrass me, why wouldn't I try and find the damn thing and take it with me?"

"So you think the murderer had no idea she was writing about all of this."

"That's my best guess. There was no indication in the house of any kind of search. No one's fingerprints on the computer except the victim's."

Kovacevic nodded. "So we're back to the question of motive."

"The murderer might have figured out what she was up to. Could have been jealous. Or angry over being played. Or concerned she might start talking."

"Assuming it was not her husband."

"Even if it was," Walker sighed. "We'll have to start by checking out Knoebel's alibi in New York. I'll handle that. And we'll need to speak with Nettie Sisson again."

"Want me to set that up?"

"No, let's surprise her."

"Right."

"Then there's this list of people we need to check out." He shook his head. "We have to run down every one of these leads without ruining a dozen lives and disrupting the whole community in the process."

"You sound like the chief."

"Heaven forbid. I just don't want to kick up a lot of dirt unnecessarily."

"So what do you want me to do?"

Walker thought it over. "We've got to figure a way to determine which of these people knew what Elizabeth Knoebel was doing, and that's going to be tricky. Let me meet with Randi first, see what she has to say."

"Randi?"

"Doctor Conway."

"You're on a first-name basis now?"

Walker stood up. "Not yet, but I'm working on it."

CHAPTER 20

That evening, as she pulled off the parkway and turned her car onto High Ridge Road, Randi Conway was still preoccupied with the anonymous notes, worrying once more if she should mention them to Walker. She had spoken with Bob Stratford and his advice had remained the same—she needed to protect the rights of her patients. Even if the police might seek a court order forcing her to divulge information confided to her by Elizabeth Knoebel, Stratford warned her to keep the faith for the time being. Only then did she tell him about the notes and, although he expressed his concern, his position remained unchanged.

"Meet with Detective Walker, hear what he has to say, but be careful."

"Careful of Walker?"

"In a way, yes," he said, then filled her in on what he had been told by his friend Chief Gill about Walker's New York City background, his brash style, and his tendency to break rules when he saw fit.

So, on the way to the restaurant, Randi found herself thinking about Anthony Walker, faintly amused at his clumsiness in asking her to dinner, suspicious of his motives, and reluctantly curious about seeing him again.

She drove on into the rainy night and, in her mild state of distraction, failed to notice the sedan that was following her, less than a hundred yards behind.

❖   ❖   ❖

Walker was at the bar when he spotted Randi entering the restaurant. He watched as she stopped at the hostess desk. When she removed her coat, he was pleased to see that she was dressed in a silky, maroon blouse and black skirt, nothing festive exactly, but something she probably had not been wearing on a Saturday in the office. She certainly is tall, it occurred to him again.

It also occurred to him that he had not had a date for months, not since he went out with the attractive divorcee who ran dispatch in Norwalk Police Headquarters. He was working on a case with her department, and one afternoon she offered up a provocative look that led to a suggestive conversation that led to dinner and ultimately to bed. It was fun, and neither of them had any complaints, but there were no repeat performances, since they both realized they were a lousy match. He had generally done all right with women, so he knew there was no point forcing the issue when things are not a good fit. Even in the face of a relatively long dry spell, he told himself there would always be someone else to meet.

Even if he didn't believe it.

He had always been a one-woman guy and years ago, when he met Mary, he figured he had found his mate for life. He took the marriage seriously and his split-up hard. He did his best to get over it, trying to convince himself that everyone is entitled to a mistake, even a big one like that. But his experiences with women since then had ended up as one-night stands, or two or three at best. Women seemed to like him well enough, and he knew his way around the bedroom, but the reviews he got were usually the same—he was damaged goods, emotionally distant, unready or unwilling to have another go at real commitment. Those brief encounters generally concluded with the same final scene—a kiss on his cheek and the offer to have him call again, but only when he was ready to have a real relationship.

Who was he to argue?

Tonight was not really a proper date, he reminded himself again, but he was looking forward to it all the same, and he felt glad when Randi looked in his direction and smiled.

He stood up, polished off what remained of his bourbon, and walked toward her.

"Detective Walker," she said as she extended her hand.

If she was at all nervous about meeting with him, there was no evidence of that in her warm grip. He said, "Look, if we're going to have dinner, the least you can do is call me Anthony."

Randi smiled. "Are you buying?"

"I am," he said.

"All right then, Anthony it is. At least for this evening."

"Okay if I call you Randi?"

She gave him a look that told him the bashful act wasn't going to cut it.

"Right," he said. "They're ready for us."

They were shown to a corner table. The waiter removed the card marked 'RESERVED,' then held Randi's chair for her. Walker asked if she would like a cocktail.

"I think I'll have some wine with dinner," she said.

Walker wanted another bourbon but resisted the notion. "White or red?"

"Let's start with white."

"Start with, huh? I like that." Before she could respond he asked for the wine list, had a quick look, and made a selection. As the waiter went off to fetch the bottle, he said, "You have to admit, this is a little more relaxed."

"Than what?"

"You know, than talking in your office. Or mine."

"I see. You asked me to dinner instead of hauling me downtown."

"Hauling you downtown?" Walker laughed. "Before, on the phone, you asked if I was calling you in for questioning. You watch a lot of crime shows, do you?"

She straightened out the cloth napkin on her lap. "I've seen my share. And my friend Bob Stratford warned me about you."

"First Selectman Stratford, huh? You start right off with the big guns."

"Bob's my lawyer, and a friend."

"I see. And what'd he have to say about me, since he and I don't even know each other?"

"He said he checked you out with your chief. Said that I shouldn't be fooled by your rough New York City style."

"Uh huh. Fooled like how? Like I'm really a softy underneath?"

"Not exactly, no. More like you may be shrewder than you seem."

"What'd you say?"

"I said you'd have to be."

"Ouch."

"You walked right into that one."

"I guess I did. So, Stratford is a close friend of yours."

"We've known each other a few years."

"So you said. But known each other how? An old romance?"

"That's a rather personal question."

Walker looked around the room. "This is a personal setting."

"I see. So this dinner is more than just an alternative to the third degree at the old station house?"

"There you go again, sounding like an old episode of *Law and Order*." She laughed.

"You didn't answer my question."

Randi paused, realizing that it was the first time she had really taken a good look at him. He was not a handsome man, but he had pleasant features, and his gray-brown eyes had an unmistakable hint of kindness that surprised her. "Bob was my lawyer when I set up my office in town. We became friends."

Walker grinned. "So you said."

"He's given me some good advice over the years. Issues come up all the time in my profession." When Walker continued smiling, she added, "He's married."

"Uh huh. So how about you, you ever been married?"

"I'm sure you've looked into one of those intrusive police files you have on me by now. You know the answer already, don't you?"

Walker hung his head slightly.

"It's all right. I suppose I should be flattered by the attention."

The waiter came, displayed a bottle of Nickel & Nickel chardonnay, then opened it and poured a little into Walker's glass.

"My lady friend should taste it. Probably knows more about these things than I do."

The waiter poured for her. Randi took a sip and told the waiter it was delicious.

"So, what about you?" she asked after the waiter filled their glasses, placed the bottle in a bucket of ice, and went on his way. "You ever been married?"

"Was. Didn't take. My wife wanted something I just couldn't give her."

Randi lifted her glass, waiting. He liked the way she held it by the stem. "Like what, for instance?"

"Money," he said. "Honest cops never see much of it." He picked up his glass. "Cheers."

"Any children?"

"Yes, two wonderful girls."

"Visit with them much?"

"I try. They live with their mother. And her new husband," he added, then started to say something else but stopped himself. "They're teenagers now, so they basically view me as a dinosaur. But they're great." He tasted the wine and gave an approving nod. Then he said, "In the interests of full disclosure I should tell you that I also heard from Robert Stratford today. Left me a voice mail, but you probably knew that."

"I didn't, actually." Her surprise seemed genuine. "Now it's your turn to tell me what he said."

"Nothing much," Walker replied. "Said I shouldn't be fooled by your sweet, all-American looks. Said you're tough as nails under that soft exterior."

"Come on."

"He said he was worried about protecting your professional ethics."

"So am I."

"I'll call him back Monday," he told her with a shrug. "No offense, but I hate talking to lawyers, even the mayor of the town. I'll just have to remind him I can get a court order and subpoena you."

"So you've said." Randi frowned. "And Bob's well aware of it."

"Funny, you know? He's worried about trampling on your patients' rights. I'm concerned about just the opposite."

"How's that?"

"I'm worried one of your patients might start trampling all over you."

She stared at him. "Gee, Anthony, you certainly know how to sweet talk a woman."

"I'm not kidding."

She continued looking at him without speaking.

"I've got a murderer to find, and I'd like to keep the number of victims at one. You want to help me?"

"You know the answer to that."

"All right. I brought some things you might find interesting." Walker pulled a few snapshots from a brown envelope. "Have a look at these."

They were the photographs of Elizabeth Knoebel, lying dead in the bedroom, that eerie bedroom decorated with dark wood and Victorian furniture.

"You showed me these before. Having another go at shock value?"

Walker shook his head. "It always amazes me. Doesn't matter how smart a person is, we're all victims of our training, right? You're a psychologist, so you look at everything from that point of view. What people say, their body language. You ask yourself, 'What did she mean by that?' Or, 'Why would he say such a thing?' You listen to the words and the tone of voice and you try to judge a person's emotional state. My job isn't that much different from yours, but I have another perspective. I'm trying to solve another sort of riddle, so I spend more time on the physical evidence than you would."

"I can see that," Randi conceded impatiently. "Are you going to give me another hint or are you about to tell me what I'm not seeing?"

"You're not necessarily missing anything. It's just an odd scene, don't you think? I mean, leaving aside that she was murdered."

"Kind of tough for me to do."

"I understand. But just think, for an afternoon in the suburbs, it looks more like a bordello than a married woman's bedroom. Especially since she knew her husband was not coming home that night."

"I'm not going anywhere near that one."

"Okay. But consider that there's no sign of forced entry into the house and no sign of a struggle. And remember, she was naked. The killer could have undressed her after she was dead, but there would have been blood on her clothes, or marks on the bed that would show she was moved. We found nothing consistent with that sort of activity. Our people think she was lying there, just as she died. So tell me, what have we got here?"

Randi Conway shook her head as she slowly pushed the photos together. "I don't know," she said.

"Whoever did this was someone she knew well. Someone who could get that close and pull the trigger."

Randi did not respond.

"Maybe a lover? Maybe someone else? Maybe she never even saw the gun before the killer raised it to her head and shot her."

Walker watched her face as she handed the pictures back to him. He took them, shoved them in his jacket pocket, and picked up his menu. "I guess I shouldn't have hit you with all that first thing, huh?" He shook his head. "Sorry."

She looked again into his gray-brown eyes. "It's all right."

They spent a silent minute studying their menus. Their waiter came by to describe the specials and, when he was done, Walker told him they'd need a few minutes. Then he returned to the large brown envelope that sat on the table. "This is interesting too. Not gruesome like the photos, but something I think I should share with you."

She watched as he unfastened the clip.

"I understand you wrote a book a couple of years back."

"So, you really *have* been doing your homework on me."

"Called it *The Cheating Heart*. Interesting title."

"It was therapeutic for me to write it, never thought anyone would publish it."

"About unfaithful spouses."

"Unfaithful fiancé, in my case."

"Which explains why you're still single."

She had another taste of the wine but said nothing.

He removed the papers from the brown envelope and, without looking up at her, he asked, "Did you know Elizabeth was writing a book?"

"A book? What sort of book?"

"Not sure how to describe it. You might say it has a similar theme to yours, although it comes at the issue from a completely different angle." He held out the pages, showing her the top sheet that bore the title, *SEXUAL RITES*. "We found it in her computer. Split up in sections."

Walker was watching her, but Randi's eyes revealed no sign of recognition.

"It seems Elizabeth Knoebel turned sex into a kind of hobby. Some of the characters may have been from the couples in your groups. If we believe what she says here, she went after some of the husbands you work with."

She seemed more curious than surprised. "Went after them?" she asked.

Walker nodded. "According to her journal, or whatever this is. Cute little act." He shuffled through some of the pages. "She doesn't use last names in here, but it wasn't tough to put it together."

"How did you get her files? You said they were in her computer. Her husband let you have all this?"

Walker nodded.

"This may sound like an idiotic question, but did Doctor Knoebel understand what he was giving you?"

"The question is not idiotic. We really don't know yet."

"You think he gave this to you in the hope of identifying her murderer."

"That's what we assume."

"What if it's all fiction?" Randi asked. "Isn't that possible? Maybe she made things up based on what she heard in group."

"It could be fantasy. We've considered that."

"I mean, how would she get to meet these men?"

"We're not sure. She might have used information their wives spilled in your group to meet them and seduce them."

She groaned, as if she had just had the wind knocked out of her.

"We're probably going to have to speak with each of them."

"You're not serious."

Walker nodded. "The women too."

As their eyes returned to the pages on the table, the buzzer on Randi's cell phone went off.

"Sorry, occupational hazard," she said as she pulled it out of her purse. "Always on duty."

"Me too," he replied with an understanding smile.

She put the phone to her ear and said, "Yes," then the muscles in her face tensed as she listened. "All right," she said, "hold on please." She placed her hand across the phone and looked at Walker. "You need to excuse me for one minute. I'm not getting much of a signal in here." She held up the phone to show him, as if that proved it. "I'll be right back."

She stood and so did Walker.

"You okay?"

"Fine, I'm fine," she said. "I'll be right back."

As she headed toward the front of the restaurant, he took a moment to admire her attractive shape. He would have much preferred if their dinner conversation did not have to revolve around murder, not to mention the consequences his investigation might have on her professional life. He realized he didn't like having to upset her, which was not his usual sentiment when examining a potential witness in the course of a homicide investigation.

When she turned the corner out of his view, Walker placed his napkin on the table and walked across the room to the bar. He was holding Elizabeth Knoebel's manuscript in his hand as he asked for a bourbon—something told him Randi was going to be a bit longer than the minute she had promised. Then he went to the window overlooking the parking lot and watched her.

CHAPTER 21

Randi stood just outside the front door, holding the phone to her ear. When she received the call inside, the display screen had declared "CALLER ID UNAVAILABLE."

When she answered, she found the voice was being electronically distorted. All the same, the words were clear. The caller demanded that she leave the restaurant to have an urgent discussion.

Now Randi stepped farther outside, past the edge of the terrace, where the air was turning cold and a light drizzle was beginning to fall.

"Who is this?" she asked.

"Elizabeth trusted you," the voice said angrily.

"Tell me who this is or I'm hanging up right now."

"Elizabeth trusted you," the voice repeated.

"I'm hanging up and calling the police," Randi said.

"You're already with the police," the voice reminded her.

Randi's sense of outrage was suddenly replaced by fear. "How do you know where I am?"

"You have no right to betray her."

"Who is this?"

There was a pause, then the voice answered with a question. "Did you get my notes?"

Randi felt her stomach go cold and tense. "What notes?"

"Don't play games, Doctor Conway."

"I'm not the one playing games here."

There was silence on the other end.

"What do you want from me?"

"I want you to remember your obligation to Elizabeth," the voice told her. "And to the rest of us."

Randi was standing under the outside lights in the front of the building, and Walker could see the look on her face. He gulped some of his drink and placed the glass on the bar. Then he walked to the front of the restaurant, grabbed Randi's coat and his jacket, and opened the door. She was standing with her back to him, facing the drizzly night. He waited, watching her for another moment, then began walking slowly toward the edge of the portico.

"Hey," he said, holding up her coat, "it's raining out here you know."

The caller had just ended their connection and Randi lowered her hand to her side.

Walker reached her and placed the coat over her shoulders. "Anyone we know?"

Randi pulled her arms into the sleeves. "It was nothing."

"You don't look so great for someone who just got a call about nothing."

"I'm all right, really."

"You look a little soggy to me." He looked up at the sky, then held his hand out, palm up, beyond the overhang at the entrance. "Smart woman like you should know to come in from the rain."

She nodded absently. "It was a patient, needed to talk with me for a minute, that's all. I walked out here to get a better signal."

"That so?"

"Just a little problem, couple of questions, no big deal."

"No big deal, huh?" Walker took a step forward and looked up again, letting the soft rain hit him in the face. "You know, I have this theory that bad liars are bad because they don't lie enough to get much practice."

Randi responded with a weak smile. "Is that supposed to be a compliment?"

Walker ignored the question, took her by the hand, and led her toward the door. "If you can't say who called, can you at least tell me what was so urgent?"

"Please don't ask me. Don't ask me anything right now."

"It's my job to ask."

"Do you have to be a detective all the time?"

He studied her lovely face, her complexion pale now, her soft skin moist from the rain. "No," he said.

She reached out and touched his arm. "None of this is easy for me. You understand that, right?"

"Yes," he said, "I think I do. You have a pretty good game face though. Most of the time."

She managed a better smile this time.

The rain was becoming heavier. Walker gently placed his hands on her shoulders. "Why not let me help you?"

She looked at him, her soft brown eyes searching his face for something. "I want you to, I truly do."

"All right. Then start by telling me what just happened. And don't give me any baloney about doctor-client privilege. That was no therapy session and you don't owe anything to a murderer."

Randi began to turn away, but Walker reached out and took her by the arm.

"Give me some time, please," she said.

"All right," Walker sighed.

"Thank you."

He offered her a crooked grin. "You really did get wet out here."

"I guess so."

"You need some dry clothes. How about we skip the restaurant and I make us something to eat at my place? I'll go inside and give Roberto his table back. I live just a few minutes from here."

"Your place?" she asked with a wary look.

"It's a small apartment, but I happen to be a great cook."

"I'll bet. What's your specialty?"

"Breakfast," he said.

"Not funny."

"I'm not kidding," he told her. "Come on."

As they turned back toward the restaurant, neither of them noticed the car with its lights off, sitting across the wide street, just beyond the parking lot. Neither of them saw the car as it rolled forward, still dark, then made a turn around the corner where the headlights came on and the sedan disappeared from view.

CHAPTER 22

Randi accepted Walker's invitation but insisted on following him in her own car. She peered through her rain-dappled windshield, concentrating on the two red taillights of his SUV just ahead. She needed these few minutes to herself, to collect her thoughts, to simply calm down. It also gave her an opportunity to notice how comfortable she was at the prospect of a quiet dinner with this man who had suddenly entered her life under the most unwelcome circumstances.

She realized that she felt safer knowing that he was keeping an eye on her. She wanted to know about the book Elizabeth had written. She wanted to tell Walker about the anonymous note, about the threatening phone call she had just received, about her fears concerning several of her patients, and Elizabeth Knoebel. But not yet, she decided. Not yet.

When they arrived at his place she pulled into the parking spot beside his car. The building was part of a complex of two-story structures.

"I'm up a flight," Walker said, then stopped at the base of the stairway and asked her to wait for a moment. He knocked on the door of the ground-level apartment.

"It's Anthony, Mrs. Shapiro. You all right?"

He waited a few moments, then heard the voice of an elderly woman call back, "Yes, dear, thank you. I'm fine."

"Okay," he said, "good night." Then he led Randi upstairs to his landing. "Nice old lady," he explained in response to her inquiring look. "Lives alone, I just keep an eye on her, let her know when I'm here." He unlocked his door and showed her in.

His apartment was small, as advertised. Randi followed him into the living room.

"Sorry for the mess," he said. "I don't do much entertaining." He dropped the brown envelope containing Elizabeth's diary on the table. "You need some dry clothes," he said. "Be right with you." He turned back as he was leaving the room. "Make yourself at home."

Walker left her alone to stare at the envelope. She thought about picking it up, then decided she would wait. Instead she had a look at the various photographs he had on display. They were all shots of Walker's daughters, ranging from infancy to what she guessed were their current ages, somewhere in their mid-teens. When he returned, he was holding a fleecy NYPD sweatshirt. "Sorry," he said, "didn't have any clean sweatpants. This all right?"

"Fine," Randi said. "It's all I need, thanks."

They stood there looking at each other for a moment.

"The bathroom?"

"Right. Just down the hall," he pointed. "I'll get the food going."

Carrying her purse, she walked the short length of corridor and shut herself in the bathroom to change. She hadn't realized how wet she had gotten, her blond hair dark from the rain. She searched the cabinet for a dryer but there was none to be found. This was decidedly a man's bathroom, clean but disorganized, with the white tiles and white towels and white fixtures seeming to cry out for anything with color. She removed her soggy blouse, toweled herself off as best she could, then pulled on his sweatshirt. She took a brush from her purse and combed her hair back, then put on lipstick and had a look in the mirror. Not a fashion statement, but at least she felt warm and dry.

Randi opened the door and switched off the light. Stepping into the hallway she found herself facing his bedroom, directly across the way. She peeked inside, smiling at the rumpled, unmade bed and the clothes on the floor. Then she saw an easel set up in the corner. She moved inside and had a look at the notes and photographs that were pinned to the corkboard. There were familiar names, snapshots of Elizabeth and the Knoebel home, and various ideas scribbled on index cards and scraps of paper.

When she joined Walker in the kitchen he was busy preparing dinner and setting the small oak table for two.

"Here," he said in response to her offer of help, passing her a loaf of rye bread. "You can handle the toast."

"You really weren't kidding about breakfast," she observed as she dropped four slices of bread into the toaster. "I thought it was just a line."

Walker looked up from the stove, where he had three skillets going—in one he was sautéing mushrooms and in the other he was frying off several rashers of bacon. The third was for the scrambled eggs he was whipping up. "Sometimes it is," he admitted.

He held her soft gaze for a moment, until she asked, "You're sure I can't do anything more than watch the toaster?"

Walker pointed to a wire basket on the counter. "How about slicing up some of those tomatoes?"

As they worked together, Walker poured them each a glass of the chardonnay he had brought from the restaurant. Then he went back to turning over the bacon and sliding the mushrooms around in the pan. They talked about his years as a policeman in New York and her years as a therapist. She asked about his daughters, and he was happy to share some details, to brag a bit about how well they were doing in school and to admit how sorry he was not to see them more often.

"I don't know," he said, "maybe people live too long nowadays. Maybe that's why marriages don't last."

"Not the first time I've heard that theory."

"I'll bet," he said. "Let's face it, when they invented marriage, people got hitched at fifteen and died before they were thirty, right?"

"So, you're not only a cynic, you're also a social historian."

"Think so?" Walker poured the eggs into the pan and stirred them with a wooden spoon, then lifted the small skillet with the mushrooms and added them. "Maybe I am." He folded the eggs over a couple of times as Randi grabbed the toast and buttered the slices. "These preserves are great," he told her as he set a heavy jar on the table. "Oregon black raspberry."

"Sounds delicious," she said.

He laid out the bacon on paper towels, spooned the eggs onto their plates, then placed everything on the table. They sat down, soft strains of music coming from the stereo system in his living room.

"Who is that?" she asked as she took a piece of toast and dipped her knife into the dark-purple jam.

"Jenna Mammina," he said. "Good, isn't she?"

"Yes. She is."

They were quiet for a moment, then Randi said, "The divorce must have been tough on you."

"On a scale of one to ten, it was depressing as hell."

Randi watched him as he picked up a strip of bacon with his fingers. She said, "We tend to learn more from depression and dissatisfaction than from happiness."

"Maybe I didn't need to be so smart."

Randi smiled.

"Unfortunately, I wasn't given much of a choice."

"Hard for me to believe. A tough guy like you, seems you're the type that makes the rules most of the time."

"That's the key qualifier—most of the time." He thought about it as he took a bite of toast. "I knew the move to Connecticut was going to be a financial stretch. Lower pay, higher cost of living. Especially the house. I couldn't even afford to live in the town where I worked. You believe that?" He shook his head. "It's different in New York City. Police and firemen are part of a huge middle class. Here in Fairfield County we're on a much lower rung of the ladder." He grabbed another piece of bacon. "But I figured they were compromises worth making. Better schools for my daughters, better life for the family."

"So where did it fall apart?"

Walker uttered a bitter laugh. "It fell apart when my wife got a look at the money all around us and decided she wanted to move out of the cheap seats. We were happy when we got here, or at least I thought so. Suddenly she hated my job, my salary, our car, and especially the house we were renting in Norwalk. Like I say, back in New York City we fit in, here we were second-class citizens."

"You felt that way too?"

"Not me. I'm a cop, always have been, always will be. I had the grades in college, could have gone to law school, could have trained to be a stockbroker or something, but that's not what I wanted."

"So what happened?"

He went at the eggs, then washed them down with some wine. "Mary's a good-looking dame. She took the easiest route she could find to get what she was after—had an affair with a divorced real estate broker. Guy was making a lot of dough, took her and my two girls to live with him in Westport. The divorce was a joke by Fairfield County standards. Mary didn't want anything except the statutory minimum for child support. She married the broker and now my daughters live in one of those large houses along the Gold Coast. Over three years ago now."

"And you stayed in Connecticut."

"I considered heading back to New York. Had this fatalistic sense of 'That's where I really belong,' but I couldn't bring myself to do it, not with my daughters here. I gave up the small house, been in this apartment ever since. My little castle." He forced a half-hearted laugh. "I do all right."

"And the anger and sadness and . . ."

"You asking if I need a shrink to talk this through?" He laughed. "No, it's over. The most surprising thing is that I don't miss Mary, not at all. Didn't even miss her very much in the beginning, after she first left. Never expected that, but it's the truth. If she felt I wasn't good enough for her, then the hell with it, right? Miss my girls like crazy, though."

"I can see that," she told him as she pointed to the photos on the counter.

"So what about you? What happened with that fiancé of yours?"

"I'm not sure."

"Quite an admission for someone with your experience."

"Some of my friends think I've always been searching for the perfect guy."

"But you don't buy that."

"No, I don't. I was going to marry the miserable sonuvabitch, till

I found out he was screwing everything that moved. I'm still not sure why, or what I missed along the way."

"That's too bad. But it shouldn't sour you on marriage."

Randi smiled. "Quite a piece of advice, coming from someone with *your* experience."

Walker laughed.

"I don't know. Maybe I see so many problems in the marriages I handle, maybe it scares me off."

"Professional hazard."

"We all have them," she said.

"What do you mean?"

"I noticed the bulletin board in your bedroom." He responded with a look that prompted her to add, "I wasn't prying. I saw it there, after I changed."

"Uh huh."

"Not the type to leave your work in the office."

"I do some of my best work at night," he said, then had a gulp of wine. "That's a line I use once in a while too."

Randi gave him a knowing look.

"So what'd you think?"

"I didn't read any of it."

"Come on. You saw enough to know it wasn't my grocery list." She picked up her wine glass. "You've created quite a gallery of suspects."

"More like a bunch of disorganized clues, actually."

"More than that, I would say."

"So you *did* read it," he said with a grin.

"A couple of names caught my eye. Especially mine. Am I under suspicion?"

"That depends."

"On what?"

"On what you mean by 'suspicion.'" He swallowed a forkful of eggs, watching her. "Good, right?"

"Delicious," she said.

"I forgot to ask if you like mushrooms."

"They're great."

Walker nodded. "Let's face it," he said, "I'm a suspicious person, by nature and profession."

"So am I," Randi admitted.

"So the truth comes out."

"Meaning what?"

"Meaning that we have more in common than you might want to admit."

She could not suppress a slight smile. "I doubt that, Anthony, I truly do." She went after a crispy piece of bacon with her fork. When it broke in two, she placed the fork down and picked it up in her fingers.

"All right," he said, "at least it explains why you're so edgy."

"My suspicious nature, you mean?"

"Exactly. Why not put some of those feelings to work and help me with my gallery of suspects, maybe trim it down a bit?"

She shrugged.

"Why not start by telling me about that phone call?"

Randi thought it over. "All right," she said. Then she told him, leaving out only the reference to the notes. She was not certain why she still withheld that, but she had the feeling she should wait until she had more time to consider things.

"And that's everything?"

"Yes, it is. Does that help you with your list of suspects?"

"Not if you don't know who the caller was."

"I truly don't."

"You should lend me your phone, let me run a trace."

"Oh no."

"All right, we'll table that for now, but don't delete anything please. Meanwhile we could go through some of the names. Let's start with Nettie Sisson, for instance."

He saw her flinch slightly at the mention of the name. "What would she have to do with this?" Randi asked.

"I'm not saying she has anything to do with it, but so far, she's the only person we can place in the house, right?"

"Why would Nettie want to murder Elizabeth?"

"I have no idea, but I read her confidential police file and spoke to a sergeant in Kettering, Ohio. You know her history better than I do. Took a butcher knife to her husband, then spent five years in a state psychiatric facility."

Randi stared at him without speaking.

"And she is your patient, as was Mrs. Knoebel."

"You play rough, Anthony."

"Homicide is a rough line of work."

"Nettie's husband was a violent, abusive alcoholic who didn't even have the courtesy to lay down and die when he should have."

"From what I was told, I believe that's all true."

"Thanks." Randi took another sip of her wine.

"Then we'll leave Nettie Sisson alone for a minute," he said. "How about we get back to Elizabeth's book?"

"I've been wondering when we would."

"You probably know all the players she mentions, or most of them anyway. Maybe you could have a look, let us know whether you believe the stories are real or fantasy. Might actually jog your own thinking some."

"Maybe."

"You know a woman named Celia?"

Randi shook her head. "I don't think so. You have a last name?"

"Wish I did. It's in one of the chapters there." He smiled. "She's not one of your patients you're not telling me about?"

"You don't give up easily, do you?"

"Depends what I'm after."

"So what are you really after here?"

"You know the answer to that."

"Elizabeth's murderer."

"For one thing," he said, holding her gaze for a moment.

"What else are you after?"

He hesitated, then broke into an embarrassed smile. "More wine?"

"I thought only psychologists are supposed to answer a question with another question."

He picked up the bottle and refilled their glasses. "What was the question?"

"Never mind," she said. "Are you asking me to read her diary?"

"I would like you to."

"All right."

"Then you'll help me?"

"Let me read it first."

"Fair enough," he said.

As they finished their meal he asked her why she chose to live in the suburbs. "I told you how *I* got here," he said. "But you're an attractive single woman. Assuming you haven't given up on finding a new relationship, what's the point of living in the midst of all these married couples."

"And divorcees," she reminded him.

"Well good," he said with a grin, "if you're after a divorcee, that makes me a candidate."

She wiped her lips with the paper napkin, placed it on the table and said, "It's late, I really should go."

"No dessert?"

Randi laughed. "I generally don't have dessert after breakfast. Anyway, it's been a long day."

She stood, leaving Walker no choice but to get up too.

"Let me help you clean up," she said as she picked up her dish.

"No, it's okay. Gives me something to do." He fumbled for the right words, then settled on the truth. "I wish you weren't leaving so soon."

"Thank you," she said in a quiet voice. "I should go."

"I understand," he said.

They were face-to-face now. "Your, uh, sweatshirt, I . . ."

"Don't worry," he told her. "Actually, don't worry about anything." He picked up the brown envelope and handed it to her. "This copy is for you. It's highly confidential, of course. Please don't let anyone else see it, and get it back to me when you're done."

She looked down at it, feeling guilty for not telling him about the notes.

He said, "I think you owe it to yourself to read this."

It seemed to her an odd thing for him to say, but she let it go.

When he walked her to her car they found the rain had stopped and the dark sky was clearing in the moonlight.

He said, "Maybe we can do this some other time, without the interruptions."

Randi hesitated before saying, "You know, I think I'd like that."

Walker laughed. "Don't sound so shocked."

She tossed her damp blouse in the back seat and got in her sedan, the envelope in hand. She started the engine and rolled down the window. "Next time, I won't have to wear the sweatshirt, will I?"

He smiled. "You know, maybe you're not as edgy as I thought."

She nodded, waiting.

"But you definitely have a quality," he said.

"A quality? Now there's a neutral review if ever I heard one."

"No, no, I mean a good quality."

"When you figure out what it is, you be sure to let me know."

He began to say something, but she just smiled and pulled away before he could answer.

As Walker trudged back to his apartment he shook his head and said, "Damn," out loud.

"Is that you Anthony?" Mrs. Shapiro called from inside.

"Yes," he said.

"Are you all right, dear?"

Walker told her he was fine, bid the old woman good night again, and headed back up the stairs. He opened the door and had a look around his empty apartment, then switched on the television to see what happened in the Yankee game as he went about clearing the table.

CHAPTER 23

The next morning, Mitchell Avery was going to leave town whether his wife liked it or not. He had traveled on business trips for years. Joan should have gotten used to it by now. Instead, she seemed to be complaining more than ever.

Before he left for the airport, she decided this was the moment to remind him again that he was not doing his fair share in raising their children, that he needed to devote more time to their upbringing.

"When was the last time you helped any of them with their homework? Or asked what they were doing in school? Or looked at one of their book reports or science projects? Why should the entire responsibility fall on my shoulders?"

Mitchell decided to take a pass on her inquisition. He said that he loved his children. He reminded her that he took them on trips and bought them things, although at the moment he could not recall which trips and what things. He told her that he felt all of the appropriate paternal feelings he should feel toward his son and daughter. He believed in quality time, not quantity of time.

Joan laughed in his face. "Name any of the children's teachers."

He responded with an angry glare.

"Go ahead, Mitchell, take a guess what grades they're in."

At least he got that one right.

Then she mentioned Kyle. Not "the children" this time, but Kyle. "You think I don't know?" she asked angrily. "You think I'm a fool?"

He assured her he did not think her a fool, but that was as far into the topic as he was willing to delve.

"You can't run away from the dangers here, Mitchell. You can't run away from the possibility . . ."

But he cut her off. He told her there was no real danger, and that they had time to deal with the problem.

"No," Joan told him, "the dangers are real and the time is irreplaceable." She told him to save the nonsense about quality time for his sessions with Dr. Conway and his comrades in group therapy. His son needed him and, by the way, so did she.

"We need you at home, not off on some boondoggle playing golf or sitting watching baseball and football games at the country club. And when you *are* home, we don't want you reading business reports or napping in front of the television. We want you fully engaged with us, we want you to be part of this family."

Jesus, thought Avery as she went on and on, *what the hell does the woman expect from me? I earn a great living. My family lives a comfortable life. We live in a wonderful house, travel everywhere, buy everything we need. What am I supposed to do? Sit around the living room with the kids and have discussions about video games and the problems in the Middle East? I work my ass off most days. Am I supposed to come home from the office and then act like I'm some stay-at-home father from a fifties sitcom? Where the hell is this woman coming from?*

But he knew exactly where she was coming from. He knew this had nothing to do with his children and nothing to do with the time they spent together. This was about the trip he was taking this morning, telling her he would be spending two days at business meetings in Nashville, knowing he was lying.

He marveled at her ability to sense these things, even though there was no way she could possibly know that he would actually be spending those two days in Miami. For Joan, it was enough that she suspected the truth, because at this point she trusted her instincts far more than she trusted him.

And yet, even after all this time, and all this therapy, and all the guilt and tears and arguments, and all the rest of it—even now the affair was too sweet, too great a temptation for him to resist. And this time he was certain there was no risk of Joan finding out again, because this time he was going to be especially careful.

So, when she finally began to run out of steam and stopped ranting at him, Mitchell told her that he loved her, making the statement with all the sincerity of a used-car salesman, went downstairs to bid his children good-bye, and set off for the airport.

Later that day, when his plane was supposed to be landing in Tennessee, he actually arrived at Miami International. He decided to call home at once, get that part of the program out of the way. He walked into the main terminal, took out his cell phone and dialed the number.

"Hi, it's me."

"Hello Mitchell," his wife said.

"The kids okay?"

"Fine. Where are you? It's noisy, I can barely hear you."

"I'm in the airport at Nashville," he said. "Just got in."

Joan could hear the garbled sound of various announcements and boarding calls in the background. "Oh," she said.

"I'm looking for my contact here. He's going to pick me up. I'm not sure where I'll wind up today, so I figured I'd call you now, before things get too hectic."

The public address system behind his voice was becoming more distinct to her.

"You know how it goes with these deals," he said, oblivious to the loudspeaker that announced arrivals and departures in the background.

Joan nodded at the phone. The words coming from behind him were unmistakable now.

"Look, I'll call you when I get settled somewhere. I should wrap this up and be home on the early flight day after tomorrow."

"All right," she said numbly.

"Love you," he said.

Joan only said, "Good-bye," and hung up, but the words still echoed in her head. The first time she thought it was her imagination. The second time it was clear. The loudspeakers inside the terminal had been shouting it out, as if wanting to be sure that she heard. She could not even draw a deep breath, the pressure in her chest was so painful. All she could do was listen to the words echoing in her brain.

"*Welcome to Miami International Airport. Baggage claim is located on level . . .*"

CHAPTER 24

Randi Conway spent her Sunday reading *SEXUAL RITES*. One chapter after another leapt off the pages. As Walker predicted, she certainly knew the players. She was familiar with their descriptions, and too many of the incidents.

She also knew this was no fantasy, this was a catalog of Elizabeth Knoebel's predatory conquests, narrated with a cynicism Randi recognized as Elizabeth's true voice.

Yet, among all of these graphic anecdotes and derisive musings about men and women, there was one chapter that left her trembling with rage.

SEXUAL RITES
By Elizabeth Knoebel
Notes for Chapter 11

I was in New York City one evening after attending a seminar at the Hilton. I met him after the last lecture, in the hotel bar. He was having a cocktail with another man. I stood there, looking around for a colleague. He asked if I needed help. I told him a girlfriend was supposed to be meeting me, but it appeared she had changed her plans. He offered to buy me a drink but I refused. Then, after he insisted, I reluctantly accepted.

We eased into a conversation, and he asked me what I did.

"I'm a therapist," I told him.

"What kind?"

"Private and group counseling."

"Marriages? Divorces?"

"Among other things."

"Marriage," he said with a wry smile. "An imperfect condition, even in the best of circumstances, which I guess is good for your business."

I suggested he might be in need of some therapy, not to mention an original thought.

"That's cold," he said with a grin, but told me he would consider therapy if I would stay for another drink.

I told him I had to leave.

"Now I'm the one who's being stranded," he said. He pointed out that his friend had already gone on his way. Then he called to the bartender.

"I'll stay another minute," I told him, "but I'm not so sure about a second drink."

"You're a careful woman, aren't you?"

"And you're very inquisitive."

"Maybe. If I become too inquisitive, let me know."

"I think I already have," I told him.

I was handed a second vodka tonic.

He was comfortable with himself, a handsome man with dark hair, blue eyes and a determined look that told me he was accustomed to getting what he wanted.

After the drinks at the bar, we had dinner. Later we went to a club where the band played jazz on a small stage that looked out into a dark room. He asked for a table in the rear where there was less of a crowd and the music was not as intrusive. I excused myself to visit the ladies' room. He said he would order cocktails for us. He told me he would choose "something special."

I returned and, after a few sips of the fruity drinks he had selected, I began to feel far more intoxicated than I had earlier.

"This is strong," I told him.

He nodded his agreement and said, "Good."

He told me he was from Boston, in town for a few days on business.

I told him I was single, but I don't recall if I told him that I lived in Connecticut. I do remember admitting that I was already in no condition to drive home that night.

Later, seated side by side on a banquette in the rear of the jazz club, he leaned toward me and we kissed. I felt no inhibitions about embracing in public that way, which is quite unusual for me. I was overcome by a sense of relaxation that was mixed with confusion. I was also feeling extremely aroused.

We ended up back in his hotel room,

although I was not able to recall how we got there.

He ordered champagne, even though the additional wine was unnecessary. I recall the bottle in a frosty silver ice bucket on the credenza. I can still see him tearing off the foil and using his thumbs to work the cork free, sending it bouncing off the ceiling before it fell to the floor. The frothy wine spilled over the neck of the bottle as he lifted it and poured my glass full. I only took a sip, barely able to stand now, almost dropping the glass. He took it from me and placed it on the nightstand. Then he took me in his arms.

He kissed me gently at first, the tart flavor of the wine on our lips. We were standing in the middle of the room, the lights soft, the quiet strains of music coming from somewhere I could not identify.

I remember laughing, then falling sideways onto the bed.

He began to undress me, unbuttoning the front of my chiffon blouse, his hands reaching in to feel my breasts. He lowered his head to kiss them, then gently bit at them. He stopped to unbuckle his belt, undoing his pants and letting them drop to his ankles and kicking them away. He pulled off his shirt and tossed it aside. All I could do was lie there on the bed and watch, feeling as if any sense of self-restraint had somehow vanished.

He finished opening my blouse, then slipped off my skirt. His hands moved up and down, massaging my breasts, stroking my skin. I was wearing nothing now but filmy, white satin tap pants, and he reached down and caressed my ass underneath the silky panties, then pulled those off too.

He slowly brought his palms along the inside of my thighs, running up and down, repeating the motion again and again. I grew wetter under his touch as he leaned over and kissed me on the mouth, his bare chest pressed against the softness of my breasts.

I felt as if I could not move.

My desire was mixed with the muddled notion that I had abandoned my own instincts. His tongue found its way down my breasts and across the flat of my stomach. Then he shoved his fingers inside my pussy, not tenderly now but with force, and roughly stuck a finger up my ass.

It was as if he had become a different person, but I felt detached from the event, as if all I could do was observe it from somewhere above.

He pushed me on my side, one hand still jammed inside me, and began using the flat palm of his other hand to slap my bottom. He hit me harder and harder, the smacks against my fleshy ass stinging as they became more forceful. When he returned his attention to my breasts, he was no longer gentle with his touch. He squeezed my nipples between his strong fingers until I uttered a distant-sounding scream. He told me to shut up and, when I didn't, he slapped me across my face several times, hard enough to make my jaw ache.

I lay there helplessly as he pushed me onto my back and climbed on top of me, grabbing me by the hips and lifting me to him. He forced himself into me, jamming his cock in as hard as he could, the pain making me cry out again. I began to sob but he ignored my tears, rocking back and forth and thrusting with an angry energy. Then he abruptly stopped, pulled away, and forced me onto my stomach. I remember him binding my hands behind my back, perhaps with his necktie, I could not see. Then I felt a searing pain as he rammed his way into my ass.

He held my arms tight as he fucked me from behind. I wanted to scream, but my face was pressed to the bed. All I could do was weep uncontrollably as he heaved and groaned until he was spent, then collapsed onto me with all of his weight.

Even when he was done, I could not move. It was late, I had too much to drink, and I had too much of whatever he had slipped into my cocktail at the jazz club. Soon I fell into an uncomfortable and fitful sleep.

When I awoke in the hotel room early the next morning, he was gone. As I began to recall what I could of the brutal night, I dragged myself out of bed. I was so sore that I limped as I walked to the bathroom. There were black-and-blue marks on my ass and neck and breasts. My wrists were sore. My jaw was swollen and bruised.

I took a long hot shower, scrubbing myself, desperately trying to wash away the awful events of the night before. I dressed, then left the hotel, with a scarf around my discolored neck and face. I moved as if I were a fugitive, hurrying through the hotel lobby, relieved that there was almost no one around to witness my departure at six in the morning.

As I drove home I felt angry and mortified and physically shattered. The only satisfaction I could muster was the belief that I knew who he was. I would have my revenge, and soon.

It turned out he had given me a phony name—at least the name I recalled—and that was no surprise. But the hotel had records and I knew the room number. It took some effort, but I tracked him down.

He was stunned to receive my call in his office the next day, even more astonished when I told him what I intended to do.

I told him I had photographs of my injuries and the hotel record for that night, and I could easily retrieve copies of the restaurant and jazz-club receipts.

I expected him to be contrite, to apologize, to beg my forgiveness. But instead he was incredibly arrogant. He said I was just a horny bitch he had picked up at a bar, a woman who wanted to be roughed up, who had willingly gone back to his room to be fucked. The bartender in the hotel saw us drinking together, the people in the jazz club saw us kissing. He told me I could do whatever I wanted, but in the end I was only going to be humiliated in the process.

As you might expect, I could not prove he had placed drugs in my cocktail, nor that he had forced me to do any of the things he did to me. I never contacted him again, and it was the last time we saw each other.

All that was left to me was to learn from the experience.

When Randi finished reading the chapter she read it again, and then a third time.

This was not one of Elizabeth's memories, not something Elizabeth had experienced. This was an eerily precise description of what Randi had suffered, less than a year ago, when she attended a conference in New York City. Every detail, every nuance.

Randi sat there, staring at the pages, her hands trembling as she relived the horror of that night. She had never shared this with anyone. She had certainly not divulged a single word of this to Elizabeth Knoebel.

So how? Randi wondered. *How could she have known?*

Unless, of course, Elizabeth had engineered the entire event. Unless Elizabeth had set her up.

It was so unthinkable, so malicious, Randi could not even fathom the evil that could drive someone to this.

But there it was on the printed page. There was no other possibility.

And then she recalled how, a few days after the rape, when she returned to her office still bruised and enraged by the event, she found a single red rose taped to her door. Without a note. Without explanation.

Until now.

CHAPTER 25

Monday morning, after an early session with a new patient, Randi Conway was seated at the desk in her office, the printed pages of Elizabeth Knoebel's journal before her.

The final chapter was so utterly different in tone than the rest of the diary it felt as if someone else had written the scene. For a moment Randi was tempted to go back to the beginning and read it through all over again, but she was still too shaken by what she had read the day before. Instead, she pushed the pages away and stared at them, wondering what to do next.

Walker had been right. Elizabeth had made a pale effort to disguise the various players and, despite the coded names, Randi knew most of the people portrayed. The character traits, the descriptions, the intimate details Elizabeth revealed, it was all painfully clear. Elizabeth had used her, and had exploited the other women in her group. She took their secrets and then tracked down their husbands, attempting to seduce each of them for the sheer sport of the chase, for the mere experience of the conquest.

And the women were not immune from the twisted game Elizabeth was playing. She tormented Fran Colello in ways that went far beyond what Randi had witnessed in group. She took advantage of Nettie Sisson's weakness, something Randi had long suspected but now acknowledged as something she should have faced. Elizabeth manipulated Phyllis Wentworth and Joan Avery, encouraging fears about their failing marriages, pushing them to the limits of personal despair. Even Lisa Gorman came under her sway, forced to question the prospects for her young family.

And then there was the pain of what Randi had been made to suffer.

Not only was it now clear that Elizabeth was behind that brutal assault, but there were also the taunts she had leveled against Randi in their private sessions.

As a therapist, Randi understood that patients play all sorts of games that are inspired by many different psychological forces. Transference. Role-playing. Fantasies. Egotism. Narcissism. Randi was trained to deflect these gambits in an effort to bring the patient in touch with his or her true feelings.

But Elizabeth was motivated by sheer malice, and Randi had never broken through the veneer that hid the causes for her malevolence from view.

Now she had to wonder—why had she failed, and why had she put up with it?

At dinner on Saturday Walker had mentioned Randi's book, *The Cheating Heart*, and she surprised herself by admitting that it had been written as a therapeutic exercise. It was never intended as a serious treatise, it was pop psychology, something she created to deal with the pain of her broken engagement. In some ways, it was payback for the way that miserable sonuvabitch had walked out on her.

It became evident that Elizabeth had read the book, dissected it for use in her sessions, and turned many of their discussions into attacks on Randi rather than counseling for Elizabeth.

Again, Randi was left to wonder why she did not take another approach, or resign as the woman's therapist altogether.

And then there was the issue of Elizabeth's marriage.

Randi asked Walker why he thought Knoebel allowed the police to see Elizabeth's journal, but Walker had no reasonable explanation. While that remained unanswered, this much was obvious—Stanley was an intelligent man with a controlling personality—whatever he did, he did with purpose.

Elizabeth had written the scene about Randi, disguising the incident as if it had happened to her. But Randi was the lynchpin around which Elizabeth's entire scheme of seduction revolved. Her overtures to Randi, although rejected, should have made it into the diary, should they not? Were there things Elizabeth wrote about her that had been deleted? And if so, by whom? What might Elizabeth have written that did not survive?

Randi slowly opened the desk drawer, took out the anonymous notes she had found in her office, then placed them atop Elizabeth's manuscript. The first said:

DR CONWAY
YOU MUST NOT BETRAY HER.
YOU MUST NOT BETRAY ME.

The second typewritten note said:

DR CONWAY
I AM SORRY

Walker was right again, she told herself. Elizabeth's murderer lived in the pages of this journal. As the police sought to decipher the clues depicted in these torrid, angry scenes, Randi knew that she was better qualified than anyone else to make sense of it all— and the one person to whom the danger of that reality was the greatest.

She picked up the phone and dialed Bob Stratford's office.

"You don't sound like you're having a very good morning," he said.

"I'm not," she replied, making no effort to conceal her gloomy mood. "You have a few minutes to talk?"

"I'm all ears."

She began by returning to the notes, then told him about her dinner with Walker and the threatening phone call she received while they were at the restaurant. She said that she had described the call to Walker but, for reasons she could not explain, had not told him about the notes.

"We'll figure out how to handle that," Stratford assured her.

"After I told him about the call, he said he wanted to take my phone and have it traced."

"Understandable."

Randi took a deep breath.

"I take it there's more?"

"There is," she said. "The main thing I wanted to talk with you about is something that Walker gave me, something Elizabeth Knoebel had written. A diary of some kind. A book, really."

"What sort of book?"

Stratford listened silently as Randi described SEXUAL RITES, recounting some of the scenes, explaining that the people were identified only by a single initial, but she was certain some of them were her patients. For now she said nothing about the chapter describing her own date rape. When she was finished, Stratford remained quiet.

"Bob?"

"I'm here. Just trying to get my mind around it, that's all."

"Me too. Walker told me not to show it to anyone, to keep it strictly confidential. But obviously I had to tell you."

"Of course," he agreed, then thought it over for a moment. "You say that you recognize some of the people this woman wrote about. How real do you think her stories are?"

"I think they're very real."

"But you had no idea she was keeping a journal like this?"

"Of course not. How would I?"

"She might've said something about it."

"She didn't. I told that to Detective Walker."

"And he believed you?"

"I can't see why he wouldn't, it's the truth. Why would that matter anyway?"

"It might bear on their decision to get an order to compel you to divulge what she disclosed to you in therapy."

"God, I didn't even think of that."

Stratford became quiet again. Then he said, "Forget what she was writing. Did you know she was seeing these men?"

Randi paused. "I, uh, I didn't know, not for certain."

"But you did suspect that she was?"

Randi took a deep breath and exhaled slowly. "*Fear* would be a better word than *suspect*. Looking back I should have seen more. But nothing like this," she added.

"What else did Detective Walker say about her diary?"

"That was it. He wanted me to read it and give it back to him."

Neither of them spoke for a moment. Then Stratford said, "Her murderer must have known about this diary."

"I don't think so," Randi disagreed. "She was murdered in her own home. Walker says if the murderer knew about it, the computer would never have been left behind."

"Right, right" he agreed, "I see his point."

"But if it comes out that she kept this sort of diary . . ."

When she hesitated, Stratford finished the thought for her. "That would put you front and center in helping to identify the people in the book."

"Walker thinks it's even worse than that."

"It puts you directly in harm's way."

"Yes," she said quietly.

"Assuming the murderer never knew of the diary but finds out about it now, you become a real threat. You're the person most likely to unravel the truth in whatever this woman had written."

"Exactly."

"All the more reason to honor Walker's request that you keep this strictly confidential."

"I know. But something like this, I mean, how long is it going to remain a secret?"

Stratford thought that over. "Good question. I'll put a call in to Walker. I phoned him the other day, left a message to let him know I was keeping an eye on you."

"He told me. Thanks."

"I'll make sure I speak with him today."

"Okay. But remember, you can't say anything about the diary."

Stratford said he didn't like that. After all, they had an attorney-client privilege, and she was entitled to confide in him.

"Just for now, Bob, please."

"I'll call Gill first, ask him about the investigation. He'll tell me about it, that way the information didn't come from you." He hesitated. "You going to be all right?"

"I'm not sure," she admitted. "I guess we'll find out."

✜   ✜   ✜

It was Monday morning, and Fred Wentworth was sitting at his small desk in the modest gray cubicle he was assigned in the company's Manhattan showroom. It was the first day of market week, and outside the fabric-lined panel dividers that defined his tiny work space he heard the voices of his coworkers as they made their pitches to buyers and then confirmed their sales. Their schedules were crammed with appointment after appointment, but Fred was not busy.

Fred was the husband of the matronly Phyllis, each of them participants in Randi Conway's groups. He was a large, oafish man with coarse features and suspicious eyes, a garment-center salesman with a million stories to tell and the need to share every one of them. His artificially darkened hair, combed straight back, was a touch too long for his fifty-five years. He wore Italian suits and loud ties that were typical of an industry where current styles often prevail over good taste. His overall appearance was that of a man struggling for a youthful look when he was well past the point where the effort was reasonable.

Wentworth fought back his anger as he sat quietly at his small desk.

It was not all that long ago that he was one of his company's top producers. He was well liked. Respected. Known throughout the industry.

Now he was little more than a relic from another era.

His large frame filled the swivel chair, his elbows resting on the black plastic arms. He was waiting for Sam to call back. Sam was an old customer. He could always count on Sam to place an order. If they wanted to know how Fred Wentworth was doing in market week, they would find out as soon as Sam called in a large order.

Wentworth rearranged his desk, moving the position of the tele-phone and his diary and his pen set, the one Phyllis had given him years ago with the engraved silver plaque that read FRED WENTWORTH in block letters, and *World's Greatest Salesman* underneath. He shifted everything around until he was satisfied that each item was in its proper place. Then he stared down at his blank order pad. He knew he would be filling out several pages of the printed forms, just as soon as Sam called.

Hell, it's market week, he told himself. Sam was probably at appointments elsewhere. Wentworth understood that. He had called Sam several times last week to set something up. But Sam was in con-ference. Or on the other line. Or out of the office. But his assistant said Sam would be sure to call back. Just this morning Wentworth was told that Sam was with a group of wholesalers and reps from Hong Kong. As soon as that meeting was concluded, Sam would call back.

So Fred waited, knowing that however the day went, at least that evening he was going to meet Thomas Colello for drinks. That would be interesting.

He smoothed back his thinning black hair with the palms of his hands and had another look at the pad of order forms. Then he decided the telephone would be better situated off to his left, so he began to rearrange the things on his desk again.

CHAPTER 26

Walker was in his office, and his Monday morning was not feeling any more productive than Fred Wentworth's. He was poring through the Knoebel file again when Chief Gill summoned him on the intercom.

Walker marched down the hall and stood in the chief's doorway.

"Shut the door and sit down," Gill said.

"What gives?"

"Lawyers," Gill said as he handed Walker two message slips.

One was from Bob Stratford, the other from a Roger Bennett, counsel to Dr. Knoebel, with a New York City phone number.

"They want to talk to me?"

"Both of them. I already had a brief conversation with Knoebel's lawyer."

"Uh huh."

"Says his client had a change of heart about you and Blasko snooping around his wife's computer."

"A change of heart? Isn't Knoebel missing the essential piece of equipment for that maneuver?"

Gill frowned.

"When did our friend Dr. Knoebel have this epiphany?"

"Last night. Knoebel called the guy at home and told him to get his wife's computer back, and pronto."

"Of course." Walker made a note of the timing, but did not mention anything about his dinner with Randi Conway on Saturday, the phone call she received at the restaurant or—most important—that he had entrusted her with a copy of *SEXUAL RITES*. He knew that last item would send the chief into orbit.

"These computer files, how important are they to your investigation?"

"Nothing helpful in the e-mails, and Teddy went back quite a way."

"What about the diary?" Gill asked, enunciating the last word with all the distaste he could muster.

"She didn't mention anyone who wanted to kill her, if that's what you're asking, but I'm betting the name is in there."

Gill thought it over. "Do you think Knoebel's lawyer had any idea how personal her writing was?"

"Not sure," Walker admitted.

"I already spoke with town counsel. He says we should give it back. Unless you can demonstrate that the files bear directly on the case, he doesn't want to risk a lawsuit."

"Now there's a bold legal position."

Gill shook his head.

"We got a warrant for it."

"This lawyer Bennett, he mentioned that. Claims it was obtained after the fact and without his client having any say in the matter."

"His client may become a suspect. I don't think the judge needed his permission to issue the warrant."

"Fair point. Call Bennett and see what he has to say."

Walker stood to leave. "What about the other call?"

"Bob Stratford? He just said he wanted to speak with you, is all."

"Right."

"You want me to get the State Police involved?" Gill's voice made it clear how little he liked that idea.

"I don't think so," Walker said, "but if I stumble into quicksand I'll be sure to holler."

As he turned away, the chief said, "Give me your best read on this. Are we going to bring someone in?"

Walker looked back, his lips pressed together, as if squeezing out the thought. "Yeah, I think we will. Problem is, right now I have too many suspects."

Back at his desk, Walker decided to tackle the tougher call first. He punched in the number and said, "Detective Walker for Roger Bennett."

Bennett got on the line, they exchanged the usual pleasantries, then the attorney went into the old soft shoe, speaking in that maddeningly verbose manner characteristic of a profession that charges by the minute rather than the result.

"So you see, Detective, my client feels great remorse in having shared his late wife's private computer. We believe it will be in the best interests of all concerned if you return the laptop and all of the information, and the less said about it the better."

Walker grinned at the telephone. "I wonder if I might ask, Mr. Bennett, what was the sudden cause of his remorse?"

"Come now, Detective. My client has been extremely distraught. Anyone could understand how the circumstances of his wife's death might cloud his judgment. He has no idea what his wife kept in her computer, but he feels it only appropriate to protect her privacy, as well as his and his daughter's."

"This case is still active, and some of the contents of Mrs. Knoebel's computer may be critical to our investigation."

As the lawyer thought that over, Walker nodded to himself. Bennett's billing clock was running whether he was talking or not, like waiting time on a taxi meter, only spinning a lot faster. Finally the attorney said, "Have you found anything in these records that suggests the identity of someone who might have wanted to do Mrs. Knoebel harm?"

Up to now Bennett was proving to be fairly unshakeable, which annoyed Walker no end. "Depends how you read this stuff," he replied. "But no, she didn't type the name of her killer after she was shot, if that's what you're asking."

He could almost hear Bennett allowing himself a smug little nod as he said, "Then I daresay, a court might express its displeasure with your department entering my client's home, removing his wife's computer without proper, written authorization, and then refusing to return it when asked."

You miserable shyster, Walker thought. He said, "We obtained a warrant, as you are well aware."

"Of course. However, as I understand the time line here, you removed the computer without a warrant, inspected its contents and then tried to cover your tracks by obtaining the court papers after the fact. As *you* are no doubt aware, Detective, that does not sanitize your actions."

"This is a murder investigation, Counselor. I doubt a court would be outraged by that set of facts, especially since Dr. Knoebel gave his permission, as you say, after the fact. And, by the way, Elizabeth Knoebel is not a suspect here, she's the victim."

"Indeed, indeed. And I'm sure you believed you were acting properly under the circumstances. Unfortunately, Dr. Knoebel was not in a state of mind where his knowing consent could have reasonably been given. And I don't believe you ever obtained any written release." The lawyer paused, giving Walker just enough time to stand up and kick himself in the ass. "I should also add that Dr. Knoebel's bereaved condition has required him to begin counseling with a qualified psychiatrist in New York. And, of course, at the time he discussed the matter with you, he did not have the benefit of counsel's advice."

So, Knoebel was getting set to see a shrink in the city, maybe setting up a polite little insanity defense. Probably using one of the hired guns a firm like Bennett's called in whenever they needed an expert to say that a client was crazy. Not too difficult to buy that sort of testimony. After all, who isn't crazy in New York?

Walker wondered what Randi Conway's reaction would be when she learned she'd been replaced, not by a mere psychologist, but by a qualified psychiatrist, as the lawyer made a point of saying, which should add an extra sting to the news. Might get her mad enough to loosen up her professional reserve and spill some information.

"Detective Walker, are you still there?"

"Yes, I'm here, I'm just not sure how to respond, Mr. Bennett. Are you asking me a question or are you just practicing your technique in subtle threats?"

"Threats? Come now, Detective. I don't think we need to resort to those tactics. Once you've had a chance to consider the situation with your superiors, I'm sure you'll conclude that the only fair and reasonable response is to return Mrs. Knoebel's laptop. Printed papers and all copies. Computer disks as well."

You unctuous little slimeball, Walker thought. "I tell you what. I'll do just that, I'll take it up with my superiors. We'll get back to you."

"That'll be fine. Can we expect a response by the end of today? I need to know whether I'll be required to file a motion with the court."

"I'll get back to you tomorrow. And while I check it out on my end, Counselor, you may want to ask your client how he really feels about bringing this to a judge. I'm not sure how much you or your client know about what Mrs. Knoebel kept on her laptop, but I doubt her husband will be keen on airing his wife's personal writing in a courtroom filled with reporters."

The silence on the other end had a frigid feel. When Attorney Bennett spoke again, he kept his tone even. "We would, of course, demand a private hearing in chambers. But since you have raised the issue, let me warn you that any attempt to exploit Mrs. Knoebel's writing in the interim will be met with the most vigorous legal action. Do we understand each other?"

"We do."

"And I can expect an answer from you no later than tomorrow morning?"

"Right."

"Good. In the meantime, none of these materials are to be shared with anyone outside your department."

Walker sat up straight in his chair. "Got it."

"And, naturally, from this point forward, neither you nor anyone from your department is to speak with Dr. Knoebel unless I am present. Understood?"

"Naturally."

"Very well then," the lawyer said, and hung up.

"Eat shit and die," Walker growled at the dial tone. After these strong-arm tactics from the mouthpiece from New York, he figured his next conversation would feel like a coffee break.

He dialed the number and Stratford, after saying "Thanks for getting back to me," quickly added, "When I didn't reach you this morning I checked in with Chief Gill. Just want to let you know it wasn't an attempt to go over your head."

"I appreciate that. If this is about Dr. Conway, I'm sure the chief told you she's not a target of the investigation. At least not at this time," Walker added. "Our interest is getting her to cooperate in finding this woman's killer."

"She wants to cooperate, I assure you. We're just concerned about the effect this will have on her professionally. You're asking her to divulge sacred confidences. I don't want this to end up destroying her practice."

"I understand, I really do. But I've got a murder to solve. And I may have a murderer who might not be willing to wait to find out if Dr. Conway is going to name him or her, if you catch my drift."

"I do. Randi's safety is of paramount importance to me."

"Well that's good. As I've told Dr. Conway, and I'll tell you, I can get a court order to force her to open up." He didn't admit that Chief Gill had put the kibosh on that idea, at least for now. He hoped Gill didn't divulge that to his old pal, First Selectman Stratford.

"We can make that decision later, can't we?"

Walker was not sure when he and Stratford had become "we," but he said, "Not too much later."

"What do you say you and I get together? We're on the same side here, maybe I can help."

"Fair enough."

"Let's meet for a drink. That work for you?"

"Sounds like a good idea."

"How about tomorrow at six, my club, that be all right?"

"Fine," Walker said, then waited, but Stratford seemed to be finished.

A voice over the intercom said, "Call for you on oh-three."

Walker told Stratford he had to go. Stratford gave him the name of the club, Walker thanked him, then hit the button for the next call. It was his ex-wife, phoning to say that his daughters would not be coming to see him for dinner on his scheduled night.

"Why?"

"They've been invited to a birthday party, Anthony. They'll have dinner with you one night next week. I'll have them call."

"Perfect," he said. "Got any other good news Mary? Your stock portfolio jump up today?"

She said, "Good-bye, Anthony."

He said, "Make sure they call me," but she'd already hung up.

He slammed the phone down, then looked up at Kovacevic, who had just walked in. "Bitch," he growled.

"Problem sir?"

Walker had a look at the junior officer. "Not anymore," he said. "At least not every day. Come on, let's go."

Outside headquarters, as Walker and Kovacevic made their way to the parking lot, they were intercepted by three television units that materialized from vans parked on the street, each team consisting of a man supporting a shoulder-mounted camera and a reporter intent on shoving a microphone in Walker's face.

"Detective Walker." A young, attractive blond was the first to reach him. "We have an unconfirmed report that there's been a development on the Elizabeth Knoebel murder investigation. Would you care to comment?"

Walker looked at Kovacevic, then back to the woman. "No," he said, and kept walking.

A well-dressed young man took his shot. "Is it true your department is narrowing the search for a suspect in the case?"

This time Walker didn't look at anyone as he replied. "I have no comment."

The third reporter gave it a try, but Walker simply said, "There's an ongoing investigation and I have no comment at this time."

"Does that mean you'll be making a statement sometime soon?" the first woman asked.

They had reached Walker's SUV. He turned around and, instead of answering the question, said, "You know, your vans are illegally parked in front of the station house. I'd get them out of here before I have them all towed."

Then he and Kovacevic climbed into the Explorer and slammed the doors shut.

"What was that about, sir? What new development?"

"Not sure, Kovie, but three television crews showing up on the same morning, just a couple of days after we crack the code for Elizabeth Knoebel's diary? This is not good."

CHAPTER 27

It was an unseasonably warm Monday afternoon, less than a week since Elizabeth Knoebel's body had been discovered. The four remaining members of her therapy group were meeting for the first time without her.

As expected, the discussion immediately turned to Elizabeth's death and who might have taken her life.

"Her husband," Fran Colello announced with as much certainty as if she had witnessed the crime.

When no one else responded, Randi asked, "Why would you say that?"

"He must have known about her lovers and finally had enough of it. Or maybe he just found out. Anyway, her husband did it," Fran repeated.

The other three women were silent.

Randi said, "I don't recall Elizabeth ever discussing lovers in this group."

"What was there to discuss?" Fran challenged with a knowing look. "Does anyone here have any doubts that she was a slut?"

The others maintained an awkward silence.

"Elizabeth never made any admission of infidelity in the group," Randi reminded them. "She may have cultivated a sexy persona, but she never shared anything about infidelity that I can recall." In fact, Randi Conway was tempted to concede, Elizabeth rarely shared anything other than her contempt. Instead she turned back to Fran and said, "You sound very sure of your accusations."

"There are some things a woman just knows," Fran said. Then she nodded her head, as if confirming a thought.

"If she did have a lover, maybe *he* was the one who killed her," Lisa Gorman said. As the youngest member of the group, she was usually careful not to confront the others. Today, however, she had a secret she wasn't revealing, and a special sense of importance—the police had called her to help them with the case. "Maybe she and this man, whoever he was, maybe they had a fight or something."

"No," Fran snapped. "It was the husband," she said.

Phyllis Wentworth cleared her throat, as if seeking permission to enter the discussion, and the others turned to face her. She was adorned in her usual tapestry-like clothing, her affect forlorn, her posture uncomfortably stiff. "Maybe Lisa is right," she suggested. "It could have been a lover's quarrel. You hear about that sort of thing all the time."

Fran was not having any of it. "Bullshit," she said.

Dr. Conway decided to move away from Fran's anger. She directed herself to Joan Avery. "How do you feel about all of this?"

"Me?" Joan had not said a word up to then. Now she slowly looked around the room as if she had never seen these women before. "I don't give a good goddamn."

She suddenly had everyone's attention.

"What is it?" Phyllis asked. "What's wrong?"

Joan sighed, as if the entire matter was too boring for her to bother about. "I didn't care about Elizabeth Knoebel when she was alive. Why should I care about her now?"

"Bravo," exclaimed Fran Colello.

Joan settled her distant gaze on Fran. "To be honest, I don't really care much about your problems either. I'm sick of this whole thing and I quit. I'm finished. I only came here today because we agreed to talk it out before any of us left the group. Now that I'm here I realize I don't really have much to say. I'm just done."

Phyllis Wentworth rose from her seat. The others watched as she stood there, visibly shaking. She wanted to move toward Joan, but she could not. She slowly sat back in her seat and said, "I wish you wouldn't leave." She spoke those words softly, her gaze cast downward. It was as much as Phyllis could manage.

The room became quiet. Then Joan said, "Thank you, Phyllis. That's actually the nicest thing any of you has ever said to me."

After another uncomfortable silence, Randi asked, "Why do you feel you want to leave?"

"There are any number of reasons."

"Please share some of them with us," Randi urged.

Joan managed a weak smile as she said, "Of course. You want me to share." She shook her head as if recalling some piece of bad news she would have preferred to forget. "My marriage stinks. Let's face it, that's why we all came to you in the first place, right? So guess what? After all these hours of group and private session, and after all this sharing, my marriage still stinks. In some ways it's worse than ever. I don't know, maybe these sessions exposed problems I didn't even know existed. Maybe ignorance really is bliss."

"Damn right," Fran said, but no one even looked at her.

"And now Elizabeth is gone. Whoever she was—and believe me, she was no friend of mine—she created a certain dynamic in this group, a tension that got us to react with real emotion. Think about the sessions when she wasn't here. What a waste of time they were, the four of us just sitting around and complaining about what assholes our husbands are."

Phyllis recoiled at the statement, but Joan went on.

"Especially you Fran," Joan went on. "You really are a bitter person, Elizabeth was right about that. But you aren't all wrong either. You talk about being ignored and unloved by your husband. I think that's why we're all here. I feel abandoned by my husband, emotionally and sexually. I'm not twenty-five years old anymore. I can't compete with the young women we see on television and look at in magazines, these fantasy girls our husbands salivate over. I can't excite my husband the way I once did, because I'm not that same person anymore. But it's not something we're going to fix by sitting around and griping."

Fran's anger evaporated. "It's all true," she said in an uncharacteristically somber voice. "I keep hoping there's a solution, but there is none, is there?" She looked at Joan, who held her gaze as Fran added, "The worst part is that I still love the rotten bastard. Isn't that just a laugh?"

"No," Joan said. "It's not a laugh at all. It's to your credit, don't you see? You're here because you have hope. Because you still believe that your commitment and your love will mean something in the end."

Fran smiled, something she rarely did in this room. "What about you, Joan?"

"I've given up that hope," she said.

No one spoke for a moment. Then Randi said, "Joan, you mentioned Elizabeth, how she was a catalyst here."

"I don't know who Elizabeth really was or what she was after. I know that she did some evil things. I may know even more about that than the rest of you. But whatever she did or did not do, it's finished now. As for me, I have some things to figure out, but I'm not going to do it by sitting here complaining about my husband. For me, the circle is broken." Joan forced another wan smile. "Death is not the only escape," she said.

When the session was over, after the other three women said their good-byes to Joan and made their way out, Randi asked her to stay behind for a moment.

They stood alone in the pale, harshly lit room, amidst the small circle of empty chairs, two players without an audience.

"So, your mind is made up?"

Joan nodded. Then she told Randi about the call from Mitchell. "After all of this," she said in a weary voice, "after everything he's put me through, he's back with that whore in Miami."

"Do you want to talk about it?"

"I'm not sure," Joan said. "There really isn't much to say, is there? I mean, the purpose of all this therapy is to work on our problems, right? Well I've finally decided I don't have any problems—with one major exception, of course—I'm married to an egocentric, immature man. And that's easily corrected, no?" She waited for a response, but Randi just stood there, watching her. "I sat home all morning, imagining what it would take to save my marriage. I actually tried to think of every good marriage I know, as if that might give me some sort of inspiration. You know what?"

Randi waited.

"There just aren't that many good marriages around. At least I don't see them."

"That's not true, Joan."

"Really? How would you know? No offense, but you only deal with the bad ones, right?" She didn't wait for a reply. "I'm so tired of it, Randi, I feel utterly worn out." She sighed. "There's no excitement, no energy in my life, nothing new, just the same old stuff. Maybe Mitchell has the right idea."

"Do you believe that?"

There was another pause as Joan struggled to remain composed. "No, I suppose not. But it appears I'm in the minority. People don't seem to care about their personal history, not the way I think they should. They don't give a damn for the value of shared experience. And commitment? My God, commitment is the biggest scam in the world. I see women willing to surrender their identities just to hold a marriage together. They fill their breasts with silicone, have their faces injected and lifted, they don't even live for themselves anymore. And where are their husbands, these wonderful men they're struggling to hold onto? Oh right, there they are, moping around, doing a lousy job of pretending not to be bored. Why do they pretend, you ask? Because they don't want to face a divorce they're afraid they can't afford. Or maybe they don't want to give up their comfortable little house and their familiar little life. Or maybe they're just too lazy to leave? So what do people do? They drink too much, lie too much, and cheat on each other in all sorts of ways. Not just sex. They cheat emotionally, deprive each other of their time, their attention—they even cheat on themselves. You know what I mean? So, where's the commitment?" She shook her head. "It's all pretty hopeless."

"Hopeless? No, I don't think it is."

Joan conjured up one of the saddest smiles Randi had ever seen. "Of course you don't. Your whole profession is about hope, isn't it? You sell the promise of a happy ending, right?"

"Not a promise," Randi said.

"The hope of a happy ending then, that's what you sell."

"Maybe I do."

Joan nodded. "You know, I used to think you would really have an answer for Mitchell and me. That we would get to a point where we would say, yes, that's it, that's the solution. But yesterday, after I got his call, after I knew he lied to me again, I finally faced the reality that there is no answer. It's very disappointing, believe me."

"That sounds incredibly familiar."

"Something Mitchell said?" she asked anxiously. "That there really is no answer?"

"Let's just say that people often come here believing that I have the solution for their problems, when the truth is I only have questions. Probably the same questions I have for myself. You and Mitchell need to be willing to search for your own answers. That's how it works."

Joan thought that over for a minute. "Sounds like psychobabble to me. What did Mitchell say?"

"Basically the same thing."

Joan laughed, a light, staccato laugh. "What a strange business you're in. This therapy, the counseling you do, it's almost like a religious thing, isn't it? I mean, if you believe in it, then maybe it works. But if you don't believe, it all seems a silly charade. You see that, don't you?"

Randi nodded. "Sometimes I do. Not always," she admitted. "Sometimes I get so caught up in what I do, I forget it's all based on that sort of faith."

"That's the word. *Faith*. And Mitchell has no faith. He's just like Elizabeth was. They have nothing but their selfishness." She nodded in silent affirmation of her own judgment. "More than anything, I'm just tired of the selfishness," she said. Then she turned and walked out of the room.

CHAPTER 28

Walker stopped off in the squad room to tell Kovacevic about his discussions with Chief Gill, Robert Stratford, and Knoebel's lawyer, then left the junior officer to follow up on some leads while he headed to his car, intending to spend the rest of the unusually warm autumn day in New York City.

First, however, he was stopping off to visit with Nettie Sisson.

On his way, he wondered about Dr. Knoebel's initial indifference to the news that they had taken his wife's computer, then his change of mind about it. Not only did he change his mind, but he had his attorney call to threaten Walker and the entire Darien Police Department if the computer and all of the documents downloaded from it were not promptly returned. If that was not enough to raise Walker's level of suspicion a notch or two, there was that little matter of the good doctor's eagerness to have his wife's body cremated. For once the chief surprised Walker, unexpectedly backing him up by issuing an order that the body be held until all possible leads were fully developed. Walker doubted that the coroner's office had missed anything, but the delay in releasing her remains might at least create some emotional pressure while the department struggled to pull together whatever they could and try to make sense of it all.

The department consisting, in essence, of Anthony Walker.

If Knoebel knew about his wife's diary, why did he not issue an immediate protest and demand the computer back the first day? Why give the police as much time with it as he had before taking action? One possibility was that Knoebel wanted Walker to have a shot of piecing together some sort of puzzle that might lead to the identity of his wife's killer. But if that were so, why insist on having it returned now?

A more logical answer was that Knoebel knew nothing of

SEXUAL RITES then, but he knew it now. Which begged the obvious question—who told him?

Walker therefore decided, before checking out Dr. Knoebel's alibi at the hospital in New York, to satisfy his curiosity about the housekeeper with the violent past. Among other things, he wanted to find out what she knew about Elizabeth's diary and—more important—what she knew about the authenticity of what had been depicted in such vivid detail by the murdered woman.

Nettie lived in a development of small units set in a series of nondescript, two-story buildings in Port Chester. The layout was not much different than the place where he lived, Walker observed with a wry smile. This was the real world, where the working class exists for the opportunity to serve the privileged class.

He shook off his cynicism by the time he found his way to her apartment. He knocked twice and waited.

When Nettie opened the door her face betrayed a mixture of concern and fear, a reasonable reaction to an unannounced appearance by a homicide detective. But there was something else in her eyes—she had been expecting him.

"Lieutenant Walker."

"Mrs. Sisson."

"Can I help you?"

"I think maybe you can."

Without waiting for him to ask, Nettie showed him inside. There was no foyer, the apartment just opened into a small living room. She pointed to the couch, then sat across from him in an old club chair, her posture ramrod straight. She did not offer him coffee nor did she engage in the sort of nervous banter he was accustomed to when he intruded on someone this way. He accepted it as a tacit invitation for him to get right to the point.

"You've worked for the Knoebels for the past couple of years."

"Yes," she said.

"How would you characterize their marriage?"

"I wouldn't," she replied, her unblinking gaze holding his. "As an experienced policeman, I'm sure you've done some sort of background check on me, or whatever it's called. I think it's fair to say that I'm in no position to make judgments about anyone else's marriage."

Walker could not suppress a slight smile. "You are a blunt woman, Mrs. Sisson."

Still staring into his gray-brown eyes, she said, "I think it saves time, don't you?"

Walker responded with an appreciative nod. "I've had the same thing said about me."

"If that's so," she said, "why not ask me what you came here to ask me."

"Which would be what, exactly?"

"You obviously know what happened between me and my husband, which means I am capable of murder. Or attempted murder, at the very least. Don't you want to know if I had any reason to kill Elizabeth?"

Walker rubbed his chin, thinking it over. "I cannot tell a lie, I am familiar with your background, but my conclusion about the incident with your husband was that you acted in self-defense. Fact is, from what Sergeant Fitzgerald told me, I wonder what took you so long. He sends his regards, by the way."

She said, "Thank you."

"Given your history, I don't really see the psychological profile of a serial killer. Am I wrong about that?" It was apparent that Nettie Sisson was not easily amused, but Walker thought he saw the makings of a grateful smile playing around the edges of her mouth. His next question caused any trace of that smile to vanish. "But, since you've raised it, did you have any reason to want to see Mrs. Knoebel dead?"

"No," she told him, her homely features now wearing a puzzled look. "That isn't really what you came here to ask me, is it?"

"No. Actually you're the one who brought it up."

Her gaze finally released his and wandered around the small room for a moment. "Elizabeth was not a good person," she said simply.

"You're obviously not the only one to feel that way. I mean, someone felt the need to put a bullet in her head." The harsh description was given with purpose.

Nettie's calm reply told him she was having none of that. "And you want to know if I can tell you who might have done it?"

"Can you?"

She frowned. "It's all I've thought about these past few days."

"Then tell me what you know about Elizabeth's diary."

"I see. So that's why you're here." She nodded, as if a riddle that had been gnawing at her was solved.

"Yes," he admitted. "I really don't believe you had anything to do with her death."

Nettie said nothing.

"I also believe that if you had any idea who the murderer might be, you would have said something by now. So my hope is that you'll tell me what you know about the diary. The people she wrote about. I'm guessing you had a pretty good idea of whether her stories were real or fantasy, or maybe a combination of the two."

Nettie was already shaking her head. "Oh no, it was all very real. The men were real." She hesitated. "And the women." She looked down at her hands, which were now tightly clasped together in her lap. "It was all very real."

Walker gave her a moment to compose herself. Then, in a gentle voice, he said, "Tell me."

And so she did. Something in his manner made it easy for her to tell him the truth. Or perhaps she simply needed to tell someone what she knew about Elizabeth's infidelities. She told Walker that she had never discussed it with anyone, not even Randi Conway. When she discovered that Elizabeth was writing a diary, she knew what it was about, but had again remained silent.

"What about Doctor Knoebel? You never said anything at all to him?"

Nettie shook her head. "Especially not him." She insisted that her loyalty had always been to Dr. Knoebel and his daughter, and that it still was. She even confessed that there were moments when she loathed Elizabeth, but she had still kept the faith.

"Why?" he asked.

"I could never be the cause of such heartache for her husband."

"But Doctor Knoebel must have had some idea of what she was up to."

Nettie could not deny it. "He did," she admitted. "But it was his choice to stay with her, don't you see?"

Walker thought he did. "Then Doctor Knoebel knew about the diary?"

"No, I don't believe he knew."

"You ever get the chance to read it?"

Nettie hesitated for a few seconds, then said, "Yes. Some of it."

"With or without her permission?"

"Without." When there was no follow-up question, she said, "There were times when I would be cleaning the den and she'd leave her computer on."

"You snuck a peek."

"Yes."

"How much of it did you see?"

"Whatever was on the screen at the time. I don't know anything about computers. I was afraid to touch it."

"I feel the same way," Walker admitted with a grin.

"She would always have it off when he was home."

Walker nodded, then moved on to other questions.

Nettie denied knowing the identity of any of Elizabeth's lovers, even those mentioned in the few snippets she had read. She said that Mrs. Knoebel was always careful not to have any witnesses to her trysts. Walker prodded Nettie on the issue, but she would not be moved. He suggested that she must have seen someone coming or going from the house, but she told him she had not.

"If she brought anyone back to the house it would have been on my days off."

Walker warned her that withholding evidence in a murder case is a serious crime in and of itself. That earned him the closest thing to a laugh he had yet seen from the woman.

"Detective Walker," she said evenly, "you admit that you're familiar with my history. I was a victim of abuse for decades and voluntarily spent nearly five years in a mental institution. Do you really believe there is any threat you can make that would intimidate me?"

"No," Walker conceded, "there probably is not."

Nettie took her time answering each of his remaining questions, but she did not hedge or stall. She was actually quite forthcoming, he thought, for someone who was still holding something back.

Later, as they were saying good-bye at her front door, he stopped to confirm one more thing. "You're still working for Stanley Knoebel?"

"Yes," she said.

He stepped outside, squinted into the afternoon sun and then had another look at her. "I'll be in touch."

"I assume you will," she replied pleasantly, and without saying good-bye simply shut the door behind him.

Back in his car, heading down the East Side Drive, Walker kept replaying Nettie Sisson's comments in his mind as if there were more to what she said than he was seeing, as if there were some way to reconcile her contradictions.

She believed that Dr. Knoebel knew something of his wife's infidelity, yet elected to remain with her. Whatever else Nettie knew about that part of their marriage, she was keeping it to herself. The way Nettie saw it, the doctor had made his choice. There was nothing to be gained by piling on more information, more evidence of Elizabeth's betrayal. The only result would be to intensify his pain.

Nettie instinctively understood that every man has his breaking point, and she was unwilling to push Dr. Knoebel to the edge. What if he found out more than he could handle? What if he learned that his wife had more than one lover? Or more than two? What if he discovered the diary?

Dr. Knoebel may be a respected member of the community, as Chief Gill insisted, and he might be worthy of Nettie Sisson's devotion, as she described it, but he did not deserve to be protected from a murder charge. As Walker drove on he prepared himself for his next round of questioning. He was heading into New York to personally verify the distinguished surgeon's whereabouts on the day of his wife's death. He wanted to know whether or not Dr. Knoebel should be his prime suspect.

CHAPTER 29

Linda Stratford did not usually visit her husband in his office and so, when she showed up there on Monday afternoon, he did not do well hiding his surprise. They shared a perfunctory kiss, then she sat in the chair across the desk from him.

"I was shopping," she explained before he could ask, "thought I would stop by and say hello."

"Well I'm glad you did."

She responded with a look he had seen countless times—a slight tilting of the head and narrowing of her eyes that said, *Save it Robert*. After the moment passed, she asked, "What's new and exciting?"

"New and exciting? In my humdrum workaday world?"

"Any word from your friends in Hartford about the nomination?"

Stratford drew in a deep breath and sighed. "Nothing good, unfortunately. Kelleher called. We talked it over and he told me I don't have enough experience to make a run at a national office."

"National office? How much experience does it take? Our congressional district is about as big as a trailer park in upstate New York."

Stratford laughed. She could always make him laugh. "You're probably right, but running Darien is not an obvious launching pad for the United States Congress."

"Maybe not," she admitted, "but nowadays what is? We've had everything from haberdashers to community organizers in the White House, right? And the party doesn't have anyone half as appealing, one-third as electable, or one-tenth as bankable as you. When are they going to get their small minds around that concept?"

"I think they're beginning to understand the bankable part," he told her. In a wealthy state, there were many wealthy men and women inclined to spend large parts of their own fortunes to gain political office. Even in that arena, it was well known that Robert Stratford, with his wife's family money behind him, was more willing than most to write the checks necessary to advance his political career.

"They better wake up and smell the roses. They need a winner in this election and you're it."

Stratford nodded, comfortable in the role of a politician acknowledging someone's support, even his wife's.

"So," she said, "what's new with our local whodunit?"

"Not much to report I'm sorry to say." He shook his head. "Frankly, it's becoming a source of concern for me. The media interest in an unsolved murder isn't going to do my chance at a candidacy any good. Death by gunshot? Reporters looking for a scandal under every hedgerow? This is not going to have a happy ending, and remember, right now I'm the face of this town."

"You know what they say my dear, there's no such thing as bad publicity. You just keep getting that handsome kisser of yours on television, the Internet, and in the paper. Later on people won't remember why they saw you, they'll just remember that they did."

"Maybe you're right," he replied, his tone telling her he was unconvinced. "But if things go wrong, I'm the man on the front lines. As you can imagine, Gill wants to have as little to do with this as possible." He shook his head. "Can you believe that's how a police chief behaves when there's been a murder committed in his own town?"

"Gill's been on the force since I went away to boarding school, and he's the same candy ass now as he was then. There isn't a toe in Darien he avoids stepping on. That's how he's kept his job all these years."

Stratford frowned. "Might be a lesson in that for all of us. Meanwhile, he's dumped the whole thing on this detective that came up from New York a few years ago."

"Lieutenant Walker."

"You know him?"

"I cannot tell a lie Robert, I've been following this story, just like the rest of your constituents. Walker is getting more media coverage than you and Gill combined."

"I've noticed, and it's amazing to me. Word is that he's a good cop, and very low-key when it comes to drawing attention to himself."

Linda's eyes narrowed again. "Maybe yes, maybe no. And maybe he's not as dull-witted as he appears." When Stratford reacted with a puzzled look, she said, "I've seen him on television."

"He's been interviewed?"

"No, just shots of him leaving headquarters this morning, refusing comment. A stoic type."

"If you're saying our friend Detective Walker is someone we need to keep an eye on, I'm already on it. Meeting him for drinks tomorrow night. Good?"

"That depends."

"On what?"

"If he solves the case, you're going to want to stand right beside him in the spotlight. On the other hand," she said with a wry grin, "if he screws it up, you'll want to stay as far from him as possible. Might even make sense for us to be out of town."

Stratford appeared to be giving that notion serious thought. Then he said, "I wonder if Chief Gill has any travel plans yet."

His wife laughed. "Gill is a wimp, but he's not stupid. I guaranty you he's figuring this the same way I am. He'll orchestrate things so success will be a duet, but failure is going to be a solo act starring Detective Walker."

"I think you're right."

She paused for a moment, then asked, "What about your friend Randi?"

"What about her?"

"The Knoebels were her patients and you're her lawyer. That puts the two of you right in the middle of all this. Is that going to be an asset or liability for you?"

"I wish I knew. This is already causing her some serious issues."

"And you want to be her knight in shining armor." When he responded with a disapproving look, she said, "I know that's who you are, my sweet. But this is one time you need to think about yourself first. To think about us."

"Of course."

Linda leaned forward and said, "Is that really what has you worried? Is it about her?"

He sat up and met her intense gaze. "Absolutely not."

"So what then?"

"I'm not sure," he said. "I just felt that things were going so well, that we had a real shot at the nomination."

She liked his use of the word *we*. "We still do," she insisted.

"Maybe so, but I can't shake the feeling that a lot is going to depend on how this murder investigation plays out."

Linda sat back and offered him a warm smile. "Yes, and I realize how much you absolutely despise not being in control of every situation."

Stratford smiled. "You know me too well."

"Well enough to know that it's not just the situation you want to control."

"You mean . . ."

"Yes. The outcome too."

CHAPTER 30

Prior to his drive into the city, Walker had telephoned from his office, arranging to meet the two doctors Knoebel claimed he had drinks with the night Elizabeth was shot.

He arrived at the main building of the medical center and was shown to a small conference room and told to wait. The two physicians were paged, but it was more than thirty minutes before they finally walked in.

Walker ignored their lateness—they were, after all, doctors. But he did not hesitate to express his surprise that they had combined the two appointments into one. It was not Walker's preferred method of conducting an interview, and he had made it clear they were to be separate discussions.

"We're not violating any rules, are we officer?"

Walker felt at home in New York, but also knew he was way outside his legal jurisdiction. All he could offer in response was a knowing smile. "Not yet, you're not," he told them.

They got down to business, each of the doctors quickly confirming that they had indeed been with Knoebel for drinks on the evening in question.

"Why are you so sure of the date and the time?" he asked.

That was easy, they told him. First, each of them carried an iPhone that kept tabs on every minute of their lives, past, present and future. Second, their hospital and office records corroborated the times they made rounds that day, the patients they saw and so forth. They assured him that they had each verified all of that in anticipation of this brief interview—putting special emphasis on the word *brief*. Finally, each man distinctly recalled hearing the news the following day that Knoebel's wife had been murdered. Naturally, that fixed the events of the prior evening indelibly in their memories.

"Naturally," Walker said.

They were also certain of how much time they had spent with Knoebel, which matched his recollection to the minute.

The interview over, Walker visited the administration office. The hospital records, which they pulled for him minus anything that might be a potential violation of HIPAA, also matched Knoebel's story. He was in surgery until the afternoon, then made his rounds, seeing patients. There was a brief period that was unaccounted for late in the day, before he met the other two doctors for cocktails, but in that window of time it would have been impossible for Knoebel to make the drive home to Connecticut and return to join his colleagues back in New York at the hour they had all confirmed. The only possibility was that he returned to Connecticut afterward, but if that were the case, he would not have gotten home before nine that night.

Jake had placed the time of death around four and Mrs. Fitzmorris spotted the sedan speeding away from the Knoebel driveway around five.

Walker completed his disappointing review in the administration office, then telephoned the coroner's office.

"Nine o'clock? No way," Jake told him. "She was dead for hours by nine o'clock."

"Uh huh."

"Any chance Knoebel had time to make a quick run back and forth to his house in between any of his appointments?"

"No," Walker told him. "Between his rounds and the operating room records here, Knoebel barely had time to change his mind that day. The only time slot unaccounted for is less than an hour."

"Not enough time for a round-trip to Connecticut."

"Right."

Walker left the hospital and strolled three blocks to the indoor lot where he paid an exorbitant fee for the privilege of parking his car for less than two hours. In the old days he could have ditched his car in the middle of Times Square and not worried about a thing. He would have just snapped down the visor and clipped on his NYPD decal.

Things change.

"Autumn in New York," he said to himself as he slid behind the wheel and prepared to make the drive home. He wished he had the Sinatra disc with that song on it. "Autumn in New York." Brings back memories.

When Walker and his wife first moved to Connecticut they made trips into the city all the time. Visited friends. Went to their favorite restaurants in the old neighborhood. Came into town for movies that were never going to make it to the multiplex in the burbs. After a while, though, the trip seemed to get longer, the friends in New York fewer and the visits less frequent. They had created a new life someplace else.

He just never anticipated how different that new life would become.

Walker was surprised at how melancholy that made him feel today. He decided to take a detour, heading slowly down Fifth Avenue along Central Park, then turning left on Seventieth Street and coming back up on Madison, passing the overpriced boutiques and art galleries that line the avenue on both sides.

He was thinking about those old friends, feeling the urge to visit one of the watering holes where he spent too much time during nights gone by, maybe stop by his old precinct. But he knew it would be a letdown, he knew it for sure. There would be different faces, the roll call at the old station house full of unfamiliar names. He remembered Lieutenant Kenny, the best superior officer he ever served under. Had cancer a few years ago, retired to Arizona or Nevada or something. Walker would love to have a beer with Brian Kenny someday, but he knew it was never going to happen. He figured that was all right, just part of the deal.

What upset him, what really depressed him, was the sense that every trace of his existence in this city had been completely washed away. He had risked his life, day after day, year after year, chasing down drug dealers and thieves, doing his job like a good cop should, putting the villains away and protecting the public. And now, looking back, what was it all about? As soon as he moved out of New York, the city had forgotten him. He even lost his wife and daughters along the way, and now he was alone.

What a waste.

Jesus, he thought, *you're a morbid sonuvabitch*. He tried to shake it off, but the feeling stuck. He found himself driving even more slowly as he continued north on Madison, looking at the shops and restaurants, new places, names he never saw before. *Hell*, he thought, *if I go downtown I probably won't even find a bar I would recognize*.

He finally made a right turn, found his way to the East Side Drive, then headed up the interstate for what had now become his home, for the good and bad of all that.

CHAPTER 31

By the time Walker arrived back in his office from his visit to New York it was after seven. Sitting at his desk, he pulled out the printed version of Elizabeth Knoebel's diary. He picked up the pages that had been stored under JWJCR.DOC and read them again.

SEXUAL RITES
Notes on the Mechanics of Sexuality

Like most men, J was inept when it came to solving the sweet mysteries of femininity.

Bred as egocentrics, men learn early on all there is to know about their own genitalia. Even before puberty, a boy becomes obsessed with his penis, exploring the sensitivity of the under-side of the glans, running his fingers along the frenulum, endlessly touching himself and playing with his testicles. His first erections and ejaculations constitute a rite of passage that arm him for a lifelong pursuit of satisfaction, just as the primitive hunter must have felt when he finally honed the tip of his spear to a sharp point and embarked on his search for prey.

Oddly, there are very few men I have ever known who have the same curiosity about the physiology of the vagina that they have for their own equipment. They tend to view a woman's pussy as a goal to be achieved rather than part of a process to be enjoyed. The vagina becomes a receptacle for penetration, nothing more. If the pussy is wet, the easier it is to enter. Whether the lubrication comes from within—as an expression of the woman's arousal—or is abetted by a cream or an oil, does not matter to most men. They believe the point is to find their way in and then employ all the subtlety of a jackhammer in driving home their stiff cock with thrust after thrust until the inevitable conclusion.

Inevitable, that is, for the man.

Even men who enjoy fondling, touching or licking a woman's pussy often fail to understand what pleases and what does not. Rough sex does not mean unpleasant sex. Would a man enjoy a woman painfully squeezing his balls? Or digging into them with her nails? Or scraping his cock with her teeth?

The first thing a man should realize is that the vagina is as sensitive for a woman as the underside of a man's scrotum is to him. The interior membranes are incredibly thin. The clitoris is something to be worshipped with tenderness, not chafed or bitten or lapped at like a thirsty dog drinking water from a bowl.

There can also be too much of a good thing. Constant rubbing or touching or licking in the same area can become more irritating than exciting. A woman has innumerable erogenous zones, all of which should be investigated and caressed before zeroing in on the ultimate target. A woman's neck, her nipples, her ears, her ass, and—that most overlooked source of pleasure—her skin itself, when properly approached and stroked and caressed, can leave her pussy dripping wet even before the man arrives there.

When it is time for the vagina to be fondled or kissed, it should not be attacked. Care must be taken. The outer lips should be gently parted, not shoved aside. The inner skin should be treated with delicacy, not assaulted with a stiff finger jammed inside. The clitoris should be lovingly embraced, not chewed or jabbed at.

This should all be obvious to any man who has ever left a woman unsatisfied, which includes virtually every man engaged in the journey of sexual discovery. Yet so many of them fail to see what is apparent, ignoring the needs of the vagina, even as they ignore the emotional needs of the woman herself. They should learn to enjoy the complete experience, they should understand that the pleasure they give will only enhance the pleasure they receive.

> J neither understood nor seemed to
> have any interest in learning.
>   Unfortunately, as we have seen, most
> men are fools.

Walker could not help but smile as he put the pages down. Whoever and whatever this woman was, it would have been interesting to meet her.

He shook off the thought when he saw a note on his desk to call town counsel, Ben Youngman. The message said that Chief Gill had spoken with Youngman about Dr. Knoebel and his attorney, so Walker picked up the phone and made the call.

"I'm walking out the door," the lawyer told him.

"Okay. Just wanted to know if you had a chance to think it over yet."

"Yes, actually." There was a pause. "Legally, I don't see why we have to give any of it back. I've spoken with the prosecutor's office. Cohen feels the same way."

Walker nodded to himself. "But?" He knew that any time a lawyer gives an answer with his voice rising at the end of the statement, there was always a *but*.

"An hour ago I got a call from Knoebel's lawyer."

"Mr. Bennett is really getting around."

"He threatened a suit against everybody—you, the department, the town."

"Did the chief tell you what we found on her computer?"

"He gave me a general idea."

"Then why don't you tell Attorney Bennett how pleased we'd be to fight this out in court? I'm not so sure Dr. Knoebel will see that as such a terrific idea, having a battle over a diary that says his wife was humping half of Fairfield County."

"TMI, Walker. I told you, Gill only gave me a vague description of what you found."

"And I'm telling you they won't fight us."

"Maybe not. I want you to return it anyway."

"What?"

"That's our position."

"Your position? What the hell sense does your position make? What if we need this as evidence?"

Youngman hesitated again. There was nothing he liked about this discussion, and he obviously considered Walker a nuisance. "Is Knoebel a suspect? A target?"

"Probably not. I verified his alibi in New York today."

"And you've been through the woman's files, right?"

"Yes."

"Have you found anything in the computer that's material to your investigation?"

"I'm not sure."

"That's not good enough, Detective. The man's wife is dead. If you don't think he's the one who killed her, and you've discovered no material evidence in her laptop, why give him a hard time?"

"There's something about it that doesn't feel right."

"Could it be the bully-boy tactics coming from the lawyer in New York?"

"I'm used to that crap. It's just a feeling I have, that's all."

"A feeling?"

"The stuff in her files is about people she knew. You said Gill gave you the *Reader's Digest* version?"

"I got the summary."

"Then you understand the situation. At the very least one of these stories might help us prove a motive if we ever finger the murderer."

Youngman hesitated. "All right. Get me the computer. I won't give it up until I speak with Cohen again."

"Okay," Walker agreed. Cohen was a hard-nosed prosecutor, and he would take a tougher line than Youngman. Walker was going to call him first thing in the morning and offer his version of the facts.

"You know," Youngman said, "the guy was an idiot not to demand her computer back in the first place."

"Except this guy is no idiot," Walker said. "So why did he do it? That's what I can't figure. At first I thought he was trying to help the investigation, a natural instinct to help us find his wife's murderer, right? Then I read the stuff." Walker shook his head. "What's he up to, Ben? Did he know what was in there or not? Is he trying to implicate other people to cover his own tracks? Did he just want someone to see what his wife was all about?"

"Easy there, cowboy. I'm not a detective or a psychiatrist, I'm just a lawyer. You say his alibi checks out. If that's true he's not a suspect, he's just the grieving widower. Get me the laptop in the morning and I'll speak with David."

"I'll drop it off myself."

"And Walker."

"Yeah?"

"Don't do anything stupid."

"Me?"

"Yeah, you," the lawyer said.

When they hung up, Walker dialed Blasko. "Can you make me a disc with all those files from the Knoebel laptop? Strictly on the down low?"

"No problem."

"I need it by first thing in the morning. We've got to give up the computer."

"I'll stop by, it'll take me all of two minutes."

"You're the best, Teddy."

Walker hung up and sat back in his chair. *Damned lawyers*, he thought. He checked his voice mail and found that Jake had phoned from the coroner's office. He returned the call.

Jake said, "I had a thought, after I spoke with you. You say Knoebel was in surgery that day."

"Uh huh," Walker replied wearily.

"Did you check the roster or the actual OR records?"

"The roster? Yeah, I think that's what the nurse showed me."

"Did it list more than one surgeon?"

"I think so, but they wouldn't let me take copies with me. Once I confirmed Knoebel was there, I didn't fight it. Why?"

"That's just it. You don't actually know if Knoebel was there. I thought of this after we spoke. Knoebel could have had residents performing surgery under his observation. He might have come and gone during the procedure. If it was a simple operation, he might not have been there at the end. Unusual, I admit. But possible."

"All right. How do I find out and how do I prove it?"

Jake thought it over. "The patient charts wouldn't show it. You need actual OR transcripts. That's the only place it might appear. The surgical abstract. It's a narrative of what happens during the operation, it says who does what. This is a long shot, I admit. And you may need a court order if they get tough with you."

"Uh huh."

"Or you might find a friendly resident who could tell you."

"I'll take a crack at it. Thanks Jake."

Walker hung up and returned to Elizabeth's diary. He wasn't giving these printed pages back, that was for sure. And he was going to hang on to the disc Teddy would make. That meant Randi Conway had the only other copy. He would have to get that back from her.

He was lost in thought when his intercom buzzed. "Someone here to see you, Lieutenant. I already sent him up."

"Okay," Walker said. He did not have to wait long before a familiar face appeared in the doorway. It was Kyle Avery.

"Sir?"

"Hey, come on in."

The boy stepped inside, looking around. They were alone.

"How are you?" Walker asked.

Kyle began nodding his head. "Good, I'm good."

"Sit down."

"Oh, that's okay. I just, uh, wanted to come here and, well, you know, just say thank you. For your help I mean."

The kid was so nervous Walker thought he'd better sit down before he fell down. "You're welcome," he said. "Sure you won't grab a seat for a minute?"

Kyle scanned the room again and figured it was okay. "Fine," he said, then came over and lowered himself into the wooden chair beside Walker's desk. "Saw you on television."

"That right?"

Kyle nodded.

"How'd I look?"

The boy shrugged.

"I don't think Hollywood's in my future."

Kyle uttered a short laugh.

Walker thought the boy looked different—it was his hair, he decided, it was cut a lot shorter—but he seemed just as jumpy as the night they met on the bank roof. "Everything working out for you at home?"

Kyle tilted his head slightly. "Not so much. They keep an eye on me all the time, you know, like I'm on suicide watch or whatever they call it." He offered up an embarrassed smile. "I'm okay, though."

"Guess you are, if you came to the police station to say thanks like this. Not easy to do." When the boy did not respond, Walker leaned forward, his chin on his hand, and smiled. "Your mother's idea?"

"No," he said with a determined shake of his head. Then he asked, "You remember that night?"

Walker nodded. "Sure do."

"Well you were right about what you said. Woulda been a whole lot worse if I didn't listen to you."

"Glad you figured that out. Your folks doing any better?"

Kyle looked down at his sneakers. "Nah. Mom and my sister and me, we moved out."

"Moved out?"

"We're staying with a friend in town for a while," Kyle told him, "This way Nina and I can still go to school here. Mom is really pissed about something. I'm not sure what." The way he made that last statement, Walker had the sense the boy knew exactly why his mother had taken them out of the house. "I don't think Dad even knows we left. He's away on a business trip. Gets home tomorrow."

"That's got to be rough for you."

"Yeah. Rough for everybody." He lifted his head, and Walker realized it was only the second time the kid had ever looked right at him. The boy had clear, intelligent, frightened eyes. "Wish you could talk to them. The way you talked to me."

Walker pressed his lips together, wanting to say just the right thing. "I know this is going to sound like bullshit, Kyle, but things really do have a way of working out."

"That's what you said to me that night."

"At least I'm consistent, right? But they do."

"Yeah, I suppose. One way or another." He thought about something, then said, "Remember how I told you I screwed up?"

Walker nodded.

"I wasn't talking about going up on the roof."

"I figured that. I mean, you had to have a reason to go up there in the first place."

"Yeah."

"You want to talk about it now?"

Kyle thought it over, staring down at his sneakers again. "That's what everyone keeps asking me. In the hospital, Doctor Conway, my mother."

"Your father?"

That got the boy to look up. "Not him, not so much."

Walker waited.

"Maybe some other time we can talk about it. Would that be okay?"

"Any time."

That appeared to please the boy.

"There's something else on your mind."

Kyle nodded. "This murder. The reason you were on TV."

"Yes?"

"You know who did it?"

"Not yet. That's what I was working on when you came in." Now he fixed the young man with a serious look. "If you have a theory, I'm willing to listen."

Kyle shook his head. "No, no I was just curious is all." When Walker continued to stare at him, Kyle said, "Well, I guess I should go," and stood up to leave.

Walker said, "Hey. If you ever do want to talk, I mean about anything at all, I'll be here."

Kyle hesitated for a moment, then said, "Thanks."

"I mean it," Walker told him.

The boy answered with a sad smile that made him look a lot like his mother. "I know you do," he said, then turned for the door and was gone.

CHAPTER 32

That evening, Thomas Colello and Fred Wentworth stood shoulder to shoulder at the bar of the Black Swan, a bistro in the center of Darien.

Colello was not one of this suburb's wealthy elite. He had a reasonably successful contracting business, which afforded him a small house with a large mortgage on the less fashionable side of town, and the right to claim inclusion in this exclusive community, even if he received little attention from the established country club set. To that well-entrenched group, Colello was not even an *arriviste*, since he had not really arrived. As in other communities along Fairfield County's Gold Coast, those actually required to work for a living were regarded with both suspicion and disdain by those who have no such need.

Whatever hopes Colello had of gaining acceptance from that upper crust, he was certainly not going to find any help from Fred Wentworth. Wentworth did not make the grade either, financially or in terms of style. The large, garrulous garment-center salesman was, as they might say at a meeting of one of the local club's membership committees, the wrong fit.

Nevertheless, Colello found Wentworth amusing at times, the only one in their dreary group therapy sessions who ever made him laugh. If the man was a bit loud, at least he could be fun. Tonight, however, Colello's motive in asking Wentworth to stop by for a drink had nothing to do with entertainment.

Colello had skipped last week's group session, the gathering that was held after Elizabeth was murdered, and he wanted to know what the others had to say.

Wentworth lifted his drink and then craned his leonine head around, surveying the rich wood paneling and architectural molding of the restaurant's grill room. "Beautiful," he pronounced, as if someone had asked him his opinion. Then he took a long pull of his Johnny Walker Black on the rocks. "Great work," he added.

"Thanks," Colello said. His company had built the interior space and kitchen, and he was now a regular customer.

"Yeah," Wentworth was saying, "you sure did it up right."

Colello was athletically built, with Mediterranean features and complexion, his dark, wavy hair combed back, neatly in place. He wore navy blue slacks that were crisply pressed, a white polo shirt open at the neck and black loafers with no socks.

Wentworth was still dressed in the suit he had worn to work. He gave Colello a gentle elbow to the ribs and said, "Bet you charged them enough too."

Colello responded with an embarrassed smile but gave no answer. "Glad we could get together tonight," he said.

"Me too," Wentworth told him as he had a gulp of his scotch.

"You have your usual one-on-one with our friend Doctor Conway on Saturday?"

"Sure," Wentworth said, "I did my penance. Beats going to church, eh?"

"Sometimes I'm not so sure."

Wentworth laughed. "What about you? We missed you in group."

"Yeah," Colello said, "something came up." He waited a beat, then asked, "How is Randi doing? She must be taking this pretty hard."

Wentworth reached into a pewter bowl, his hand the size of a bear's paw, and scooped out some bar mix. "The Knoebel thing, you mean?" He began chewing on the nuts as he said, "Yeah, seems to be."

"She say anything about it in group?"

"What do you think? She wanted us to talk about Stanley, what we thought when we heard about his wife's death, how we felt about him, all that crap."

Colello waited as Wentworth took another big swallow of scotch. "And?"

"What the hell is there to say? Guy's cold enough to kill his own mother, know what I mean?" He shook his head. "She wanted us to share our feelings, but there was one little problem—none of us had any. Mitchell couldn't give a shit and Paulie wouldn't know what to do with an opinion if he tripped over one." Wentworth polished off his drink in a final gulp.

"So that was it?"

"Basically, yeah."

Colello knew there had to be more, Dr. Conway would have pushed them to discuss the Knoebels, but he decided he would circle back to that subject later. He waved to the bartender. "Do us again, would you Marcus?"

As a new round of drinks were being poured, Colello said, "I've got some interesting news about the murder investigation. A good friend in the police department here in town fills me in on what's going on from time to time."

"That right?"

Colello nodded. "What I've got to tell you stays between us."

"Absolutely," Wentworth said as he picked through the dish in search of cashews. "What'd he say?"

"The scuttlebutt is that the police found Elizabeth Knoebel's diary."

"Her diary?"

"That's right. And it's supposed to be seriously X-rated."

Wentworth ignored the bowl of nuts and looked up. "What does that mean?"

Trying to sound casual about it, Colello said, "Let's just say it's not a list of her favorite restaurants."

The bartender served them fresh drinks and Wentworth lifted his glass and took a swig. Colello was eying him carefully, about to say something else when he noticed Robert Stratford stroll through the door. Stratford was still in his professional uniform, dark suit, powder blue shirt with contrasting white collar, and yellow Hermès tie with a geometric print. He turned in their direction and gave Colello a brief wave, then came over and the two men shook hands.

"Bob Stratford, say hello to Fred Wentworth," Colello said. "Bob's our First Selectman in Darien."

"I know who you are," Wentworth said genially. "I voted for you."

"Well thanks," Stratford said with his practiced smile. "I appreciate every vote I get."

Colello said, "Bob's also a successful lawyer and, among his many illustrious clients, you know who he represents?"

Wentworth shook his head and gave his wide shoulders a theatrical shrug.

"Bob is counsel to our good friend Doctor Randi Conway."

"That so?"

"Guilty as charged," Stratford said, then asked the bartender for a vodka tonic. "All right if I join you two for a little bit?" He looked at his watch. "I'm meeting someone but I guess he's running late."

"No problem," Colello said, doing what he could to disguise his disappointment at the intrusion.

"So," Wentworth said, "you represent Doctor Conway."

"I do," Stratford said. "I take it you know her."

Wentworth shot a conspiratorial glance at Colello. "We've met," he said.

Colello said nothing.

"Guess she's got her hands full," Wentworth said.

Stratford did not reply. He took the drink the bartender handed him and said thanks.

Wentworth was a man who regarded silence as positively painful. He filled the current void by saying, "Almost all murders wind up being committed by someone in the family, did you know that?"

"You suggesting she was shot by her husband?" Stratford asked.

"Thomas and I were just getting around to that," Wentworth said.

Colello figured if anyone knew what was going on, it would be Stratford, so he decided to run with it. "We were discussing a rumor that the police have found the woman's diary." He gave the First Selectman a searching look. "I assume you've heard that, am I right?"

Stratford had first been told about the diary by Randi, then by Chief Gill. He said, "My lips are sealed. Even in a personal chat like this, I have to respect the fact that there's a police investigation in progress."

He did his best to hide his concern that the secret of Elizabeth Knoebel's journal had already become a topic for barroom chatter. Instead he took a sip of his vodka tonic, forced a grin, and told them, "That doesn't mean I'm not willing to hear what you have to say."

"Well," Colello responded, lowering his voice slightly, "the buzz is that Mrs. Knoebel was involved in some steamy extracurricular activities, and was writing about them." Colello strained to keep a neutral demeanor as he spoke—one of the reasons he was here was to gauge Wentworth's reaction to this news, face-to-face. "May have named names, too."

"Names?" Wentworth asked.

"Actually, it seems she used some sort of code. That's the story I heard anyway."

"A code," Wentworth repeated.

"The police have already cracked it, so now they can track whatever leads she might have left behind."

When Stratford offered no reaction, Wentworth said, "If it's true, Stanley'd have reason enough to pull the trigger, know what I mean?"

Colello took a moment to make it appear he was mulling that over. It was apparent that news of Elizabeth's infidelity had come as no shock to Fred Wentworth, even if word on the diary did. "You may be right, Fred, but there are some serious issues to deal with before you even get there. First, like you say, you have to believe what she wrote is fact and not fiction. Then there's the question of whether Stanley knew. And what about the people she mentions?"

"What about them?"

"Maybe a lover did it. Or an ex-lover. The authorities have the diary and maybe it's a road map for them to solve the case."

"An interesting thesis," Stratford said.

"Who else knows about this diary?" Wentworth asked.

"I have no idea," Colello said.

Stratford certainly was not answering that question.

"What about Doctor Conway?" Wentworth looked from Colello to Stratford.

When Stratford again offered no response, Colello said, "Far as I know, the police aren't showing it to anyone."

"Mm hmm," Wentworth murmured, then picked up his glass of scotch. "I sure would like to get my hands on a copy. More reasons than one, know what I mean?"

Neither Stratford nor Colello gave any indication that they knew what he meant.

"Bob," Colello said to Stratford, "this all stays here, right?"

Stratford shook his head. "I should really ask who told you, but there are barroom rules. It stays right here."

"Thanks."

Wentworth liked that, and said so. "You're okay for a politician. And I really did vote for you, true fact."

Stratford smiled. "I believed you the first time."

"So," Colello said, returning to the subject at hand, "this could get messy for a lot of people. I mean, take my situation. And Fred's. Our wives were in Randi's group with Elizabeth Knoebel. And the two of us are in group with Stanley." He turned to Wentworth and said, "Hope you don't mind my telling Bob."

"Too late now," Wentworth replied affably, already two and a half large Johnny Walker Black Labels into the program. "But why should any of this make it messy for us?"

"Who knows?" Colello said. "Maybe the police end up questioning all of us because we knew them from group."

"I see your point," Wentworth replied. After an uncomfortable silence, he added, "Hey, maybe we can help the cops."

Stratford nodded thoughtfully. "Better be careful what you wish for. Like Thomas says, you could end up getting served with a subpoena."

That appeared to bring Wentworth's sense of civic duty to a screeching halt.

"Only kidding," Stratford responded with a smile and a slap on the big man's arm. Then he had another look at his watch. "I better make a call and find out what happened to my friend. Nice to meet you Fred."

They shook hands, Stratford bid Colello good night, then he headed outside to use his cell phone.

Colello stood there, silently drinking his bourbon, not looking at Wentworth.

"Yeah," Fred said, his expression serious now. "I sure would like to see what she wrote. More reasons than one, know what I mean?"

CHAPTER 33

South Beach is Florida's answer to the Cote d'Azur, albeit a decidedly American answer. It proclaims its sensuality without finesse or tradition. It is straight-ahead, unrelenting and without apology. As sexual parades go, South Beach is both alluring and honest.

The main strip, Ocean Drive, runs north and south, bordered on one side by a wide stretch of sand that leads to the sea. During the day, a dazzling assortment of beautiful women populate the beach, showing off their firm, tanned bodies in skimpy bikinis that become more expensive the less fabric involved in the design. Eager men of differing vintages and description variously ogle, pursue, or pair off with these young lovelies.

As night falls, the action moves across the street, where the west side of the avenue is fronted by restaurants and bars that proclaim their trendy, often foreign-sounding names in gaudy neon that glows to life as darkness replaces sunlight. Provocatively dressed women and stylishly attired men pack the walkways and saloons and bistros, working hard at having fun as they move in rhythm to the Latino beat of the music thundering from every open door and window.

Mitchell Avery absolutely loved the place. He did not care that he was among the older denizens, he saw his age as an asset, just as he had described to Randi Conway. He reveled in the openness of the sexuality, the free, uncaring attitude of the singular voices, the sensual poses, the utter frankness of everything that surrounded him. And the best part was that he could afford whatever it cost to participate in this nonstop party.

This is me, he told himself.

If every man has a place that defines him, this place was surely Mitchell Avery.

South Beach was where he met Maria, during a business trip to Florida more than a year ago. She was standing at an outdoor bar, having a *mojito* and swaying to the sound of the insistent beat that poured through the speakers positioned all around them. Mitchell stepped up beside her, ordered a martini and said hello. Maria smiled.

She was wearing a black, thigh-high skirt, Jimmy Choo stilettos, and a chocolate brown, open-neck satin blouse that provided a generous view of her shapely breasts. It was difficult to be heard over the loud music, so when Avery offered to buy her a fresh cocktail he pointed to her nearly empty glass, and she nodded. Over the next half hour they managed enough conversation to agree they should have dinner together. Mitchell chose another busy spot on the strip where he pressed several bills into the hand of the maître d', and was promptly shown to a table. Later they make their way to a crowded rooftop lounge where they had another round of cocktails, and eventually wended their way back to Avery's hotel.

Since that first meeting Avery had seen her several times. He had seen her even after his wife had learned that his trips to Florida had nothing to do with business. He saw her even though the mention of this young woman's name could send Joan Avery into paroxysms of rage. He saw her because Mitchell needed to see her, regardless of the risks, despite his promises that the affair was over.

Now, after taking special care to pretend he was on his way to Nashville, he was seeing her again, without realizing that Joan knew he was in South Beach.

Avery booked a suite overlooking the sea in one of the best hotels on the strip, but at the moment he was not spending his time enjoying the accommodations or the view. Instead, he was devoting his attention to Maria.

She was wearing a beige skirt and cream-colored blouse that contrasted nicely with her tanned, olive skin. She stood on the balcony looking out at the ocean and, when she turned to him, she smiled, her teeth gleaming white, her eyes as black as her long, wavy hair. Avery was seated on the couch in the living room, watching her, admiring her shape. Her hips were rounded, her waist impossibly small, and the pronounced curves of her ass and full breasts provided an irresistible carnal symmetry.

And she was there for him.

Avery delighted in their relationship, the pure sexuality of their encounters, the complete lack of pretense. She was willing to fulfill his fantasies. He could ask her anything and she would oblige. He would match her generosity with his own, expressing his gratitude with dollars and gifts.

Was there ever a more honest basis for a relationship?

She turned away from viewing the sea and came into the room, moving slowly, performing an undulating dance to the music that poured from the hotel stereo. Then she began to strip for him.

He loved watching her undress, and she took her time doing it. She began by slipping off her skirt, then carefully unbuttoned her blouse. She rocked her hips to the rhythm of the music, clad only in her thong panties, which she wriggled out of and kicked aside so she stood before him, still in her stiletto heels, tanned and naked.

He admired her firm young breasts, her long slim legs, her flawless tawny complexion. He imagined her lying nude somewhere beneath the Florida sun, beads of perspiration covering her unlined skin, picturing the moisture along the line of her smoothly waxed vaginal lips as they were exposed to the light of day.

She moved closer, so that he could reach out and touch her. He drew her to him, and she reached down and undid his belt, then pulled his pants to the floor. Mitchell was still seated on the couch, so she kneeled beside him, her buttocks round and smooth, poised for his touch, his caress, even the gentle slap of his hand. He pulled her across his lap, leaned forward and began licking her from behind, the taste salty, the aroma a mix of perfume and her own musky scent.

She moaned as his tongue searched deeper between her legs, then she yanked on his shorts, pushing them to the floor. He was already firm, so she rose up again and took him in her mouth, running up and down on him, her tongue wet and hot. He reached for her breasts, squeezed her ass, then began to play with her pussy, wonderfully moist to his touch.

He lost himself in her suppleness, in the sublime feeling that he was as alive as he ever felt. He gently pushed her head away, took her by the hand and led her into the bedroom. He threw back the covers and sheets, laid her on her back, then got on his knees and entered her. They began moving together in a transcendent rhythm that bathed them in perspiration and pleasure. She came in three convulsive spasms, then pushed him away, turned around and had him enter from behind. He slid inside and reached around, holding the weight of her breasts in his hands as he thrust himself into her, the pace quickening until she cried out again and he spent himself in the sweet effort.

They rolled onto their sides and lay still for what seemed a long time. Then she rose, kissed him on the cheek and climbed out of bed. He watched her, marveling at her perfect naked ass, long sinewy legs and firm torso. She never looked back, disappearing into the bathroom to spend the time it would take for a beautiful young woman to put herself together again. Avery stood, pulled on a robe, went into the living room and made himself a drink. He stepped out onto the terrace, sat in one of the chairs and stared into the night.

These were the moments, shortly after the sex was finished, when he understood what should always be apparent to him—all they had between them was sex. It was great sex, no doubt, but these were also the moments when he was at his most lucid, when the truth of who he was and what he had done swept over him, undistorted by the deceit of lust.

What the hell am I doing here? he asked himself. Then he had a gulp of whisky.

He felt the familiar emptiness that followed this betrayal of Joan. He felt pangs of concern for Kyle that had become increasingly frequent since his encounter with Elizabeth Knoebel and his son's ensuing visit to that rooftop just a few days ago. He felt worried over how the entire Elizabeth Knoebel thing would play out.

Then he wondered at his own selfishness, allowing himself to be drawn back here again as if some primal urge drove him.

"*What the fuck*," he said out loud.

He had been through all of this before, of course. Once his physical needs were satisfied, once he was spent, he was left to ask himself the same irritating question.

Was it worth it?

The time, the expense, the effort, the obvious risk to his marriage and family—in these moments of clarity his egotism actually seemed ludicrous to him. Ludicrous, that is, until a bit of time passed and his libido recharged.

He thought, *I am such an asshole*, knowing he would get no argument from his wife if she were asked.

He had the sudden, irrational wish that he could simply snap his fingers and be transported back home, seated in his den with a scotch on the rocks, watching television.

And then, of all things, he began thinking about the office.

Avery had long been a success in business, wealthy by any reasonable standard, and he provided his family a superb lifestyle. Yet it was not lost on him that he was getting older, that the young bucks and bright young women who were joining the company had energy and ideas and a familiarity with the modern world of technology he would never match. They came to him for advice because his experience was still respected, but it would not be long before he would become an anachronism.

And then what?

The irony was that Mitchell enjoyed being around younger people. He learned from them and felt invigorated by them. But they also frightened him. Some days he was fine with that dynamic, while other times he felt as if he were walking a tightrope. He was nothing if not a realist, he knew there were fewer years in front of him than behind, both in business and in life. He looked at beautiful young women and handsome young men and felt adrift among them, fearful of being found out, terrified of losing his balance.

So here he was, with Maria, having once again indulged his selfish impulses. *What the hell for?*

To prove he could still cut it? To prove he could be with this sexy girl and keep her happy?

What bullshit! We both know why she's here, he told himself. If all she wanted was a good fuck, she could get one from any of those muscle-bound morons on the beach across the street.

He slugged down the rest of his drink, went to the bar, and poured himself another.

After Maria had put herself together and looked sensational all over again, he felt a stirring he would rely on later to complete their night. For now it was time for him to put aside his doubts and regrets and join the South Beach carnival.

Mitchell made a reservation at a popular Italian restaurant, his favorite along the strip, which was packed as usual. He took good care of the maître d', and they were promptly seated at a table in the middle of the action. The tables were so close they were practically touching people on all sides, but that was part of the fun. They were surrounded by a din of earnest chatter, and Mitchell watched as three young men and three young women at the round table to his left engaged in a lively debate that left them oblivious to his curious stare. Their table was cluttered with espresso cups and wine glasses. Their voices were unhurried but energetic. He turned back to Maria.

"Another drink?" he asked.

"I'll wait for the wine," she said.

To his right were two couples, one of the men holding court on some issue that seemed to bore the women. One of the women turned to Mitchell, regarding him with an unsmiling gaze that was neither inviting nor damning. She returned her attention to the dull monologue, and Mitchell reached out for Maria's hand. She moved forward, awkwardly leaning across the table to place a kiss on his lips. Mitchell was usually uncomfortable with that sort of public display, but he said nothing. She made it seem all right. This was South Beach.

"It's amazing how crowded it is, even on a weekday night."

She nodded. "It's always crowded here."

"You mean you come here without me?" His smile meant to tell her that he was teasing, but his eyes did not. "I thought this was our special place."

"I pass by once in a while," she replied.

The waiter brought the wine list and Mitchell ordered a Barolo. His drink was finished, so he asked the waiter to bring the wine straight away. "You like Barolo?" he asked Maria.

She shrugged. "Sure." Then, with no hint of embarrassment, she asked, "That's red wine, right?"

Mitchell laughed. How could a question that would seem foolish from someone else seem so beguiling? "Very red," he said. "You'll like it. Trust me." He reached for her hand again, this time taking it to his lips. "I didn't realize how much I missed you."

"You should miss me," she said, her dark eyes zeroing in on him. "You should miss me all the time."

Of course I do, thought Mitchell. And then, inexplicably, he recalled the softball team his company sponsored when he was just starting in business, just after he and Joan had married, when he first went to work in New York. He found himself thinking about how much fun he had playing second base on those worn-out fields in Central Park. Warm summer evenings spent fielding ground balls, running around the bases, drinking beers and laughing. He tried to recall if it had been as much fun then as he imagined at this moment. It made him think of Joan again, and he found it difficult to dismiss the images.

As if reading his mind, Maria leaned forward and whispered, "I have a special treat for you tonight."

"A special treat?"

"When we get back to the hotel I will perform two dances," she said.

Mitchell responded with a puzzled look.

Moving even closer to him, she said, "We'll put on the music in our room, and the first dance I will strip for you. But you cannot touch me, you must only sit there and look. That will be my dance."

He smiled, waiting.

"The second song will be your dance. I will dance again for you, but this time you can do anything you want. Anything."

Just then the waiter arrived and went about uncorking the bottle. Mitchell gave the wine a quick taste, then said, "Pour away."

The waiter filled their glasses too high. He was busy and had no interest in coming back to their table any more often than was absolutely necessary. Which was just fine with Avery.

Maria lifted her glass and said, "A toast to you."

"No, to us," Mitchell said and they each took a long drink.

"This is good," she told him. "Barolo, right?"

"Right," he said. He wanted to return the discussion back to her plans for the night ahead, but Maria said something he did not hear. "What's that?"

"You haven't even asked me how I'm doing in my new job," she repeated.

Mitchell did not remember she had a new job. "I'm sorry. We got so wrapped up in other things." He grinned. "How's it going?"

"Good. The girls there are really nice. I like the people a lot."

Mitchell nodded approvingly, waiting for more. He had no recollection of what sort of job she had taken, so there was nothing more for him to say.

She took a sip of her wine, then asked, "Whatever happened with that woman who was murdered?"

Mitchell responded with a blank stare.

"The woman in your town," she said, as if it should be obvious to him.

"Not sure, I guess the police are investigating."

"Oh," she replied, then had a look around the crowded restaurant, leaving Mitchell to wonder why he had no recollection of ever having mentioned Elizabeth's death to her.

CHAPTER 34

The following morning, when Randi Conway opened the door to her office, the first thing she noticed was her desk chair. It had been moved in front of the window. *Odd*, she thought as she stood in the doorway. With everything else in utter disarray, she focused on her chair.

She stepped inside slowly, leaving the door open behind her. She took off her coat and threw it on the couch, moving cautiously forward, all the while struggling to comprehend the chaos that lay before her. Papers were scattered across the floor. The lock on her file cabinet had been pried open and the drawers hung open. Forms, correspondence and patient charts were everywhere.

Randi wheeled her chair in place behind the desk and sat down. "Oh God," she said out loud.

She had the sensation that she had been physically violated. It reminded her again of that night in New York. It was a hollow feeling, as if this was another attack on her personally, not just the records and files in her office. Shock turned to upset, as she was struck with the realization that she would need to compare every file with her patient register, that she would need to determine if anything had been taken. She would have to reconstruct each folder, knowing the task would be nearly impossible. Her shoulders slumped at the thought of the damage that had been caused, the time it would take to put things together, and the risk that something was missing. She shook her head. Even if a file was there, how could she be certain that one or two of the pages had not been removed? Or copied on her own machine? It was hopeless.

She bent down and picked up the folder at her feet, which was sitting apart from the other piles, on the floor off to the side of her desk. It contained Paul Gorman's records, and it had been pulled apart.

Without thinking, she began to rearrange the disorganized pages. When she was done she placed the file down, slowly opened the desk drawer and removed the envelopes holding the two printed notes.

They had not been touched.

She knew she would have to call the police. She would have to call Anthony Walker. But first she telephoned Bob Stratford. She told him what happened and asked him to come by.

"All right, but be sure not to touch anything," he warned, "they're going to have to look for fingerprints."

"Oh God. They'll be looking through every confidential file in my office."

"I'll call Walker right now and have him meet me there. I'll explain our concerns." He hesitated. "You okay in the meantime?"

"I'm fine. Whatever they wanted to do is already done, right?"

"I don't mean to alarm you, but are you certain they're gone?"

Randi instinctively got to her feet. "I just assumed," she said, her head turning quickly back and forth as if she might find someone standing there.

"Yes, yes," he reassured her, "they wouldn't stay around, it makes no sense. I'll make the call and be there straight away."

"Thanks."

"And Randi," he said, "lock the door."

She hung up and slowly, quietly moved to the door to her group therapy room. She pulled it open with a sudden jerk.

No one was there.

She hung her head, clutching the doorknob as if she might fall down without the support. At least she was satisfied she was alone. She went to the front door, shut it and turned the latch. Then she made her way back to the desk where she again faced the typewritten notes.

She turned away from them, having another look at her ransacked office and, as she pondered the clutter of open folders and scattered papers, she became increasingly angry. *Strange*, she thought, how that had not been her first reaction. Now, however, rage was replacing upset and fear.

Her private file cabinets had been invaded, her professional con-fidences desecrated. *Who would have the nerve?* she wondered. She became aware of her own breathing as it became uneven and labored. She clenched her teeth. She wanted very much to punch someone in the nose.

She stood again and walked around, not touching any other files, conducting a random survey. Somehow she became overcome with the suspicion that nothing had been removed. She didn't know why she believed that, it was just a feeling.

She stood amidst this clutter, slowly turning, trying to take it all in, making a mental photograph as if that would help her regain a sense of order. Perhaps it would help her understand what they were after as they searched through these papers. Randi wondered whether they really wanted anything at all, or if this was just some sort of warning.

✣   ✣   ✣

A short time later Walker knocked on the door and Randi let him in. Kovacevic and the forensic team were right behind.

"You all right?" Walker asked.

She nodded.

"Good." Walker quickly reviewed the scene. "You touch anything?"

"Nothing but the doorknob," she said. "Uh, except my chair. I moved it back to the desk. And the one file I picked up from the floor."

"Good," he repeated, then barked some orders to his men. They immediately set about dusting for fingerprints, taking photographs and marking various papers for identification. When Walker turned back to Randi, he saw the concern in her soft brown eyes. "Stratford called, he told me you had some letters to show me."

Randi nodded, then led him to her desk and the two typewritten pages. "Here they are. Maybe I shouldn't touch them again?"

"Too late now. You had to pick them up to read them the first time, right?" Walker pulled a handkerchief from his pocket and lifted the letters off the desk. "No sense in putting my prints on there too." He looked them over, then directed Kovacevic to place each in a separate clear cover.

As the other officers pulled on their latex gloves and went about their work, Stratford arrived. Walker watched with some interest as he hugged Randi and she teared up, for a moment seeming as if she might cry.

"It'll be all right," Stratford assured her, giving her a pat on the back and then turning to Walker. "I'm Bob Stratford," he said. "I had other ideas about how we would meet for the first time."

"So did I," Walker agreed.

Stratford said, "I'm curious to see these notes."

Walker pointed to them. They were on the desk, now encased in plastic.

Stratford read them, then turned to Randi. "Tell the detective whatever you know about these."

Randi explained how she discovered the letters under her door. Remembering the envelopes, Randi pointed to them and Walker also had those placed in a clear sleeve. "I got this first note Wednesday morning. I found the second on Thursday morning," she admitted with a hint of embarrassment, refusing to meet Walker's disapproving gaze. He remembered picking it up when he came to meet her that day.

"I guess you'll find my fingerprints on the envelope," he told Kovacevic, then added, "I'll explain later." Turning back to Randi, he said, "Go on."

"You asked if I touched anything. This one file was right there," she said, pointing down, "there on the floor. I picked it up and put it back together, sorry. That's all I touched, I think. Except for the telephone."

"And the doorknob and the chair," Walker reminded her.

"Right."

"Are you sure that's it?"

Randi nodded.

"Can I see that?" Walker gestured to the Gorman file.

Randi looked to Stratford, then said, "I don't mind if you want to look for fingerprints or something. Reading a patient file is another matter."

"Let him see it," Stratford said.

She reluctantly passed the manila folder to Walker, who accepted it with handkerchief in hand. He and Stratford sat down, side by side in the two armchairs, and began skimming the information together, page by page.

"The data sheet is on the left," Randi said. "Why do you need to read my notes?"

Walker looked up at her. "We have a murder, two anonymous letters, a threatening phone call and now a burglary." He saw her expression and said, "Breaking into your office and vandalizing it is a felony."

"How can reading that file help?" Randi asked.

"Maybe Paul Gorman knew Elizabeth Knoebel and you have a note in here about that."

Randi shook her head.

"Okay, maybe not, but you get the idea."

"Paul Gorman had no connection to Elizabeth. Not that I know of, anyway, so there couldn't be anything in my notes."

"Wasn't his wife in the group with Elizabeth Knoebel?" Walker reminded her.

Randi nodded. "And he's in the group with Doctor Knoebel."

"There may be something else they were looking for, something less obvious."

"Whatever," she replied helplessly as the two men returned their attention to Gorman's records.

When he finished his preliminary read-through, Walker looked up. "Since we're speaking of your patients, it might interest you two to know that Doctor Knoebel hired a high-priced lawyer in New York, not to mention a fancy Park Avenue psychiatrist." He leaned back and had a good look at Randi. "Any comment?"

Randi turned from Walker to Stratford, then back to the detective. She said nothing.

"Who's the lawyer?" Stratford asked.

"Roger Bennett. Know him?"

"Rings a bell," Stratford said. "I can check him out if you like."

"That'd be helpful." Walker turned back to Randi. "I know you haven't had much of a chance to look, but does it appear anything is missing? Something obvious maybe?"

"No," she said. "Not that I can tell."

"Uh huh."

"What a nightmare," she said.

Stratford nodded. "You're right, Randi, it is. But if the woman's murderer is the same person who left you these notes and burglarized your office, Detective Walker needs to know what information the killer has taken." He paused, then had a serious look at his friend. "Your safety has just become a major issue."

Before she could respond, Walker looked up from Paul Gorman's file. "I couldn't agree more," he told her.

CHAPTER 35

The police spent most of the morning scouring Randi's office, looking for anything that might help them determine who broke in and trashed her records. They dusted for prints throughout her office and looked for anything that might be helpful in and out of the building. They searched for marks on the carpet in the corridor and surveyed the parking lot out back.

But they found nothing.

Randi watched the technicians who went through her papers. As she told Stratford and Walker, it was one thing to search for evidence, but quite another to allow them to read through confidential patient files. She hovered over them like an eagle protecting her flock.

When the forensic team was finally done they told her she could begin the thankless task of putting her records back together. They had snapped enough photographs and collected a sufficient number of exhibits. Now it was up to her to make sense of things and determine what, if anything, was missing.

By the time Stanley Knoebel arrived at her office for their late-morning appointment, she had just begun the reconstruction. When he knocked at her door, Randi did not let him see the disaster her private office had become, instead steering him into the room where her groups met. When he sat down she had a fleeting thought that his rigid bearing was actually better suited to these straight-backed chairs of cane and chrome than the comfortable sofa inside.

For his part, Knoebel did not ask why he had been relegated to this antiseptic meeting place. It was clear from the start that he had little interest in being here and wanted to have done with this meeting as quickly as possible. "When you called yesterday and asked to see me, I felt I owed you the professional courtesy of this final visit," Knoebel announced with his customary formality. "I should tell you that I won't be coming to see you or your group again. I have begun seeing a psychiatrist affiliated with my hospital in New York."

"So I understand."

This appeared to amuse him. "And how might you have come to learn confidential information about my medical treatment, Doctor Conway?"

Randi could not believe her blunder at revealing what Walker had just told her that morning. A very rough day was becoming worse. "It's not important."

"Indeed. Well let me hazard a guess. Could it be that you learned it from our local constable, Detective Walker?"

Randi folded her arms across her chest and clutched her elbows in her hands. "It's not important."

Knoebel's chilly smile remained frozen on his lips. "Was it also your friend Detective Walker who suggested that you call me to arrange this meeting?"

"No, of course not."

"Of course not," he repeated with an extravagant show of skepticism.

"You're my patient," Randi said. "At least you have been up to now."

"Of course." His Eastern European affect seemed more imperious than usual today. "My attorney advised the police that they are no longer authorized to contact me without him being present. Are you aware of that?"

"What?"

"Is this meeting an attempt to circumvent that directive by having you interview me on their behalf?"

"I have no idea what your attorney said to the police. I asked you here because I've been your therapist and I felt, under the circumstances, we should meet."

Knoebel leveled his cold stare at her again. "But you admit you have been speaking with the police."

"Naturally. Detective Walker wants to find Elizabeth's murderer and he wants my help. I've told him that the discussions I have with my patients are confidential."

"Oh, excellent," Knoebel said. "Apparently we all want the same thing. We all want our rights protected."

Now it was Randi's turn to stare at him. "Shouldn't we also want the truth?"

"Do you, Doctor Conway?"

"I do."

Knoebel nodded his head slowly, watching her. "I'm not so sure."

"Why would you say such a thing?"

"There is much about Elizabeth none of us ever wanted to know." He paused before adding, "She inspired such hatred," then seemed to let the thought go.

"She inspired enough hatred for someone to murder her."

The statement roused him from his brief melancholy. "I've met Detective Walker and I must say, you're beginning to sound a bit like him." Knoebel folded his arms across his chest, showing that he, too, was capable of striking a pose. "So, who hated Elizabeth enough to murder her?" He sighed, as if the matter were too troublesome to consider. "Everyone and no one, I suppose. My wife had a great facility for drawing out the worst in people, as you well know. Homicide is quite another matter, and far beyond my comprehension." He paused. "Perhaps you're in a position to guess the identity of her murderer."

The suggestion caused her an imperceptible shudder. "I'm not sure that I can. But I think I can guess at your frustration and upset."

"Really? I'm not sure I believe that."

"What *do* you believe?"

He thought it over. "I believe you had a reasonable appreciation of how miserable our marriage was."

"I'm not sure I ever understood your marriage, certainly not from your perspective. To be candid, I really don't think I ever came to know you at all." Randi allowed herself a smile. "I think you're the only patient I've ever addressed by last name after spending so much time together. It's probably best that you'll be seeing someone else."

Knoebel nodded. "That may be," he said, appearing to think it over. "Unfortunately, whomever I see will not have had the benefit of knowing Elizabeth." That thought quieted him for a moment. Then he said, "My wife and I loved each other in a totally destructive way. We actually hated each other more effectively than we loved each other. Surely you saw that."

"I saw two people who were more comfortable with bitterness than with tenderness."

"Perhaps."

"Is that what kept you together?"

"A bond of hatred, you mean?"

"I'm not sure what I mean," Randi admitted. "There was so much hostility between the two of you, yet neither of you ever wanted to deal with it."

Knoebel rubbed the inside corners of his eyes with the thumb and forefinger of his left hand. "Did you know my wife was sleeping with some of your other patients?" He posed the question as if this were some tiresome piece of business he simply had to get out of the way.

"Whether I knew such a thing or not," Randi replied evenly, "I would not be at liberty to say."

"You knew, didn't you?"

"I'm sorry, but your wife's confidences survive her death. Even in speaking with you."

"Were you sleeping with her?"

Randi drew a deep breath. "Why would you think such a thing?"

"I didn't say I thought it, I was merely asking."

Randi offered a blank look in response.

"Did she ever ask you?"

Randi hesitated, then said, "Your wife was an extremely flirtatious woman. When she wasn't dealing with her anger, she traded on her beauty and her sensuality to manipulate men. And women. There's no reason to believe she amended her behavior in a clinical setting."

The immediacy of that concept hit Knoebel hard, knowing that Elizabeth had talked with Randi, revealing things about him, herself, perhaps her other lovers. "Did you know she was keeping a diary of her exploits?"

This time Randi was determined not to betray Walker. "Again, whether I knew such a thing or not is of no consequence. I think you are the person we should be talking about, not Elizabeth."

With a sudden flash of anger, Knoebel said, "We are talking about me, don't you see?" It was the first time Randi had ever heard him raise his voice. "She was the biggest part of me, everything she did, all the pain we inflicted upon one another, every moment we lived, whether separate or apart. What else is there for me to speak of? My medical practice? My own infidelity? Is that what you want to hear about, Doctor Conway?" He shook his head. "It's too late for that. The game is over."

"The *game*?" It was Elizabeth's word.

Knoebel rose from his chair and Randi flinched as he stood, realizing in that instant that she was not really sure who he was or what he might be capable of doing. "You simply did not understand Elizabeth," he said angrily as he glared down at her.

"I suppose not," she replied, trying not to reveal her anxiety as he stood over her.

Knoebel took a deep breath, attempting to calm himself. "Probably because she never meant you to," he said, then nodded to himself. "Or perhaps you simply never fell into her trap, not completely, and that is very much to your credit."

It was clear that Knoebel was not about to sit down again, so Randi got to her feet. "It appears that you and I are left to protect her secrets," she said.

"Are we?"

"You said so yourself," Randi told him.

He responded with a sad nod, as if this came as a relief. "Perhaps you are right."

Randi drew a deep breath. "Is that why you wrote those notes to me? Was that part of the 'game,' as you call it?"

His blank look in response seemed as genuine as anything he had ever said to her. "What notes?"

"Never mind," she said, shaking away the thought of the two type-written slips of paper the police had taken with them. Instead she found herself wanting to ask him about the diary, but she knew she must not.

Knoebel saw the conflict in her eyes. He said, "This part of the drama is not done. You realize that, don't you?"

"What isn't done?"

She waited for an answer, but Knoebel gave none. He formally offered his hand and she took it. "Good-bye," was all he said. They shook, his grip firm, but his hand was much colder than she had expected. Then he turned and was gone.

CHAPTER 36

Mitchell Avery was on his way home from the airport, and he was worried.

He had not been able to reach Joan since he arrived in Miami. That was the last time they had spoken. Her tone seemed more distant than usual, even cold, but he had not asked why. He was not in the mood to have an argument over the telephone. He was in Florida to have fun.

Yesterday he telephoned the house several times. No one answered, and the voice mail system had been turned off. He tried her cell phone, but got nothing. So this morning, as he rode in the back of the taxicab, he was worried. Joan must have suspected something. She must have discovered he was in Florida.

Isn't that perfect? he asked himself. He had not spoken to his wife or children for two days, had no idea where they were, but his first thought was not about their safety, it was about whether she had found him out. He shook his head, knowing what she would say if she could hear his thoughts right now.

"In the end it's all about you, Mitchell." *That's exactly what you would say, right Joan?*

He tried to shake it off. At the moment, he just wanted to know where they were.

The taxi pulled in to the semicircular driveway of their large colonial. He took great pride in the place, always pleased to come home, to have others know that this grand home belonged to him.

This morning he had no such feeling.

He paid the driver, slid his bag off the back seat and hurried to the front door as the cab drove away. Things were unusually still.

He tried the polished brass knob, but the door was locked. He rang the bell and listened to the chimes as they echoed inside. There was no answer. He dropped his bag and made his way to the kitchen door around the side. That door was also locked. He cupped his hands around his eyes and placed his face to the glass.

No one was there.

He went to the end of the driveway, where they kept a spare key hidden beneath the mailbox in a magnetic holder. He found it and let himself in the front door.

"Joan," he called out. "Joan, I'm home."

There was no response.

He left his bag in the foyer and took the stairs two at a time, heading up to the master bedroom. Everything looked as it always did. Until he noticed the blank space on one of the walls.

Joan's favorite painting had hung there. A small oil of no great value, a Paris café scene at the turn of the century. A man in a wide-brimmed hat, sitting at an outdoor table, bent over a sketchpad, oblivious to the activity behind him. She loved that painting.

It was gone.

Instinct led him to her walk-in closet, knowing what he would find when he flung the door open. It was empty. Only hangers remained, some suspended naked and askew on the long, wooden rods, others having spilled to the floor, lying in a mangled heap.

He went to his own closet and opened the door. Everything was just as he had left it.

Mitchell ran down the hall to his children's rooms. As he went from one to the other, he found that some of the clothing had been removed—their closets had not been emptied in the same dramatic style as Joan had done with hers. He noticed that all of the beds were made. Everything else appeared to be in its proper place, just as if they would be returning at any moment.

But he knew they would not.

The silence in the house was numbing as he went down to the kitchen, looking for something, some sort of explanation. That would be the place for it, of course, that's where they left messages for each other.

An envelope with his name printed on it was taped to the refrigerator door. He pulled it down and tore it open. The note was in her handwriting.

Dear Mitchell,

I hope you enjoyed yourself. Unfortunately, you will finally learn that the cost of selfishness is high.

Joan

When he placed the envelope down, Joan's gold wedding band fell out. He watched as it rolled across the granite countertop, onto the floor, and bounced two or three times on the ceramic tiles before coming to rest at his feet. He slowly bent to pick it up, held it in his hand, then carefully studied it as if it were something he had never seen before.

She must be at her sister's place, he told himself. He would start making phone calls. She probably had a lawyer by now. He wondered if he should call his own lawyer first.

Then he turned back to the refrigerator. It was not yet noon, but a beer seemed like a good idea while he figured things out.

He pulled the door open, flooding the room with an awful, sour smell. He looked inside and saw that Joan had emptied the refrigerator, unplugged it, and left a half-gallon carton of milk, open, to spoil within.

Avery began to laugh out loud, but there was no merriment in the sound.

He sat on a stool at the counter and continued laughing, the refrigerator door still open, the nauseating odor of rotten milk permeating the entire kitchen. He laughed so hard his whole body began to shake until he could not distinguish between amusement and sorrow, between his own heartbreak and the anguish he knew he had caused her. He continued to sit there, his body beginning to shudder, feeling more alone than he had ever felt in his life.

CHAPTER 37

The anonymous notes had concerned Randi, but they had not really frightened her. In her profession this sort of communication was not uncommon, nor were telephone messages from patients disguising their voices, or unattributed gifts.

The trashing of her office was another matter entirely.

Now, after confronting Stanley Knoebel, her concerns had only grown.

As Walker's men went off to assemble their clues and Stratford worked to protect her legal rights, she decided it was time for her to seek the guidance of a man she had trusted for nearly two decades. She made a call, canceled her afternoon appointments, got in her car and drove more than three hours west, to the university where they had first met.

For as long as Randi Conway had known him, from their very first faculty-student conference all those years ago, Leonard Rubenfeld maintained his office in a constant state of purposeful chaos. Folders, forms, periodicals and books were haphazardly piled everywhere, documents were scattered about, and the place looked as if it hadn't been dusted in years.

She stood in the open doorway for a moment, watching as he pored over some papers, feeling the urge to rush over and hug him. But she hesitated, knowing how the professor felt about physical displays of affection. When he finally looked up from his work, his rumpled face broke into a wide grin. Then he stood and, as Randi approached with her arms outstretched, he grudgingly allowed her to wrap him in a warm embrace.

"All right," he said as he backed away, "are we all done with that now?"

Rubenfeld was several inches shorter than Randi, his paunchy physique earned from endless hours hunched over a desk. His nose was a touch too large, his mouth a touch too small, and he was almost completely bald, the few surviving wisps of hair giving him something of a monastic look. He had a weak left eye that regularly floated off to the side, making any effort to meet his gaze through his thick-lensed glasses a virtual impossibility.

As she took a step back Randi saw that he appeared much older than the last time they met. They kept in touch over the years, occasionally speaking on the telephone, running into each other at professional conferences, exchanging e-mails and articles and so forth. Still, it was sad for her to see how he had aged.

He waved her toward one of the two old-fashioned leather armchairs in front of the cluttered bookcases that lined the walls of the musty old room. They exchanged some pleasantries but Rubenfeld, in his brusque manner, soon cut that short. "I was happy to get your call, but you didn't come all this way to make small talk. Let's begin with the headlines, shall we?"

"I've got a few issues," she told him.

Rubenfeld removed his tortoise-shell glasses and wiped them with a crumpled tissue he found amidst the papers and books on his untidy desk. He studied her for a moment, then replaced the smudged spectacles and made an impatient wave of his hand. He was exceptionally fond of hand signals. "Go," he said.

"First, one of my female patients was murdered a week ago." She gave him the headlines, as he would say.

"I actually read something about it when I saw it was in your part of the world. Didn't have any idea she was one of yours. Tell me everything."

Randi did, including the involvement of Anthony Walker, the discovery of Elizabeth's diary, the anonymous notes and the vandalism of her office.

"Hmmm. I certainly didn't read anything about a diary," he said, zeroing in on the key piece of information.

"It's not public knowledge yet, but based on what she wrote, the police believe she had affairs with some of my male patients, husbands of the other women in her group."

"Is it true?"

Randi sighed. "I think it is."

"Nice girl," the professor observed with a frown.

"I also believe she had a brief sexual relationship with at least one of my female patients." Here Randi paused again. "A woman I introduced her to."

Rubenfeld nodded solemnly without comment.

"The other woman had an extremely difficult background. She was an abused child of an alcoholic father. Then she was an abused wife."

He shook his head. "Abused child becomes abused wife. Textbook stuff." Rubenfeld was well respected in his profession—an academic who had forsaken private practice and lucrative offers to write pop psychology manuals, choosing to remain at the university, conducting his classes, engaging in research, issuing scholarly papers and maintaining the purity of his intellectual purpose. It was a rewarding position, leaving him free to pursue anything that piqued his interest. "So now we have two victims, so to speak."

"Not that simple. This other woman was not only a victim."

He responded with one of his lopsided looks, but said nothing.

"Several years ago, in the midst of an attack by her husband, she stabbed him with a kitchen knife. Spent five years in a psychiatric facility."

"Killed the sonuvabitch. Good."

"No. He didn't die."

"Just ventilated him for a while, eh?" He made a slashing motion through the air with his right hand.

"I guess you could say that."

"And you figure Lizzie Borden might be the one who did in Madame Bovary?"

Randi shook her head. "No, I don't."

"All right, what about these men she was sleeping with. You know who they were?"

"I have a suspicion about who three of them were."

"Only three, eh? And is this just a suspicion?"

"None of them ever admitted it to me outright. One of them is a patient I don't feel I know all that well, I only see him in group, but he made some comments to me a while back. And Elizabeth said things. Nothing specific . . ."

"Have you asked any of them about her? Since this Elizabeth woman was killed, I mean."

"Not directly."

Rubenfeld leaned forward, now peering at Randi over the top of his glasses. "This isn't one of those 'I've got a friend with a problem' deals, is it?"

"No, no, no. Of course not."

"You weren't drawn into this little web yourself, were you?"

She did her best to meet his off-kilter gaze and said, "No." She replied to his dubious look by saying, "I would tell you."

"But she took a run at you, am I right?"

Randi sat back. "Yes," she admitted.

"All right," he said with another wave of his hand, "go on."

"The police want me to cooperate with their investigation. If they have it their way I'd tell them everything I know about each of my patients, just on the chance it might help them solve the murder."

"And this is only topic number one?"

"Yes."

"What's next, world peace?"

Randi managed a wan smile. "No. The next two subjects are my personal life and my future as a practitioner."

Rubenfeld started to laugh so hard he doubled over and began coughing. "You really are some piece of work, you know that?" He rubbed the palm of his hand across the top of his mostly bald pate. "Well, I don't have a class until day after tomorrow. Maybe if we talk until then we can make some headway."

She watched as Rubenfeld lit his pipe. It was part of an age-old routine. He would light it, take a single puff, then ignore it as it went cold again.

"Let's start with the ethics problem," he said as he exhaled a small amber cloud of smoke. "Honoring the confidences of your patients is more than a matter of your personal integrity, it is an absolute obligation."

"I understand that. But this is murder."

"And murder is a terrible thing. But so is forcible incest. Spousal abuse. Molestation. Where do you draw the line on where you're allowed to betray these confidences? Will you reveal the confidences of a murderer but protect a sodomizer of children? How about an adulterer who contracts HIV and may infect a spouse?"

"I understand the issue."

"Oh, good. Do you also understand the difference between someone threatening to commit a heinous act and someone who confesses a horrible deed that is already done? And, by the way, who gets to make these moral judgments? You? Who the hell died and left you in charge? A secret is a secret, a confidence is a confidence. There is no ambiguity here, it's black and white." He struck another match. "Unless you're being warned about a crime that is about to be committed, you have no right to share these secrets with anyone. That leaves you with the problem of how to protect your patients, your practice and, by the way, yourself." He lit the tobacco remaining in his pipe, then blew out the match just as it was about to burn his fingers. "But you've omitted one critical piece of information." He stared at his former student through his thick lenses. "Do you actually know who murdered this woman?"

Randi Conway stared back at him, this man she respected and trusted more than any she had ever known. "I'm not sure," she said. "I'm afraid that I might not be seeing things I should."

"The abused woman who stabbed her husband, for instance?"

Randi nodded. "For instance."

"You simply can't bring yourself to believe she'd be capable of murdering this Elizabeth, eh?"

"No."

"Of course not," Rubenfeld responded with a rheumatic chuckle as his pipe went out again. He drew on it, saw it was dead, then tossed it on his desk, cold ashes flying out of the bowl, scattering among the others already strewn amidst the clutter. "No decent therapist wants to believe a patient is capable of a horrible deed like murder. Before therapy, fine, that's perfect. They had problems, that's why they came to see you in the first place. Or worst case, they do something terrible after your therapy is completed, when they're not your patient anymore. Not so terrific, but what the hell, she was beyond your influence, you can forgive yourself. But doing something terrible while a patient is still in your care? That's the ultimate proof you've failed, you've cocked it up completely, you're an imbecile and that's that. Am I right?" When she hesitated, he said, "Of course I'm right."

"I see your point, but I still don't believe she's the murderer."

"Fine," the professor responded with a dismissive flick of his wrist, "that's good enough for me. We've decided this woman is not guilty. So who's the next suspect? Let's get back to all the men this Elizabeth was screwing. Any of them you don't like?"

Randi shook her head.

"What about the husband? Don't the police think it was the husband? You're telling me the woman was cheating on him all over town, right?"

"The police say he had an alibi."

"Ah, an alibi." He rolled that one again on his tongue. "An alibi. Good, now we can start talking like TV show detectives. Alibi," he repeated derisively. "Forget the alibi. Give him the third degree. Work him over. Throw the book at him."

Randi tried to force a smile, but Rubenfeld waved it off.

"Don't humor me," he told her. "Tell me who else you aren't looking at."

"I really don't know."

"Yourself?"

"Me?"

"Hey, don't look so upset, I don't mean that you murdered this woman. I mean you were never any good at looking at yourself. That's why I was always so concerned about you. You've always avoided your own feelings. You lose yourself in your work, you hide behind the problems of these strangers you treat."

She wanted to say something, but just stared at him dumbly.

"What about this policeman you mentioned?"

"What about him?"

"When you started telling me this saga, you mentioned your personal life. The way you talked about him, I was wondering..."

"Detective Walker," Randi interrupted, as if stating his name would explain something.

"Is that what you call him, 'Detective Walker'? How intimate."

This time Randi could not help but laugh. "We're not intimate. And sometimes I call him Anthony."

"Ah, now we *are* getting someplace."

"I thought you wanted to discuss who might have murdered Elizabeth."

"Is that what you thought, that I'm interested in solving a murder? Not my line of work, young lady. My only interest here is you."

She stared at him.

"All right, all right. Let's get back to these guys who slept with this Elizabeth. The men you know about."

Randi shook her head slowly. "They're patients. One of them I don't see privately, only in group. I don't feel I know him very well."

"So you said," Rubenfeld reminded her impatiently. "Tell me, Randi, do you think I'm not listening or am I starting to look a touch senile?"

She sighed.

"So then," Rubenfeld announced triumphantly, "the man you don't know very well, he must be the murderer, because you had the least influence on him. It's obvious, no?"

She lowered her head and looked at him with a disapproving grimace.

"Fine," Rubenfeld said, announcing his willingness to abandon criticism for the moment. "First you have to be honest with yourself, which, as I've said, is not your long suit. If you really don't know anything specific that would identify the murderer, you have no right to disclose a random selection of secrets you've learned from your patients just so the police can pick through them to make their own misguided judgments. If there is something concrete, if you have direct information that could help solve the case, that's when the true dilemma arises."

Randi nodded obediently. "And then what?"

"The police can compel your testimony in a murder case. You know that of course."

"They've threatened that more than once."

"But they haven't done anything about it yet."

"No."

"How interesting." He appeared pleased. "It sounds like your friend Detective Anthony Walker may have more interest in protecting you than in finding a killer."

The look she gave him said she had already wondered about that herself. "I do know that Anthony is concerned I'm in harm's way. With the discovery of Elizabeth's diary, I may be the best person to piece everything together and figure out who killed her. If the murderer finds out about the diary, well, you see where it goes from there."

Rubenfeld scowled at her. "Of course I see, what am I now, a moron?" He thought it over for a moment. "But you said the diary is not public knowledge. We don't know that the murderer is even aware it exists."

She shook her head.

"Well hopefully he never does. Or she, eh?" Rubenfeld studied his protégé for a moment, then picked up his pipe and looked inside the bowl. There was still some tobacco remaining, which he tamped down with his forefinger. He lit another match and fired it up. "In the meantime it sounds to me like this policeman is protecting you. That's a good thing."

"Yes," she said. "I've come to realize that."

"Look, I know this has you worried about your future as a practitioner, but you shouldn't be, it will all work out." He smiled at her. "You always worried too much, you know that? You're bright. You're capable. You care. Maybe you care too much. I hope it's your worst sin as a therapist."

"You're right," she agreed as she watched him inhale some smoke and then blow it out slowly.

"You said you wanted to discuss your love life. What about it?"

"I wish I had an answer for you."

"An answer for me? How about an answer for yourself?" He gave a wistful shrug of his shoulders. "Still playing hide-and-seek with your emotions, just like when you were a student." He took another pull at the pipe, which was still yielding some smoke. "You're a beautiful woman, full of intelligence and life and compassion. And how do you live? Like you're trapped inside yourself, waiting to be rescued."

She nodded slowly, her soft brown eyes sad, yet willing to hear what he had to say.

"This detective. He's interested in you, surely you see that."

"I think so. At least I believe he's trying to protect me."

"Well that stands for something, doesn't it?"

"We're so completely different, he and I. He's difficult and he's tough and he's got issues."

"Ah, how terrible that must be for a young woman in search of perfection." He chuckled, emitting a small gray cloud in the process. "Perfection is a death wish, Randi, a guaranty of failure. People are not perfect. Love is not perfect. And, if you ever stopped to think about it, perfect is boring. People are always looking for something new, something better, something different, something that will make things *oh so perfect*." He raised his eyebrows and gawked at her once more from above the rim of his glasses. "Then again, most people are nincompoops." He laughed again. "Life can never be perfect, that's what makes it wonderful. It's a landscape that never stays the same, with beautiful sunrises and sunsets and everything that can possibly happen in between. So what do people do? They look for the never-changing horizon. Eternal youth. Young skin, hard bodies, images from fashion magazines and pin-up posters. Photographs of models. False idols. They want immediate gratification, as if that's where they'll find romance and excitement. They don't want to deal with truth, with history, with the realities of life. Sadness, pain, love, hurt, joy, all of the wonderful passions that make life worth living. No, they'd rather be lied to," he said, his voice rising. "What complete rubbish! All they end up with is disappointment, and then they want to know why they're miserable. They don't understand, and obviously neither do you."

"Maybe I don't."

"Well then, I'll tell you the secret. But you remember what I'm saying now, and I hope for your sake I never have to say it again." He leaned forward and looked at Randi with an intense gaze that for this one time did not waver. "Life is about taking risks. Risks of the heart, risks of the mind, risks of the soul. You take chances and you find relationships, you find yourself, you find the truth. All the rest of it is false, and the people who refuse to take those chances are cowards. They deserve the small, pathetic, unfulfilled lives they earn for themselves." He sat back. "You should know all this by now, but I realize sometimes you have to hear it again because sometimes you're a nitwit, so I have to remind you. Like I have to remind you to call me more often, eh? So come on, let's go through your laundry list of problems again. If I can't straighten out your personal life in one afternoon, maybe I can help you solve a murder."

CHAPTER 38

When Walker and Stratford parted ways at Randi Conway's office that morning, they agreed to keep their date to meet at the end of the day for drinks. The forensics team would have some time to study whatever they gathered from the invasion into Randi's files, and they would have an opportunity, as Walker suggested, to kick some theories around.

They met at Stratford's country club. It was an exclusive place, and Walker admitted to his host that he had never seen the inside before.

"A lot of things in this town are simply a function of how long you've been here," Stratford said, even though both men knew the truth was more complicated than that.

Walker responded with a knowing grin.

They were seated at a small table in the far corner of the dark grill room, overlooking the golf course. It was a quiet weekday night, giving them an opportunity for a private discussion.

After Stratford ordered their drinks he began tossing out some ideas. Walker listened politely, then offered his own view.

"Let's say I discover someone was having an affair with Elizabeth Knoebel and I figure out who it was. Let's also say I do this without Doctor Conway's help." He took a sip of his Jack Daniel's. "Now, what if this guy wasn't the murderer, but he's concerned that the world might find out he was doing the dirty deed with the late Mrs. Knoebel?"

Stratford nodded thoughtfully. "Based on what Gill told me about this journal, it's a fair assumption that Mrs. Knoebel was having at least one affair. Maybe more. But that doesn't get us any closer to the murderer, assuming your hypothetical adulterer was not the killer."

"Agreed," Walker said. "But what if this guy knows something about her death? And what if he's keeping quiet to maintain the peace on his own home front? Now I come along with enough information to finger him as the dead woman's lover. Not a very happy result for him."

"Makes sense."

"And what does this mystery man know about the murder?"

"Not important, let's just stay with the theory."

Stratford was listening.

"The closer I get to identifying this guy with the information, the more dangerous this guy becomes for the killer. And," Walker added as he stared at the lawyer, "the more dangerous it becomes for Randi Conway." He waited for a reaction, but Stratford gave none. "So, let's take the boyfriend first. The shooter has no way to be certain this guy actually knows anything that might help us solve the case. Still, the more I push, the more anxious the killer becomes. Then there's Doctor Conway, who remains the X factor. Who can be certain what she knows about Elizabeth, or what she's willing to say? It might make sense to get her out of the way. Or maybe it's worth it for the killer to take them both out. He pulled the trigger once, maybe he can do it again."

"You keep referring to the killer as 'he.'"

Walker smiled. "Point taken. It's just a theory, at least for now."

Stratford sipped his martini as he thought it over. "The theory's a bit far-fetched, don't you think? For starters, how does the killer even know about the boyfriend? And suppose he does, why would the murderer think they can identify him? Or her."

"Remember—it's likely our murderer was the one who went through Randi Conway's files last night, maybe made a guess who Mrs. Knoebel's boyfriend was, then spread the rest of the papers around so we wouldn't know what or who he was looking for. I should also admit to you, strictly off the record, we may have a lead that supports my theory."

Stratford leaned forward. "Now that is interesting."

"Let's stay with the danger to Doctor Conway, a more obvious issue. The murderer has no way of knowing whether she had information from the Knoebel woman that could help solve the case, or if she may start spilling it to the police."

Stratford swallowed some more of his gin. "Anyone ever tell you that you sound like an Alan Ladd movie?"

"I love those old flicks."

"Me too."

"I thought I was more in the Dick Powell style."

"Maybe. Definitely not Bogart, though."

"I agree. Anybody tries to do Bogie, they wind up sounding like an asshole."

Stratford picked a piece of white lint off his navy blazer. "What if it turns out that the boyfriend *was* the killer, have you considered that?"

"Sure, but so far the facts don't fit that result. A timing issue."

"A timing issue?"

"Strictly off the record again?"

Stratford held up three fingers. "Scout's honor."

"Okay." Walker paused for proper effect. "We can place a car at the Knoebel house on the afternoon of the murder."

"What does that mean?"

"Not sure yet."

"I assume this car is not owned by the Knoebels."

Walker nodded. "Correct. But we may have figured out who did own it."

"That so?"

"Uh huh," Walker said. "Here's another interesting tidbit. We found scratch marks on Elizabeth Knoebel's neck. The coroner says they were made only a day or so before she was killed, consistent with some sort of scuffle. We're trying to determine who Mrs. Knoebel might have tangled with."

"That could be extremely interesting."

"We may also have another angle. Someone with a troubled past might come into play here."

"A troubled past?"

"As in violent," Walker said, then had another drink of his whisky.

"Again, interesting. But you haven't even mentioned Elizabeth Knoebel's husband."

"The most obvious candidate."

"What do you think about him?"

"Not sure what I think about him, to be honest. At the moment he has an alibi."

"At the moment?"

"Something we're still checking out."

"I see."

"So, let's get to the real point of this cozy little get-together. Is your friend going to get into this with us, or is she going to keep floating out there like a sitting duck on a deep pond?"

"Somehow I don't see those as her only two options."

"You do recognize the risk she faces?"

"I do," Stratford said.

"That's a start."

They were quiet for a moment, then Stratford said, "I understand you're not married."

"No."

"Divorced?"

"Totally." Walker waited, but there weren't any other questions coming along that line. "You're married."

"I am."

"But you didn't say happily."

Stratford smiled. "Blissfully."

"Blissfully is good."

"It is. My wife is an extraordinary person."

"You're a lucky man, then."

"I take it you weren't."

"Let's just say I hope to do better next time."

There was another pause, then Stratford said, "Let's get back to this someone with the violent past."

Walker shook his head. "Not yet." He took one more swallow of whisky. "First I want to know what you're going to do to get Randi Conway talking. Then you and I can really get to work on this jigsaw puzzle."

CHAPTER 39

Randi Conway arrived at her building early Wednesday morning, walked upstairs, unlocked the door to her small suite and found the office in the same awful condition she left it the day before.

She realized, with a sense of bemused disappointment, she had an irrational hope her papers might have been miraculously replaced, or that the intrusion was no more than a passing nightmare. Instead she was obliged to spend another frustrating hour organizing things into several neat piles before she met her first patient of the day.

As she worked to put her files back together, she considered everything she had been forced to confront yesterday under Professor Rubenfeld's relentless inquisition. He helped her see past some of the emotional barricades she relied on, the obstacles she placed in the way of awareness, understanding, and even passion. In some ways he made her feel like she was once again his undergraduate student, and there was nothing flattering in that.

All the same, he had somehow filled her with the sense that—as he told her more than once—things were going to work out.

This morning, after she had enough of collating documents, she went to her desk and prepared to meet with Phyllis Wentworth. These private sessions with Phyllis were usually painful excursions into frustration and sorrow, but this morning Randi was glad to get back to work. She also felt some satisfaction from the knowledge that Phyllis relished the chance to complain, to become irate and to sometimes simply cry her heart out. This was a place where she could indulge the emotions she would never allow herself at home.

"'Having sex,' Fred calls it. 'People have sex,' he says. He makes it sound so antiseptic." Phyllis shook her head. "He makes it sound like a fast-food order. 'I'll have a cheeseburger, some sex and large fries.' I want to make love, Doctor Conway. Do you see?" The level of her anger was already rising. "There, I said it. And you know what the worst of it is?"

Dr. Conway offered a suitably curious look.

"At this point, even if he said he just wanted to have sex I'd say yes. Yes, I'll have sex. I'll have plenty of sex. But he won't let me touch him. He doesn't touch me and he won't let me near him. There's no affection, there's no love at all." And then she began to cry. "Women like me, we were brought up without any real goals." She took the tissue Randi held out for her. "Today it's different," she said between sobs. "Women today are smarter. They grow up with ideas and dreams. They have careers. Ambitions. But that's not how I was raised. Girls today are raised like men. It was different for us. We had no life plan. We were taught to live day-to-day. See that the kids are happy. See that your husband is happy." She looked up. "Was there something wrong with that? Did I waste my life?" she asked, but she was not waiting for an answer. "What are we supposed to do, all of us discarded, used-up women? Wither and die? Have plastic surgery and pretend we're twenty-five years old?" She suddenly looked as though she wanted to hit something, or someone.

"You're raising a few different issues, Phyllis, but that's fine. Let it all out and then we'll look at each item, one at a time."

Phyllis uttered a bitter laugh. "You want to look at something, Doctor? Look at tennis balls."

"I'm sorry?"

"I'm telling you, you'll be a wealthy woman if you can figure out what to do with used tennis balls. I play in a doubles league, and after we're finished playing we leave the balls on the court or drop them in the basket for the pro."

Randi nodded.

"Someone hits them a few more times, but eventually they run out of air and what can you do with them?"

Randi waited for the punch line.

"Nothing," Phyllis announced. "They're useless. They're not even biodegradable. They're a blight on the land. Are you following me?"

"I think so."

"If you can figure out what to do with used tennis balls you'll be rich. Then you can figure out what to do with all the used-up, middle-aged women after we've been bounced around until no one wants us anymore. You'll probably win the Nobel Prize."

Randi permitted herself a restrained laugh. "You know, Phyllis, it never fails to amaze me how different you are in our private talks. You never say anything like this in group."

Phyllis nodded, busily wiping away the latest round of tears. "I need this time with you," she admitted simply. "More than you know."

"Why don't we talk about that a little bit?"

"All right." She had no idea what she was agreeing to discuss, but she had already expended a good deal of her emotional currency, so she was willing to have Dr. Conway take the lead for a while.

"I want to know what causes the difference in your attitude, between here and group. And I want to know which of these two Phyllises your husband sees at home. Can you tell me that?"

Phyllis smiled for the first time. "He doesn't see much of this, I can tell you."

"Why not?"

Phyllis was stunned by the pain that simple question caused her. Words rushed into her mind in a furious jumble, words she did not want to hear or speak. She tried to avert Dr. Conway's gaze. "I can't," she replied meekly.

"You can, Phyllis. I actually think you must."

She found the strength to look up. Her eyes were filled with tears, but this time it was not from the flood of outrage that came so easily to her in the sanctuary of this office. Now she felt despair as she confronted the absolute truth of her hopelessness. "He's so angry," she said slowly. "He's always so angry. He thinks I don't know how bad things are for him at work, but I do." She looked at Randi, as if ready to impart some deep secret. "I got a call the other day from the administrator of his pension plan, or something like that. They were confirming an early withdrawal he made. Can you imagine? He won't tell me he's borrowing against our future just to pay our bills, and I can't even discuss it with him. I have to pretend I don't know."

"Did you tell him about the call?"

"Of course not. I'm afraid. Don't you see?"

"You're afraid of your husband?"

She shook her head ever so deliberately. "Afraid of Fred? No, Doctor Conway, I'm afraid *for* him, for what he might do. He's all I have. I don't want to be alone." Her sobs came from a wellspring so deep inside her she feared that once released they might never end. Her shoulders rose and fell and she gasped for breath as her chest heaved with the weight of her awful grief. "I'm so afraid."

Randi hated herself for not going to her, for not holding this sad woman in her arms and telling her it would be all right. *This is not a profession for human beings*, she thought. But she knew she must stay where she was. She must sit and watch this wretched woman suffer the ordeal that she ultimately faced alone.

"I'm sorry," Phyllis muttered.

"For what?"

She began wiping at her face with a handful of tissues. "I'm making a spectacle of myself."

"No Phyllis, you're not. You're showing the courage to confront your fears. That's the beginning of solving any problem. First you have to face up to it."

Phyllis managed one of the saddest smiles Randi had ever seen. "Words, Doctor. Just words." She took a deep breath and let out a long, uneven sigh.

"What would you like instead?"

"Instead of what? I don't understand."

"Words. You say we're dealing in words. The alternative would be actions, correct?"

Phyllis nodded.

"All right. What would you like to do? Or what would you like the two of us to do? Or what would you have Fred do?"

Phyllis spoke slowly now. "I want to feel loved. I want to feel that everything I've given, everything I've done for all these years actually means something. That it has value. I don't want anyone giving me anything out of obligation. I've been married more than thirty years. I don't want anyone doing anything for me like it's some kind of a favor, okay? I've earned something here. I want what I've earned."

"What do you believe you've earned, Phyllis?"

"Love," she said. "First I want to feel loved. Then I want to enjoy myself. I want to laugh and have fun. And I want someone who wants to be my partner, to share that with me." She was staring at Randi now, her frightened eyes those of a woman who understood more than she wanted to know. "Sometimes he scares me. And sometimes he infuriates me. But even with that, even with all the things I want, I know what I don't want."

Randi waited.

"I don't want to be alone," Phyllis said.

But this time she did not cry, and Randi knew there was another conversation she needed to have with Fred Wentworth.

CHAPTER 40

Once Phyllis was gone, Randi returned to her files. She was kneeling over a pile of papers, putting them in order, when she heard the knock at her door.

She opened up to find Mitchell Avery.

He trudged past her into the room, not taking notice of the mess he was obliged to step around as he made his way to the couch and dropped himself down.

"What are you doing here?" she asked, not meaning for the question to sound as harsh as it did.

"I think the better question is, 'What are you doing here?' You're supposed to be saving marriages, right? How're you making out on that score?"

Randi stood, closed the door, and took her seat opposite him, in the black, leather swivel chair. "What are you talking about?"

Avery explained what he discovered when he returned home yesterday morning, including Joan's note. "I called her sister in Vermont. She says Joan's okay, but she won't tell me where she is. She said Joan won't speak to me, but she and the kids are fine and I shouldn't worry." He gave Randi a look that said it might be the craziest notion he had ever heard. "*Shouldn't worry*? All I've done is worry. And by the way, I've been trying to reach you since I got back."

"I had to go out of town yesterday. I didn't get your voice mail."

"I didn't leave one. Figured I would catch up with you in person." He leaned forward. "So where the hell are my wife and kids?"

"I don't know," Randi admitted.

"Well what the hell *do* you know?"

Randi took a deep breath. "I saw Joan Monday. She told us she was leaving group, but she wasn't prepared to discuss her reasons. I called your house afterward, hoping she might be willing to see me privately, but there was no answer." Randi's calm tone only intensified Avery's anxiety.

"That's it? You didn't do anything else?"

"There was no voice mail so I couldn't leave a message," she said. "I thought I'd hear from her."

"Great," Avery said abruptly. "What do we do next?"

"Would you like me to try and reach her?"

"Now *there's* an idea," he snapped. Then he gave her the name of Joan's sister and her telephone number. "I was going to drive up to Vermont, but I don't know that she's there. What the hell, I should go anyway. Maybe I can beat the information out of her."

"Out of who, her sister?"

"Of course, damnit. Who do you think?"

"First, you need to calm down Mitchell. Then you and Joan should come and see me."

"Are you listening? I can't even find her, how am I going to get her to come and see you?"

"We'll find her, then we should all talk."

"What the hell for? You're a marriage counselor. I don't have a marriage anymore. I don't even know what I'm doing here. I should go and see someone in the missing-persons bureau."

"What happened in the past few days, Mitchell?" she asked, not divulging what Joan had told her about Miami.

"I was away," he said, then became silent as Randi waited. "I was in Florida," he admitted, his voice somber, even hoarse. "Remember that girl I told you about? In Miami? Joan must've found out I was there."

"Mitchell," she began, then stopped. "Are you sure this only has to do with Florida?"

"What is that supposed to mean?"

"It's a question, Mitchell."

He wasn't paying any attention to her now, speaking to himself as he muttered, "I don't know how the hell she could have known."

"Joan's note, did it say anything else?"

"Huh?"

"You said she left a note. What did it say?"

"Not much. Some bullshit about the cost of selfishness."

"Anything about Elizabeth Knoebel?"

"Elizabeth Knoebel?"

"Could this have anything to do with her?"

"What the hell are you talking about?"

"I think you know," Randi said.

Avery shook his head. "What the hell are you running here, Doc?" He stood up and began to pace back and forth behind the couch, for the first time noticing the jumble of papers and files on the floor. "Jesus, what a mess."

"I'm reorganizing."

"You may need some help," he said.

"Talk to me, Mitchell."

"About Elizabeth?"

"Yes."

He shook his head.

"You told me you knew her. Tell me what happened."

He stopped and stared down at her. "I met her in a bar one night." He resumed his pacing. "Had no idea who she was or what she was up to, not in the beginning. She came at me like I was Don Juan, but I've been around too long for that sort of applesauce. I figure if something looks too good to be true it usually is. I actually thought she might be a pro, so I blew her off. She was none too pleased with the brush but, hey, I'm no George Clooney, and when a good-looking woman starts draping herself all over me before we've said a how-do-you-do, I know there's danger ahead, Will Robinson." He forced a bitter chuckle. "That's when she tells me that she's in Joan's therapy group. Heard all about me and how terrific I sounded, how she also knows my marriage is a mess, and wouldn't we be something together." He stopped his pacing and looked down at Randi again. "Really, Doc, what the hell are you running here?"

"You never slept with her?"

"Are you kidding? Not so much as a catnap. She was some kind of bitch, though. I gave her the firm no-thanks, so then she tells me she's Stanley's wife. Said if I didn't go to bed with her, she'd tell her husband and my wife that we had a torrid affair, or some such bullshit."

"And?"

"And I told her to pound sand, what do you think?" He held out his hands, palms upward, and said, "You know where she went from there, don't you?" Then he resumed pacing.

Randi drew a deep breath, then asked, "Why don't you tell me?"

Avery stopped and engaged her in a staring contest the therapist quickly lost.

"Did she ever tell Joan anything about meeting you?"

"Not that I know of."

Randi waited.

He finally said, "Go ahead, I know you want to ask me."

She hesitated, then said, "You knew about Kyle, didn't you?"

"Not at first," he admitted as he gave up wandering around the papers on the floor and slumped back on the couch. "But I saw something was different. Let's face it, I'm not the world's greatest father, but I know my son. I realized something was up."

"Did he tell you?"

"Eventually." Avery shook his head. "What a rotten whore, going after a kid like that. Why? For revenge against me because I shot her down? How warped is that?"

"Very," Randi admitted.

"The worst came afterward, when she told him that she'd done me too."

"But you were never with her."

"I'm telling you the truth, Randi. No goddamned way. I've been straight with you about the women I've been with, haven't I? Trust me, Elizabeth's story was a total lie."

"But she told Kyle the two of you had been together?"

"Why do you think my son was so upset? After the incident on the bank roof, that's when he and I finally talked it through." He stared at her, his disbelief still evident as he said, "My poor kid actually thought about taking a swan dive off the bank building he was so confused. I was furious, believe me. But by then she was dead." He let out a long sigh. "Solved one part of my problem anyway."

Randi shook her head. "I don't know what to say."

"For starters, you could tell me if you knew."

"I didn't," she admitted. "But I suspected." Randi said nothing about the existence of Elizabeth's journal, nor the mention in her diary of the seduction of a young boy.

"Well now you know, and that stays just between us, right? My son believes me and, if anything, we ended up closer. By the way, Joan also suspects, but she doesn't know anything for sure, okay?"

"How awful."

"No kidding."

Randi nodded. "Do you know anything about Elizabeth and other men in your group?"

"I don't, but I wouldn't be surprised. She thought she was completely irresistible, she made that pretty clear." He shook his head. "She was good-looking, I'll give her that, but even a fool could see she was poison."

"Yes," Randi agreed in a quiet voice, "she was."

"Look, the woman struck out with me. Who the hell else she scored with is none of my business. I wasn't about to bring it up in group because I had no reason to humiliate Stanley."

"You're right," Randi said.

"Well at least we agree about something. So, if you want to keep playing Sherlock Holmes, why not put your mind to something useful, like finding my family and helping me get them back."

CHAPTER 41

Later, after Avery was gone, Randi received a call from Walker.

"You with a patient?" he asked.

"Just finished with one."

"Have a minute?"

"Sure."

"You don't sound good. Rough session?"

"You could say that."

"Want to talk about it?"

"What do you think?"

"Can't blame me for trying."

She didn't say whether she wanted to blame him or not.

"I met with Bob Stratford last night. He wants to help with my investigation. Unfortunately, he's not the person who can give the help I need."

"And I am."

"You've never told me, did you finish reading Mrs. Knoebel's journal?"

"I did."

"And?"

Randi hesitated. "I'm not sure what to say."

"You can say whether or not you're ready to identify her murderer."

"I can't."

"Can't or won't?"

"What I mean is, I don't have an answer for you, even if I could give it."

"Let me help you, then. We have a pretty good idea of who some of the people were that Mrs. Knoebel was writing about. My guess is that you also recognized some of them as your patients."

"Yes," she admitted.

"One of the chapters talks about a woman we believe to be Nettie Sisson."

Randi waited.

"I've already told you, we know all about her background."

"That doesn't prove she had anything to do with Elizabeth's death."

"I didn't say it does. What it does do, however, is point to a tendency toward violence and an unbalanced mind."

"Is that it?"

"Oh no. As you saw in her diary, Mrs. Knoebel claims she and Mrs. Sisson had much more than a homeowner-housekeeper relationship."

"But you don't really think she had anything to do with Elizabeth's death . . ."

"Actually I don't, for what that's worth. But it's something I have to consider. Then there are the various men Mrs. Knoebel bedded. We think we can prove one of them was at her home the afternoon she was murdered."

"Is that true?"

"It is. It's also possible that he was the one who shot Mrs. Knoebel, although I have cause to doubt it."

Randi said nothing.

"Whoever broke into your office Monday night, what do you think they were looking for?"

"I don't know."

"My guess is that they were looking for the journal."

"But I thought no one knew about her diary."

"Secrets are tough to keep in a small town. Who knows that better than you? Where was it?"

"I had it with me," she told him. "At home."

"That was fortunate, at least so far."

"Meaning what?"

"Meaning it was lucky they didn't come after you for it."

Randi wanted to say something, but remained silent.

"You've had some time to look through your files. Anything missing?"

"Not that I've found so far."

"Uh huh."

"If you're trying to scare me, you are."

"I consider that progress."

"Very funny."

"Not meant to be."

"Anthony, even if you put aside the problem of my professional ethics, you're glossing over a critical factor here. I don't actually know who murdered Elizabeth Knoebel."

"Maybe not, but there are people who might believe you do. Word of the diary is starting to leak, and I'm afraid it won't be long before the media gets hold of it. Gossip is a bitch."

"So you think people will be looking to me if her diary becomes public knowledge."

"Yes, I do."

"One of those people being her murderer."

"Precisely. So do us both a favor and help me with something that's become even more important to me than solving this case."

"What?" she asked.

"Protecting you," he said.

After the call, Walker returned to Elizabeth's diary. He picked up the section under SHAKE.DOC, called "Notes for Chapter Six." Like the Nettie Sisson episode, it involved a woman rather than a man. Here, however, Elizabeth did not use an initial, she used a name.

Celia.

Was that a real name or another code?

Walker had another look at those pages.

```
Sex with a woman is a completely dif-
ferent experience for me. No matter how
gentle a male lover intends to be, there
is always some intrinsic violence in the
act, an explosion, a sense of finality.
```

Women have different orgasms, especially together, as well as the ability to continue to enjoy multiple climaxes. There is none of the dynamic arc that exists with a man—the sex act as a parody of creation, life and death. Women can go on and on pleasuring each other, which sets up a myriad of unique opportunities.

✤ ✤ ✤

Celia was special to me, in her way, not least because I was her first. She was a virgin in this sort of sexual liaison. That is far more appealing to me than a committed lesbian, who brings with her preconceived notions about roles and responsibilities. Celia was nervous, guilt-ridden, and filled with anxiety about my seduction of her. But she was also curious, intrigued, and incredibly needy.

The first time we were together there was so little physical expression the connection between us was almost chaste. The second time, however, we shared a bottle of champagne, and I provided a setting that was entirely private and secure.

After our first long kiss I insisted that we disrobe. I convinced her that the embarrassment and restraint she felt would be alleviated if we could simply see each other, fully naked, and she complied.

We were face-to-face on the bed, our bodies touching for the first time. She felt the softness of our breasts pressing together, and it seemed a revelation to her. As we kissed I moved two fingers ever so carefully around the entry to her wet pussy, and she shuddered at the sensation.

Only a woman can really understand how to manipulate the clitoris, careful to ensure it is lubricated, then pressing and squeezing, but not too hard, with just enough movement to send shivers up the spine.

I took my time, sure that she reached her first climax before I went at her with my tongue. In no time, we were a moist tangle of legs and breasts and lips, and she finally came with such force that she broke down and cried.

Walker felt very much a voyeur reading various sections of Elizabeth's diary, and this chapter was giving him that same queasy feeling. He skipped past the rest of their sensual encounter and got to the end.

It was a shame that I would have to break Celia's heart, but I knew the time for that would fast approach. As we continued to meet, I felt she also suspected that was coming, although her hunger for my body and how I made

her feel seemed to increase in reverse
proportion to the time we had left
together. Even her ability to please me
increased.

Unfortunately, it was not a relationship that could survive.

Well, Walker told himself after he placed the pages back into his
drawer, *it didn't matter to Elizabeth Knoebel whether she was doing a
man or a woman, she played no favorites.*

She meant to hurt them all in the end.

So who the hell was Celia?

CHAPTER 42

Kovacevic strode into the detectives' squad room and dropped himself into the chair beside Walker's desk.

"How was your trip to the big city?" Walker asked him.

"It was interesting." He pulled out his notebook and copies of the hospital records he brought from New York. "Are you ready for this one?"

"I'm ready."

"Jake knows his stuff," the young officer said as he thumbed through the papers. "The day in question, when Dr. Knoebel was scheduled with a full slate of surgery, things might not have been everything they seemed when you were down there."

"I'm listening."

"It's like Jake said. The actual operating-room records show which doctors and nurses were present during the procedures, who did what, all that stuff. The afternoon of Elizabeth Knoebel's death, the chief resident actually performed the surgery. Knoebel was there, got him started, then the other guy did the job."

"The other guy did the job?" Walker smiled. "Is that some new sort of technical medical jargon?"

"Sorry. The other surgeon performed the procedure."

"Meaning what? That Knoebel could have walked out of the operating room, jumped in his car, and made a quick run up to Connecticut."

"It's possible."

Walker grabbed the main file and sifted through his papers until he found a white sheet with his own notations. "What time could he have left the OR?"

"According to these reports," which Kovacevic held up for effect, "he could have split sometime around two."

"And my notes say that the next time he made a confirmed appearance in the hospital was just after four o'clock, during his afternoon rounds."

"That's what I came up with."

"So now we've given him a little more than two hours to make his round-trip."

"Seems so," Kovacevic said. "He could have done a turnaround in that time. I got up here in under fifty minutes just now, without heavy rush-hour traffic, same as he could've done."

"Understood. How sure are we of these OR procedures? If Knoebel turned the surgery over to the resident, wouldn't he be there to complete the procedure, close it up or whatever they call it? Just to be sure there were no screwups?"

"The way I get the story, that's customary, but not always done. The big cheese gets to go off and make money somewhere else. A lot of the time the patient never knows who did what while he's under the knife. Point is, there's no notation in the records that Knoebel did anything after the surgery was started."

"So maybe he was there, and maybe he wasn't."

"Right. The woman I spoke with said these doctors and nurses are involved in so many operations, it's impossible for them to remember if or when a staff surgeon goes in and out of the room. I get the feeling nurses don't love surgeons and Knoebel's one of their least favorite, if you get what I'm saying."

"I've seen him in action."

"Bottom line, he may have had a window of opportunity that afternoon."

Walker slowly drew a deep breath, then let it out all at once. "How about that?"

CHAPTER 43

Paul Gorman arrived early for group that evening.

Gorman was a handsome young man with sandy-colored hair, an athletic build and the self-conscious look of a midlevel executive nervously reaching for the next rung of the corporate ladder. He was the youngest member of Randi's Husbands Group, as his wife Lisa was in hers. He thought himself a good patient, not because he ever shared anything truly personal, but because he never missed a session. The other men viewed him as a neophyte in the battle between the sexes, and Wentworth seized every opportunity to make him feel a fool. Randi found it fascinating that they all seemed to begrudge Paul his youth far more than the women in the Wives Group did Lisa.

"I'm sorry to bust in on you this way, but I have something I need to say. Privately."

"All right. Have a seat."

Gorman glanced at the file folders that were now neatly piled in the corner of the room, but decided not to ask. He sat in one of the squat leather chairs that faced Randi across the desk. "I wanted to talk to you about leaving the group. I thought I should mention it to you before I bring it up tonight."

"All right."

Gorman shifted nervously in his seat. "No offense, but I'm not getting a lot out of these sessions. Lisa feels pretty much the same about hers. Don't get me wrong," he added quickly, "we like seeing you when it's just the two of us. We know we've got things to work on and you've helped us, you really have. Lisa and I are communicating much better than we did before."

"Good," Randi said, feeling as if he was looking for a pat on the head.

"But the groups, they just don't seem to be doing anything for us. For me, well, these other guys are not really a good fit. I think you understand."

"You realize Doctor Knoebel will not be coming back."

"I figured that."

"Tell me your concerns about the others."

He shrugged. "I feel like Mitchell and Fred take over and no one else gets a word in edgewise. Not that Doctor Knoebel ever wanted to. I mean, I'm sorry about his wife, but for all the good he did himself or anyone else here, he could have stayed home. And Thomas doesn't even show up half the time. So I get stuck listening to Mitch and Fred talk about the problems of middle-aged marriages. But I'm not as old as they are, and I don't feel any connection."

"It's my fault," Randi replied.

"No it isn't," he said. "I've watched you try and control them, but they always go back to the same things. Then if I try to say something they ridicule me, like I'm just a kid. You've seen it."

"I have," Randi admitted. "I was actually thinking about inviting some new people into our sessions to change the dynamics. Without Stanley Knoebel we only have four. I was considering two or three new people. Thought we'd try it out. If it doesn't click maybe I'll restructure the entire group. Would that make a difference?"

Gorman managed a half-hearted smile. "It might. You want me to hold off discussing my feelings tonight?"

"Not at all. I wish you'd say exactly what you've just told me. Might do the others some good to hear it."

"All right," he said. "I will."

When the other men arrived, Randi was pleased to find Thomas Colello in attendance. Not only had he missed too many sessions, but tonight his presence might prove helpful to Paul Gorman, if the younger man was actually going to voice his concerns. She began the session by telling them what she had already told Paul—that Stanley Knoebel would not be coming back. That came as no surprise. Then she suggested they invite two or three new participants, and credited Gorman with the idea.

To her amazement, they all agreed that some new life would be a benefit.

"Although having Knoebel here didn't count as a real person anyway," Wentworth volunteered with a brittle laugh.

Most groups tend to develop an insular pattern over time, and the introduction of someone new can upset that balance. The lack of cohesion among these four men, however, caused them to welcome the prospect of new members. An interesting commentary, Randi ruefully acknowledged to herself, not only on their personalities, but on her failure as their therapist.

Paul Gorman volunteered a watered-down version of his concerns about the group dynamic, to which little response was given because Mitchell Avery interrupted with the announcement that his marriage was over.

The others fell silent as Avery described what he found when he returned home, the details of the event seeming to evoke more curiosity than empathy. The empty closet. The note. The spoiled milk in the refrigerator. These factoids seemed to fascinate the other men, and their reactions made Randi want to scream.

In the end Avery wanted their support, and that was offered easily enough. This was not a forum where he was going to be condemned for his infidelity and tonight, given the circumstances, Randi was not going to push the issue. She allowed Avery to go on complaining about his situation for most of the session, until even he could not bear to discuss it anymore.

"So," Randi said, returning to Gorman's concerns about the group, "how do you all feel about what Paul had to say earlier?"

"Let's face it, Doc," Wentworth said, "none of us really want to be here to begin with. I mean, you're not a bad egg, but this group thing is about as much fun as waterboarding. We talk the same bullshit every week. Whose wife is pissed off because she's not getting enough attention. Who's cheating. Who's getting caught. How lousy it is to get old." He looked over at Gorman. "Paulie here, he doesn't have to worry about getting old yet. But soon, young fella. You're just getting a preview, know what I mean?"

"I wish you wouldn't call me 'Paulie,'" Gorman said in a quiet voice, but no one paid any attention.

Randi was looking at Wentworth. "What do you find so objectionable about these discussions, Fred?"

"Objectionable? Nothing. I just don't see what it gets us. Thomas and I went to a bar just the other night, had a few drinks, talked things over. Mitch and Paulie here can join us if they want. It's the same thing, isn't it?"

"Is it?"

Avery uttered a loud sigh.

Wentworth turned to him. "Look Mitchell, it all boils down to the same thing," he said. "Whether it's business, money or life in general. It's all about sex."

When Avery did not reply, Randi asked, "In what way is it all about sex?"

"Come on Doc, it's not like you don't know. Why the hell do men care what clothes they wear or the cars they drive? Why do women jump up and down, doing all that aerobics crap? Why do they polish their nails or blow their hair dry? Why do they have tit jobs and face lifts? It's all part of the same game, isn't it? Feel young, feel sexy, make sure you're attractive before it's too late."

"Too late for what?"

Wentworth rocked back and forth in exasperation. "Too late to be taken seriously, that's what. Too late to get it done."

No one responded.

"It's a different world today. Women are different. Stronger. Independent. They want it as much as we do, know what I mean? It's tough to stay married nowadays."

"Tougher than you know," Avery muttered.

"What about that, Doc?" Wentworth asked Randi. "You figure it's getting tougher to stay married?" Fred looked around at the others and, before Randi could respond, he added, "I bet you hope it is. Good for business, am I right?"

When the little joke fell flat, Randi said, "I can't speak for marriages in general, Fred. What about discussing yours?"

Wentworth stared at her for a moment, then said, "There was this woman I want to tell you about. We did it in her house. Her own bedroom. While her husband was at work," he added with a malevolent smile. "That'll put some extra lead in the pencil, know what I mean? Not that I needed any help, because this lady was friggen gorgeous."

"Don't you ever meet any woman who isn't friggen gorgeous?" Avery asked impatiently.

Paul Gorman laughed, but said nothing.

"You may think that's very funny," Wentworth said to Gorman, choosing to go after the younger man rather than Avery. "Scoff all you want, but I'm telling you something you can learn from." Wentworth looked around the room at the other men. "That's the only reason I'm bringing it up. I'm not sitting here trying to brag or anything. I'm just telling you, you meet a woman like this and it makes you wonder how the hell you can stay married."

Randi asked, "Is that why you're sharing this, Fred? Because you're thinking about leaving Phyllis?"

"I don't know. I mean, the thought crosses my mind, I admit that. Phyllis is a good dame, don't get me wrong, but this woman was something else. Took me to her bedroom, a beautiful place, all done up dark and mysterious. Panels of wood, fancy drapes, all that crap. I swear it could have been a high-class cathouse in New Orleans."

Randi noticed Colello sit up in his chair as he asked, "What was it got you so excited, Fred, the lady or her interior decorator?"

Wentworth turned to him, not sure if he meant it as a joke or not. "I don't get it."

"Neither do I. Maybe you should write for *Architectural Digest*," Colello said, forcing a laugh. "Go on. It sounds interesting."

"Interesting?" Anger began to color Wentworth's complexion.

"We're listening," Colello said. "Tell us what happened."

"What do you think happened?"

"Tell you the truth," Colello said, "I don't know. You always start these stories about fabulous-looking women, but you never finish them."

Wentworth was surprised to have the attack come from his flank. He thought that Colello was his friend. "Hey, what is this?"

Colello stared at Wentworth as he said, "Why don't you tell us. A minute ago you were talking about leaving your wife for this woman's headboard."

"Whoa," Wentworth said.

Colello shook his head. "Go ahead, finish the story. Did you screw her or did you take photos of her curtains."

Wentworth was red-faced now. "Damn right I screwed her."

Randi Conway interrupted. "The point here is not to invalidate one another, the object is to find ways to support each other."

Colello looked her straight in the eyes. "That doesn't mean we give up our right to question or criticize, does it?"

"No," she admitted. "But it's important for those reactions to be constructive. I hope you all agree with that."

When no one replied, she said, "We're done for tonight. Next week I may have a guest or two sitting in, all right?"

They each mumbled some form of assent as they stood and made for the door, four convicts on parole.

Randi said, "Thomas, you have a minute?"

As the other three departed, Colello followed Randi into her private office.

She said, "I don't meet with you or Fran one-on-one, but it's clear to me that you have some things going on that you're not sharing in group."

Colello nodded. "I'm working on it."

"I respect that, although the point of these sessions is to provide an opportunity for each of you to get input from the others. You can only do that by letting us know what's going on with you."

Colello responded with a nod that conveyed no enthusiasm for the idea. "Let's be honest. I come here because it makes Fran happy. If you believe I'm likely to get any help with my marriage from Fred, or Paul, or even Mitchell, then I'm in worse shape than I thought."

"I'm also here, you know. And I'm available if you want to talk privately."

"I appreciate that."

"One other thing." She saw the residual anger in his eyes. "Fred said something tonight that seemed to set you off. Can you tell me what it was?"

Colello twisted his mouth in a thoughtful expression. Then he said, "Let me think on it, okay?"

"You're sure you don't want to discuss it now?"

"I'm sure."

"All right. Call me if you change your mind."

"Okay," Thomas Colello said, then bid her good night.

Outside the building, Colello walked quickly to his car. Before opening the door he slammed down on the top of the sedan with the side of his fist and growled, "Sonuvabitch."

✤   ✤   ✤

After a full day in private sessions and an evening with her Husbands Group, Randi Conway arrived home nearly exhausted. She changed into jeans and a sweater, poured herself a glass of white wine, then went into the dining room and collapsed into her desk chair without troubling to switch on the light. She sat there, her eyes adjusting to the darkness, her feelings becoming a thought, the thought an idea.

Fred Wentworth and Thomas Colello. Something happened between them when Wentworth described his latest fantasy conquest.

The men were sitting in her small group therapy room, suffering indulgently as Wentworth ran on with another tale of sexual conquest. It was the sort of story Wentworth frequently told in group, and it was doubtful he had a single believer in the room. They usually endured

Fred's yarns in the name of good fellowship. Some of the stories were even entertaining. But tonight Thomas Colello had a different reaction, and Randi was not clear why.

Until now.

The bedroom. That was the part of the story that had triggered the angry response from Colello, the details Wentworth gave of the bedroom. The dark furniture. The tapestries on the walls. The large headboard.

The description now triggered something for Randi. The photographs Anthony Walker had shown her. The photographs taken at the scene of Elizabeth Knoebel's death. Randi now envisioned what Thomas Colello saw. Fred Wentworth had not been creating another of his fantasies, he was describing a room that really existed.

The bedroom where Elizabeth Knoebel died.

Coincidence? Perhaps. Was Wentworth's description so filled with detail that Colello found it unmistakable? Not necessarily. There was something more, more than the room. What was the something more?

Did Wentworth know her? If so, was he trying to provoke the others with his comments? Perhaps, but why? Was he challenging the others to find out if they recognized the scene? Did he want to know who else might have paid a visit to Elizabeth's bedroom?

And what of Colello's anger? At the time it seemed out of all proportion, but now Randi was beginning to understand. It had to do with whatever he knew about Elizabeth's death. He and Wentworth had also mentioned something about seeing each other outside the group a couple of nights ago. Was that discussion part of the problem tonight?

Randi sat back and took a sip of the cold wine, then checked her messages. When she heard Walker's voice, she felt at ease for the first time that evening. He said he wanted to see her again. And she realized that she wanted to see him.

She thought about calling to describe what had just happened, but what could she tell him? She could not divulge what was shared in group, even though she truly had no idea what had been shared. The only thing she had was a suspicion.

More than one suspicion, actually.

She stood up, looked around the small room, and listened to the quiet for a few moments.

Then she decided to go for a drive.

CHAPTER 44

Walker was watching television in his living room when he heard the knock. His first reaction was to check his watch. It was nearly ten.

When he opened the front door Randi said, "I'm sorry to bother you so late."

He looked past her, as if he expected to find someone else there.

"Can I come in?" she asked.

"Of course. Sorry. Come in. Buy you a drink?"

"That'd be great."

He led her into the living room where she sat on the sofa. He switched off the television and went into the kitchen.

"Highball okay?" he called out.

"Highball?"

"Something I call an American Tragedy. Jack Daniel's corrupted by ginger ale."

"Sounds good."

He fixed the drinks, came back and handed her a glass. "So, to what do I owe this pleasure?"

She watched as he sat in his arm chair, took a swallow of the drink, and said, "This is good."

"Goes down easy this time of night."

Randi had another taste, then said, "Something happened in group. It's hard to explain, but I believe two of my patients have been in Elizabeth Knoebel's bedroom." She took another gulp of the cocktail.

"Easy," Walker said with a smile. "Don't let the ginger ale fool you, it's a real cocktail."

She nodded. "Maybe even more than two of them." She took another long gulp of the highball.

"I don't suppose you want to give me the names."

When she looked at him he saw something in her eyes he had never seen before, something he couldn't identify. "I want to tell you, please believe me. I just can't."

"How about I throw out some names and you tell me if I'm right?" Randi said nothing.

"One of them was Thomas Colello?"

Her expression was all the answer he needed, but she said, "Please Anthony, don't ask me anything about it tonight." Her look softened as she said, "That's not why I came here."

"All right." He took a sip of his drink. "So, you're telling me you didn't drive all the way over here to tell me that you've got something to tell me that you're not ready to tell me, have I got this right?"

"Yes," she said with a smile. "That's right."

They stared at each other for what seemed a long time. Then he placed his glass on the table, got up and sat beside her, not speaking, never taking his eyes from hers. He tenderly reached out and held her face in his hands, and then it all seemed so natural, so right.

The way they kissed, the way he slowly undressed her, the way they laid back, side by side on the couch, and kissed some more, until she reached down, tugging at his belt. He got up, removed his shirt, kicked off his trousers and pulled off his shorts. He slipped off her panties, she whispered his name, then wanted to say something else, but stopped. There was no need for her to say anything, not now.

As he knelt over her she felt as if she was falling backward, as if that was how she would give in to the oncoming pleasure. They kissed again, and she reached out for him and, as she stroked him, all of her remaining tension evaporated. He lowered himself over her and she helped guide him in, wanting it to happen before she could think, before her own fears got in the way.

They began slowly at first, then with a faster, more insistent motion that felt perfectly in time.

She had so many thoughts, but for now she pushed them away. She wished away every doubt as she surrendered to a sublime rush of sensations that left her biting his neck and digging her nails into the flesh of his firm ass. She cried out as her body arched, convulsed, then exploded. She was lost in recurring waves of satisfaction that washed over her as he drove more deeply in a final series of thrusts until he too was spent, and she had a final climax that left her weak and damp and filled with joy and confusion and the need to believe that this really was all right, that everything was going to be all right.

CHAPTER 45

Anthony and Randi awoke early, in his bed, the reality of the new day arriving for them even before the light of first morning broke. He stared into the darkness as she began to rouse herself into consciousness.

"You all right?" he asked.

She did not answer at first. Then she said, "I've never done anything like this before."

"Which part do you mean?"

"Don't be funny. You know what I'm saying. Showing up here like this."

"Uh huh."

"I mean it. It's important that you believe me."

"All right then, I do."

She turned to look at him. "I mean it Anthony."

"You know, I have this theory that when people do unusual things—and by that I mean things that are extraordinary for them—they're really just acting on their most basic impulses. What I'm saying is, those are the moments that actually define us."

She studied him in the faint light of dawn. When he reached out, she allowed herself to be drawn against him. "You're truly a policeman with a philosophy for every occasion."

"I'm a detective, not a policeman," he reminded her. Then he kissed her softly on the lips. "By the way, I do believe you," he said, still holding her close, not wanting the morning to intrude on them, at least not yet.

"Good," she said. "That's good."

When she paused again, he asked, "What is it?"

She smiled. "Wish I brought a toothbrush."

Walker got up and found her a new toothbrush, then made coffee and they drank it in bed.

"It's not even sunrise," he said.

"Good," she replied.

And they made love again.

Later, still in bed, Randi was wearing his robe and Walker had pulled on sweatpants. They were laying on their sides again, facing each other.

"I really have to go," she told him.

"Already?"

"I've got to get home to change. I have an early session." She kissed him on the lips. "Okay if I take a quick shower?"

"Take a long shower, if I can watch."

She smiled.

"Will I see you later?" he asked. It was not quite seven o'clock.

"You mean at my office?"

"Come on, you know what I mean."

"You mean I'm not a policeman's one-night stand?"

"Detective, not policeman. And no, this was no one-night stand. At least not for me."

"I'm so relieved."

"Good. Now that we settled that, what about our other discussion?"

Her smile vanished. "I'll call you later, when I'm ready."

"Good. And after that, I'll buy you dinner."

"I certainly hope so," she said.

CHAPTER 46

Randi was mindful of the fact that Nettie Sisson knew more about Elizabeth Knoebel than almost anyone else. She was also beginning to realize, as fear for her own safety was increasing, that Nettie might have similar concerns for herself. On the one hand, Nettie might be a suspect in Elizabeth's murder. On the other, she was a potential victim.

In keeping her early appointment with Nettie, Randi needed to balance her obligations to this sad, battered woman with a growing inclination to address the entire spectrum of problems that Elizabeth's murder was creating.

When Nettie arrived she immediately opened the door to that discussion, confirming Randi's basic assessment.

"I'm so frightened," Nettie said as soon as she took her place on the sofa. "It's bad enough that I know things I shouldn't. What's worse is that I don't know enough to protect myself."

"What does that mean?"

"Don't you see? I know who Elizabeth really was. I knew what she was doing." She almost shuddered as she added, "I also know what she was capable of, but what I don't know is who killed her. I honestly do not, Doctor Conway. Isn't that worse?"

"Worse than what?"

"Than knowing. If I knew, I could tell the police. I could get protection. The way it is now, whoever murdered her probably believes I have more information than I do." She sighed deeply, as if about to cry, but Nettie Sisson had used up all of her tears long ago. "Am I making any sense at all?"

Randi wanted to tell her that she was making more sense than she could possibly know, since they now shared the same precarious ground. "Have you been threatened, Nettie? Has anyone contacted you?"

"You mean other than the police? No, no, nothing. Not yet. I've spent the last two days alone, not even leaving my apartment. I don't know what to do."

"What you need to do," Randi counseled with less than total commitment to the idea, "is to live your normal life. There's no reason to believe anyone means you harm."

"Doctor Conway, I have a good idea who some of these men are. Whoever did this thing to Elizabeth, don't you think they realize at some point I could be giving the police a list?"

"Calm yourself, Nettie. The police already have a list, and it's far more extensive than anything you could provide."

Nettie responded with a puzzled look.

"The police know about the Knoebels' participation in the groups I run."

"You gave them names?" Nettie asked.

"Of course not. They spoke with Dr. Knoebel, got the names from him. I believe the police had other information as well."

Nettie gave an expectant look.

"I'm not sure what else they have but believe me, they don't need you as a source."

"The diary?"

"You know about it?"

"Of course."

"Do you know what it contains?"

"Yes," Nettie admitted.

"You've told this to the police?"

"To Detective Walker."

"Well, in a way that makes you even less important for now, which is a good thing, right?"

The older woman thought it over. "What about confirmation?"

"Nettie, let's put this in perspective. Were you at the Knoebels' home when Elizabeth was shot?"

She shook her head.

"Were you there at any time that day or night?"

"No."

"Do you have any idea who might have been visiting Elizabeth that day?"

"I don't."

"Then I think your worries are somewhat exaggerated. Which is not to say that you are not entitled to be concerned," she added hastily, "but we need to keep our focus. I understand why you would react with fear in this situation, I do."

Nettie responded with one of those expressions Randi had witnessed from her many times, a look that declared, 'I realize I've got problems, but I'm not insane.' She said, "That's very helpful, Doctor."

"Good. Now let's devote some time to your feelings about what happened here. And about your relationship with Elizabeth."

A reluctant nod and another familiar look from Nettie, although this time it was not nearly as sanguine. It was an acknowledgment that it was time to visit that dark place again, whether she wanted to go there or not.

CHAPTER 47

Walker also arrived at his office early that morning, made some calls, reviewed his notes, then summoned Kovacevic. It was time to meet with the suspects they had identified, starting with Thomas Colello. Then they would work their way through the others on his list.

One of the entries in Elizabeth Knoebel's journey was almost certainly about Colello. The file was designated TLROT.DOC, which Blasko's code breaking had it reading as THOMS. That, together with other facts Walker had run down, made it clear who the passage was about. The chapter had a different tone than most of her other writing. He took a moment to read from the printed pages.

```
         SEXUAL RITES
      By Elizabeth Knoebel
     NOTES FOR CHAPTER 14
     Try a Little Tenderness
```

We had never stayed overnight together. Up to then our meetings had the hallmarks of a typical affair. A man's affair. Starting with drinks. Then dinner. Followed by sex. A shower. And then home.

This time we arranged to meet out of town and the result was a surprise, at least to me. The level of intimacy was heightened in part by the knowledge that we would have the entire night ahead, and in part by the tenderness he displayed. It was something I had not seen from him before, an interest in me that I had not expected.

We had certainly enjoyed evenings of wonderful carnal excitement before that. He was a man who knew how to touch me, how to be masculine without being rough. He would never rush anything. He was always careful that I reached my climax at least once before letting himself go.

And this time we had the luxury of time. This would not just be sex punctuated by sleep, it promised to be a more complete experience. After we got to our room we made love, then drifted into the sublime post-coital twilight. His leg was draped over mine, our bodies still touching, an expression of both physical and emotional intimacy.

We did not rest for long. I was still aroused. I opened my eyes and, in the dark, could make out his features. In repose there was something kind about his face, something I had not seen before.

He was on his stomach, breathing gently, and I felt the need to touch him. I began by using my long nails, running my hand slowly up and down his back, from his neck to the base of his spine. As he began to stir I traced circles with my fingers, moving to the swell of his firm ass. Then I slid down and reached for his thighs, still employing very little pressure, tickling rather than rubbing him.

When I slid my hand between his legs I could feel he was already growing. Without a word I got to my knees, spread his legs apart and pressed my face into the dark warm crevice, licking him as I reached underneath with my hand and softly massaged the tip of his cock.

He asked if I wanted him to do something to me, but I told him to relax. I insisted he enjoy what I was doing, and he did. I turned him over and went down on him, using a long slow motion, cupping his balls in one hand while using the other to rub his chest. All the while my head moved up and down, slowly increasing in speed and intensity until he exploded in my mouth.

Later, we lay side-by-side, whispering in the dark. I wanted to say something to him, something about how much pleasure I had derived from pleasing him, but I could not. All I could bring myself to say was how I hoped he enjoyed it.

Instead of the expected response, he took me in his arms and held me, and for an instant I thought I might cry.

It truly was a night of surprises.

Kovacevic walked in and Walker placed the pages in his desk drawer with the rest of Elizabeth's journal, then they headed out.

Walker drove, with Kovacevic riding shotgun. They traveled on the

Post Road west, toward a part of town where more modest houses can be found—this was not the neighborhood where the Averys or Knoebels resided. They reached the modest ranch-style home where the Colellos lived, pleased to see all the cars were still in the driveway.

Walker stepped up to the front door, rang the bell and waited. When a dark-haired man opened up, the detective showed him his identification and said, "Mr. Colello?"

Thomas Colello stood in the entrance, gripping the door knob as if it were the only thing holding him up. He was dressed for work, but he saw his plans for the day were about to change. He stared at Walker's police badge, remaining motionless for a moment, then blinked. "Yes, I'm Thomas Colello," he said. "Is there a problem, Officer?"

"I'm Detective Anthony Walker. We need to talk." Walker glanced past Colello into the small house. "This is probably not the best place."

Colello stepped outside and pulled the door shut behind him. "What's this about?" For the first time he saw Officer Kovacevic standing beside Walker's Explorer at the end of the short driveway.

"It's about the death of Elizabeth Knoebel. It'd probably be better if we have this discussion at the station house."

Despite Colello's initial reaction, it was clear that this visit had not come as a complete surprise. "Do I need to call my lawyer?"

Walker said, "That will be entirely up to you." Then he nodded at the young officer, who quickly stepped forward and positioned himself beside his superior officer. Kovacevic took out a small card and read Thomas Colello his legal rights.

"I understand," Colello said when Kovacevic completed the litany. It was apparent from the look on his face that his legal rights were not his primary concern at the moment. "I've got to tell my wife I'm leaving." He said it as if he was asking the two policemen for their help.

Walker nodded his understanding. "Just tell her we're investigating Mrs. Knoebel's death."

"How the hell can I say that?"

"Tell her we need to speak with you because you're acquainted with Doctor Knoebel. We know you were in a therapy group together.

You can tell her we'll also be talking with her and some other people who knew the Knoebels."

"Is that true?"

Walker nodded. "Afraid so."

"Jesus," Colello groaned. Then he shook his head and said, "Okay," although the expression he wore now made it clear he would rather tell his wife the bank was foreclosing on their mortgage. "I'll need a minute, all right?"

"Sure. Go ahead."

When Colello disappeared inside the house, Kovacevic gave Walker a puzzled look.

"What's the matter, kid? You think he's going to scoot out the back door and make a run for it?" Walker smiled. "Trust me. He's in there giving his wife some bullshit story, maybe even telling her what I suggested. Then he's calling his lawyer."

Walker was correct on both counts. After a few minutes Colello rejoined them on the front steps. He told them he would drive his own car to the police station. It would be unseemly to have his neighbors witness two cops shoving him into the back of their car and driving off with him.

Walker looked around. There wasn't a neighbor in sight.

It would also be more convenient, Colello added, since he could make his own way home afterward.

Walker gave that a skeptical look too.

There was a third reason, Colello admitted. He had indeed phoned his lawyer, who demanded they have no further conversation with him until they all convened at the police station.

A half hour later, in the detectives' squad room, Walker was prepared to conduct what he regarded as a fairly polite interview, given that Colello was nominally a suspect in a murder investigation. Chief Gill was on hand, and Officer Kovacevic was operating the recorder. Colello's lawyer, a local criminal-defense attorney named Mark Silverstein, had arrived. He and Walker were acquainted, which was the warmest possible description of their relationship. Silverstein had known Chief Gill for years, and the lawyer realized the situation had to be serious if Gill was sitting in.

"We're entitled to a clarification," said the attorney. "Before we go through any preliminary matters, I would like to know if Mr. Colello is a target of your investigation."

"Yes, Counselor," Walker replied. "He is."

"In that case, we should suspend this meeting until I've had a further opportunity to confer with my client."

"You want a few minutes to talk?" Walker asked, "is that what you're saying?"

Silverstein bristled. "Look, Henry," he said, ignoring Walker and directing himself to Gill, "I don't like the way this is being handled. Your man barges into my client's home without a warrant, and now he wants to bulldoze us into this interrogation." He stood up, making it clear that he and his client were ready to walk out.

Before Gill could respond, Colello placed his hand on the lawyer's arm. "Take it easy, Mark. We're going to get to this eventually." He turned to Walker. "Go ahead and ask your questions. I didn't kill Elizabeth."

"All right," Walker said, avoiding the glare directed at him from Mr. Silverstein. He figured, given Colello's statement, the best plan was to jump right in. "You and Elizabeth Knoebel were lovers, that right?"

"That's right," Colello said without hesitation. "We were."

Now Silverstein collapsed, rather than sat in his chair, but when he tried to protest again Colello shut him up. Walker simply ignored him.

"How long?" the detective asked.

"A few months. Not long."

"Where did you first meet her?"

"At a bar, near my office. Lots of singles and cheater action there."

"Uh huh. And this was a few months ago?"

"Right." Colello took a deep breath. "A Wednesday night, I think. Maybe it was Thursday, I can't remember."

"How many times did you see her after that?"

"Not sure. Five times, maybe six." He tried to sound casual about it, taking a moment to smooth back his dark hair.

"Which was it?" Walker asked with a skeptical look. He had already concluded that an evening with Elizabeth Knoebel was not something a man was likely to forget.

Colello and Walker stared at each other for a moment. "Six times," Colello said. "Including that first night."

"Did you know who she was when you met her?"

"You mean, did I know she was Stanley Knoebel's wife? No, of course not."

"What do you mean, 'of course not'?"

Colello rolled that one over once or twice before answering. "Knoebel was in my marriage counseling group. If I knew she was the guy's wife, I wouldn't have made a play. It wouldn't be my style, you know?"

"I think I know," Walker replied amiably. "But at some point you did learn she was Knoebel's wife, right?"

Colello nodded.

"When?"

"I think it was the fourth time we were together." When Walker responded with another dubious look, Colello said, "The fourth time."

"Uh huh. And where were you *together*?"

Silverstein didn't care much for Walker's tone and said so, but his client talked right through the interruption. "We arranged to meet in that same bar the first couple of times. From there we'd go to a motel." He paused, then added, "It didn't start off as an affair of the heart, if you catch my drift."

Silverstein tried to stop their colloquy again. "Just hold on, Detective Walker." Turning to his client he asked, "Don't you think we should talk this over?"

Colello said, "We already talked it over, Mark," the admission in front of the police only further infuriating his counsel. "I didn't kill the woman, but they already knew I was seeing her. Isn't that right, Detective?"

"That's the information we have," Walker agreed pleasantly.

"Who gave you the information?" Colello wondered.

Walker smiled. "You save your questions for the end. I'll do the asking for now, okay?" He looked from Colello to his lawyer, then back to the suspect. "So Mr. Colello, at some point you did learn that she was married to Stanley Knoebel, correct?"

"Right."

"A man you knew from your group therapy."

"Right."

"And by then you also knew Elizabeth Knoebel was in your wife's therapy group, correct?"

"Yeah. At that point I knew exactly who she was."

"How'd you find out?"

Colello chewed at his lower lip for a moment. "She told me."

"Just like that?"

"Just like that."

"What'd she say?"

"She spelled the whole thing out. Said she knew who I was, right from jump street. She came looking for me, or at least that's how I had it figured by then. Said the things my wife told them about me in their group made me sound interesting." Colello gave them a nervous imitation of a smile. "She said I sounded interesting, can you imagine? Meanwhile, Fran would come home and tell me about this bitch in her group that she hated." He looked slightly embarrassed about mentioning his wife. "You don't need all the details, do you?"

"Details are helpful."

"Elizabeth handed me all this crap about how Fran made me sound like a man's man. How she thought my wife didn't understand me." He began laughing. "That's supposed to be the guy's line, right? 'My wife doesn't understand me.' Elizabeth snowed me like a Colorado avalanche."

"But you did go on seeing her after that?"

"After what?"

"After you knew she was Knoebel's wife."

"Yeah," he admitted with a sigh. "Yeah, I did."

Walker played with the papers on his desk, then looked up at Colello. "You were at her house the day she was murdered, isn't that right?"

This time, when Silverstein spoke up, Colello and Walker both remained quiet. They listened as the lawyer went back and forth with the police chief about Colello's rights, whether they were charging him with murder, and the Fifth Amendment. Their argument became increasingly heated, until Colello held up his hand.

For a moment everyone was silent. Then Silverstein said to his client, "It's time for you to stop talking Thomas."

But Colello shook his head and looked at Walker. "I told you I didn't kill her, and that's the truth. But I was there that day. You want details, right?"

"Right."

The attorney tried one last time to stop him, but Colello told him to forget it. "The only way to clear myself here is to tell the truth, Mark. They already know I was at the house that day." He turned back to Walker. "That's why you brought me in here, right?"

Walker nodded. "That's certainly a big part of it."

"Okay. It was late in the afternoon. Elizabeth called me that morning, asked me to come over, said she would be alone."

"You know we can check the phone records on that," Walker said.

"Why would I lie about it?" Colello asked. Then he became quiet. They all watched as he shook his head, remembering.

"I need something to drink. Could I get a cup of coffee?" Colello asked. "Black."

They all waited as Kovacevic got him a cup and Colello took a sip.

"Where was I? Oh yeah. Elizabeth called me, told me her husband would be in New York till the next day, I should meet her at the house." Colello stopped again. "What a complete numb-nuts I was. I mean, what if Stanley came home early? Or someone else stopped by to see her? It was totally idiotic on my part, I know that now. But you've got to understand something about Elizabeth. She was the kind of woman who made you do stupid things. Even after I knew who she was I couldn't bring myself to stop seeing her. And it wasn't just because she threatened to tell my wife about us."

"Did she make that threat?"

"Not in those words. She would just drop remarks about how much she and Fran hated each other. How it would kill my wife if she knew about us." He rubbed his face roughly with the palms of both hands. "She would say things that made it clear she was on some sort of mission. But that didn't matter to me either. That's the crazy part. None of it mattered because she was such an incredible woman. I mean, I don't really want to get into all of that if I don't have to, but trust me, there is no other word for it. She was incredible." He paused, lost again in the memory of Elizabeth Knoebel.

"You were going to her house," Walker prodded him gently.

"Right. So I got there and I rang the bell a couple of times and got no answer. So I tried the door and it was unlocked. I figured, what the hell, some more of Elizabeth's games. So I go inside, just like a lemming upstream, right? A real genius."

"Go on."

"It's strange when I think about it now, and I've thought about it plenty, believe me. I don't know why I just didn't get back in my car and drive away."

"Had you ever been in their house before?"

"Never. I didn't know if I was walking toward the kitchen or the living room. I'm just standing in the middle of the entrance, the foyer or whatever, and I call out her name. Another good idea, huh? What if someone other than Elizabeth was there? Like her husband, for instance, with a gun or a baseball bat? But there's no answer. I call out again, still nothing. I tell myself, 'Thomas, get the hell out of this place.' But instead I walk upstairs, I figure this is just Elizabeth's way of testing me, so I call her name a few more times, start looking in different rooms until I got to the bedroom. And we all know what I found there."

"No we don't. What did you find?"

"She was dead. Naked, on the bed, blood all over the pillow. Jesus,

I almost threw up. I just stood there, staring, like I couldn't move. I just stood there until I realized, hey, what if the killer is still somewhere in the house? Or what if someone heard the gunshot and the police are on their way? So I slammed her door shut, ran down the stairs, jumped in my car and beat it outta there."

"I want you to really think about this for a minute. Did you touch anything in the house that day? Anything at all."

Colello mentally retraced his steps that afternoon, an exercise he had engaged in countless times during the past week. "I don't think so," he said. "Except the front doorknob, I guess. And the doorknob to her bedroom." He gave Walker a guilty look. "I have to admit, I wiped them both with my shirt tail."

Walker nodded. "How did you know she was dead when you saw her?"

"Jesus, man, I'm no expert, but dead is dead."

"What time were you there?"

"It was five. I'm sure of that. I was supposed to be there at five and I was right on time. I mean it was her house, and she said the house-keeper was off and her husband wouldn't be back that night. I wasn't going to take chances with the timing. I said that already, right?"

"More or less." Walker looked down at his notes again. "What did you do after you left the house?"

"What do you think I did? I drove outta there fast, then went for a drink. Several drinks, actually. I told my wife I would be out at a meeting until late that night, so I couldn't go home. I really didn't want to go home. There was no way I could face Fran. So I got good and drunk."

"Mr. Colello, do you know if Elizabeth Knoebel had other lovers? I'm referring to the period of time when she was seeing you. Did she ever mention anyone else?"

"No. But now as I look back on the whole thing, it wouldn't sur-prise me. You want to know something?" He looked Walker in the eyes again. "Nothing about Elizabeth would surprise me."

Walker studied him carefully as he asked, "Did Elizabeth Knoebel ever discuss her diary with you?"

Colello shook his head, and looked away. "Never."

"But you knew she had a diary, is that right?"

"I didn't, no. I mean, not then. I just heard about it the other day."

"And where did you hear that?"

"Some guy I know. Jesus, I shouldn't have said anything, don't want to get him in a jam."

Walker, Gill, Kovacevic and even his own lawyer stared at Colello.

"Sir," Walker said politely, "I wouldn't worry about getting anyone else in trouble right now."

Colello shrugged, then tried out a look that was supposed to persuade them he was a tough man to intimidate. It was less than convincing.

"Tell us about the diary."

"A guy I know in Town Hall, said he heard about it from a friend of his in the police department."

"The man's name, please?"

"Damnit," Colello said.

"Tell them," his lawyer advised him. "You've already told them every other bloody thing."

"Yeah," Colello said. "I suppose you're right." He puffed out his cheeks and exhaled in one blast, then he gave him the name.

Gill and Walker exchanged a look. That was something they would follow up on later.

Walker turned back to Colello. "Did you ever tell anyone else about Mrs. Knoebel's diary?"

Colello hesitated.

Walker fixed him with an intense look, his gray-brown eyes seeing through the man. "Mr. Colello, who did you tell about the diary?"

Colello wilted under the detective's gaze. "Only one person. Fred Wentworth," he said. "Guy in my therapy group with Doctor Conway."

"He's the only one?"

"Oh yeah, Bob Stratford was there when I told Fred, but I had the feeling he already knew."

"And that's it?"

Colello nodded. "That's it, I'm sure."

"All right," Walker said, pausing to glance at his notes again. Without looking up he asked, "When did your wife find out about you and Mrs. Knoebel?"

It was the first question that truly startled Colello. "What do you mean? My wife never found out."

"Are you sure?"

Walker watched as the man's shoulders sagged, his head lowered slightly and he glanced at his lawyer, who by now was too dumbstruck by his client's admissions to interrupt. "Sometimes Fran looks at me and I think she knows things she has no way of knowing. We pretend we're working on our marriage, but it's all bullshit. I thought I knew Fran better than I ever knew a living soul. Now I'm not sure of anything."

"Is it possible Elizabeth Knoebel told her?"

The thought had occurred to Colello more than once. "What isn't possible? You tell me."

"We're going to have to speak with your wife."

"I realize that now," he said hopelessly.

"It's not my job to give out information and it's not my purpose to ruin anyone's marriage."

"Like it isn't screwed already," Colello said, then looked up at Walker again. "I know it was all wrong. It was even worse to go on once I knew the truth. When I knew she set me up."

"Set you up?"

"She planned the whole thing, like I'm telling you. When she picked me up the first time, that was no casual meeting in a bar. I have the feeling you already know that, right?"

Walker nodded. "That's how we figure it."

"At the very least, when she told me Stanley was her husband, that's when I should've let it go."

"That's not the issue right now," Walker replied in a flat tone. He paused. "The issue is why you have kept silent, why you didn't come forward on your own."

Colello shrugged. "Pretty obvious, don't you think? I never saw anyone else at the house. I just saw Elizabeth lying there and then I made tracks. I honestly don't know anything that can help."

"Maybe so, but we're going to need to go back over all this in more detail. You never know what you might have seen that you may not realize."

"Okay." Colello took out a cigarette. He was so unsteady that Kovacevic looked to Walker, who nodded. *The hell with the rules.* Kovacevic reached out and lit it for him. "Look," Colello said, "I know I'm not about to win any good citizenship awards, but I want you to believe I'm telling you the truth here, all right?"

"It's not important what I believe. I just put the facts together and let the state's attorney make the decision." Walker looked up at Chief Gill, then turned back to Colello. "Okay," he said, "let's take it from the top. Step by step."

CHAPTER 48

Stanley Knoebel was sitting in the den. His vacant gaze fell on Elizabeth's computer. It had been returned to him by Officer Kovacevic.

He stared at the machine, wondering at what his life had become. He could see nothing. He could hear nothing. He was spiritually blind. Emotionally deaf.

No man is a success if he attains all of his goals. Such a man is without purpose, hollow and spent. Yes, Stanley Knoebel thought, that was precisely how he felt. He was bereft of purpose. His only dreams came at night, unwelcome and unforgiving, thrust upon him, spoken without invitation, leaving him with unbearable sorrow.

My God, Knoebel thought. *Is there nothing remaining of me?*

Memories are the only things we truly own, the only things that can never be traded or stolen or given away. We create our memories, shape them, edit them, hold them for as long as we need or want them. Memories are not always real, but they are ours. Memories can be counted on, even when the people we are remembering have long since disappeared or disappointed, even after our own emotions have let us down.

Emotions are not faithful in the way memories are. Emotions live their own lives, beyond our control.

Happiness leads an evanescent existence, easily destroyed and impossible to resuscitate at will. Examine happiness too carefully and it evaporates, like a bubble that floats on the breeze until you try and take hold of it for a closer look.

Sadness is made of sturdier stuff, standing up to scrutiny and reason, usually surviving intervening thoughts and events that would easily crush delight. If you observe happiness too closely, some or all of it will fade. Explore sadness and you will only grow sadder. We are under its spell, like it or not.

Love can be more powerful, and far less predictable. We can often identify the source of our happiness or sorrow, even if we have no ability to govern those feelings. But love is mysterious. It controls us, and we willingly give ourselves up to its control. We covet its magic like nothing else in creation.

Stanley Knoebel wished he had never fallen prey to its fascination, but it was beyond his control, he had truly loved her. He had loved Elizabeth as much as he would ever love anyone.

Yet hate, as he came to see, exists in the underbelly of love's power. Hate has its own great force, with an appetite unmatched by all other feelings combined. It eats away at everything we are and, in the end, unless we can struggle free from its grasp, it leaves us with nothing.

Nothing, that is, but our memories, however we choose to see them and hold them and keep them for ourselves.

He had loved Elizabeth, but he came to understand that she did not love him. She might have, in the beginning, he allowed himself that much, but ultimately their marriage became her prison. She was locked inside the wealth and comfort he provided and, coupled with her own fears, she found it was a confinement she could not escape. Instead she became determined to punish him for her own disappointment.

How could she have failed to see who he was, to gauge his limitations? He wanted to provide what she needed, but she would not forgive his imperfections, his remoteness, his inability to be what she wanted him to be. She continually tore him down, ripped their marriage apart, and destroyed their lives in the process.

He drew a deep breath, then let it out in a rush as he stood up, crowbar in hand. He raised it high above his head and paused. What would his lawyer say? What would the police claim? That he had destroyed legal evidence? That it proved he was her murderer?

To hell with them. His lawyer, the police. To hell with all of them.

He brought the heavy metal bar crashing down. Then again. And again, as the metal and plastic yielded to his forceful blows. Sparks were sent flying and crunching sounds resonated through his head as he destroyed Elizabeth's computer.

CHAPTER 49

That evening, Fran Colello waited for her husband to tell her the truth. About his discussion with Detective Walker. About Elizabeth Knoebel. About everything.

She waited, but so far he had not told her anything.

"What happened?" she finally asked. "What did the police want?"

Colello said the police had brought him in for routine questioning because he was acquainted with Stanley Knoebel through group therapy.

"Routine questioning? The police came to our door without warning, for all of our neighbors to see. No phone call, no request for you to stop by and meet with them. What sort of routine questioning is that?"

Colello shrugged. "I don't know. Maybe that's how they do things in a murder case," he told her. "They don't care who they upset."

"What did they ask you about Doctor Knoebel?"

"You know, the usual stuff. What do I think of him, did he ever say anything strange, did I think he was the kind of a guy who would murder his wife, that sort of thing."

"What about Mrs. Knoebel? Did they ask you about her?"

"Why would they? What do I have to do with Elizabeth Knoebel?"

"Elizabeth?"

"Sure. That was her name, right?" He fixed her with an angry stare. "What is this? I already got the third degree from the police."

"The third degree? I thought it was routine questioning."

"Sure, it was routine. But it's a murder case. They break your chops, you know?"

"I don't know, I really don't. Tell me."

"You'll find out soon enough. They want to talk with you. I guess they want to talk with everybody who ever met these people."

"Should I bring a lawyer, Thomas?"

"What is that supposed to mean?"

"You called Mark, and he went with you. Should I call him too?"

"I don't think I like your attitude. What's with the attitude?"

"It's a simple question. I don't understand why you needed a lawyer to answer routine questions about Stanley Knoebel. You hardly know the man, right?"

She watched as his anger visibly rose again, then fell, the color having flooded his face, then quickly drained away. He stood up and stomped around the room, acting as if he were ready to explode, then backing off.

He was not sure how to respond, and his uncertainty made everything plain to her.

"Tell me, Thomas."

"Tell you what, for chrissake?" When she didn't respond he said, "Let's just drop it, okay?"

"Tell me," she said again. "It's all right. Just tell me the truth. I'm entitled to know."

"Know what, for crying out loud. There's nothing to tell. You'll see for yourself. They'll ask you a bunch of bullshit questions and that'll be the end of it."

"That's not what I'm talking about. You know goddamned well what I'm talking about. I have to know. I have to hear you tell me."

"Tell you what? What? This is a sick conversation. I don't understand what you're saying and I don't understand what you're asking. What do you want from me?"

"The truth."

"I told you the truth."

"No, I mean the truth about Elizabeth Knoebel."

"Listen to me, Fran. There is nothing I can tell you about Elizabeth Knoebel. There is nothing else here that means anything. You're looking for something that isn't there. Okay? Please try and see that."

"You're wrong. You don't know how wrong you are. It doesn't end here. You'll see. It's worse than you think."

"What? What the hell is worse than I think? Speak English, will you please?"

"It's worse than this, don't you understand?"

He looked at her and saw something in her eyes that was completely unnerving. He hesitated, then in a softer voice said, "Look, I know it's upsetting. This woman gets killed, we have to talk to the police about it. I know it's upsetting. But don't make it into something it isn't. Are you listening to me, Fran? Don't make it into something it isn't."

Fran Colello did not want to make it something it was not. She said, "With everything that's happened, and everything that's going to happen, all I ask is that you tell me the truth."

Colello felt like punching his hand through the wall, or something worse, but instead he stormed out of the room, out of the house, jumped in his car and headed for the Black Swan to get drunk. He went without telling her the truth.

A short time later, when Detective Walker called Fran to set a meeting for her interview the next day, she knew it was too late.

CHAPTER 50

Back in his office the next morning, Walker was arguing on the telephone with a hospital administrator in New York.

"What are you telling me?" he demanded. "Was Doctor Knoebel in the operating room that afternoon or wasn't he?" He looked up at Kovacevic, his frown displaying part exasperation and part accusation, a signal to the junior officer that somehow this was his fault.

Kovacevic remained standing while Walker had the woman on the other end of the call explain it to him one more time.

"Okay," the detective responded, "I think I got it. The answer is that there is no answer. You're telling me there's no way of verifying the times Doctor Knoebel came and went from the operating room that day, other than questioning every nurse and doctor in the entire hospital." He nodded at her reply. "All right. Well thank you again," he said, then slammed the phone down. "Damn."

"No good, huh?"

"No good. She says Knoebel could have been anywhere. He might have gone up to the gallery to observe the surgery from above. He could have been in and out of the OR. He could have been in the john for all they know. There's no way to check for sure, unless everyone who was in the hospital that day is willing to say he wasn't there during those critical afternoon hours."

"Fat chance."

"Exactly. No one is going to sink him that way, especially since they're not in the habit of looking at their watches while they're in the middle of surgery. How the hell could anyone be sure, unless they saw him get in his car and leave?" Walker scrawled a note to himself in the file. "Run another check with the parking garages around the hospital. Find out where he normally parks, but if he really murdered her we've got to figure it was planned well in advance. He wouldn't have used his regular garage." He looked up. "All the same, if he's going to rely on this alibi, it's got some holes in it."

Kovacevic nodded.

"Okay, what else do you have?"

Kovacevic paused.

"What is it?" Walker asked.

"It's Doctor Conway, sir."

"What about her?"

"I keep thinking about those anonymous notes."

"What about them?"

"Maybe they were supposed to work as some sort of reverse psychology or something. They help to rule her out as a suspect, don't they?"

Walker studied the young officer for a moment. "Sit down," he told him.

Kovacevic planted himself in the chair beside Walker's desk.

"So, you think Randi Conway should be a suspect?"

"I don't know, sir. What do you think?"

Walker responded with a frown. "I've considered it, believe me." He scratched his chin and stared straight ahead for a moment. Then he shook off the thought. "You know Kovie, I think this job is turning you into a cynic."

The junior officer smiled. "I suppose that's a compliment, coming from you sir."

Walker laughed. "Whatever it is, don't lose that edge. So tell me, where's her motive?"

"What if Mrs. Knoebel did something to Doctor Conway we don't even know about?"

"Possible. But what about our gallery of cheaters and disgruntled spouses? It takes a lot to drive someone to murder. "

Kovacevic nodded.

"It's possible Doctor Knoebel murdered a cheating wife. Then we have Elizabeth Knoebel's lovers. Maybe one of them got an idea of what she was up to, diary or no diary."

"Like you said, it takes a lot to turn someone into a killer."

"What about the wives? It seems every one of those women hated her."

"They had good reason to, if they knew what she was doing."

"Yeah." Walker rubbed his eyes. "It's like I told Gill, we've got too many damned suspects. But let's go back to those two anonymous notes for a moment. There's something about them that bothers me too." He thought it over. "It's all too easy," he said.

"Sir?"

"Everything points to one of Randi's patients."

"Randi, sir?"

"Doctor Conway," he said with a grin. "But think about it, Kovie. She gets two notes. Her office is ransacked and her files scattered around. What do the notes mean? Nothing, far as I can tell. She doesn't believe any of her records are missing from the break-in. Sure, someone might have read something, but so what? Or they might have been looking for the diary. But somehow it all feels manufactured. I mean, what if the murderer is not one of her patients? What if it's someone who knew Elizabeth Knoebel, knew Randi Conway was her therapist, and has been doing everything possible to send us in the wrong direction?"

"If you're right, it's working."

Walker nodded. "People have affairs every day. And they get caught every day. But they don't resort to homicide. I'll grant you that the Knoebel woman is an extreme case, and the stuff she was writing takes things to another level. But did any of our unhappy players know about the book? Except Nettie Sisson? I don't think so, or at least we have no indication that they did. I don't even think Randi Conway knew, based on her reaction when I showed it to her. But maybe our killer did."

Kovacevic nodded.

"I'm asking you, do you really believe Colello went off and shot Elizabeth because his wife might find out about their affair?"

"No, I really don't."

Walker shook his head. "Neither do I. Can I see Fran Colello shooting her? Maybe. But there's got to be someone with more at stake here. Or a combination of real danger and a warped mind."

"Which leads us where, sir?"

Walker picked up the phone. "I have a message from Doctor Conway, says she wants to meet with me. Asked me to bring the photographs of the murder scene." He punched in her phone number. "Time to make that date."

CHAPTER 51

An hour later Anthony Walker arrived at Randi's office. She was working her way through a cup of coffee.

"Got any more of that?"

"Help yourself." Randi pointed to the machine on her credenza. "That's a refrigerator underneath, if you need milk."

"Black is fine."

"Did you bring the photos?"

Walker casually dropped an envelope on her desk, then went over and picked out a ceramic mug and had a look inside. "Anyone ever wash these things?" he asked.

Randi smiled weakly. "Sometimes I do, sometimes the cleaning lady. Sometimes no one. Pretty grungy, huh?"

"This one doesn't seem to have anything moving in it. Should be all right." He filled the cup and sat down in the chair across from her.

She looked at him, a flush in her cheeks as she asked, "Will we be okay? You and me, I mean."

"Yes," he said. "I think we will."

"I do too," she said with a smile.

He waited as she began to study the photos, then asked, "So what gives?"

Some of the pictures were more gruesome than others. Each of them offered a stark portrayal of Elizabeth's violent death. "The room. I told you, I believe more than one of my patients was in that room."

"I already told you, I know one of them was Thomas Colello." She began to say something, but he showed her the palm of his hand. "It's okay. He already told us he was there, at least once."

"He did?" Randi shook her head. "All right, I'm not even going to ask about that right now. I'm more interested in the other man. He was talking about this room in group the other night. I'm sure of it." She returned to the photographic images. "It didn't hit me at first. I've never been to the Knoebels' home and I had only seen these pictures. But Thomas knew right away. Strange. I couldn't figure out why he became so angry. I was looking for something deep-seated, you know? Some issue between him and the other man." Now she looked up at Walker. "The weight of knowledge can really slow you down sometimes."

"I wouldn't know. I've never had enough for it to get in my way."

"Save the 'aw shucks' routine, Anthony," she said with a smile. "Use it on someone who hasn't heard your theories on life and marriage."

Walker wrapped his hand around the mug, ignoring the handle, then slowly drank some of the hot coffee. All the while, he watched Randi. "So? You going to tell me who this was or should I start guessing?"

"Look, I wouldn't have called you here if I didn't want to cooperate."

"Uh oh. Sounds like I should start guessing."

"No, it's not like that. I want to wait for Bob. I called him, wanted to make sure we're doing this correctly. After all, it may amount to nothing. It seems there may have been a lot of people in Elizabeth's bedroom. I hate to say it that way, but it appears to be true. What if this other man *was* there? It doesn't mean he killed her, right? I mean, that would be a pretty extreme leap of faith, wouldn't it?"

"I don't know."

"Suppose I give you his name. Then you'll go and question him, correct?"

Walker took a sip of coffee. "That would be the general idea."

"Then he'll know I put you onto him. And what if I'm wrong? What if it was a coincidence? What if he had nothing to do with her death? Where does that leave me? I violated a sacred trust, my professional ethics. Then what?"

Robert Stratford opened the door, catching the last of Randi's questions. "I hate to sound like a lawyer, but I think it's safe to say you'll get sued. What would remain of your practice is hard to say. I sure wouldn't want to be telling you any of my secrets once the story got out that you were sharing patient confidences with the police. How about you Lieutenant?"

"Good morning," the detective glumly replied.

Stratford went over and fixed himself a cup of coffee. He was dressed in a navy blue suit, white shirt with gold cuff links and a yellow tie with little red pindots. His black shoes were as shiny as the hood of a new car. "I'm not trying to be obstructive, just realistic." He came over and sat in the chair beside Walker. He looked into his mug, then placed it on the desk. "God, Randi, when was the last time you cleaned out that machine?"

"It's not the coffee maker," Walker assured him. "It's the cup."

"Oh good." Stratford picked up the mug, had another good look at it, decided it would be all right and took a sip. "I guess the heat of the coffee should kill the bacteria, right? Now where was I? Oh yes. Randi filled me in on the phone." He turned to her. "You've looked at the photos?"

Randi gestured toward the group of pictures spread out before her.

"And?"

"And I think I may be right," she told them.

"Okay. And now we have to decide what to do about it," Stratford told her.

"I understand."

"What you told me on the phone this morning," Stratford said to her, "you still feel the same."

"I do."

"Look," Walker said, "If it helps at all, I promise I'm not going to barge in and tell this guy I know what happened in his group."

"Of course not," Stratford agreed.

"I'll do everything I can to be discreet," Walker told them. "I'll make it clear that the questioning is part of a series of routine interviews I'm conducting of all the people in both therapy groups, Mrs. Knoebel's and Doctor Knoebel's. I've already begun that process, so there's no reason for it to seem that you breached any confidence whatsoever. I've made it known that you didn't supply the names of your patients, which is true, I put that together with help from Doctor Knoebel and Mrs. Gorman. All you'd be doing by giving me his name is saving me some valuable time." He looked to Stratford, then turned to Randi. "This is a murder we're talking about. Somebody took a gun, put it to that woman's head and pulled the trigger." He leaned forward and began tapping his fingers on the photographs. "Have another look."

Randi felt ill. Then, as if she had no choice, she stared once again at the images of Elizabeth Knoebel. She was on the large bed with the dark mahogany headboard, her life gone, her once beautiful face distorted, the blood everywhere. She looked at Stratford.

Stratford stared back at her. They did not speak, but the sudden tension between them was as real as if they were yelling at each other. Walker began to sense he might be getting more than one answer today.

Stratford finally said, "Give him the name."

Randi turned to Walker, her eyes weary. For an instant she thought of Nettie Sisson, of what the woman knew and what she did not. Then, before she could speak, Walker held up his hand.

"It's Fred Wentworth, right?"

Both Randi and Stratford turned to him.

"Yes," she said, not hiding her surprise, "it is."

Walker stood. "Thanks," he said. "Just wanted confirmation. For the record, you still haven't told me a thing." Then he turned and headed out of her office.

CHAPTER 52

When he finished with Randi Conway and Robert Stratford, Walker went outside and climbed into the Explorer. Kovacevic was waiting in the driver's seat.

"You get anything?" the young officer asked.

"Fred Wentworth."

"She gave you his name?"

"Not exactly. I gave the name, she confirmed that he was the guy who got Colello upset in her group the other night."

"You don't sound very enthusiastic about the lead."

"Let me ask you something. Did you believe Colello when he said he didn't know anything about the diary until after Elizabeth Knoebel was shot?"

Kovacevic nodded. "I think he was telling the truth about that."

"Me too. So, when he told Wentworth about the diary, that was almost a week after the murder."

"I'm with you so far."

"Colello never said anything about Wentworth being upset when he told him. Nothing about any sort of strange reaction."

"True."

"Colello also mentioned that they ran into Stratford at the bar that night, remember?"

Kovacevic nodded.

"When we went through everything the second time, Colello said that Stratford would not discuss the case."

"I remember."

"If Wentworth had some sort of violent reaction to news of the diary, Stratford would have said something to me just now."

"I would think so."

"But when Randi and I put those names together just now, Colello and Wentworth, I never said anything about knowing they all had a drink the other night."

Kovacevic waited.

"Yet Stratford never mentioned seeing them. Maybe it's nothing, maybe they never said anything to him worth repeating."

When he paused, Kovacevic asked the obvious question. "But why wouldn't he at least mention seeing them together?"

"Exactly." Walker pulled roughly at his chin with his thumb and forefinger. "There's something just doesn't feel right about how this is unfolding."

"How do you mean?"

"Maybe I'm uncomfortable about Randi Conway's relationship with Stratford." Walker shook his head. "Although I hate to admit it." He forced a dry laugh and borrowed one of Thomas Colello's lines. "Not my style though."

"I wouldn't think so."

He was about to say something about how utterly stupid it was to have slept with a woman who was either a key witness or a suspect in a murder case, but he kept that to himself. "No," he repeated, "it isn't my style at all."

"Could it be something else?"

"I don't know." Walker sat back and covered his upper lip with his lower in the way he did when he was thinking. "You drive, I'm going to try and reach Wentworth, set up an interview with him as soon as we're finished with Colello's wife."

Walker tried to reach Fred Wentworth at his office and on his cell with no success. Meanwhile, Kovacevic drove them to the Colello home for their appointment with the lady of the house. A short time later, she and Walker were seated at her kitchen table as Fran listened to Officer Kovacevic rattle off the required list of legal warnings.

She could remain silent. If she chose to talk with them, anything she said could be used against her later. If she said anything that incriminated her, or incriminated anyone else for that matter, she could be sure that would be used. She had a right to have an attorney present, but that was up to her. If she could not afford a lawyer, the state would provide one. Kovacevic asked her to sign a piece of paper acknowledging that she understood all the rights he had just explained.

"Did my husband sign one of these?"

Walker said that he had.

"But his lawyer was with him. Why did he have his lawyer with him?"

Walker shrugged. "That was his right, as the officer just explained to you. You can have a lawyer here if you want."

She read through the form. "Why would I need a lawyer?"

"I don't know, Mrs. Colello. Nowadays people seem to have lawyers around for everything. It's entirely up to you," he repeated patiently.

She was still looking at the form. "You met with my husband at your headquarters, or whatever it's called."

"We didn't want to disturb you. Didn't know if you had children at home at that hour. Like I told you on the phone last night, we can go to my office if you prefer."

She looked up from the papers and studied Walker for a moment. "Pen?"

Walker handed her his ballpoint and she signed her name. Kovacevic, who was standing alongside Walker, bent over and witnessed her signature.

Fran looked up at the younger man. "Wouldn't you be more comfortable sitting? Or are you standing guard so I won't go running out the door?"

Kovacevic looked at Walker, who nodded. "Thank you," the officer said. He took a seat at the end of the large, antique wooden table and switched on his hand-held digital recorder, leaving Walker and Mrs. Colello facing each other across a three-foot width of oak parquet.

She said, "You want to know about Elizabeth Knoebel, right?"

"Yes."

"I hated her. Does that answer any of your questions?"

"It might."

Fran Colello brushed back her dark, straight hair with a casual sweep of her hand. Not a bad-looking woman, Walker thought. Just a few pounds over fighting weight and a bit careless with her grooming. A woman, he thought, who didn't give a damn anymore.

"So, Detective, are you going to tell me that my husband was having an affair with Elizabeth Knoebel?"

"No, ma'am, I'm not."

"He was, you know. You should know that if you're a detective." She calmly examined his face again. "But you already knew. It's obvious. Is that why you're here, Detective Walker? To find out if I shot that bitch because she was screwing my husband? Is that what you want to know?"

Walker smiled, wishing he hadn't.

"You see something funny about this?"

"No ma'am, just the way you said it, is all. What makes you think your husband was having an affair with Mrs. Knoebel?"

Fran noticed some toast crumbs on the table, remnants of her family's breakfast. She began to carefully push them together with the edge of her right hand, corralling them from four sides in an ever-decreasing square of tiny, dry pieces of crust until they were in a small pile. Then, with violent backhand motion, she swept them off the table onto the floor. She looked up at Walker. "How do I know? Is that your question?"

Walker nodded slowly. "Yes."

"You'll have to do better than that if you want to find your murderer, Detective Walker."

"We're doing the best we can, Mrs. Colello." He took a deep breath and started again. "Look, I realize this is difficult, but you were the one who brought up the subject of your husband and Mrs. Knoebel."

"Mrs. Knoebel." She repeated the name like it was some disagreeable taste. "Suppose we just refer to her as 'the bitch'? Would that be all right?"

"I'm afraid that'd make me a little uncomfortable, referring to a murder victim that way. You can suit yourself."

"How accommodating you are, Detective Walker. Anything to get me talking, is that the drill?"

"I'd simply like to have my questions answered."

"Fine. Answer number one. I knew because women know these things. It wasn't just the way he behaved, or the nights he stayed out late, or the scent on his jacket that seemed familiar but wasn't mine. It wasn't only that. It was her. The things she said in group."

"What sort of things did she say in your group that made you suspicious?"

"I can't really remember any specifics," she admitted. "We discussed so many things in group, private things, personal things. Even so, there were things she knew about me I couldn't remember saying."

"Can you recall one example?"

"No," she said. But now, as she was forced to think of Elizabeth, Fran did begin to recall, the memory rising up in her like a burning sensation of hate that made her want to scream.

She heard Walker ask, "Was it something she said in your group that caused you to attack her. I'm talking about the day before she was killed."

"Ah, so you've been speaking with Doctor Conway."

"No ma'am. We spoke with other members of your group."

"I see," she replied coldly. "Well then, you already know what happened. She was insulting and vulgar and horrible and I grabbed her by the throat. What's your question?"

"Do you recall what she said? Did she say something about your husband?"

Fran Colello bared her upper teeth, about to say something. Then she paused. "Wouldn't that be convenient for you? But no," she added with a quick shake of her head, "she called me a used-up old housefrau. That's when I tried to choke her."

Walker decided to drop that subject for the time being. "Did your husband ever say he was sleeping with Mrs. . . . uh . . . with her?"

"My husband? Start telling the truth? Why ruin his perfect record? No, Detective. Thomas never told me. He won't admit it even now. Isn't that the proper procedure in the handbook for cheating husbands? Deny, deny, deny. No matter what. If you're caught with your pants at your ankles and the girl on her knees, just deny. Say your belt buckle broke off and she's helping you find it." Walker noticed that Fran Colello's smile was almost indistinguishable from her sneer. "When man was created, the Lord said, 'Denial shall be yours.' Isn't that the way it works?"

Walker felt he should say something. Instead he glanced at Kovacevic.

"I'm sorry," Fran Colello said to the younger officer. "Did you expect me to break down and cry or something? I don't think so, gentlemen. My husband is an unfaithful bastard and she was a bitch, and I'm glad she's dead. But I didn't kill her if that's what you want to know. Although I would've been happy to if I had the chance, or if I thought it would have made a difference in my life."

"Do you remember where you were the day she died?"

"I was right here doing my chores, just like a good little housefrau."

"How are you so sure you were home that day?"

"I'm home every day, Detective. And I remember hearing about it the next night, on the radio. I remember wondering . . ." She stopped.

"Wondering what, Mrs. Colello?"

"About the previous day, I guess." Her eyes would not meet his now.

"That's not what you were going to say, is it?"

She looked down at her clean tabletop. "I remember, that's all. I remember how I felt. Pleased and angry and sad, all at the same time. And I remember thinking about where I was the day before. At the time she was killed. I wanted to fix that in my mind. It helped me enjoy the moment."

"What else were you wondering, do you recall?"

She shook her head.

"Were you wondering where your husband was that day?"

She shook her head again.

"Is that what you were wondering?"

She reacted by treating her own hands to a withering stare.

"What time did your husband arrive home that night? The night of Elizabeth Knoebel's death. Do you remember?"

"I don't know."

"I don't expect you to know exactly. I'm only asking for your best recollection."

"That's not what I meant. I meant, I don't know if I should be answering these questions about my husband."

"Let me ask you something along a different line. When you were in group together, did Mrs. Knoebel ever mention having affairs? I'm not referring to your husband. Did she ever mention any other men she was seeing?"

"Why would she? She was always too busy criticizing me. Or Joan. Or one of the others."

Walker leaned back for a minute and looked into Fran Colello's cold, hazel eyes. "I really need to ask you some questions about your husband. Are you certain he was sleeping with Elizabeth Knoebel, or is it just something you suspected?"

She grimaced at the direct question. "I knew then and I know now," she replied.

"How do you know?"

She paused, thinking through what she was going to say. She took a moment to study Walker's weathered face, the relentless gray-brown eyes that hinted at compassion but gave little away. "I followed him one day," she admitted. "I followed him to a bar. He met her there. I waited across the way until they came out. They got into her car and drove to a motel just down the road. My loving husband didn't even notice me there. It was as if I was invisible."

"Is that the real reason you attacked her in your group therapy session? Because you found out she was sleeping with your husband?"

"Yes, Detective. And in answer to your next question, I wished she was dead. I'm glad she's dead now. But I'll tell you again. I didn't kill her. And neither did that bastard I'm married to."

CHAPTER 53

Fred Wentworth told himself he had to learn to keep his big mouth shut. He had the salesman's habit of talking too damn much, a lousy occupational hazard.

He liked Thomas Colello and thought they were becoming friends. Now he had done something to make Colello angry and he couldn't figure out what it was. Thomas had become upset in group, and all Fred knew was that it had something to do with Elizabeth Knoebel.

She was still a problem for him, even now.

He should never have bragged about knowing her, about being in her bedroom. Maybe that was the reason Colello turned on him. But why?

Damn, Wentworth cursed himself. In the end, what had she meant to him anyway? Humiliation. Derision. She had stood there laughing at him, and he should have caved her head in then and there.

Now he had received the phone call, early this morning, something that could not be ignored. He had been summoned to a private discussion about Elizabeth and her diary. He was told it would be best if they met before he spoke another word about it to anyone. Before the police came knocking on his door. Before he suffered a public embarrassment. There was trouble ahead, he was told, and he was going to need help.

It was an appointment he had to keep.

This was another day when he had no appointments scheduled at work anyway, so leaving the office was not an issue. He headed up the highway from New York, through Westchester into Fairfield County, exiting onto an access road, then turning onto a winding, two-lane stretch that was lined with colorful trees of red and orange and purple leaves.

They agreed to meet at an out-of-the-way coffee shop in back

327

country Redding. No sense in having their discussion interrupted by anyone they knew in town. No point in even being seen together until this blew over.

Fred would be pleased to do anything that would keep things from getting worse.

He had been traveling for several miles on the back roads, worrying over how all of this would play out for him at home, at work, and with the police, when he brought his station wagon to a halt at a stop sign. There was no other traffic at this hour, except for a sedan he noticed in his rearview mirror. The road ahead was otherwise quiet, he was early, and he didn't need someone pressing him from behind. He took the first right turn, but the sedan did the same, staying close.

At the next intersection Wentworth headed left, but the car in back of him also took that turn. As the sedan drew close up behind him, Fred stuck his arm out the window to wave the driver on, pulling his wagon along the shoulder and slowing it as the sedan sped past and continued around the bend ahead. Fred did not get a look at the driver.

Once he saw that the sedan was gone, Wentworth increased his speed, returning to a consideration of his problems and how he intended to deal with them. He was lost in thought as he came around the next turn where he spotted that same sedan, off to the left side of the road, amidst some trees.

In that instant Fred knew. Somehow he understood. Before he could react, the sedan leapt across the blacktop, heading straight at him. Fred stepped on the accelerator, his heavy station wagon careening to the right, his tires spinning in the dirt and gravel alongside the edge of the road as he tried to surge ahead. But the sedan was faster, and it was already alongside him, coming from an oblique angle that gave it all of the leverage, forcing Wentworth's vehicle into a thicket of trees as they raced around the curve of the bending road, both of them going too fast now, no other cars in sight.

The sedan veered harder to the right, forcing Wentworth up a slight berm and then into a shallow ravine. The sedan then swerved left as the station wagon went crashing off the side of a large tree and then smashed sideward into another where it came to a loud and violent stop.

The driver of the sedan stopped and had a look around before getting out of the car to survey the damage. Staying clear of the steam and smoke that was gushing up from underneath the crumbled hood of Wentworth's car, the murderer stepped toward the open window. Fred Wentworth was slumped to the side, the front airbag having deployed and deflated, now just an empty balloon sitting on his lap. It had been no help with the brunt of the lateral impact.

Too bad it had to be Wentworth, perhaps the least deserving of all the possible candidates for this thankless role. After all of the planning, Wentworth would never have been the first choice, but there it was. The decision had been forced by the actions of others, and now it was done.

The murderer, with a hand gloved in latex, felt Wentworth's neck. He was already dead. The murderer then drew the pistol from a coat pocket. Having to use the gun to fake his suicide would clearly have been an unwelcome complication. Instead, the murderer simply placed the handle of the revolver in Wentworth's lifeless hand. Once the fingerprints were made, the murderer took the pistol, walked around the wagon and, leaning through the passenger side window, placed it inside the console between the front seats.

With nothing else to be done here, the killer crossed the deserted road, climbed back into the sedan and proceeded on, turning left at the next intersection. In a few miles this car, which had been taken from an unsuspecting suburbanite from North Stamford who had left it in the driveway with the keys above the visor, would be abandoned deep in the woods where the murderer's own car waited to be used to keep another appointment.

CHAPTER 54

Walker was becoming increasingly frustrated. He could not reach either of the Wentworths. He had tried their cells and home with no luck. When he called the main line in Fred's office all he learned was that Wentworth had left early that morning to keep an outside appointment. No one had any details beyond that.

They were finished questioning Fran Colello, so Walker and Kovacevic drove across town to the Wentworth house, but again came up empty. No one was there. After waiting a while in the driveway, Walker thought better of leaving any sort of message and told Kovacevic it was time to return to headquarters.

They spent the balance of the afternoon in the detectives' squad room, reordering their thinking about the Knoebel case. If Wentworth was their man, they wanted to do as little as possible in the way of further disrupting the various fractured marriages they had already intruded upon. To that end, they put additional interviews on hold until they interrogated Wentworth.

As night fell they were about to take another run past the Wentworth house when Chief Gill summoned them both to his office.

"What the hell is going on here, Walker?"

"Could you be a little more specific Chief?"

"I told you to keep this investigation low-key and to get it wrapped up as soon as possible, did I not?"

"That would certainly be the preferred method in every homicide."

"Spare me the New York City sarcasm. I've got attorneys for not one, but both Colellos complaining about your treatment of their clients. Doctor Knoebel's lawyer says that you two are spending so much time in his hospital they're going to start charging our department rent. You're in Doctor Conway's office more than you're here.

And now rumor has it that you've become drinking buddies with the First Selectman, a pairing that has not gone unnoticed by the local gentry and the media. Is that your idea of dancing around like Fred Astaire?"

Walker wondered what irked Gill more, the disgruntled citizens or the idea that he had become cozy with the First Selectman. "I'm heading up a murder investigation, Chief, not to mention the B and E of Doctor Conway's office. Unfortunately, suspects and clues are not generally delivered to headquarters. You have to go out and find them if you want to solve the crimes."

"Is that so? Well tell me then, what crimes have you solved so far?"

Walker sighed. "I met with Doctor Conway and the First Selectman this morning. They confirmed a name that may be helpful."

"A name?"

"A suspect."

"Another one? Perfect. And whose life are you going to ruin tonight?"

"Fred Wentworth. Another of Doctor Conway's merry men. He made comments that led some members of his therapy group to believe he'd been in Elizabeth Knoebel's bedroom."

"According to you, who hasn't?"

Walker's cell phone had been buzzing in his pocket. He ignored it the first two times. Now he said, "Hold on Chief." He looked at the incoming number. "It's coming from one of ours." He hit the green button and said, "Yeah Kevin."

Walker sat there, phone in hand, staring at Kovacevic as he listened to Kevin Chambers say, "That guy you wanted us to locate for an interview, name of Fred Wentworth. Something just came across the computer from the State. Troopers found a car off Route 35, up near Redding. Crashed into a tree sometime today. Driver alone in the vehicle. Dead at the scene. Preliminary identification is Fred Wentworth."

Walker told the officer he was about to go on speaker, hit a button and had Chambers repeat the information to Chief Gill and Kovacevic.

When Chambers finished, Walker asked, "The State's on it?"

"Yeah. Troopers are at the scene."

"He drove his car into a tree?"

"That's what they're telling me."

"Drunk? Heart attack?"

"Not sure yet, but the trooper says there were marks on the side of car."

"Meaning what, Kevin? What sort of marks?"

"The car was very banged up. Hit a ditch and scraped a lot of bushes and smaller trees before it hit the large oak where they found it. But even with all that, there are marks that might have come from another vehicle."

"They look like new marks?"

"Seems so."

"What do the troopers think?"

"Not saying yet. He could have hit something before he went out of control. Or it may have been a hit-and-run."

Walker looked to Gill, who was doing his best not to react.

"One more thing Anthony," Chambers said.

"We're all listening."

"The troopers found a revolver in the center console between the seats of Wentworth's station wagon. It's a .38 caliber."

Everyone was silent for a moment. Then Walker said, "Be sure no one touches that revolver, assuming they haven't screwed it up already. We need prints and then we need it sent to ballistics."

"I'm on it," Chambers said.

"Keep me posted," Walker told him and hung up.

CHAPTER 55

When Mitchell Avery picked up the private line in his office, the last voice he expected to hear was Joan's.

"Oh Mitchell," she began, then started crying.

Joan was not given to emotional outbursts, and so Avery's insides froze as he asked, "Joan, what is it? Are you all right? Is it one of the kids?"

"No," she managed to respond as she tried to pull herself together. "It's Phyllis Wentworth." She took a deep breath, then told him, "Her husband is dead."

Relief washed over Avery like a huge wave, followed by a moment of guilt. He was glad it had nothing to do with either of his children or Joan, feeling as if a firm grip on his insides had suddenly been released. But then he asked, "Fred Wentworth is dead?"

"Yes."

"What happened?"

Joan drew another uneven breath. "I came to Doctor Conway's office. I had an appointment with her—to talk about us. When I got there, she was sitting at her desk crying. It was awful."

When she paused, he pressed her. "Joan, what happened to Fred?"

"He was in a car crash. Ran into a tree or something. Randi just heard."

"Jesus, that *is* awful."

"There's more," she said.

"Was someone else hurt?"

"No, no, nothing like that. He was alone. No other car involved, or however they say that."

When she hesitated again, he said, "I'm listening."

"The police told Randi they found a gun in his car. They say it might be the gun that was used to murder Elizabeth."

Neither of them spoke for a moment. Then Mitchell asked, "Where are you?"

"In my car, outside Doctor Conway's office."

"All right. I'm leaving New York right now, heading back to the house. Meet me there, okay?"

Joan began crying again. "I'm not sure. I don't think I can do this right now."

"Please Joan. There's so much we have to talk about, so many things I want to say. Just meet me at the house, I'll be there as fast as I can."

She thought it over, then said, "All right. I'll go there now."

"Good, I'm on my way."

"But Mitchell," she said, then paused again. "No more lies."

CHAPTER 56

The ballistics test of the pistol found in Wentworth's car was rushed through forensics the next day. The match with the bullet that killed Mrs. Knoebel was perfect. The serial number had been filed off the revolver, so there was little chance of tracking down the history of ownership. The case was open and shut.

The local news had the story within hours and the murder was declared as having been solved. This seemed to delight everyone involved in the investigation.

Everyone that was, except Anthony Walker.

Sitting at his desk, reading the ballistic results, Walker told Kovacevic, "It's the murder weapon all right, handed to us on a platter."

The younger officer understood the reason for Walker's sullen demeanor. Everyone wanted the case closed, and Walker's dissenting views were not welcome. He went to Chief Gill, arguing that there was nothing to connect Fred Wentworth to the murder except the gun found in his car.

"And his fingerprints on it."

"Not too hard to manage, since he was dead when they found him."

"And aren't you the one who told me he made statements in front of several witnesses where he placed himself in Mrs. Knoebel's bedroom?"

"But not on the day of the shooting. This is all circumstantial."

"Are you kidding me?" the chief demanded. "What do you need, Walker, a full-color photo of Wentworth pulling the trigger?"

"Chief, I realize everyone wants to hang this on Wentworth and, because he's dead, it's easy and convenient and it closes the file. But what about the marks on the driver's side of his car? Where did the other dents come from?"

"Who knows? Maybe he caromed off something on the other side of the road. Maybe it was some sort of half-assed suicide."

"Suicide? If he wanted to kill himself, there was a gun in the car, remember? Who the hell kills himself by running a station wagon into a tree?"

"Look Walker, ballistics says the gun is a spot-on match with the bullet that killed Mrs. Knoebel. It was found in Wentworth's station wagon. With his fingerprints on it."

"I understand that, Chief, but what kind of a moron commits murder and then keeps the weapon right there in his car?"

"What do I know? Maybe the kind of moron who manages to crash into a tree on a dry sunny day." Gill gave his head a vigorous shake. "Look Walker, we have witnesses who'll say Wentworth made statements placing him inside the Knoebels' bedroom. We've got the murder weapon with his prints on it. We have a diary with information on various men the victim knew, and you admit one of them matches this guy. So, when I have some spare time I promise I'll paint the picture for you in oil. Meanwhile get back to work and close this file."

CHAPTER 57

Walker could not be convinced that Wentworth's death was an accident, and the State Troopers involved in the investigation agreed. Unfortunately, Gill ordered the file closed and the State had no jurisdiction over the Knoebel case. They could, however, look further into the car crash.

"You want us to get involved here," asked a trooper Walker knew from Bridgeport, "try to find the other car?"

"The one that ran him off the road?"

"Exactly. If our forensic team gets their hands on that, we might find something."

"Do what you can," Walker said. "My chief has shut me down."

"I'll see what I can do," the trooper promised.

Meanwhile, no one else was interested except Anthony Walker.

And Phyllis Wentworth.

She was incapable of containing her grief, which was intensified beyond comprehension by the unbelievable notion that he had murdered Elizabeth Knoebel. She sought comfort from Randi Conway, never guessing that their therapist might, in some measure, have been an instrument of Fred's death.

Randi was riddled with guilt, but could obviously never reveal her discussion about Fred with Walker and Stratford. Instead, the two of them spent the best part of an hour expressing their shared anguish, with Phyllis never knowing how deep the therapist's remorse ran. At the end of the session, Randi suggested Phyllis speak with Anthony Walker. She told her that he was the one person who could see through everything, who might make sense of it all.

Phyllis was astonished. "You want me to go to the police? The people who are saying this about my Fred?"

"No," Randi replied, barely able to meet Phyllis's tormented gaze. "I don't want you to go to the police. I want you to go and see Anthony Walker."

And so, not sure what else she could do, Phyllis surprised herself by making the phone call and inviting the equally astonished detective to her home.

Walker could not shake the sad irony of this meeting. He had been sitting in the Wentworths' driveway the day Fred died, trying vainly to reach the man, not knowing he had already been targeted for death. Imagine if he had gotten to him first. Imagine how differently things might have turned out.

Phyllis showed him into their modest living room, offered him some water—which he declined—then launched into protests of her husband's innocence that ranged in emotion from raw anger to primal heartache.

Walker allowed her to vent until she finally ran low on tears and energy. "You're preaching to the choir, Mrs. Wentworth."

"What?"

"I don't believe your husband murdered Elizabeth Knoebel. Apparently Doctor Conway didn't share my views with you."

The woman was genuinely surprised. "No she didn't. She only said it would be helpful if we could talk."

"Well, we're talking. Unfortunately, no one else seems interested in listening to us."

Phyllis took the handkerchief away from her eyes. "You really mean what you say?"

"Always," he told her.

"Then let's do something about it."

"What do you suggest?"

"I think you should find Elizabeth's real killer."

"I've been ordered to close my file, to which I have objected quite strenuously. I've told my chief that if we find her killer, we'll find your husband's murderer too."

The sudden look of horror in her eyes made it clear this was something she had never considered. "His murderer?"

Walker drew a deep breath, puffed out his cheeks and blew the air out slowly. "I apologize. I realize you've been through a lot. It never occurred to me..."

"You think Fred was murdered?"

"I'm afraid so."

She looked away now, shaking her head in response to the latest aftershock of this tragedy. "I thought, I mean, they said it was an accident, right?"

"I'm sorry, but I don't think this was an accident. I think your husband was forced off the road. I also believe the murder weapon that was used on Mrs. Knoebel was then planted in his car."

She reacted with another of her looks of bewilderment, of which Walker was learning the poor woman had quite a repertoire.

"Do you have any idea what your husband was doing on that road the day, uh..."

"No," she interrupted. "That's one of the things I kept saying to the State Trooper who came here. Fred was supposed to be at work. I don't know why he left early, or why he'd be driving around up there. It makes no sense."

"I'm sorry I have to ask you this, but where were you that morning?"

"Where was I?" She paused, the day fixed in her memory. "I was running errands. In the market, at the cleaners." Her eyes began to well up again. "I remember thinking about that, once I heard about Fred. Trying to place exactly where I was at . . . at that awful moment."

"Mrs. Wentworth, I tried several times to reach you on your cell phone that morning. There was no answer."

Phyllis responded with a sad smile. "You know what Fred used to say? He would say, 'Phyllis, why do you have a cell phone if you never use it?' Ah," she sighed, "it was probably in my purse, as it always is. I never hear it ring. I almost never look for messages either." Then she hesitated. "Do you think if . . ."

"No, it wouldn't have mattered, I just wondered why I couldn't reach you." He studied her for a moment, then said, "Let's get back to why your husband would have been on that road that day. Do you think he might have been meeting someone?"

"Perhaps. But who?"

"I was hoping you might have a guess for me." He paused. "Ma'am, I'm going to have to ask you some tough questions here."

She responded with a tentative nod.

"Is it possible he was on his way to see a woman?"

Phyllis gave him as weary a look as he had ever seen. "My husband is dead. People think he was a murderer. You believe *he* was murdered. What isn't possible? If you're asking me if I think it was likely, the answer is no."

"Are you aware that there are people who believe your husband had a relationship with Elizabeth Knoebel?"

"Yes," she said without hesitation. "I know he saw Elizabeth."

"When you say, 'saw,' how do you . . ."

"Elizabeth was not a good person, Detective Walker. And Fred was a weak man. The sad truth was that nothing came of it except embarrassment for Fred."

"And you know this to be true?"

"I do."

"May I ask how?"

"Not that it matters, but Elizabeth was such a vicious woman . . ." She stopped here to shake her head. "She actually told me. Can you believe that?"

"She told you that she had seen your husband?"

"Oh yes. She told me how she mocked him when he, when he couldn't . . ."

"I get the picture."

"And then she ridiculed me for being married to him. She was a horrible person, Detective Walker."

"Did you ever tell that to your husband?"

"Never. How could I? He'd suffered enough humiliation from Elizabeth."

"Mrs. Wentworth, do you believe there is any possibility—and I mean even the remotest chance—that your husband would have murdered Elizabeth Knoebel?"

"Of course not."

Walker managed a slight smile. "That's the answer of a loyal wife. But if she subjected him to that sort of ridicule, well, there are all sorts of crazy motives for murder. I want you to take a moment and search your heart and tell me honestly. Is there any chance at all?"

Phyllis took his admonition seriously. She sat back and closed her eyes for what seemed a long time. When she sat up again she looked directly at him and said, "As I've said, Fred was a weak man, much as I hate to say it so soon after we've placed him . . . well, you understand. But it's true. I knew he was a failure at work. He thought he was fooling me about that, but he wasn't. He was a coward in many ways, and not much of a husband over the past several years. But I loved him, you see, and love is a strange thing. You make allowances. You forgive. You overlook. But it does not render you completely blind." Now she permitted herself a painful smile. "Fred could never have shot that woman, no matter how she shamed him." She shook her head. "I knew Fred too long to miss anything, believe me. I knew all about Elizabeth Knoebel and what she did to Fred. And you must know this—whatever she did to him or said to him, he didn't have it in him to murder her."

CHAPTER 58

Walker realized that Phyllis Wentworth's insistence on her late husband's innocence was certainly not enough to keep the case open, even when coupled with his own suspicions. No matter how strong the arguments he presented, Chief Gill refuted every one. More important, the chief had ordered that there be no further investigation. The world believed that Fred Wentworth murdered Elizabeth Knoebel, he was conveniently dead, the media had happily tied a ribbon around the entire package, and so everyone could return to life as usual.

Even in the face of that opposition, Walker was still in contact with the State Troopers. He also had some other ideas, and First Selectman Robert Stratford was the person he wanted to discuss them with.

When he phoned for an appointment he found he no longer had direct access and had to negotiate his way through two different secretaries. Now that the Elizabeth Knoebel case had been solved, Detective Walker was yesterday's news.

Even so, he pressed the issue, managing to arrange a meeting and suggesting the perfect spot.

Walker phoned Randi, explained that he wanted to use her office for a private discussion with Robert Stratford that night, and said he wanted her to be there. He was not surprised when she resisted, first telling him it was a bad idea, then suggesting she should not be involved in the discussion. He told her it was important and she ultimately relented.

So it was that Walker organized one more gathering among the three of them, a sort of post mortem on the Knoebel–Wentworth matter.

Stratford arrived first and found Randi seated at her desk, alone.

"I didn't think you'd actually come," she said.

Stratford looked surprised. "Why wouldn't I?"

The sadness was evident in her soft brown eyes. "Do you really want to do this now? With Anthony coming?"

"Anthony?" he said with an amused look. "What exactly is it we don't want to do in front of Anthony?"

She stared at him without speaking.

"Come on Randi, you and I have no secrets."

"Don't we?"

Stratford turned away and began arranging magazines and newspapers on a side table.

"Elizabeth," Randi said, pronouncing the name as if it were toxic. "We need to talk about Elizabeth." She was staring at his back as she said, "I read the diary, Robert. I read about you. I haven't said anything to Anthony, but it's time for you and me to face the truth."

"Ah. The elusive truth." Stratford gave up his busywork and walked past her to the window. The moonless night had grown dark. "I don't know what the truth is anymore," he said, still not looking at her.

"This was more than one of your casual affairs."

For a moment Stratford did not speak, he didn't even move. Then he nodded, keeping his back to her as he stared out the window. "Much more," he said. "Until I discovered I was just one of her laboratory animals."

"She was a troubled woman, surely you saw that."

When he finally turned to face her his features were set hard against the backdrop of the ebony night. "Troubled? No Randi. Evil. She was the incarnation of evil, which is something you should know better than anyone. What she did to me, to you, to others. And then, as if all that was not enough, she intended to expose us, to destroy us all."

"She didn't deserve to die, Robert."

"Didn't she?"

She sat back, staring at him. "What about Fred Wentworth?"

"What about him?" Stratford asked.

"Don't play games with me."

"Games? Let me tell you one of the basic truths of life, Doctor

Conway. Whatever happens to people, in the final analysis, they've brought on themselves. People make choices, you and I included." Stratford took a few seconds, as if to give her time to contemplate the idea. "I suppose you think you made no choice in all of this."

She offered no response.

He sat in a chair across from her. "No matter," he said pleasantly.

"No matter?" Anger rose in her voice. "You need help, Robert, and I can't be the one to give it."

"Help? I don't think so. My problem is solved, and so is everyone else's. Elizabeth is gone. Fred Wentworth murdered her, and now he's dead too."

"Fred Wentworth did not murder Elizabeth."

"Didn't he? The police certainly think he did. The press thinks he did. Once you confirmed his name to your friend Anthony, you helped to close the circle."

She winced. "You were supposed to protect me, not use me."

"I did protect you. I did everything I could to stop you from divulging your patients' confidences, didn't I? Didn't I make sure the police kept an eye on you? Maybe not directly, but you had enough attention that you were safe. Then events began to build and, like an old-fashioned pressure cooker, something finally had to give. Once you and your new boyfriend were convinced that it was a matter of life and death—as the police are so fond of describing it—you told him what he needed to know. The anonymous notes. The phone call at the restaurant. The break-in. When you gave him Wentworth's name the rest was as easy as painting by numbers."

A voice came from behind Stratford, startling the two of them. "Painting by numbers? Mind telling me who or what was the subject of this artwork?"

Stratford spun around to face Anthony Walker. The detective stood in the doorway, waiting for an answer.

"We were just discussing a theory of the Knoebel case," Stratford said. "Why Wentworth would have murdered her."

Walker looked to Randi, but she turned away.

"Precisely why I asked you to meet me this evening," Walker said. "What theory have you come up with?"

"Nothing solid yet." Stratford twisted uncomfortably in his seat to face the doorway behind him as he spoke, but Walker wasn't moving. "Seems clear this fellow Wentworth was the man."

"Uh huh." Walker appeared to be thinking it over. Then he said, "Phyllis Wentworth swears her husband was incapable of murder. For what it's worth, I believe her."

Stratford shook his head. "She's a grieving widow who can't bring herself to believe her husband was a cold-blooded killer. Sorry Detective, not a very persuasive witness."

"Maybe not," Walker said. Then he circled behind Randi, dropped a large envelope on her desk, and leaned against the windowsill, facing both of them. "What I've learned about Wentworth does not exactly conjure up the profile of a murderer."

Stratford nodded amiably. "All right, but what about the woman's diary? I'm basing this on limited information since I never saw the entire thing, but I am told that her writings include an episode about a man now believed to be Wentworth. Her story indicates things did not go well for him. Perhaps she threatened to reveal his inadequacy. That might provide a motive. Or maybe the shame itself was too great."

"Maybe, but then we'd have to explain why Fred Wentworth's car was run off the road."

"Wentworth was run off the road?"

"Oh yes. His death was no accident. The marks on his station wagon made that obvious, but we decided not to release the information until the other vehicle was found. The troopers have it now. It was abandoned in the woods, ten miles or so from the scene of the crash. Their forensics team is going over it as we speak."

"I wonder what they'll find," Stratford said.

"We'll know soon enough."

The threesome was quiet for a few moments. Then Stratford said, "Since you have more information than I do, why don't you go on."

Walker folded his arms across his chest. "All right. Let's say the murderer didn't know about Elizabeth Knoebel's journal at the time of the killing. If he had, he would have looked for copies or, at the very least, he would have taken her laptop. But he didn't, which suggests to me that he simply didn't know. Whatever his motive for killing her, it had nothing to do with her journal. Later, when the diary was discovered, it created both a problem and an opportunity. Assuming the killer was one of the men identified in her writing, that created an unforeseen risk. On the other hand, the stories about her other playmates offered a chance for him to cast suspicion on someone else. All he had to do was let our investigation play out a little bit, and create some misdirection along the way."

"Misdirection?"

"Sure, the things you just mentioned. The anonymous notes. The break-in of this office. The phone call Randi got when we were at dinner. False clues, all of them, staged to send us in the wrong direction while the murderer created a story around them that was just plausible enough to lead us to a believable fall guy. There were several of Randi's patients who might have worked just fine. Some that you and I have already discussed. Nettie Sisson. Fran Colello. Thomas Colello. Fred Wentworth just happened to fit the bill."

Stratford remained silent.

"I must say, the Wentworth ploy was risky, especially since he had to be killed to really make the plan work. There was no way to allow him an opportunity to exonerate himself. No, he had to be removed, and there was real danger in the way it was done. I mean, look at the possible flaws. First, there was the risk of being seen switching cars. Then you had to be sure that Wentworth died in the crash. And, of course, since you had to leave the revolver behind, someone could have driven by at the moment you were planting the gun, another chance of being spotted. But the true genius was in engineering things so that Randi gave us his name. Once you learned that Colello suspected Wentworth had been in the Knoebel house, well, the rest was truly inspired."

Stratford stared at him wide-eyed "You actually believe I murdered Elizabeth Knoebel and Fred Wentworth."

"I do.

"You're insane."

"Am I? I tell you what, even an unregistered gun like the one they found, it'll ultimately be traced. Don't look so skeptical, the State is working that angle. And the car that ran Wentworth off the road. Whatever you did to clean it out when you ditched it, they'll find something. I know you must've been wearing gloves, but maybe you left behind a hair or two, or breathed too hard on the windshield. Or perhaps you left tire tracks from your own car near the exchange point."

"You really believe this hogwash?"

"I do." Walker stood, picked up the brown envelope on Randi's desk and tossed it into Stratford's lap. The lawyer reflexively caught it as Walker continued. "Unlike Fred Wentworth, you really did have a motive, didn't you? You have a political career at stake, and you couldn't afford to have the truth about your relationship with Elizabeth Knoebel made public. Killing her was one thing, but then you had to bring our investigation to an end so the diary would be buried before anyone identified you in there."

"You are way off base here, Detective."

"Am I? I admit, proof beyond a reasonable doubt is a tough hill to climb, that's true, but even if you manage to skate on the criminal charge, you're through." He pointed at the envelope. "Once we determined that the RSETU file was actually an encoded name for ROBRT, it was easy to fill in the blanks. Personally, professionally, you're done."

Stratford held up the envelope. "Please Detective, not this woman's deranged fantasies. Please tell me that's not the basis of these slanderous accusations."

"Deranged? Maybe so. But they weren't fantasies, which we've already established from others mentioned in her diary. There's another piece to the puzzle you didn't know about, something we didn't tell anyone. You see, Elizabeth Knoebel kept a schedule in her computer. She recorded all of her meetings, dates and places, chapter and verse. Shouldn't be tough to get corroborating testimony from bartenders and waiters and motel clerks. You know the drill, Counselor."

They stared at each other, waiting. Then Stratford stood up, casually brushed off his suit jacket and smiled. "The day Fred Wentworth died. What time was he found?"

"Just before noon."

"Yes. That's how I recall it. And the coroner's report indicated his time of death . . ."

"Was an hour or so before that."

"Exactly what I was told by Chief Gill. So, before you came here tonight with this Alice in Wonderland story, did you bother to check my whereabouts that morning?"

"I did. You were not in your law office or in Town Hall."

"High marks for addressing the obvious. What you did not know, however, was that I was in a private meeting with three representatives of my party from Hartford. We kept our gathering a secret to avoid unnecessary speculation about what you have referred to as my political career. We took a small conference room at the Hyatt in Greenwich, all of which you can easily confirm. I arrived there before ten and did not leave until after one."

Walker did not reply.

"As for the death of Mrs. Knoebel, I'm sure I will be able to account for my location that day as well, should it come to that. You'll find I am also quite meticulous in keeping records of my schedule."

Walker remained silent.

"So then, I think it's fair to say that your desperate speculation is nothing more than grounds for a slander suit." Turning to the forgotten person in the room, he said to Randi, "You should really choose your new friends more carefully." He came around the desk and bent down to kiss her on the forehead, but she pulled away. Stratford straightened up and had another look at the envelope in his hand, then returned his attention to Walker. "You're a small man with a small mind, Detective. Whatever you think you know about me is nothing more than wild conjecture."

"That so?"

"Oh yes. And then there is the small matter of your own breach of professional conduct." He smiled again as Walker and Randi waited. "Do you think I don't know you two have been sleeping together? Please, don't look so shocked, and don't waste time with idiotic denials. You have suggested that I am a clever and careful man, and you are correct on both counts." He strolled toward the door, then turned back to them. "Any attempt to tie me to Elizabeth Knoebel will force me to reveal that the detective in charge of this investigation was having a sexual relationship with a woman who was not only a key witness in the case but, in addition, a potential suspect. I'm sure Randi has shared with you stories of her own difficulties with the late Mrs. Knoebel. All of that would also have to be revealed. Then there is the added complication that your new lover is a client of the very man you would be accusing. Take some time to employ your limited imagination and see how all that will play out. You will be fortunate not to end up in prison yourself. You will most assuredly lose your job, and likely forfeit any chance of ever working in law enforcement anywhere at any time in any other jurisdiction in the country."

Neither Walker nor Randi spoke.

"I see I've made my point," Stratford said, then turned and walked out.

When he was gone, Randi looked up at Walker, tears welling up in her tired brown eyes. "Oh my God," she said.

"Are you all right?"

"You really believed he killed them both?"

Walker walked around the desk and slumped in the seat opposite Randi. "I did."

"But he must be telling the truth about his meeting that day, the morning Fred . . ."

"I'm afraid that's probably so," Walker agreed as he began to rethink his entire view of the case. "He wouldn't lie about something that would be so easy to disprove."

"What about those things you said, about the car?"

Walker got up and walked to the door, just to be sure Stratford was gone. Then he returned, sat down, and let out a long sigh. "They did find the car, but not so much as a single print. It was wiped clean. There were a couple of hairs, but we don't have a match. They likely belong to the owner the car was stolen from."

"What about Elizabeth's date book, proving that Bob was seeing her?"

He shrugged. "There is no date book."

"So he was right. You were bluffing."

"I played him, that's all. Just like he's been playing me. And you, for that matter."

"But why? If he didn't kill Elizabeth . . ."

"I'm still not convinced he didn't kill Elizabeth. He seems to have a strong alibi for the day Wentworth died, but he still hasn't told us where he was the day she was murdered." Walker nodded to himself. "My guess is, he'll find a way to work that out too."

"Typical Bob," Randi said, "to have himself covered that way. Now he'll go home so he and Lady Macbeth can discuss damage control." More to herself than to Walker, she said, "I wonder if she really has any idea."

Walker looked up. "What did you say?"

CHAPTER 59

Outside, at the far end of the parking lot behind Randi's building, Robert Stratford sat in his Mercedes, the engine idling, the map light casting a glow across his face, the CD player sending soft strains of *La Traviata* throughout the leather-upholstered interior. The envelope Walker had given him was on the passenger seat. He had removed the pages and was reading through the notes Elizabeth had made about their relationship.

Vain men are the easiest to control. They are willing to accept as true anything that strokes their ego, believing as they do in their superiority.

These men are convinced they are worthy of your attention. They make mistakes, behaving carelessly, and act with little regard for your feelings or the consequences that will be suffered by those they are betraying.

Sexually, such men are often a disappointment. Their sense of entitlement leads them to believe it is their pleasure that is important, not yours.

R, as we shall call him, was a particularly easy target. His opinions of himself, who he was, his place in society, all were informed by arrogance. He was a successful attorney, a respected man who had married for money

and was intent on preserving that afflu-
ence and the façade of respectability.

Like so many of his ilk, R's initial
charm evaporated in the overwhelming
imperative of his selfishness. These are
the men who deserve to be exposed for what
they are. Their smug existence, their
careers and especially the counterfeit
personal lives they lead—all the truths
of their duplicity need to be bared.

When I told R it was over, that I was
finished with him, his incredulity was
pathetic. So much so, in fact, that I
was actually delighted for the opportunity to laugh in his face. Who did
he think he was, I demanded to know—a
question that cut to the core of his
narcissism. In the end, he was so much
less than he wanted to believe.

He angrily gathered up the papers, shoved them back into the
envelope, hid it under the floor mat, put his car in gear and decided he
would drive around a while.

✢   ✢   ✢

Linda Stratford was waiting in the kitchen when her husband finally
arrived home. "Well?" she asked. "What did he want?"

"Walker doesn't believe Wentworth murdered Elizabeth Knoebel."

"You're not serious."

Stratford looked at her for a moment, then went to the cupboard
and, without another word, pulled out a bottle of Glenlivet, took a
crystal tumbler from the shelf and poured himself a drink, no ice.

"Why would he say such a thing?" she asked.

Stratford took a long pull of the scotch as he searched for an appropriate reply, allowing the whisky to course through him with a pleasurable, dulling sensation. Linda knew of the diary, of course, because Linda knew everything that happened in Darien, but he had never told her anything about his relationship with Elizabeth, and this was no time for a confession. "I don't know," he said.

"Why is he bothering you at this point? The case is closed."

"He won't give up on that journal the Knoebel woman was writing. She obviously intended it as an X-rated *Peyton Place*, and Walker seems hell-bent on using it to ruin as many lives as he can."

"There must be more to it than that Robert. You're not telling me everything."

Stratford took another gulp of his drink. "He accused me of murdering Fred Wentworth. He said Wentworth's car was run off the road, and he thinks I'm the one who did it. Can you imagine?"

"But we both know where you were that morning."

Stratford responded with a curious look. It was not the reaction he expected.

"What is it, Robert? Did you expect me to ask why he would think such a thing? Why he would believe you had a reason to kill that man?"

"It crossed my mind."

"After all these years, do you really take me for a fool? You think I didn't know why you became so involved in a police investigation that you normally wouldn't make a phone call about?"

"Her murder was becoming a scandal for this town," he replied, but it sounded as false to him as it did to her.

"Please," she said, as if she could not bear another affront to her intelligence. "I know all about you and Elizabeth, and I know you're scared to death her diary will become public."

Stratford was barely able to reply. "You're wrong," was all he could manage.

"Am I? If there had never been a diary, we would have had no problem. The 'diary matter' as you kept calling it, that changed everything."

"Stop this."

"You think I don't know that you're the one who called Knoebel's lawyer? Told him the diary was becoming an embarrassment to the whole town and would end up humiliating Doctor Knoebel? Once you found out about it you tried to contain the damage, but it was too late."

"Enough."

"Enough? That phone call might be the one piece of hard evidence they can track back to you, but it doesn't prove you're the murderer."

He stared at her. "What are you saying?"

She spoke slowly now, as if to a child who simply wasn't getting it. "The day Wentworth died, you can cover that time fairly well with the meeting you had. But the day Elizabeth was shot. What are we going to do about that?"

Before he could respond, the doorbell rang. Stratford placed his glass on the counter and went to answer it. He opened the front door to find Lieutenant Walker and Officer Kovacevic standing there.

Stratford said, "I think I've had just about enough of you for one evening, Detective."

"We're not here to see you," Walker told him. "We're here to speak with Mrs. Stratford."

"What?"

Linda Stratford was already standing behind her husband. She said, "Don't be rude, Robert, show them in."

Reluctant and anxious, Stratford nevertheless stepped aside and allowed his wife to lead the two policemen into their comfortable den.

"So," she said to Walker, "you wanted to speak with *me*?" Her tone conveyed both curiosity and amusement. Walker quickly wiped the smile from her face.

"Officer Kovacevic," he said, "please read Mrs. Stratford her rights."

"What is this," Robert Stratford demanded.

"Mr. Stratford, you either need to identify yourself as the attorney representing your wife or I am going to have to ask you to leave the room. If you refuse to either represent her or leave, we'll have to take Mrs. Stratford to headquarters for questioning."

The Stratfords stared at each other for a moment without speaking. Then Stratford said, "Of course I represent my wife."

"Good," Walker said. Then he had Kovacevic read her rights and pulled out a release for her to sign.

When the formalities were over everyone was still standing, Stratford and his wife facing the two policeman, and no one was being offered a seat. Kovacevic turned on his recorder.

"You mind telling us what this is about now?" the lawyer demanded.

Walker looked to Linda Stratford. "Please tell us the nature of your relationship with Elizabeth Knoebel."

No one missed the look of surprise on Robert Stratford's face. The room became quiet as all three men waited for her answer.

"Mrs. Stratford?"

"Why do you want to know?" she finally replied.

"I'll be asking the questions ma'am. At least for now."

Linda turned to her husband. "What now, Robert? I either answer his questions or take the Fifth? Is that the proper legal way to say it? Take the Fifth?"

Stratford ignored his wife and again directed himself to Walker. "See here, Detective, whatever vendetta you've developed against me, why in the name of decency are you dragging my wife into this?"

"I'm conducting a murder investigation. There is no vendetta against you. I just want the truth."

"Chief Gill told me this case was closed. You have no right . . ."

"The investigation has been reopened. We have new information from the State Troopers who have continued to look into the death of Fred Wentworth."

"What? When did all this happen?"

"Less than fifteen minutes ago. At our meeting earlier this evening I told you the car that forced Fred Wentworth off the road had been located. After you left I confirmed certain facts with the State. I also discovered new evidence in Elizabeth Knoebel's diary." Walker turned back to Stratford's wife. "You knew that Mrs. Knoebel was writing a diary."

Linda took her time removing a cigarette from a marble case on a nearby table. She lit up, drew deeply and exhaled slowly, then stared at the detective. "Yes, I did."

"And you've seen the diary."

"I have."

"Right now I don't care how you came to see the diary, ma'am, we can deal with that later. I need you to tell me if you knew of the diary *before* Mrs. Knoebel died?"

She shook her head slowly. "Wish I did."

"Why do you say that, Mrs. Stratford?"

"I, uh, don't know. I just said it, is all."

"You know that she wrote about her relationship with you in that diary."

When Linda offered no reply, her husband said, "My wife and I need . . ."

Walker held up his hand to the lawyer, not taking his eyes off Linda Stratford. "There was a chapter in Elizabeth's diary about a relationship she had with another woman. You remember that?"

Linda nodded slowly. "As I recall, there was more than one of those."

"The name of the file I'm talking about was 'SHAKE.' It was one of the few files Elizabeth did not name with the code she used for most of the others. We thought the word *shake* was a comment on the nervousness of the woman she was describing."

Linda Stratford waited.

"It was also one of the few files where Mrs. Knoebel used a name rather than an initial within the chapter. She called the woman Celia, right?"

"Yes."

"Celia was a character in *As You Like It*. Celia loved another woman in the play. Do you recall the play?"

"Rosalind was the other woman's name," Linda said, almost in a whisper.

"So that file name, SHAKE, had nothing to do with nerves. It referred to *Shakespeare*."

Linda stared at him without speaking.

"Celia was a woman who loved another woman, but was not actually gay. In fact, she ends up marrying a bad guy at the end."

"I remember," Linda Stratford said.

Walker looked to Bob Stratford and then back to his wife. "So the file name and the use of the name Celia was also intended as a twist on the name of Shakespeare's birthplace."

Linda nodded. "Stratford-upon-Avon."

For a moment the room became dead silent.

"Was Celia some sort of pet name Mrs. Knoebel used for you?"

Now sadness filled Linda's deep blue eyes. "Something like that. Something you and my husband and this young policeman here wouldn't understand."

"So, are you ready to tell me about your relationship with Mrs. Knoebel?"

"Unique," she said. "I would describe it as unique."

"In what way was it unique, ma'am?"

"There was nothing else like it, not in my life."

"Did you also know Fred Wentworth?"

She took some time on that one. "No, not really."

"When you say 'not really' . . ."

"Let's say we were never introduced. I came to know who he was."

Walker nodded. "I'm going to need to ask you some detailed questions about your unique relationship with Mrs. Knoebel."

"Hold on," Stratford interrupted again. "My wife has rights."

"We've already read your wife her rights, Counselor." Turning back to Linda, Walker asked if she still understood what she had signed.

"Yes," she replied quietly. "Yes, I do."

"Mrs. Stratford, it can be difficult to solve a murder case, but once a clear suspect has been identified it becomes much easier to connect the dots. Take this case, for instance. Matching the paper that was used to write the anonymous notes left at Randi Conway's office. Reviewing telephone records of calls between the suspect and victim, as well as the call to Doctor Conway the night she and I were out to dinner. Matching

DNA found in the car that ran Fred Wentworth's station wagon off the road. Tracing ownership of a murder weapon. Confirming a person's whereabouts at a given date and time. It all becomes much simpler once we believe we know who committed the crime. Do you understand what I'm saying?"

She looked at him without speaking.

"Mrs. Stratford, do you want to tell me why you murdered Elizabeth Knoebel?"

This time, when Robert Stratford began sputtering a string of lawyerly objections, no one paid him any attention. His wife and Anthony Walker were locked in a staring contest neither was willing to lose.

Linda finally relented, crushing the remains of her cigarette in an ashtray and lighting another. "It was the most difficult decision of my life," she began, her voice quiet, her attention trained on Walker. "Somehow I have the odd feeling you understand that." She searched his gray-brown eyes for evidence of that comprehension. "It became a choice between my safe, comfortable life, and this strange, alternate existence, this bond to a woman I didn't really know and couldn't trust. I had never done anything like it before, never cheated on my husband with another man, let alone a woman. Not ever."

"I do understand," Walker told her.

Linda nodded. "Elizabeth was . . . she was a special person. For all of her faults, for all of the pain she inflicted on people, she was something different." She sighed. "After a while—and it wasn't a long affair, you see—after a while I came to understand that all of her tenderness, all of the caring, all of the love, it was just pretense. She preyed upon my weaknesses, the lack of passion in my marriage, my inability to have children. I knew Robert had affairs, and I told her about them. Actually, I told her about everything. She was good at what she did, believe me. She was extremely good at drawing me out, at encouraging intimacy. For a while, even after I suspected it was some sort for game for her, I was still willing to, uh, to be with her for the way she made me feel. But when I discovered she was also seeing Robert . . ." She puffed on the cigarette again. "Can you have any idea how that felt, any idea of that pain? I was already wracked with guilt for having an affair with a woman and for betraying my marriage. Then I learned she was fucking my husband. Don't you see? This was a woman I thought I loved."

She appeared to have run out of steam for the moment, so Walker asked, "How did you learn she was seeing your husband?"

Linda paused for a moment, then let out a bitter laugh. "She told me. Can you believe it? I had reached a point where I couldn't deceive myself anymore about who she was, and I think she realized that. So she told me about Robert, and I finally saw that she was hell-bent on destroying us both, although I'll never really know why. She was just evil, I suppose, simple as that." She paused again, remembering, and this time Walker remained silent. "It was an impossible situation. There was no escape." She took a long drag of the cigarette. "I cannot count the days and nights I spent searching for an answer. Robert would be at work, or at meetings. Or with her. I would sit alone in the dark, trying to find a solution. Wondering if there was someone I could ask for help. Berating myself for having gotten into this pathetic mess. Looking for a way out. But it was clear. I knew our lives would be ruined. Our reputations. Robert's career."

"Did you ever confront her about it?"

Linda managed a sad smile. "Of course. And she laughed in my face. Told me I was weak and deluded and privileged. She called me pathetic. One of her favorite words, by the way. It was awful. This . . . this person I'd trusted, I'd shared everything with. It was sickening. I wanted to choke her then and there, but instead I just walked out, still trying to find a solution, realizing it all came back to the same choices. I had to kill her. Or Robert. Or myself."

Stratford let out an audible gasp, before saying, "Linda, my God . . ." but his wife gave him a look that brought him up short.

"She was a hideous individual," Linda said to Walker. "Actually, *hideous* is not nearly strong enough to describe her. But even so, the choice was not easy." She took another puff of her cigarette and let out the smoke. "Sometimes, when I wake up in the middle of the night thinking about everything, I fear I made the wrong choice." As Officer

Kovacevic took her by the arm and led her toward the front door, Linda Stratford turned back to look at her husband. "Some nights, I think I should have killed you instead."

CHAPTER 60

Walker's bluff had worked. When he called the State Troopers, they told him they had found nothing in the car, not a shred of evidence. Still, he never told the Stratfords they had, he had not lied to the suspect. All he did was suggest the possibility, creating the predicate for her to tell the truth.

Elizabeth Knoebel had not really kept a record of her assignations, no appointment book, nothing. Walker never even telephoned Chief Gill, never bothered to share his suspicions with him. Instead he relied on his instincts, called Kovacevic for backup, then took a run at Linda Stratford. Once he figured out that she was Elizabeth's Celia, he knew that she would tell him everything, that she actually wanted to come clean.

It was just as Linda had said about him. Somehow, Walker simply understood.

One of the ironies of the confession given by Mrs. Stratford was that her husband was never implicated in any way. To the contrary, he became a tragic figure, someone worthy of empathy. A victim of the distorted relationship between two unbalanced women. Even his political career might survive.

Phyllis Wentworth was obviously relieved to have her husband vindicated. As a bonus, she now owned the rights to a wrongful death claim against a wealthy woman who had admitted enough to ensure Phyllis a wealthy dotage.

One of the nicer by-products of the recent tragedies was the Averys' reconciliation. After Joan's call to Mitchell on the day Fred Wentworth died, he raced back to Connecticut and the two of them spent the remainder of the day together. And the night. They discussed Elizabeth

Knoebel, Fred Wentworth and, more important to them, their children, their relationship, their past, their present and their future. Joan and the children moved back home the next day, filling their closets with the clothing she had hidden in the cedar storage room in the attic. Leave it to Mitchell to not even check there.

As Professor Rubenfeld often told Randi, the best course of therapy is often the one you don't plan.

Paul and Lisa Gorman had a beautiful wildflower arrangement delivered to Phyllis Wentworth along with their heartfelt condolences. They also sent a card to Randi expressing their appreciation for everything she had done for them and telling her that, for now, they would not be seeing her again.

Fran Colello sent a handwritten letter to Randi. She said that she was sorry for the Wentworths. She also appreciated everything the therapist had tried to do for her. And, she wrote, she was filing for a divorce.

Finally, Walker went to see Dr. Stanley Knoebel to tell him everything the police now knew about his wife's death. Knoebel conducted himself with his usual formality, but at the end of the interview he handed Walker an envelope and asked Walker to deliver it to Randi Conway.

Apparently everyone in town now knew about the police detective and the therapist.

The envelope contained a short note written on an embossed card. It read, "Dear Dr. Conway, Whatever you may have thought of us, our marriage and our lives, I need to say that we thank you for trying." It was signed Stanley Knoebel, the first time he had ever used his first name with her.

All that was left then, was for Walker to close his file on the Elizabeth Knoebel murder. As he sat at his desk he needed to have one last look at who this woman really was, someone who could inspire so many people to engage in so many acts of deceit, stupidity and even murder. Before he placed the printed manuscript, along with the computer disk, into the evidence box, he turned to the final entry in her diary and read.

SEXUAL RITES
By Elizabeth Knoebel
NOTES FOR FINAL CHAPTER
What Every Woman Needs

I can recall a time when I was young,
yet not so very young. I remember him,
how he was also young, how he was trim
and muscular and how I thought him handsome. His legs were long and agile, his
arms sinewy and strong. He was ardent
and I was willing, and we enjoyed the
fever of our age. And we believed we
were in love.

I cannot recall exactly how it was
the first time we were together, but I
remember that we were in the woods, not
far from my home. I can still picture
the large trees with their green leaves
providing us shelter, hiding us from
view. I can still feel the warmth of the
rays of sunlight that traveled their
broken path through the foliage, finding
us on the soft floor of the forest. I can
still envision us, naive and awkward
in our nakedness, and so very eager to
share our passion.

We made love together many times
after that first day. Each time, when
we were done, he would hold me. Sometimes we would kiss, or he would have
me lay my head on his chest as he gently
stroked my hair. Sometimes we would
speak in a soft whisper. Sometimes we

would say nothing at all. Sometimes we would doze off, sleepy in the aftermath of passion.

We knew so little then, except how we felt. I can actually recall how we felt. I can also remember how he held me.

He was young and I was young, as I have said. I have had many lovers since, all of them more worldly. But not one of them has ever made me feel wanted and needed and loved the way he did, both during and after our lovemaking. Not one of them has ever held me the way he did, after desire released us from its convulsive grip, after he had been satisfied, when it would have been easy for him to find a reason on those sunny summer afternoons to go away.

But he always made me feel that there was no place better for him to rush off to, no reason to leave. He made me feel that there was nothing else in the world more important to him than I was at that moment. Whether that was true or not I did not know, not then and not now. The only thing that mattered was how I felt, and how I feel about it even today.

I can still see his face as it was then, and I wonder where he is now. I hope that his ability to feel love did not fade with his youth as mine has done. I wonder, if he were to hold me in his arms today, would I feel the same way I did then? I wonder, would he find a reason to leave too soon, or would he still understand what I need, just as he seemed to understand then?

I want to believe that he would, that he would hold me the same way, and that we could feel what we felt then. But there is a sad aching in my heart, a fear that tells me it would not be.

Even so, even with all that I have learned and experienced, even after seeing men and women in the harshest light, even in the face of that, all I want is to experience once more what I felt on those summer afternoons when we lay together amidst the trees, when making love was so much simpler. When life was so much simpler.

When he finished, Walker slid the pages into the brown envelope, dropped the envelope in the box, sealed it for shipment and marked it for transfer to the oblivion of closed files and forgotten lives.

ABOUT THE AUTHOR

L. T. Graham is the pen name of a New England–based suspense writer who is the author of several novels. Graham is currently at work on the next Detective Anthony Walker novel.